Lag Delay

Grace Parkowski Thrillers, Volume 1

Ryan M. Patrick

Published by Ryan M. Patrick, 2024.

This is a work of fiction. Similarities to real people, places, or events are entirely coincidental.

LAG DELAY

First edition. October 29, 2024.

Copyright © 2024 Ryan M. Patrick.

ISBN: 979-8227470423

Written by Ryan M. Patrick.

For my wife, who somehow puts up with me

Lag Delay

PROLOGUE

June 2027

    Kennedy Space Center, Florida

"Ten, nine, eight," the OuterTek webcast presenter said as Captain Michael DePresti watched the numbers at the bottom of his launch console count down towards T-0.

Everything had been building towards this moment for the last three years.

As the ILIAD mission's Shrike Heavy rocket government mission integration manager (GMIM), DePresti had worked his ass off to integrate the NASA payload headed to Venus with the rocket that it sat atop, nearly three miles away, at Launch Complex-39a outside the floor-to-ceiling windows of the historic control center that had commanded the Apollo and Shuttle missions of years past.

The sun was setting behind them and the Atlantic Ocean, a deep blue expanse to the east, stood as a beautiful backdrop to the most exciting moment in spaceflight: a rocket launch.

His heart pounded at a million beats per second in his chest.

"Seven, six, five," the presenter continued.

DePresti took a deep breath. It had not been an easy journey to get here. Keeping NASA, the Space Force, and OuterTek in line had seemed impossible at times. Still, this was the most exciting moment of his life.

"Four, three..."

He snuck a peak at the graph pinned to the top-left monitor at his quad-screen console, a line chart continually updated with live numbers from the rocket.

Just an hour before, he had been alerted by his Aerospace mission assurance lead that a string of sensors on the rocket's second stage were giving odd readings. The man, an older Ph.D. following along from Space Systems Command's (SSC) STARS facility in El

Segundo, had explained to DePresti that there wasn't much danger to the rocket - the numbers were all in-family from previous launches.

However, these parts, mostly thermistors and pressure sensors, gave different values than expected from SSC and Aerospace's rigorous pedigree review before the launch campaign. The sensitive payload needed to remain in certain temperature, pressure, and cleanliness ranges in order to prevent damage. If the sensors weren't working as planned, the billion-dollar mission's success was in jeopardy.

DePresti wasn't convinced of his team's assessment. There was no reason the numbers would be anything other than expected, especially with a mature launch vehicle like the Shrike Heavy. If the sensor values remained in-family, the launch could proceed as planned. If any of them jumped, the rocket's flight computer would abort at T-1 second and the launch vehicle would remain on the pad.

DePresti swallowed a lump in his throat. He was okay with a recycle and another launch attempt in a few days once all of the consumables had been replenished, but his parents had flown in from Philadelphia to watch the launch from a site just south of LC-39a on Banana River. Their flight back was tomorrow morning, and if the Shrike Heavy remained on the ground, they would miss his launch.

"Two, one, ignition."

The Shrike Heavy's twenty-seven main engines ignited their blend of RP-1 and LOx in a carefully planned sequence. The blast from the faraway pad was so brilliant that DePresti had to shield his eyes with his hand. He looked up at the graph showing the second-stage sensors in question. They were still within the system's limits, but still not what he had expected to see.

"Liftoff."

The giant rocket - the most powerful in the world - lifted off of the pad on its twenty-first mission.

Hoots, hollers, and cheers went up from around the firing room.

"We are off the pad," the presenter said with a thousand-watt grin.

"Liftoff," DePresti echoed to himself with a smile of his own.

He high-fived his boss' boss - Colonel Chad Hawke, seated at the console next to him - and returned to his monitor.

This mission wasn't over yet.

This was one of the most complicated mission profiles that any rocket could fly. The Shrike Heavy's second stage would place the Aering-built ILIAD payload, consisting of a relay satellite and landing module containing two humanoid robots and their associated ground support gear, in a temporary transfer orbit, then at just the right moment do an intense burn that would place the stage on a hyperbolic orbit that would hopefully put them around Venus in just a few months. A lot of things needed to happen for the payload to arrive there safely.

He used his phone to text his girlfriend, an Aering engineer who would be one of the future remote operators of the robots. But, she didn't respond, likely busy with her own part of the mission.

DePresti put his cellphone down and made a landline call to the Aerospace lead, located at a hangar at the neighboring Cape Canaveral Space Force Station. The other man should have been in the room with him but had been pushed to an overflow location due to higher-priority VIPs. "Are you watching this?" he asked.

"You bet I am," the other man said. "It's one hell of a launch."

He smiled. "Any concerns?"

"No, everything looks okay from here," the Aerospace man said. "We'll continue to monitor that string on stage 2."

"Thanks," DePresti said. He ended the call.

LAG DELAY

The rocket was completely out of view of the windows, so he tracked its progress on the webcast and via a live trajectory feed on his computer. Thankfully, using his four monitors, he could keep track of the sensors he was worried about on one while watching it ascend on another.

Most of the team was still taking it all in. Col Hawke and a few OuterTek executives were in the process of making plans for a post-launch party. Other side conversations popped up around him, but he kept his focus on his console.

Most of their jobs were done. The rocket did all of the work now.

A few minutes later, the side cores shut off and separated using small quantities of explosives. They started their trajectory back to a pair of landing sites located at the far south end of the geographic cape.

The center core continued on with the second stage and payload on top of it.

DePresti started cycling through the different video feeds available at his workstation. There was a view of the bottom of the rocket, showing the curvature of the Earth as it ascended. Another one showed the payload inside of its fairing, and yet another displayed the interior second-stage LOx tank, the blue-purple liquid pulsing in a mesmerizing fashion.

He made another call back to the Aerospace lead. Everything was still good, the engineer insisted. No concerns about the payload or launch vehicle. Everything was proceeding as planned.

The Space Force captain let out a sigh of relief, releasing all of the pent-up pressure built up inside of him. All of the hard work that he had put in was finally paying off.

The Shrike Heavy was well past max-q, the point of maximum aerodynamic pressure on the launch vehicle, and had passed the Karman line into outer space.

The next step was stage separation. The main booster separated from the second stage and began its oath to an autonomous landing barge located out in the middle of the South Atlantic.

A few minutes after that, the ground team prepared to jettison the fairing that encapsulated the payload, the two halves of which would then float down using parachutes to be captured by specially equipped ships downrange near the barge. After that, the payload would be exposed to the cold vacuum of space.

Everything was still going according to plan.

DePresti noticed something odd at about twenty seconds before that event. His mission clock, which had been counting forward from T-0, was now counting backward.

He wiggled his computer mouse to see if his terminal had frozen or locked up. Nope, everything was fine. DePresti's eyes shot up to the graph showing the sensor data that he and his team were concerned about.

They were all normal except for one, a thermistor string along the raceway. It had been showing normal temperatures but was now displaying readings that were out-of-family.

DePresti quickly switched to the anomaly net. "GMIM here, seeing some weird data," he said, then let the button go.

As he got a muffled response from one of the OuterTek engineers, a gasp went up from around the room.

Up on the screen, on the left side, the presenter had just announced that the fairings had been jettisoned. However, the live feed from within the encapsulated stack showed a dark fairing still attached to the second stage.

DePresti's mouth hung open in shock. A million possibilities, all negative, went through his mind. Had the video frozen? They'd had issues on the static fire with helium purges messing with the cameras, perhaps that had happened again.

He deftly hit a few shortcuts on the keyboard to pull up a different video feed.

It wasn't a video problem. The second stage LOx tank was still pulsing in a mesmerizing fashion.

"What the hell," he said under his breath.

The woman on the screen was just as shocked as he was.

"Cut that feed out," one of the OuterTek executives yelled.

"Anomaly team to the net," Col Hawke ordered. "Figure out what the fuck is going on."

DePresti switched his headset over to the government-only anomaly voice net as the webcast team pulled all of the video feeds down, including on his monitor.

"Everything looks normal," a senior Aerospace engineer told Hawke. "Not sure why the video isn't matching the sensor feed."

DePresti watched Hawke look up at the OuterTek launch crew, all of whom had calmed down from the initial shock, then back to his PC. "They're not worried here."

"Webcast team is bugged out though," another Space Force officer, this one physically located at the OuterTek plant in Hawthorne, reported. "They're running scared around the control room."

"What about the technical team?" DePresti asked.

"Same as y'all there, troubleshooting, but not worked up too much," the other officer replied. "The telemetry is good, and there haven't been any reported explosions picked up by OPIR."

"My money is on a camera going out," another Aerospace technical lead chimed in.

After a few minutes of technical discussion, one of the OuterTek engineers walked over to Hawke and DePresti. "We're going to outbrief in thirty seconds," she told the two military officers. "They finished their investigation."

DePresti nodded and switched over to the contractor's voice channel.

The OuterTek launch director polled his team for their findings shortly after.

Everything was nominal, save for a string of video cameras that had gone out. The ones inside of the tanks had remained operational, as they hadn't been put through a helium purge. The webcast was supposed to cut the feed when the cameras became unresponsive but instead hung with the last image received.

However, there would be no video for the rest of the launch.

"Just like an NRO launch," Hawke grumbled, referring to the black-budget intelligence agency that developed, launched, and operated the nation's spy satellites. They didn't let either OuterTek or the American Rocket Alliance, the two main launch providers, show video on their webcasts after stage separation for national security purposes.

DePresti, along with everyone else in the firing room, breathed a sigh of relief.

He tried texting his girlfriend again but didn't get a response.

Half an hour later, the second stage made its first burn into a transfer orbit. An hour and fifteen minutes after that, the second burn was made, putting the rocket stage and payload on a hyperbolic orbit toward the system's second planet.

Another round of cheers went through the room.

DePresti took an offered champagne flute, engraved with the OuterTek logo, with a smile. He sat back in his chair and took a sip as an OuterTek VP passed out mission patches. A wave of relief washed over him as the telemetry anomaly from earlier and the video feed cutout were the farthest thing from his mind. It had been nothing short of a successful launch.

CHAPTER ONE

November 2027
    El Segundo, California
    "Come on!" Grace Parkowski screamed as she slammed her fists into the steering wheel of her year-old Toyota Camry.

The traffic on CA-1 was bad, worse than anything she'd seen since moving across the country from her home city of Wilmington, Delaware to the South Bar area almost five years ago.

The twenty-six-year-old aerospace engineer had left the townhouse of Mike DePresti - her boyfriend of just over a year - in Redondo Beach at seven AM, the same time she did every day, to get to her job at the Aering Space Systems facility in El Segundo.

Normally, Parkowski wouldn't have laid on her car horn in frustration. Her supervisor, Dr. Jacob Pham, was more than accommodating. It was fairly common for people to show up late due to the crazy LA traffic.

But today was not like any other day.

On this Friday morning in the middle of November, Parkowski would step, virtually of course, onto the surface of Venus.

She would be the lone operator of one of the two ACHILLES humanoid robots on the ILIAD mission that had launched four months ago from Florida. The robots had landed on Venus just twenty-one days ago and before going through their initialization and characterization phase. They were now ready for the operators – like Parkowski – to control them through a virtual reality interface.

Parkowski's shift "on the sticks" in the Aering parlance didn't start until ten o'clock. But she had to run through the script with Dr. Pham before she could start her mission, and even getting herself into the VR gear was time-consuming. She had planned for an arrival time of eight o'clock, but the bumper-to-bumper status of Pacific Coast Highway was getting in her way. In addition, she had stayed up late to watch an NFL game that went well into overtime, waking up a little later than she had planned, and in retrospect, the late night might not have been worth it.

Parkowski cursed and checked her makeup in the rearview mirror, then pulled her dirty-blonde ponytail slightly tighter.

She had worked on different projects since she had arrived in the Los Angeles area, but none of them were as cool as this one. Parkowski had dedicated the last year of her life to learning every inch of the ACHILLES robot, every piece of software and hardware, and all of the procedures needed to operate it. She had been practicing in the VR gear for a few weeks now, and could probably do it in her sleep, but was anxious to get her first mission underway.

As a fast-riser within the aerospace company, she was angling for a promotion to a supervisory job within the next few years. Being late for her first mission wouldn't kill her Aering career, but it definitely wouldn't help it either.

She tapped her left foot on the floor, a nervous habit she had learned from her father, and waited for the idling cars in front of her to go forward.

Finally, the old Chevy SUV in front of her moved six feet. Parkowski breathed a sigh and let her foot off of the brake.

She took a moment to calm herself down and clear her head, taking in her surroundings. It was a beautiful day in Southern California. The sun shone brightly overhead and a slight breeze came in from the Pacific.

Parkowski smiled. Just like the weather, everything was going to go well today. The mission was going to be a success, she was going to blow through its objectives and finish strong at its conclusion in the early part of the afternoon. Then, she would either go home and rest, or go out to dinner with her boyfriend and his military unit at the nearby Rock & Brews to celebrate a going-away.

Nothing was going to ruin her day.

After what seemed like an eternity the traffic started moving again. As she drove she looked for the source of the delay but couldn't find it. It was as if the collective sea of cars on the road had a mind of its own.

Parkowski got off the main road before taking a few back streets through a residential section of El Segundo to the Aering plant. She parked her car in the attached parking garage and made her way into the facility with plenty of time to spare.

"Morning, Bert," she said to the security guard as she scanned her ID card at the reader at the entrance to her building.

"Good morning ma'am," the elderly dark-skinned man replied from his desk. "How do you think your Birds are going to do this weekend?"

Parkowski gave a quick laugh, then shook her head. "I'm not sure. I think we've got a good chance against the Giants, it's at home, but my boyfriend is worried. He thinks it's a trap game."

"I hope they win," Bert responded. "My Rams are probably going to be in contention with New York for the seventh and final wild card."

"Me too," Parkowski said as she quickly stepped to the large, heavy door that controlled access to her part of the facility. She liked talking with the security team, especially football with Bert, but she was in a rush. "Have a good weekend."

"You too, ma'am."

Parkowski walked down a wide, nondescript hallway with windows at the top of the walls near the ceiling, allowing the sun's morning rays to fully illuminate the space without the help of artificial light. The building was part of an old Hughes plant that had been bought by Aering when the former company went bankrupt twenty-five years ago. Most of the multi-building facility was devoted to spacecraft design and production, but this particular edifice was home to the ILIAD project and the control of the ACHILLES robots.

She turned the corner and kept walking until she found the women's locker room. There, she changed from her street clothes into a skintight black turtleneck and leggings. Parkowski thought that they looked like workout clothes, only tighter and made of a strange material that seemed to attract lint and dirt like a magnet.

Parkowski checked herself in the mirror. Her dark brown eyes looked tired, and the light makeup she had put on this morning didn't do much to hide it. She didn't feel particularly exhausted, but the bags under her eyes gave it away.

She made a mental note to go to bed earlier tonight regardless of her evening plans. It had been a long week. Hopefully, it didn't affect her performance on today's mission.

Shoeless, Parkowski went through an airlock at the far side of the locker room into a semi-clean room.

Originally a spacecraft high bay development area with forty-foot ceilings, it had been repurposed as a command center for the ACHILLES project. The space was sectioned off into multiple segments: a large cube farm for the scientists who were in theory guiding the mission, but in practice just reviewing data after it came in, a smaller one for the engineers working on the hardware and software of the ACHILLES robots, a lab area for the technicians, and a large section in the middle which appeared to be a small metal "stage" raised above the floor that almost looked out of place in the high-tech setting.

Just outside the high bay was a hallway with offices for the senior staff, as well as a pair of controlled rooms with cipher locks: one actively used and owned by NASA, another one, inactive, for a classified program that used to occupy the ACHILLES mission space.

About ten people were in the room, most of whom stood around the one person hooked up to the VR gear up the stage. A large clock hung in one corner like in her high school gym. Above the stage was a 100" flat-panel monitor that displayed a rocky landscape, obviously the surface of Venus from the sensors of the robots.

It was seven fifty-five AM. She had made it.

Her supervisor and mentor stood underneath the giant television screen that towered over him. He smiled as Parkowski approached. "How are you doing this morning, Grace?" Dr. Jacob Pham asked.

"Just fine, Jake," Parkowski responded. "How are you doing?"

The older Vietnamese-American man shrugged his shoulders. "Can't complain. Another day, another dollar."

"You're not excited?" she asked.

He shook his head, then thought for a second. "I'm not excited for myself, but I'm definitely excited for you," he told Parkowski, who at five-foot-eight stood a head taller than him. "I've been in and out of the gear and walking on Venus for the better part of two weeks. It's no longer as new and fascinating as it was the first time I was in."

Pham paused and took a breath. "It's just after eight and your shift isn't until ten," he told Parkowski. "Let's get you set up and we'll walk through your mission before you have to get on the sticks. Does that sound good?"

"Sounds great," she echoed her boss. "Let's go."

CHAPTER TWO

El Segundo, California

Parkowski followed Pham to a rack of equipment, the closer of two in a row. The older man pulled out a pair of slip-on shoes made of an exotic rubbery material and handed them to her. "Put these on first," he said. "Remember, just like going into a clean room..."

"Bottom to top," she finished with a slight smile. As she sat down and put them on, Pham walked to a nearby chest and pulled out a pair of what looked like soccer shin guards. "Do you want me to help you put them on?"

She nodded. "Of course, boss."

He bent down and strapped the attachments to Parkowski's legs - not the first time he had helped her suit up. When she had first described this whole process to DePresti, he had been defensive. "So, you're wearing your Catwoman suit, and this dude's just feeling you up and putting all of the gear on you."

Parkowski had laughed. "He's five-foot-nothing, old enough to be my father, and on top of that, he's been married for twenty years...to another guy. You don't have anything to worry about, Mike. It's just part of the job. We all help each other get ready to get on the sticks."

Pham finished putting on the shin guards and had returned to the large locker. He came back with a pair of wristbands. "Go ahead and put these on."

She slipped them on, then reached over and pulled out a pair of custom-fit gloves labeled with her last name. "Where are the helmets?" Parkowski asked, not seeing the last part of her gear.

"Over there, at the rack near the stage," Pham told her as he pointed in that direction. "The techs did a double-check last night in preparation for the missions we are running today."

Parkowski nodded, then walked to the second stand of equipment. Up on the raised platform she saw another operator, Caleb Marx, take a couple of steps.

The ACHILLES probes were controlled by a top-of-the-line virtual reality system. It had full haptic feedback in the gloves and shoes and partial feedback throughout the skintight suit that Parkowski wore.

The custom-built headset, a lightweight fourth-generation model, provided a 120° field of vision. The gloves, shoes, and bands around her wrists and ankles provided sensor readings.

Those inputs were transmitted via wired signals to a large rack of high-performance computers near the raised platform. From there, they ran through a landline to NASA's White Sands ground station in Las Cruces, New Mexico. At that location, it was uploaded to the Monitoring and Information Communication System (MICS) satellite network until it reached a high-speed communications relay at the Earth-Moon L2 point. That relay blasted a tightbeam signal at Venus.

There, it was received in synchronous orbit by a small communications satellite placed there by the ILIAD probe and sent to the ground, where it was broadcast to the ground and the ACHILLES robots. Inside, in the main computer system, the commands inputted by the user were mirrored by the robot's internal control systems.

Since Venus was nearing its closest approach to the Earth the total delay time was a little under two minutes. The computer system that powered the virtual reality environment was able to smooth that delay out to just a second or two through filtering and predictive processing. It calculated two to three dozen possible next frames for the user, so when the VR gear sent a command, it was able to give a response before the signal bounced to Venus and back.

Parkowski found her VR headset and put it on to check the fit. When it was strapped over her eyes and ears, she was completely immersed in the Venusian environment. Now, however, it was completely black.

She wondered what Marx was doing. There was a limitation right now that only one user could be active at one time, switching between control of the two robots. The system had been baselined for two active users, but bandwidth limitations had prevented that from occurring. Software engineers were furiously working on a fix, but none had come in yet from the developer.

Taking her helmet off, Parkowski looked around for her mentor and found his bald head in the row of cubicles.

As she walked to him she looked up at the screen. Marx's robot was walking in a large, barren wasteland with yellow-brown boulders strewn around it.

Parkowski originally had wondered why they had engineers control the robots, rather than the researchers, until she had gotten into the VR gear and linked into a simulated environment. The robots themselves were complex, almost to a ridiculous extent, and the UI in the VR environment displayed an overwhelming amount of information on the screen regarding battery power, control actuators, communications links, and the like. There was no way a postdoc in geology or climate sciences would be able to control the robot and get his or her research done at the same time.

She found Pham hunched over a computer screen. "What's up?" she asked.

He smiled at her. "Give me a sec and I'll pull everything up."

"No problem."

He clicked a few icons on the screen, bringing up a PowerPoint presentation and a piece of mission planning software that Parkowski had some rudimentary knowledge of onto the workstation's two monitors. "You're controlling both robots for four and a half hours today," Pham said. He motioned for her to lean over his shoulder in order to see better. "Let's go through the mission overview first, then plan your waypoints in the mission planning software and make sure you're ready to go."

She stepped behind the seated engineer and peered over his hunched form. He started the presentation. "Do you want to go through it line-by-line or just skim it?" Pham asked.

"Line by line," Parkowski replied. "Let's make sure I know every single detail."

"Copy," Pham said, clicking through the initial slides. "You are going to take control of ACHILLES 1 and ACHILLES 2 and a box of their equipment from Mr. Marx at point Alpha, which is located deep within the region of Ishtar Terra, a highland area near the planet's north pole. Alpha is roughly a thousand kilometers east of the Sacajawea volcano, and about ten kilometers from the ILIAD probe's landing site."

"Roger," Parkowski said as she squinted at the screen. Her eyes hurt, probably from the intense incandescent light pumped into the windowless high bay. "What's the lag looking like?"

"Total delay is predicted to be one minute and fifty-five seconds," Pham explained, "actual is one minute and fifty-eight seconds. The computer has been able to smooth that out to a perceived delay of point-five seconds."

"Got it," she said. The math could be a little fuzzy to her at times, but as a big-picture concept, it made sense.

"From there, you will take the two probes and the equipment they carry to point Bravo, located twenty kilometers to the northeast. There is a cave system there that the scientists want to map via ground-penetrating radar."

"What's the mass of the equipment?"

"Ten kilograms," Pham replied as he switched to the next chart in the deck, "One of the ACHILLES robots should be able to carry it easily, especially with the slightly lower gravity on Venus."

She nodded. "Got it."

"Once there, you are going to set up the gear and perform a number of radar collects on the cave system," Pham continued. "There will be a radar technician from Rayleigh, the manufacturer, on the net with you to work through the steps needed."

"Ok, sounds easy enough," Parkowski said. "What next?"

"Then, the robots are going to split up for a bit," Pham explained. "ACHILLES 1 will head back to the landing site and hook up to the recharging station at Waypoint Hotel. It has a big day planned for tomorrow and needs all of the power it can get. Then, you'll switch to ACHILLES 2 and take the radar gear to another waypoint, Charlie, located ninety kilometers from Bravo. You will leave it there for the next operator to pick up."

"Copy," Parkowski said as she stretched her arms over her head. "And all of this is going to take four and a half hours?"

Pham nodded. "That's with about twenty minutes of contingency time, but this is going to take a while. We've had comm issues with the gateway, so you may lose connection a few times. Marx had a lot of trouble in his first ten minutes in control, but the stability got better the more he used the system. The distance between the three points isn't particularly close, and trust me, there's not much to see on the planet. I'd recommend drinking some caffeine, but not too much, as you're not going to get much in the way of bio breaks while you're on the sticks."

"Ok, ok," she replied to the long-winded explanation. "I think I'm good. No further questions."

Next, the senior engineer showed Parkowski how to input her planned path into the mission planning software. It was cumbersome to use, with an antiquated interface that reminded her of some of the old video games from the nineties that her dad played on his laptop. Parkowski had once complained to one of the Aering in-house software engineers, who had shrugged. "It was bid out," the man had told her, "and we always pick the lowest bidder with a government contract. I don't think ease of use was very high on the list of selection criteria."

After thirty minutes of using the awkward software, Parkowski was done. The computer took a couple of minutes to compute the expected parameters for both of the ACHILLES robots, as well as the communications bandwidth and pathway for the entire mission. "Am I good to go?" she asked Pham.

"Yes, you are." He closed out of the software and they walked to the raised platform.

Pham helped her put her gear back on and started hooking the cables up to it. Parkowski tried to count them but lost track after ten.

A pair of technicians swooped in to help Dr. Pham as he struggled to plug one of them in. "Let me help you, doc," one of them said as he took the cable.

"Fine, fine," Pham said with a smile. He took a step back, still holding Parkowski's VR helmet in his hands. "Remember, when we first hook you up, you're in view mode only. Marx's gear is still in control."

"I remember, I remember," Parkowski said. Some operators had experienced motion sickness while viewing another person controlling the ACHILLES robots. She had not.

But, her body was shaking a little. She was so excited.

This was the closest she might ever get to being on another planet, a childhood dream of hers from watching old science-fiction shows with her dad; an aspiration that had been dashed when she found out that an arrhythmia would keep her from ever being an astronaut. "Can I have my helmet?"

"Of course." Pham handed her the slim, black helmet that covered her head and eyes. "Here you go."

He paused. "And Grace, you're going to do great."

Parkowski smiled, put it on, and fastened the strap under her chin. She saw nothing but darkness, the screen still wasn't on. Someone, she couldn't tell who, plugged a cable into the helmet at the back near her neck. Immediately a blue screen came on, showing her that the helmet's software was booting up. It then went black again.

"I'm ready," Parkowski said. "Dial me into Marx's feed."

A second later she was looking out onto the surface of Venus.

CHAPTER THREE

El Segundo, California

Parkowski steadied herself. The shock of being in the virtual environment was overpowering at first, but she got her footing as the haptic feedback of her connected shoes helped her body regain its balance.

The view was incredible.

Rather than the blue sky of Earth, Parkowski saw the same yellow-orange atmospheric hue that the Soviet Venera probes had transmitted back to Earth. Her visibility was good, allowing her to see anywhere from forty to eight kilometers in any direction. On the actual planet, the thick clouds made of sulfuric acid would have clouded her view, but inside the virtual setting, only a few were rendered.

It was like something out of a science-fiction movie, but right there in front of her eyes. She paused, remembering that she wasn't in control, yet. The scene was still.

"Comm issue, Grace," she heard Marx say. "Give us a sec."

"Ok," she replied.

The virtual environment was created by an Aering subcontractor with inputs from a variety of aircraft simulator and video game companies. Using real-time data, the simulated world was synchronized with the real one, allowing the virtual explorer to see the weather, temperature, and other features of Venus in near-real-time with incredible graphical fidelity.

The algorithms used to give feedback to the user on the sticks in the VR gear was top-notch as well. The supercomputer physically located at the Aering facility that also ran the virtual environment was able to predict the next "move" for each of the input devices and seamlessly link the virtual environment that the human experienced with the real, hostile, alien world of Venus.

The entire world started to move in front of her. Whatever issue that had popped up was now fixed. Marx took a few steps forward using his own gear, a disorienting move. "Ready to transfer."

Parkowski stretched her arms. The next time she moved, her movements would be copied on Venus. "Ready to take control."

"Switching," a technician said. "Thirty seconds."

She slowly breathed in, then out, then in, then out. Parkowski was ready to go.

"Switched," the same technician said. "Ready to go."

Parkowski took a few steps forward and looked around. The surface around her was mostly flat, save for a few shallow craters and crevasses. The terrain sloped gradually at first, then sharply, towards the massive volcano to her east named after Sacajawea. She saw a bit of aliasing in her display, a jagged edge of a ridge near the horizon reminded her that she was in a simulation and not in the real world.

There was a hiss of static, and then a new voice spoke to her. "Can you hear me?" Pham asked, his voice a little garbled.

"Yes, but not great."

A pause. "How about now?" Pham said, more clearly this time.

"That's better."

"Ok," Pham said. She heard a rustling of papers. "Grace, I'm going to need you to switch between the two robots. You are currently on ACHILLES 1, I want you to check out ACHILLES 2."

"Copy," she replied.

Parkowski used the controls inside of her gloves to pull up the heads-up display's main menu at the bottom of the VR headset. A blue translucent table appeared with several options. Using a wheel located in her right glove's thumb, she selected the icon that would allow her to switch between robots.

In an instant, Parkowski jumped to ACHILLES 2. The entire VR screen snapped to show the view from the "head" of the second probe through the electro-optical sensors located where the robot's "eyes" would be. The view was much the same, except for some more noticeable aliasing. "The image quality from the second probe is worse."

"I know, we had the same problem all morning," Marx chimed in. "The software guys think it's the simulation software itself rendering at a lower quality level to save computational power. Or something like that."

"Thanks, Caleb," she said as she took a few steps. Parkowski looked down at her feet as she did so, amazed at how her walking in the real world was instantly translated into the virtual one.

Parkowski remembered the first time she ever used VR. It was at DePresti's house, in his spare bedroom that was his office and video game playroom. She laughed internally at the memory. It had been early in their relationship, maybe the second month or so, and she was in shock that this seemingly normal, attractive man she had been dating was a giant video game nerd. Parkowski wasn't turned off or offended, her father and brothers played video games; she just hadn't pegged DePresti as the video gaming type. He had shown her his setup, which consisted of a powerful gaming computer, headset, and motion-controlled, handheld actuators. "This is the future of entertainment," he had insisted. "In five years, everyone will be playing on something like this."

She wasn't so sure. The entire setup cost over a thousand dollars for the virtual reality headset and controllers and God-only-knew-how-much for the PC, a high bar of entry for most people. However, she had let DePresti put the headset on her and had gotten her into a simple game where she'd cut open blocks coming at her with a laser sword. After about twenty minutes, she took the headset off. "That's it?" she had jokingly asked a shocked DePresti. It didn't have quite the "wow" factor that he had expected.

Back in the present, Parkowski continued walking, catching sight of the first ACHILLES robot about half a football field away.

She noticed that ACHILLES 1 was carrying a large package, an oblong box dark in color with wires sticking out of it. That must be the ground-penetrating radar. She hadn't noticed it when she had been in control of it, the VR system didn't simulate weight. Parkowski picked up her speed and caught up to the first robot.

"Alright, I've got the two together," she told Pham. "What's next?"

"You are currently at point Alpha, and need to get to waypoint Bravo," the older engineer told her. "Grace, pull up your HUD. You're missing out on a lot of information."

She groaned. Parkowski hated the HUD - it was information overload. "Ok," she replied as she used the thumb switch to pull up the full heads-up display.

Now, it really looked like a video game. There was a miniature map in the upper-left corner of her display with a blue triangle in the middle of it showing her current position. A model of the ACHILLES robot she was currently piloting was in the top right, with numbers showing stresses, strains, temperatures, and battery life for each of its components overlaid on top of it. The bottom left had the current communications settings and the health of that system. The bottom right was empty at the moment. It was customizable, allowing the user to display any number of settings or status pages that they wished.

Parkowski always considered the HUD to be a distraction to the work she was doing. Instead, she preferred to pull up individual menus as she needed them and put them away when she was done. Alerts were set for various metrics measured by the system, if any of the robot's systems were trending in the wrong direction she would deal with it then. Otherwise, Parkowski wanted to be immersed in her work - a hard task with all of the additional overlays on her display.

LAG DELAY

Parkowski turned the ACHILLES 2 robot so it was pointed in the correct direction, to the northeast. "Here we go."

She only got about a dozen meters forward when the system grew sluggish. "I'm getting some lag here," Parkowski said over the net. "I'm going to hold up and run a diagnostic."

"Copy," Pham said. "We see you stopping, but everything looks green from out here."

Parkowski flipped through her menus until she found the external communications system.

The settings and values in the menu were all normal; there was nothing out of the ordinary. Puzzled, Parkowski checked the raw signal coming into the robots from the relay in orbit. The transmission was being received by the robots, but it was well below the strength needed to maintain the minimum lag required for smooth operations. "I've got a signal strength problem, over."

"Let's check the satellite," Pham said. "Standby. Don't switch robots."

"Roger," Parkowski replied. "Standing by."

The answer came a few minutes later. "There's an issue with a power regulator on the comm bird in orbit around Venus," Pham told her. "We're switching it to the redundant string until we can figure out what's exactly wrong with it."

"Got it, thanks," Parkowski said. They were switching to the backup power system on the satellite, the only option they had if the primary power subsystem was malfunctioning.

She moved her hand and watched the ACHILLES robot mirror her movement smoothly. "Everything looks back to normal."

She walked what the HUD told her was about a hundred meters, then switched back to ACHILLES 1 to bring it back to the other robot. Parkowski was sweating in her tight clothes that didn't give her skin much room to breathe. While walking in ACHILLES 1, she checked the time - it was eleven. She had already been in the virtual environment for an hour. Time flies when you're having fun.

After bringing ACHILLES 1 next to the other robot, she switched to ACHILLES 2 and continued on her path to checkpoint Bravo. The environment showed her more clouds and the terrain was getting steeper, with plenty of pitfalls and steep ledges to avoid. She did some quick mental math to make sure the robot could get over those obstacles.

Thankfully, it didn't translate to any increase in difficulty. Parkowski was able to keep a good pace and reach the checkpoint in fifty minutes, ten minutes off of her planned time even with the communications issue.

At Waypoint Bravo, she looked around but didn't see any caves. "Hey Doc," she called out on the radio. "I'm not sure where I'm supposed to set up my radar gear."

"Huh," her mentor said. "Let me check the map."

A minute later he returned to the net. "The waypoint's a little off. The entrance to the cave system is located just past a small crater to the north. It's probably hard to see with all of the clouds and steam."

Parkowski squinted in that direction. Just behind a boulder, she saw a small dip indicating a crater. "Ok, I think I see it," she told Pham. "Let me confirm."

She walked past the boulder and into a shallow crater that reminded her of a sand trap at a golf course, just without the sand. Climbing the other side carefully, she came to a small pit that, from her view, looked like it went a pretty decent depth into Venus' surface.

"Ok, I'm here," she said. "Get the Rayleigh tech on."

CHAPTER FOUR

El Segundo, California

Using the robot's arms, Parkowski placed the nondescript metal gray box on the ground.

She wasn't sure what to do next. "Is the tech on the net?" she asked again as she brought the ACHILLES robot down to one of its "knees"

"I'm right here," an unfamiliar male voice said in her ear.

"Hi," Parkowski said. "What exactly am I supposed to do with this box?"

She heard a quick laugh. "Well, first things first, you need to move it on its side," The tech said. "The radar dish itself is recessed into the box, it's the large circle next to your left leg if the display I'm seeing here is correct."

Parkowski rotated the box so she could see the circle. She could barely see it with the computer-generated graphics. Pulling up the HUD, she created a display from the ACHILLES robot's cameras and pinned it to the upper right of her display. Despite the grainy footage, the radar dish was clearly there. "Ok, here we go," she said to herself as she rotated the radar system into the correct orientation.

"Got it," she said over the net. "What next?"

"Check the control panel," Ratliff said. It was now visible, a series of minimalist controls on the top of the box with a small three-inch LCD next to them. "Look for a row of square buttons. The largest one is the power button."

After turning it on, the Rayleigh tech helped her get the radar configured. She took a quick image using the lowest setting available, then switched the control panel to the image processing function. "I'm not seeing anything," Parkowski told Ratliff, "at least not anything useful. It looks like a completely black screen, not like a radar image."

"Huh," she heard the tech say. "Give me a sec, I have one of the engineers here with me in the room."

Parkowski stood up and stretched her legs. She was starting to get tired and hungry. That breakfast sandwich hadn't been enough; she had underestimated how much walking with all of the VR gear on would tire her out.

She looked at the landscape around her. The graphics inside of the virtual environment were almost photorealistic, immersing her in the alien planet. She almost forgot that her body was still on Earth. The sky was a different color, sure, and the clouds more ominous, but it wasn't completely out of place from hiking in Arizona or New Mexico. Except for the lack of vegetation. That got Parkowski every time. Unlike early science-fiction depictions of the planet, Venus was completely barren.

The technician came back online. "The radar doesn't have the correct settings to operate on Venus," he told Parkowski. "The magnetosphere is different from Earth's and we need to compensate. We're working on getting a correct list of parameters that you can feed into the system manually. Standby."

"Got it," she replied. Parkowski stretched her arms out, then sat down.

Five minutes passed before he spoke again. "Hey, Ms. Parkowski, sorry for the delay," he said. "We have the correct list of configuration settings for the radar. Please let us know when you're ready to input them."

Parkowski knelt next to the radar box. "I'm ready now," she told Ratliff as she readied the ACHILLES robot over the control panel.

The tech walked her through the settings, page by page, until the radar was properly configured. "Try taking an image now," he suggested.

Parkowski tried again. This time, the control panel showed a black image with white lines seemingly drawn indiscriminately across it. "What the hell is this?" Parkowski said to herself softly. "I have something, but I'm not sure if it's what we're looking for," she said over the net.

This time, Dr. Pham responded. "It looks like you've got it," he told Parkowski. "That's what a radar image looks like before any processing. I think we have the right settings now."

"Copy, thanks," Parkowski said, looking incredulously at the control panel. There was no way that anyone would be able to glean something of substance from that, she thought, but that wasn't her problem. "What do I need to do next?"

"The radar system can map the cave system below you automatically," The technician broke in. "We've got a script here at the plant in Aurora that will do that so you can continue your mission while it does its job. I'm sending it over to you in El Segundo now."

"Grace, we'll take it from here," said one of the Aering technicians. "We'll upload the script through the comm pathway to your ACHILLES unit so you can transmit it directly."

"Ok," she said. "How long will that take?"

"Once we have it? About five minutes total," Pham broke in. "Just hang tight. I know we've told you to do a lot of that today but that's part of the job, sorry. Don't worry, we're still on track to complete all of the objectives of your mission by the end of the shift."

"Got it," Parkowski responded. "Sitting tight until it's uploaded."

DePresti often talked about how in the military, especially when he was outside of his normal acquisition duties in a class or when he was in a training environment at the Air Force Academy, there was a lot of what he referred to as "hurry up and wait."

Parkowski felt like this mission was full of that. She spent half of her time waiting for other people to do things so that she could do her job.

"Uploaded to your ACHILLES unit," the Aering tech said a few seconds after Parkowski was finished with her self-reflection. "Go ahead and transfer it to the radar unit."

Parkowski pulled up her menu and turned the Wi-Fi setting of the ACHILLES unit on. The ubiquitous network protocol used in millions of households around the world was also used on Venus to transmit files between the two ACHILLES robots, their equipment, and their home base. She transferred the file, a tiny, 54 KB text file, and went back to the radar's control panel. "I'm ready to run it."

"Go ahead," Ratliff said. "We'll check the first couple of images and then you can leave and complete the rest of your mission."

She hit "play" and the script began taking images. Parkowski checked the first one on the control panel. It looked suspiciously similar to the first one captured by the radar. "Does this look correct?" she asked over the net.

"Yes, it does," Ratliff confirmed.

"Copy. Should I stick around or can I move on?" she asked.

"Go ahead and take the ACHILLES 1 unit back to the charging station," a new voice she recognized as Pham's immediate superior, Dr. Robert Rosen, said. "We're monitoring the preprocessing images as they come in and we'll let you know if there's any issues. If there are, you can switch back to ACHILLES 2 and troubleshoot. In the meantime, let's press on."

"Got it, sir," she said, a little surprised by the senior engineer's presence on her operational net. Rosen was just below an Aering VP; the project's chief engineer whose presence was felt in almost every facet of the operation. "Anything else?"

"Nope, just keep doing what you're doing," Rosen said. "Good job, Grace, and the team is doing outstanding work."

"Thank you," Pham replied, speaking for her. "Grace, go ahead and switch to ACHILLES 1. I'll help guide you to Waypoint Hotel."

LAG DELAY

Parkowski switched robots and checked her local map for the next waypoint. It was about five kilometers to the west, away from the mountains. Once the ILIAD probe had reached orbit, it had released a half-dozen charging stations, powered by large solar panels, to preplanned spots across Venus' surface near where the ACHILLES robots would be operating. The robots themselves could hold a charge in their internal batteries for only twenty hours before needing a four-hour recharge period.

The terrain was steep and uneven initially before leveling out somewhat as Parkowski continued her robot's journey. She had to carefully use her legs to get the ACHILLES 1 unit over some boulders and cracks in the ground. The sun beat down overhead, thankfully, she couldn't feel it inside her gear. However, the ACHILLES robot's temperatures were at the high range of its nominal zone.

"I'm getting high temps," Parkowski called out. "Not sure what to do, over."

Yet another tech, an older woman with a soft voice, responded a few seconds later. "I'll have the thermal team take a look, hold up for a second Ms. Parkowski," the female technician said. "I think we've seen this before during the midday hours and it wasn't a big issue. Once you get to the charging station, there are thermal dumps there that will allow the ACHILLES unit to dissipate excess heat."

"Ok, let me know what they say," Parkowski responded. "I'm maybe a klick from Waypoint Hotel. I can make it there in less than ten minutes if I push it, but I don't know how much heat that'll generate."

She didn't get an immediate response.

About ten seconds later Pham came on the net. "I had to step away for a second," the older engineer told her. "How's everything going?"

"Not too bad," she responded. "I'm about a kilometer from Hotel but I've got a lot of heat built up. They're checking to see if it's ok."

"Ms. Parkowski?" the female tech came back on. "The thermal guys say you're ok to continue."

"Ok, thanks," she said as Parkowski started her trek again. About a hundred feet from the waypoint she spotted the charging station. It was a gray cylinder, maybe the size of an oil drum, with solar panels in a cruciform configuration pointing up at the sky. She quickly found the charging cable and inserted it into the ACHILLES' charging port on the left side of the torso.

She had told them it would take ten minutes, she did it in just under eight.

Parkowski then switched to ACHILLES 2. The VR environment took slightly longer to "blink" between the two robots, generally a sign that the lag between two points on the communication pathway was getting worse. "Can I get a lag check?" she asked.

"Still one minute and fifty-eight seconds, no change," Pham replied.

She shrugged her shoulders. This was a complex software system, and a lot of the small issues and bugs were generally unexplainable. Parkowski checked the clock. One hour for her to get from her current position to point Charlie.

"Here goes nothing..." she said to herself.

CHAPTER FIVE

El Segundo, California

Parkowski began walking through the barren landscape to her mission's ultimate destination.

She was sweating profusely now. Being in the suit for this long almost qualified as a workout. It dripped down her forehead and almost into her eyes. She wished she had been able to wear less clothing, but the gear required the tight, athletic attire underneath the arm and leg sensors.

There was some more lag. She had to stop twice to let the VR environment catch up with what was happening in the real world on Venus. "Getting some spikes here," she said on an open channel. Checking the chronometer, she was at the hour mark since she had started her trek to Charlie.

"Copy, we're reading the same thing here," Pham said in a calm tone. "I've got one of the technicians calling over to NASA to see what's going on. Preliminary analysis shows heavy traffic through MICS, much more than would be expected on a Friday. We'll see if we can free up some bandwidth for you." A pause. "Is it bad enough that you need to pause or cancel the operation?"

Parkowski shook her head, a pointless gesture inside all of the VR gear. "No, let me check some settings and see if I can't make it a little better. I think I'm good for the time being."

"Very good." She heard some papers rustling in the background. "You still have plenty of time left."

"How much exactly?"

"Well, it's just after noon local, so you have about an hour and a half, but it's going to take you most of that time to get there." A map appeared in front of her blown-up version of the one in her HUD, overlaid over the VR headset's display of the Venusian landscape. "There's Charlie," Pham said, a little blue cursor circling a point, "and there's you," the cursor pointing at the blue arrow. "It's about eighty kilometers from your current position in a low-gravity setting. You'll be fine."

"Thanks, Doc," she replied as she checked the VR system's settings. Everything looked good, but she turned down some of the graphics fidelity to reduce stress on the rendering system.

Parkowski went back to her minimalist HUD and started her journey.

She was glad that she was controlling a robot a planet away and not actually on Venus herself. The ACHILLES unit had to transverse some pretty rough terrain to get to point Charlie. There was a shallow crater that didn't look too tough until she got into it. The depression was pockmarked with smaller impact holes, and to top it off, had cracks running through it up to a foot or so deep.

ACHILLES 2 got stuck not once, not twice, but three times, and Parkowski had to work carefully in order to get the robot's foot out of a crevasse or hole. She placed a large timer on her HUD to count down until the end of the mission and transfer of control.

"What happens if I miss my window to give up control of the robots?" she asked Pham out of curiosity while continuing her trek across the crater.

"Depends on by how much," the scientist replied. "If you miss it by a few minutes? That's fine, we can adjust. If you miss it by an hour or so, we could recover, but it would cause an enormous replan of the downstream schedule. You're not planning to do that to us, are you?"

"Of course not," Parkowski said with a slight smile. "Just curious, that's all."

"You're almost home free," she heard Rosen say, breaking in on the channel. "Keep it up, Grace. You're doing great."

LAG DELAY

She smiled again and continued her push forward - her future promotion was in the bag.

Looking ahead, Parkowski saw some weird effects on the horizon, a naturally jagged ridge in front of a distant mountain range.

This was aliasing, an artifact of the lag spike she was encountering. The VR system's renderer was downsampling images to preserve bandwidth but was displaying them in the same, higher resolution of the environment, leading to the jagged edges.

"Doc, are you sure the lag numbers are correct?" she asked again. "Lots of weird stuff going on."

"Still one minute and fifty-eight seconds even," Pham answered. "No alerts or alarms in our monitoring software."

"I'll take your word for it," Parkowski said under her breath. "Ok, thanks," she replied over the net. "Continuing onwards."

She managed a few more meters before her entire ACHILLES rig stopped moving, despite her continued inputs.

Parkowski groaned. "Hey doc, I'm stuck."

"We know," Pham said. "They're switching to the alternate wideband comm pathway on the relay. The NASA flight crew think that's the issue."

"Isn't MICS just a bent pipe?" she asked, meaning that the communications satellite just simply passed forward whatever it received. In this case, it should just be taking in the signals from the communications satellite around Venus, amplifying it, and sending it down to a ground station on Earth.

"It is, but something's wrong with that pipe on the bird itself," the Ph.D. told her. "Thankfully, we're fully redundant. They're switching to the alternate side now and will troubleshoot the primary later."

Parkowski rolled her eyes. "Fine, how long is it going to take?"

"One sec," Pham said. "They're putting together the script now."

She heard him ask a muffled question to someone on the other end, then come back to the mic. "As soon as they upload these commands, you should be good to go - it should be almost instantaneous. Wait a minute, then try moving forward again."

"Roger roger."

Parkowski took a deep breath and let her arms drop, trying to relax at the apex of a difficult mission, her first inside of the VR gear controlling real-life robots on another planet. Her stomach growled again. She couldn't wait to get out and go get some food.

After counting to sixty she tried again. It was much smoother now. Whatever issue they had isolated to the MICS satellite must have been fixed, at least for the moment.

She checked her map. Fifty kilometers from the target location, and plenty of time to get there.

Parkowski pushed her robot hard on the flat, rocky plain, but had to lay off her speed when they came to another crater-filled moor. She had to deftly maneuver the ACHILLES unit through the crevasses in the ground, much like near the more mountainous region earlier, to ensure that its "feet" didn't slip through.

She wondered why the unit's feet were so small, at least half the size of those of an adult man's and in the shape of an L, like a prosthetic leg/ankle/foot combination. While Parkowski was an engineer, she wasn't intimate with the "whys" behind the design of the ACHILLES robots, just their end result and how to use them. However, it would have been much easier for her if they had been made longer and wider for use on Venus' pockmarked surface.

Twenty-five kilometers to go. There were more boulders here, likely broken off of the nearby mountain range, and pushed down by wind and gravity. Parkowski could no longer take a more-or-less straight route to her destination, rather, she had to weave through the increasingly dense field of large rocks that blocked her path.

She was now within seven kilometers of Point Charlie.

LAG DELAY

Up until this point, Parkowski hadn't noticed any noise, other than the artificial sounds of her own robot's footsteps and the radio chatter in her ears. Whether it was the VR software filtering out external sounds, or her own ears and brain tuning them out, she didn't know for sure. But there was noise, the footsteps of technicians and scientists meandering around outside of her rig or static over the comm net, and even more artificial sounds from the VR environment such as the scraping of the ACHILLES unit's foot against the ground. But, she just didn't notice them.

However, there were now some strange sounds that had to be coming from inside of the environment itself. She heard a low rumble, then a weird, chirping sound not unlike that of a bird, followed by a loud roar.

Parkowski looked around, instinctively seeking the source of the sounds. They were completely out of place on Venus. But, all she saw was the desolate landscape, the same one she had traversed over the last few hours.

A little nervousness was starting to seep into her armor of confidence.

"Hey doc, I'm hearing some weird stuff," she said into her mic.

Pham came on the net. "Weird stuff?" he repeated.

"Yeah, some sounds. Did you guys hear anything out there?"

"No, nothing out of the ordinary."

"There's not anything at all? Didn't a bird get into the high bay a few weeks back?"

"No, nothing like that. Grace, is everything ok?"

"I'm fine, Doc, seriously. I just heard something odd."

Pham didn't respond. Parkowski kept moving forward towards the objective, the strange chirping sound still coming through her headset.

There was another sound now, a low rumble at a different frequency than the earlier one, but she tuned it out. It had to be some kind of bug in the software, perhaps some kind of programming artifact left in by the development team.

Not all of the sweat was from her exertion now. Parkowski worried that something was going wrong.

At two kilometers from Point Charlie, the lag started to get better and the sounds disappeared. Parkowski breathed a sigh of relief. She was almost done.

The aliasing at the horizon went away, the blockiness of the far-away ridge giving way to a more natural curve. Whatever communications issue that she had been experiencing throughout her mission was gone.

She saw movement.

A gigantic wyvern rose from the other side of the ridge. It was red and brown and about the size of a city bus with wings.

The dragon surreally flapped its wings as it hovered a hundred feet above the planet's surface.

Her jaw was on the floor.

Parkowski was stunned. Not only were dragons not real, and certainly not on Venus, but her rational mind wouldn't allow for anything, let alone a gigantic mythical creature, to fly in the thick atmosphere. But there it was, clear as day, in front of her.

She was exposed and out in the open. The field of boulders was kilometers behind her, there was no way she would make it back there if the dragon would attack.

The dragon stopped flapping its wings and went into a lazy glide in an orbit about half of its original altitude.

Parkowski breathed out. Maybe it hadn't noticed her.

But it had.

The beast made a sharp turn and came straight in her direction.

CHAPTER SIX

El Segundo, California

Parkowski screamed.

The dragon swooped down and opened its mouth wide. Flames shot out towards the ACHILLES unit.

Her survival instincts kicked in. Parkowski dove towards the planet's rocky, cracked surface. Unfortunately, she forgot that she wasn't actually there on Venus.

She fell to the floor in a heap of wires, equipment, and hardware.

It was like something out of a nightmare. Parkowski felt trapped, constrained by the wires wrapped around her body.

The sensor on her left leg slid off as she slammed, knee-first into the lightly padded floor. Her other leg hit a moment later, followed by her torso and arms.

Parkowski felt a shooting pain in her right elbow that had gotten twisted in the fall, and a slight ache in her knee.

The dragon was still there, overhead, blotting out the stars. It roared and started another dive.

She screamed again and rolled away from the dragon, entangling herself in a mess of cords and wires. Something unplugged, likely her headset, and her entire world went dark.

Parkowski paused for a second. Was she dead? Had the dragon's fiery breath gotten her? Was she in heaven...or hell? Then she remembered. She wasn't on Venus. She was on Earth, in a high bay, in the building she worked at every single weekday.

A couple of deep breaths later, she was calm. There was no immediate danger. But, she was still in a shock, a daze as everything at the moment seemed so surreal.

She tried to stand up, but couldn't. A cord or wire strapped to her leg prevented her from doing so. The skin-tight clothing Parkowski wore made it hard for her to tell just how many cables were around her, or where they were, but they were definitely constricting her body. She was only able to make it up on one knee.

There were muffled sounds outside of her headphones, some voices and scuffling of feet, but it all was a haze. "Lost connection!" she heard a male voice shout. She recognized it but couldn't put a name to it. Someone grabbed her wrist, trying to help her up, but instinctively she pulled away, falling back and trapping her left foot under her.

Parkowski took another deep breath. She was on Earth, there was no dragon, and everything was going to be ok. Another set of hands, softer ones, began detaching the cables from her leg sensors. She relaxed. Just by touch, she could tell that it was Dr. Pham.

A second and third set of hands started unwrapping from the cables from the nest that surrounded her. "Stay calm, Grace," she heard Pham say. "Everything is ok."

"Can you take my headset off?" she asked.

"No, not yet, sorry," the male voice she had heard earlier said. It was one of the technicians in the high bay. "We need to get all of the wires off before we can safely remove it."

"Ok," Parkowski replied. "Thanks, everyone, sorry about that."

She felt like shit. Everything had been going so well too.

No one responded, the team of three was in the process of slowly untangling her from the VR setup.

Finally, soft hands - Pham's - were placed on either side of her head, and the headset was lifted off. Parkowski breathed a sigh of relief. Her eyes took a moment to adjust to the bright, artificial lights of the high bay but after a few blinks she could see.

Pham, the technician named Damien, and an older woman were positioned nearly on top of Parkowski, unplugging and unwrapping, trying to free her from the mess of cables. A second set of people, Dr. Rosen and the NASA lead, Dr. Hughes, included, were huddled around a four-screen computer terminal in the front of the room.

She stood up. Her eyes shot up to the large computer monitor displaying the simulated environment. It was frozen, showing a still image of the ridgeline that she had reached before the dragon had attacked her. Something must have happened to the system, either through the communications pathway or by her own actions here on Earth.

Conspicuously, the wyvern wasn't present.

"Are you ok, Grace?" Dr. Pham asked.

She snapped back to look down at him. "I think so," she said. "Sorry about that."

"Did something happen?" he asked as the last loop around her right leg was removed.

Parkowski was surprised by his question. "Did you guys not see it?"

"See what?"

"The dragon," she insisted, her stomach giving an audible growl.

The two technicians shot her weird looks.

"Grace, you're hungry," Pham said loudly, changing the subject. He lightly grasped her elbow and steered her towards the edge of the raised platform. "Let's go eat something in my office."

"But the mission," Parkowski protested. "Is everything ok? Are the ACHILLES units safe?"

"Don't worry about them now," Pham said in a lower tone as he helped her get off of the stage. No one was looking at her. They were either working the bank of terminals, trying to reacquire contact with the robots, or cleaning up the mess she had left up on the raised platform.

He gently steered her to his small office and closed the door.

Parkowski was about to ask if he had seen the dragon when the older man shoved a protein bar in her face. "Eat this," he said, more of an order than a suggestion.

Parkowski tore the wrapper off and bit into it. It was some weird fruity flavor, not one she would have chosen herself, but with how hungry she was the young engineer didn't care.

Pham watched her as she devoured the bar. "Do you want another one?"

She shook her head. "Maybe...maybe in a few minutes?" Parkowski swallowed. "Thank you."

"Not a problem."

Pham then got serious, the amused look disappeared from his face. "You said something odd back there," he said to the still-chewing Parkowski. "Unless I was hearing things, you mentioned a dragon."

She paused. "I did because I saw one."

Pham just looked at her.

"Really," Parkowski insisted. The protein bar was gone.

He didn't respond.

"Did you not see it?" she asked.

Pham shook his head. "I have no idea what you're talking about, Grace," he said softly. "A dragon?"

"Yes, a dragon," she confirmed.

"A Chinese dragon, or a European one?" Pham asked.

She thought for a second. "A European one...wait, are you messing with me, doc?" Parkowski asked, suddenly angry.

"No, no, most definitely not," he said, almost defensively, "just trying to gather information."

"But you didn't see it?"

Pham shook his head again. "No. You were coming up on the waypoint, you were almost done, and then all of a sudden you screamed and fell. We still had a signal then, the robot fell hard to the ground, same as you, but when you started rolling we lost the connection. Not sure where along the pathway we lost it, but lost it we did. Most of the team started trying to bring it back up while a couple of the techs and I went over to make sure you're ok."

He took a breath. "It happened so fast. But, I feel like I would have remembered a dragon."

Parkowski nodded. "I know, and I know it sounds insane," she said. "But it was clear as day, right there, coming over the ridge at me, breathing fire like out of a movie or something."

"How clear was it, if I may ask?"

She bit her lip in thought. "To be honest, it seemed incredibly detailed," the engineer said slowly. "Which is interesting, because the rest of the environment had quite a bit of lag and artifacts."

"Got it," Pham said with a nod. He fished another protein bar, this one a more acceptable peanut butter flavor, out of his desk drawer. "Are you ok?"

"You've already asked me that, Jake," Parkowski replied with a forced smile. "I'm fine, really. Now that the initial shock wore off I feel great."

"Ok," he said. "Just making sure."

Someone knocked on the door.

It was another technician, this one older and with his graying hair in a ponytail. "Connection is back up, boss," he said to Pham. He turned to Parkowski. "Are you ok, ma'am? I saw you take a spill."

"I'm fine, thanks for asking. Are the robots ok?"

"Yes, they are," the tech said. "Right where they were supposed to be. Mohammed is suited up and is going to take over unless you want to stand in for him."

"No, he can handle himself," Pham said, standing up from his chair. "Give me a minute with Grace here, and I'll join you in the control room.

The tech nodded and left.

He sighed. "Not your fault, Grace, these things happen. Get out of here, take some time off, and come back Monday. I'll have some of the weekend staff pull the logs and see if they can figure out what caused the anomaly.

"We've only got a few months before planetary alignment limits our contacts and we have to go on a bit of a hiatus. Unless we run into the problem again, we'll probably not do a deep dive until then."

Parkowski nodded. She didn't agree, but she understood.

He patted her on the shoulder. "It's going to be alright. When is your next shift?"

"Shoot," she said. "I don't remember."

Pham leaned down to his desk and grabbed a notebook. "This might not be accurate," he said as he looked at it, "but it looks like you're on the sticks again on Wednesday."

"Wednesday," Parkowski repeated.

He nodded slowly. "Any plans for the weekend?"

She gave a quick laugh. "No, not really," Parkowski said. "Probably just a relaxing weekend."

"Your place or your boyfriend's?"

"Probably his, it's only a ten-minute walk to the beach," she answered.

Pham smiled. "Go for a walk, get some fresh air, hell, even get out of the city and do something," he suggested. "Whatever happened back there, get it out of your system and come back ready to go next week. You're doing great, you've got a great future here. Keep it up."

"Got it, thanks," Parkowski said. She got up, a little unsteadily, and started towards the door. "Have a great weekend, Jake," she said as she left the Ph.D.'s office.

"You too, Grace, take care of yourself," she heard Pham say as she walked down the hallway.

Parkowski headed through the high bay, sneaking a peak at Mohammed in the VR gear.

LAG DELAY

There was no dragon up on the 100" TV screen. Just the cloudy, rocky surface of Venus.

CHAPTER SEVEN

Redondo Beach, California

Parkowski had a surprisingly good time with DePresti's unit that evening at Rock 'n Brews. The dragon and the ILIAD mission were the furthest things from her mind - and she hadn't breathed a word about them to anyone after she had left the Aering building.

But, as she tried to go to sleep that night, the problems came back. Parkowski had worried about the events at Aering, replaying them over and over in her head to see if there was anything she could have done differently.

She wasn't sure if there was.

On Saturday morning, Parkowski woke up in DePresti's bed to find the Space Force captain gone.

She yawned and rolled over to check her phone.

It was just after seven. Why her boyfriend was up so early she didn't know, but the townhouse was deathly quiet. He wasn't here.

Parkowski flipped through the news on her phone for a few minutes before she heard the front door slam. DePresti wasn't the quiet type. "Mike, is that you?" she called.

"Yeah," she heard him say. "One sec."

About ten seconds later, DePresti appeared in the doorway of the bedroom, dressed in gym shorts and a t-shirt. "Sorry about that," he said. "I went for a run and didn't want to wake you up. You were out cold."

"No, you're fine," Parkowski said, sitting up. "You just scared me, that's all."

DePresti laughed. "Sorry about that. Want to go grab breakfast?"

She shook her head. "No, let's just eat here." Parkowski wasn't ready to face the world yet.

"Everything ok?"

Parkowski forced a smile. She wasn't sure if that promotion that had seemed like a sure thing a day ago was still on track. "Yes, but I would appreciate it if everyone would stop asking me that."

DePresti gave her an odd look. "Ok, fine, let's eat here, but then let's go for a walk or go do something," he said. "Something's bothering you, Grace, I can tell. We've been together long enough."

"Ugh, you're right," Parkowski said, agreeing with her boyfriend. Normally, he was wrong about almost everything, at least in her opinion. But, here, he couldn't be more right. Thankfully, he didn't press further.

She got up and out of bed and followed him to the kitchen. DePresti got a carton of eggs out of the fridge and started scrambling them while she got some strawberries and blueberries and started making bowls of fruit.

He turned on the TV to ESPN - not her favorite, but she could deal with it - and the two sat down to eat.

"So, what exactly happened yesterday?" DePresti asked.

Parkowski smiled. She had deftly avoided this topic while they were out with his unit the night before. While she was naturally curious, her boyfriend was even worse. He had to know everything going on, to the point where he could be almost borderline invasive.

She finished chewing her egg. "Well, I finished my mission.'

"That's good."

"But, in the end, I kind of screwed up."

"Why did you do that?" DePresti asked as he went to the fridge for some orange juice. He poured a glass and took a sip.

"Well, I saw a dragon."

DePresti spit out his juice. "What?"

"I saw a dragon."

"You're not bullshitting me, are you?" DePresti said, grabbing a rag to wipe up the spilled liquid.

"Nope," Parkowski confirmed.

"And then what happened?"

"I screamed like a little girl and dove to the floor. It was coming at me, breathing fire."

DePresti poured himself more juice into his glass. "I can't say I would have done much differently." He sat back down at the small table. "What happened after that?"

She took a breath. "It turned and came around for another run. I rolled, instinctively, and totally forgot that I had about a dozen wires hooked up into me."

DePresti laughed briefly, then frowned. "Wait, was there a real dragon?"

"I don't know," Parkowski said, finishing her eggs. "No one else saw it."

She sighed, eager to change the subject. "My headset turned off, I must have unplugged the power cord. Someone yelled 'lost connection' or something like that, I don't really remember. And then..."

Parkowski stopped talking - and eating. Telling her boyfriend what had happened to her yesterday helped, but also brought up how much she had screwed up. She put down her fork and left the rest of her food untouched.

DePresti must have figured out how uncomfortable she felt. "Want to go for a walk?" he asked, finishing his breakfast with a huge bite of egg.

She nodded.

They quickly cleaned up the kitchen. Parkowski brushed her teeth and got her Philadelphia Eagles sweatshirt on while DePresti did the dishes.

She stepped over her boyfriend's recently-acquired scuba gear, haphazardly thrown around the front door, and walked down the stairs to street level. Then, they walked the three blocks to the beach.

LAG DELAY

It wasn't even eight o'clock yet, but on this breezy November morning, the streets were already somewhat busy. A lot of people had the same idea as them - get a walk in before the storm threatening off the coast came in.

Parkowski wished she had put her hair up. It swept around in the wind coming in off of the Pacific, but it wasn't the end of the world. They made small talk as they crossed the narrow streets before they reached the beach.

"North or south?" DePresti asked.

"North," Parkowski answered after a quick scan. "Fewer people."

They started walking on the sand toward Hermosa Beach.

"So," DePresti said after a minute or so of silence. "How did the first part of your mission go? You know, before the dragon and all of that."

"Honestly, pretty well," Parkowski answered. She explained how she had gotten her VR gear on, how she had adapted to the environment, and the surprisingly detailed rendering of Venus.

They walked on the hard sand and she continued, explaining how she was able to control the two robots and how she was able to flip between them.

DePresti didn't say much, just nodding and asking a few minor clarification questions. He, too, was an engineer, and wanted to know the details.

She started describing the anomalies and DePresti started asking more questions. "Was the system lagging every time you pointed in the same direction?" he asked.

"I don't remember," Parkowski replied.

DePresti stopped for a second, kicking at the sand with his running shoe. "Something's weird about this whole thing."

"What do you mean?" Parkowski asked.

"I can't put my finger on it, but this isn't how my VR setup works," the Space Force captain replied. "Granted, I don't have as nice of a setup as you, but if you were getting that much lag, they should have been seeing it on the TV monitor."

"Hmm," Parkowski said, scratching her scalp. "That makes sense."

"Unless it's configured differently," her boyfriend said. "Like I said, just throwing that out there."

They kept walking north along the beach. The small waves started to take the tide back out, exposing more and more sand as they continued.

"When did you see the dragon?" DePresti asked.

She thought for a moment. "Right before I got to the last waypoint."

"And there weren't any other weird artifacts or other mythical creatures in the environment?"

"No, just some graphical tearing," she answered.

"It's just bizarre," DePresti said. "I mean, I believe you, I have to, right? But even if I didn't know you as well as I do, you don't gain anything by telling everyone there was a fucking *dragon* on Venus. You'd have to have evidence to back it up."

Parkowski laughed. "Thanks for the vote of confidence. And who knows, they might have an answer by the time I show up on Monday." It was time for her to ask a question. "Are you using your computer later?"

"My gaming rig?"

"Yeah."

"Um, I was planning to play something tonight, unless we're going out," DePresti answered, momentarily confused. "Why?"

"I want to check something out," Parkowski said, stopping again. She smiled. "Don't worry, it's wine night. I'm going out with the girls from about seven until ten or so. You can have your video game time."

"Thanks, I guess?" DePresti said, still confused. Parkowski declined to elaborate - she had a plan, but it wasn't fully hatched yet.

The two engineers made it to the Redondo Beach pier. "Want to grab lunch?" Parkowski asked.

"Sure."

\#

After lunch, a rare rainstorm passed over the coastal town. The wind from the Pacific battered the windows, but the darkened sky gave the townhouse a somewhat cozy feel. To the two transplants from the East Coast, it didn't rain enough in Southern California - it was a welcomed sight.

Parkowski started a load of laundry in DePresti's machine before going into the spare bedroom that he used as an office. He was there, working on his laptop.

"Doing anything interesting?" she asked.

"Nope, just browsing the news," DePresti responded. "Why?"

"Going to test out a theory, to make sure I'm not crazy," she said, pointing at the gaming computer on a minimalist, gunmetal-gray steel desk. "Going to use your rig."

"Is this about the dragon?"

"Yup."

He laughed. "Let me know if you need anything."

She got to work.

Parkowski had her own account on DePresti's computer for when her own Dell laptop from college wasn't enough. She logged in and got onto the Aering company portal. From there, she went to her personal folder on the corporate cloud. Parkowski had an old build of the Venus environment that she had saved there in case she wanted to run it for practice outside of work.

It downloaded fairly quickly; DePresti's gigabit fiber-optic internet line he used for online gaming with his buddies from back in the Philly area was finally good for something useful. Parkowski quickly installed it and tried to boot it up.

She saw an error message. "Do you know anything about Unreal Engine?" Parkowski asked her boyfriend.

No answer. DePresti had fallen asleep. She repeated it, louder this time, followed by a clap of thunder.

He woke up with a start, almost dropping his laptop in the process. "Yeah, I know a bit," he replied. "What's up?"

"I'm trying to run something but I'm missing a dependency."

"Google the filename of what you're missing and put it in the folder you installed whatever it is you're messing with," DePresti suggested. "If it's UE4 or newer, it should figure it out itself."

"Thanks."

She did as he suggested and it worked, bringing her to a splash screen with "Panspermia Studios - Internal Use Only" overlaid on the standard GUI that she had seen before in training. The name looked unfamiliar until Parkowski realized that it was the developer who had created the Venus environment, a recollection from a briefing long forgotten.

"Nice setup, right?" he asked as he got up to stand next to her. "Andrew Chang helped me set it up before he moved out to Barstow."

She laughed. "Why would someone move to Barstow?"

"To get off the grid," DePresti replied. "He's nuts. Like grade-A crazy. But he's a good guy."

He hovered for a minute and then sat back down.

"Mike, another question," she said. "Have you ever heard of Panspermia Studios?"

"Yeah, I have," he answered as a bolt of lightning struck somewhere to the east outside of the office window. The rain was coming down harder now. "They make video games, and I think also do some special effects stuff for movies."

Parkowski bit her lower lip. She was onto something here but was missing a piece. "Got it. Is it ok if I use your headset?"

"Go for it."

She loaded up the Venus environment with a nominal scenario: two ACHILLES robots, only one controllable, in the Ishtar Terra region. She selected minimal lag, medium fidelity, and multiple control inputs - she could use DePresti's keyboard or the VR controllers sitting off to the side.

Parkowski put the VR headset on top of her head. It was significantly lighter than the professional one she used at Aering but was still noticeable. Once the environment was fully loaded, she could control the robots with the keyboard. Parkowski pressed the "W" key and the screen moved forward as the "robot" moved on "Venus."

She placed the headset over her eyes and did the same thing. The scene in front of her moved forward, just like it had on the monitor.

Parkowski opened up the HUD - significantly easier to use here - and started going through the settings. At work, this was all handled by the techs, here she had to change them herself.

Something popped out at her.

"Mike, another question," she asked.

"What?" DePresti yelled from the kitchen.

"What is 'twinning'?"

He poked his head in the office.

"In the sense that you're using it, it means that the environment is being rendered three times - one for each eye and one for the eternal environment - and displayed on both screens, the monitor and the VR headset."

"What if I turn it on?"

He thought for a moment. "The computer would have to do twice the work," DePresti explained. "You'd have to render each frame twice, but I'm not sure why you would."

"Can I try it out?"

"Sure, you can't do any damage," he laughed. DePresti went back to the kitchen.

Parkowski toggled the setting to "on" and was given a new option - graphical fidelity for each display output.

She left the VR headset on "medium" while changing the computer monitor to "low".

Parkowski went back into the Venus environment, now with the headset on the desk in front of the computer monitor. This time, she could tell a difference between the two. The VR headset looked mostly like what she saw at work, while the computer monitor was extremely low fidelity, more like a video game from before she was born.

They were separate views of the same environment.

She pressed "W" again. This time, the VR headset lagged, taking forever to render the next frame, while the computer monitor's image moved smoothly forward.

"Getting anywhere?" DePresti asked, eating out of a huge bowl of peanuts.

"Yeah, I am," Parkowski replied, shutting down the Venus environment. "Pretty sure I figured out why I saw the dragon and they didn't."

"Good job. But not the "why" of why you saw a dragon?"

"Nope. That one is still a mystery."

CHAPTER EIGHT

El Segundo, California

"Sorry about your Eagles," Bert the security guard said to Parkowski as she badged in.

"It happens," she replied. "I still think we'll make the playoffs, but I'm not sure about the division at this point."

"Well, best of luck this week."

"Thanks!" she replied as she headed down the hallway to her work area with a pep in her step.

Parkowski had had a pretty good weekend.

Between figuring out a piece of the mystery on Saturday, to a Sunday lunch double-date with one of her boyfriend's friends from his unit and his girlfriend, the only thing that went wrong was the Eagles' loss to the Giants on Sunday Night Football.

She put her phone in her locker and headed into the high bay in her street clothes.

About a dozen people were there, mostly technicians. She looked for her boss but didn't see Pham anywhere.

One of the other operators, a woman she didn't recognize, controlled the ACHILLES robots on the raised platform. She was on her hands and knees, seemingly adjusting something.

Parkowski walked over to the TV screen. The robot was down in front of what looked like a small RC car, tinkering with a control panel on top of it.

She shrugged and walked out of the bay to Pham's office beyond it.

He wasn't there either.

Parkowski sat down in the other chair across from his desk. Hopefully, he would return soon.

Fifteen minutes later, no sign of Dr. Pham.

She got up and walked back to the high bay, looking closer this time. The woman was now walking as if on a treadmill, much like Parkowski had on her mission last Friday.

Still no sign of Pham. She asked one of the techs if they had seen her boss. The man nodded. "Check over in the cube farm."

She thanked him and walked in that direction. Pham was there, huddled over one of the hot-bunk computer terminals.

"Good morning, Grace, how are you?" he said without looking up.

"Good morning," she replied. "Working with us peasants today?"

"Computer in the office is not working," Pham said, still buried in the computer monitor. "Had to come out here."

Parkowski smirked. "Oh, ok."

"I'm working on something - a theory of what happened last week," the older man said as he furiously typed away, not mentioning the word *dragon*. She knew Pham was a hunt-and-peck typer, but he could output faster than any traditional typist, mostly thanks to his copious use of keyboard shortcuts. "But I'm not quite there yet."

Parkowski looked at the cubicles, all unoccupied, and took a seat at a computer next to him. "I worked on that this weekend, too."

He finally stopped to look at her. "I told you to not worry about it this weekend," Pham said, but he didn't seem surprised.

"I know, Jake, I know," she said, "but you know me."

Pham laughed. "I'd probably have done the same thing."

He went back to his computer for a second and then turned to face her. "I've got an hour before I have to help Mr. Marx get ready for his mission, but let's tell each other what we've found out."

Parkowski took a breath. "So, Mike has a VR setup."

"Like the one here?"

She shook her head. "Nowhere near as nice, but it works."

Pham didn't say anything, so she continued. "So, I loaded up a build on his computer, an older one, the one they gave us to play around with a couple of months ago."

"Do you remember what version?"

Parkowski thought for a moment. "Fourteen, I believe," she said.

Pham nodded. "That's close enough."

"Anyways, I loaded it up and started messing with it," Parkowski went on. "I started playing with the options and settings, and I found something really interesting."

"And that would be?" Pham asked.

"If you have multiple displays," she explained. "There's a setting called *twinning*. I had never heard about it before but Mike has. It means that the computer renders a frame once and sends it to both displays. In my case, I had a computer monitor and a VR headset - three renders total."

Pham nodded. "Isn't that what we normally do? Why would you do something different than that?"

"If you have a powerful enough computer, and you've more than two displays, it might be more efficient to show one display at a higher graphical fidelity and the others at a lower one, or vice versa," she explained. "At least, that's what my Google-fu was able to uncover over the weekend."

The older man smiled. "Got it, or at least I think I do."

"So, do you remember how I saw the dragon," Parkowski said, a little unsure, "and you didn't?"

"I do."

"Well, hypothetically, if I did see a dragon," she said. "Regardless if it was real and on Venus or just some kind of glitch, it *is* possible that I only saw it on my headset and whoever was watching it on the TV screen or streaming it on their computer didn't see it. There might be different environments."

The senior engineer rocked back and forth in his chair, deep in thought. "Fascinating," he said softly. "I never even thought of that. We'd have to check the logs, of course, and talk with the technicians who set the VR stuff up. They'd have to know how we're configured."

"Got it," she said.

"But it makes sense. And it flows nicely into what I've been thinking," Pham said.

"So, what are you working on?" Parkowski asked, intrigued.

Pham waved for her to come around to the monitor, which she did. "Let me explain," he said to Parkowski.

She nodded.

"So here are the logs," he said, pulling up a window showing a spreadsheet pulled from the VR environment's internal logging tool. "I went over them Friday night before I went out to dinner with Gus, and again this morning."

"Did you see anything out of the ordinary?" Parkowski asked, squatting down slightly to get a better look.

"Nope," Pham said. "I compared it to Marx's run that morning, and Mohammed's run after yours. At face value all 3 were nominal, save for your temporary loss of contact with the ACHILLES units."

Parkowski felt a pang of guilt. "That didn't screw anything up, right?"

"No, they were fine," the Ph.D. replied. "They're designed to be able to withstand a comm hit pretty frequently, given the distances involved. No lasting damage, and Mohammed was able to complete all of his objectives before we put the two units in station-keeping mode for the weekend."

"Phew," Parkowski said, breathing a sigh of relief. "I was scared for a bit that I had done some damage, but I kind of forgot all about it when I heard that the connection was restored."

"Don't worry about it," Pham said. "If there was any danger to the robots, we would have been a lot more worried."

He cleared his throat. "So, again, the logs. While it's a video game developer..."

"Panspermia Studios," Parkowski cut in.

"Panspermia Studios," Pham confirmed, "that made the environment, it's actually more similar to an aircraft or ship simulator than a simple game."

"Why is that?"

He laughed. "Standards, mostly. When we contract something like that out, federal mandates force us to include documents like military standards or international best practices as part of the contract for the contractor to adhere to.

"As part of these standards, the environment is made up of 'layers' and 'enumerations.' The layers are static - things like the terrain and skybox. The enumerations are dynamic, pulled from a library of objects contained deep within the code base."

Pham took a breath and went on. "The robots are enumerations, complex ones made up of subenumerations for the head, body, and each limb. They are modeled across multiple spectrums: visible, infrared, ultraviolet, and have their own complex RF signature. Others aren't as complex, simple boulders and rocks are just a wire mesh with a texture thrown over it that are more similar to an object in a video game."

He paused. Parkowski leaned back from the computer monitor. "So where are you going with this, boss?"

"Let me show you," Pham replied, going back to the keyboard. Without using the mouse he deftly sped through several windows before coming to a debugging interface. "I've narrowed down the logs from Friday to the last 300 seconds - five minutes - of your mission. This is the list of enumerations currently active." He pulled up another spreadsheet-like screen and scrolled down. "As you can see, there's a lot."

"And everything is normal?"

"Once again, at first glance, yes," Pham said. "But..."

"But," Parkowski said. "There's something."

Pham nodded. "There's an enumeration for something that doesn't exist on our system. C-458, here," he pointed at the screen. "It's a dynamic model, that's all I can tell, but a lot of the fields are either blocked or don't show up in the debugging tool.

"It showed up in the environment through some kind of trigger event, which I also can't see in the tool, and remained until we lost the connection. When we recovered it, the enumeration was gone."

Parkowski pulled up a chair and looked at the screen next to Pham. "So, what is it?" she said, almost to herself.

"I don't know," Pham replied. "What I am doing is gathering all of the information that I can, and I will send it over to our focal point at Panspermia. Hopefully, we'll get some clarity, and make sure that if it was a bug, that you didn't really see a dragon, it won't happen again."

"Thank you so much," Parkowski said, breathing a sigh of relief. "And thank you for not thinking I'm crazy."

"No problem," Pham said. "I've worked with you for a year now, and you're nothing but a rational engineer, just like me. And, there was no damage to the robots or any of the gear here. No harm, no foul. You're fine, Grace."

He locked his machine and stood up. "I'm going to go check on my computer and then fire off that email. The schedule for this week has been updated, you're on the sticks on Wednesday afternoon. We'll have a planning session tomorrow morning."

"Got it, thanks," Parkowski said as she stepped aside to let him through.

After Pham was gone, she sat down at the cube and logged into the computer. Parkowski's email inbox was full; she hadn't touched them since Thursday morning. She sighed and started working her way through them.

LAG DELAY

It was almost lunchtime when Pham stopped back by the cube, holding a piece of paper face-down. "Sorry, they fixed the PC in my office, so I just transferred my session over," he explained.

"No worries," she replied.

"I just got off the phone with Panspermia Studios," the Ph.D. said with a smile. "And you're going to like what they told me."

"What did they say?"

"They make a video game called Faerieia," Pham explained. "In addition to their work with NASA and for the military. Not sure if you've ever heard of it."

Parkowski laughed. "I haven't," she said. "Not much of a gamer, and my boyfriend plays mostly sports and shooter games."

"I hadn't either, but apparently it is a fantasy role-playing game," Pham said. "That heavily features..." his voice trailed off.

Parkowski cocked her head slightly; she wasn't sure if she was supposed to fill in the blank or not.

"Dragons." Pham filled it in for her.

"No shit," she said.

"No shit," he repeated.

"So how did it get in the Venus environment?" Parkowski asked.

"I asked them that," her boss replied. "Faerieia has a portion of the game set on a hellscape similar to Venus, so when they were starting to build up the environment for us they copied it over as part of the prototyping process. I guess some of the call-outs to the dragon model were kept by accident."

Parkowski finally let out her breath. "Holy crap."

He laughed. "They copied the event for the dragon to appear and used it for a meteorite event in our environment, but didn't delete the dragon itself - reusing some code. So when a sensor detected a meteorite, it wanted to show you it in the environment. However, for reasons that they're still investigating, it managed to 'call home' to Panspermia and get the dragon model and display it in your environment, complete with a canned animation where it flew at you. Your 'twinning' research was correct. It only did it in your model because you were the only one who could 'see' the meteorite. The feed to the TV screen and the monitors couldn't see it, so it never triggered there."

"So, I'm not crazy."

"No, not at all. Your description matches the dragon, seen here," he said, showing her the piece of paper. It was the same creature that had attacked her on Friday.

"Thank you so much for running this down," Parkowski said, rocking slowly back and forth in her chair. "I know what I saw and to have that confirmation really gives me a confidence boost."

"Well, you're going to need it," Pham said, grinning as he took the piece of paper back. "I'm heading out early today, but I'll see you tomorrow. It'll be time to plan your second mission."

CHAPTER NINE

El Segundo, California

The rest of Parkowski's day was as normal as it could be.

She ate lunch at the Rayleigh cafeteria with a couple of her work friends, finished up her emails by one o'clock, and spent the rest of her day checking out the schedule, reading the logs from prior missions, and reading the unfortunately sparse mission details for her upcoming jaunt with the ACHILLES robots.

It wasn't perfect, though. The techs avoided her for the most part, and there was an uneasy silence surrounding her in the high bay as she passed through.

She had plans to go out for a quick dinner with her boyfriend, but DePresti had sent an email to her work address telling her that he was going to be late at work preparing for a major review on one of his programs. Parkowski decided to stay late, too, so that they could eat dinner together.

At around four o'clock, she was done with her other work and decided to dig into the logs from her mission. Parkowski opened up the logging software that Pham had used earlier.

She wanted to get into the logs for two reasons.

First, to confirm what she had been shown this morning. Parkowski trusted Pham more than almost anyone else in her life, but for something as bizarre as seeing a dragon in a simulated Venus environment, she had to be sure that it was just a bug.

Second, she wanted to learn how to work the debugging and logging systems in case she had to do something similar in the future

Parkowski was surprised at how easy the software was to use compared to the mission planning software - obviously different developers. Everything created by Panspermia was modern, sleek, and designed with the user in mind. The mission planning software, the communications stuff she had seen connecting the Aering building with MICS, and some of the other UIs she had seen in her current job, had all been created by traditional defense contractors such as Aering and were more cumbersome to use.

The logs were all stored in a spreadsheet, a two-dimensional database that linked to other files and documents that contained more information. She clicked on the "C-458" enumeration and traced it to the communications log. Sure enough, when the sensor, an IR camera on the relay satellite orbiting Venus, had seen the meteorite enter the atmosphere, it had sent a message to the communications hardware. Then, in the same region where the ACHILLES robots were operating, a signal had been sent to the environment back on Earth to display a meteorite exactly where the real one had been sensed.

She laughed to herself. Parkowski wondered how much it cost for Panspermia to implement that feature. It didn't add much to her ability to do the mission, but had to have been part of the contract between Aering and the video game studio nonetheless.

Parkowski shook her head and started to follow the communications pathway that the signal traveled once the relay satellite sensed the meteorite.

The packet had left the sensor and traveled via the satellite's internal Linux real-time operating system to the communications payload. One antenna was always pointing down at the planet, the other in the direction of the satellite at the far-off Earth-Moon Lagrange point that directed the signal to the MICS satellite. The comm box had seen that its final destination was the Venus environment and sent the packet through the narrowband connection that way.

She opened up the packet in the debugging tool. In it, she could see fields in a table format like the initial log window.

Parkowski quickly scanned the packet's metadata. Most of what she saw made sense, but a number of other fields were blank.

She scrunched up her nose. That was weird.

The engineer pulled up another packet, a state-of-health telemetry report that was sent every second back to the NASA ground station operators for the satellite at White Sands. That one, when opened, had every field in the metadata filled out, with even more data available once she double-clicked on each of them.

Parkowski pulled up another packet, searching for one from the IR sensor this time. This one was old, a reading of a hot pocket of gas in a crater near the ACHILLES landing site. This packet, when opened, also had all of its fields filled out and accessible.

Another mystery, she thought.

She pulled up the initial packet, taking another close look at it.

Parkowski wasn't a communications engineer - her expertise was in robotics and control systems - but she knew enough to be dangerous. From what she saw, everything looked nominal, a normal network packet. What was different about this one, she wondered.

She double-clicked on one of the fields that was blank. A dialog box popped up. It was an error message, stating: ERROR: DATA MASKED. THIS SYSTEM CANNOT DISPLAY BRONZE KNOT DATA.

"What the..." Parkowski said, rubbing her eyes. It had been a long day, most of which had been spent hunched down over a computer screen. Maybe she was seeing things. She read it again.

ERROR: DATA MASKED. THIS SYSTEM CANNOT DISPLAY BRONZE KNOT DATA.

"That doesn't even make any sense," she said softly.

Parkowski closed the error window and tried double-clicking again.

ERROR: DATA MASKED. THIS SYSTEM CANNOT DISPLAY BRONZE KNOT DATA.

She read it a third time, this time more slowly.

"ERROR: DATA MASKED." So the software was throwing up an error because there was data "masked" or hidden from the user. That made sense at first glance, the previous screen had blanked-out fields that should have been filled out.

But, on further thought, it didn't. Why would any data be hidden from her? This wasn't anything like what DePresti did; while Aering did do work on-site for the Space Force and some classified customers, the ILIAD project was most certainly unclassified. There was proprietary information, sure, and parts of the technology were ITAR (International Traffic in Arms Regulations) controlled, but in theory, as the prime contractor for NASA, Aering, and by proxy Parkowski should have access to all of the data.

"THIS SYSTEM CANNOT DISPLAY BRONZE KNOT DATA." That made sense based on the previous sentence until she got to the word "bronze." What the *fuck* is a "Bronze Knot," she thought.

That made no sense at all.

This packet was created in the communications hardware of the relay satellite and was sent to MICS to be "bent piped" back down to Earth. It was the same as every other packet, all of which should have been unclassified, and from her spot-check of the other two, this was the only odd one.

Parkowski backed out again and tried some of the other blanked-out fields. She got the same error message for each one. However, one of them did provide more information. It wanted to open up a "BRONZE KNOT MESSAGES" spreadsheet located in a directory on a shared drive that Parkowski had never seen before. When she tried to open it she got another error message - file cannot be found.

Frustrated, but also intrigued, the junior engineer went back to the logs and tried to find some other packets that also would trigger the same error message. Parkowski tried for over twenty minutes to find one with blanked-out fields to no avail.

She sat back in her chair and thought for a minute. This was weird, there was no reason why any of the logs should be hidden from her, yet there they were - "masked" from her sight.

Parkowski sighed. She had already caused a lot of trouble with what happened on Friday, despite Pham's assurance to the contrary. There had been a repair ticket for the equipment she had damaged that had been CC'd to her email. The mission report for the time block after hers noted that it took nearly an hour to get back to a nominal state.

It seemed like she had two options.

Parkowski could bring this discovery of hers up to Pham, who being the good guy that he was, would take it up to his boss or look into it himself. She would be at the center of attention again and who knows how that would work out.

The other option was to keep this to herself. No one else would know, nothing would happen to her. She would get another chance to prove herself on Wednesday during her second mission. She'd still be on the path to that promotion she was working towards.

To her, it seemed like an easy decision. No one else needed to know what she found.

Parkowski pulled up the error message one last time. It was the same, no change from before. She took a screenshot and saved it to her personal folder on the shared internal Aering drive.

She left the office and went home.

#

The next day was more of the same. Emails and a couple of brief meetings in the morning; her afternoon was filled with mission planning.

Parkowski had been through it before during her first time in the Venus environment. It was a painstaking, almost excruciating process where every single minute of her time controlling the ACHILLES robots was planned out using the old, slow mission planning tool. Last time, it took over three hours; hopefully, now that she was more experienced, it would be a little shorter.

She, Pham, and two technicians who would be responsible for making sure all of the ground systems needed for her mission to be successful all sat in the small conference room.

Surprisingly, Dr. Rosen stepped into the room about an hour into the planning session. That meant only one thing: senior leadership was now interested in her mission. Whether it was due to the encounter with the anomalous "dragon" last week or for another reason she didn't know, but it was odd for him to be there.

It made her nervous.

Rosen didn't say anything; he just observed the planning for fifteen or so minutes before departing the room without saying a word.

Parkowski brushed it off. If she was in his position, she'd probably do the same thing. She had heard through the company grapevine that they were bidding on a similar mission to Io. Any failures during the proposal process would probably result in a loss to another contractor.

Plus, he'd probably be the determining factor if she were to rise to a higher-level position within Aering. Given how her last mission went, Rosen probably wanted to know as much as possible as to how Parkowski was performing in her current role.

The mission itself seemed fairly simple.

Parkowski was only to control one of the ACHILLES units this time; the other would stay at a recharging station for its duration. Her destination was the base of one of Venus' many volcanoes. They were all thought to be extinct, but a previous NASA mission had detected some odd readings that may indicate that some of them were dormant rather than dead. Parkowski's job was to carry a small, unmanned drone to a waypoint at its base and then launch it. She would initially control the drone and get it on an upward trajectory but then transfer control to a more seasoned operator, a former RQ-4 Global Hawk pilot, located at another part of the sprawling Aering facility.

That operator, along with a pair of co-located sensor operators, would take over control and use more refined methods - flight stick and throttle, versus Parkowski trying to manipulate actuators physically located on Venus with her robot's hand-analog - to fly the drone on a suicide mission into the volcano. This would hopefully provide the NASA volcanologists with a better understanding of the state of volcanic activity on Venus.

She went home to her apartment that night and watched a few episodes of a show with her roommate before going to bed early. Tomorrow was a big day; a chance to correct the mistakes she made the previous week and get her coveted promotion back on track.

CHAPTER TEN

El Segundo, California

On Wednesday afternoon, Parkowski sat with her head in her hands on the bench in the locker room.

She was getting herself in the right mental state to put her VR undergarment on and go into the high bay for her second mission with the ACHILLES robots.

It shouldn't be this hard, she thought. The mission was straightforward, she had the appropriate training, and the support team around her was top-notch. It was just another day in the office.

But it was hard. And her experience last time loomed large over her.

Parkowski was a perfectionist. It was part of being an engineer. You wanted to get the correct answer every time, to get the best design you could on the first try.

Her last mission in the VR environment was less than perfect.

She breathed slowly, remembering how she got ready for high school soccer games. Clear your mind, visualize yourself doing the task, and cast all of your worries aside. But, her old tricks weren't working. Dread gripped Parkowski, just like the last time in the VR gear.

Parkowski put on her Catwoman suit and headed, headset in hand, into the high bay.

Pham and a female tech helped her with the VR gear, bottom to top just like the last time she went into the Venus environment.

One of her close friends at Aering, Rachel Kim, had run the morning shift. Her job was to get the robots in position to support Parkowski's mission.

That gave her a small but much-needed boost of confidence. The seniors at Aering trusted her to do the more difficult mission of releasing the drone near the volcano despite her missteps last week.

They could have switched her with Kim but chose not to. Someone, probably Dr. Pham, still believed in her. That little gesture filled Parkowski with pride.

"Are you ready?" Dr. Pham asked. She was completely geared up, save for her customized headset which lay at her feet.

Parkowski nodded.

He clapped her softly on the back. "We'll switch over in five minutes. Did you remember to eat more this time?"

She laughed. "Yes, but hopefully not too much."

Pham gave a small smile and nodded. "Go get 'em."

Parkowski walked over to the side of the raised platform and did some basic stretches, still trying to get in the right mindset for the mission. She paced back and forth like a cat.

Finally it was time to switch. Kim stopped walking and a small swarm of technicians ran up to her to help her remove her gear. She was calm and smiling after her successful mission.

Parkowski was all nerves as she waited.

After a few minutes, Kim was disconnected from the VR setup and carefully stepped down off of the platform.

"All yours," she said to Parkowski.

"Thanks, Rachel. I'll take good care of it."

Parkowski climbed up onto the raised platform and took a deep breath.

A technician attached all of the relevant cables and got her ready.

Parkowski did one final stretch of her arms and placed the helmet on her head.

She was now on Venus, seen through the eyes of ACHILLES I. The screen was semi-frozen: she could move her head around and see the environment, but her actuators weren't controlling the robot's limbs yet.

Pham's voice popped into her ear. "Are you ready to transfer control?" he asked.

She nodded. "Yes."

There was a slight hint of haptic feedback as the VR controllers were synced to the actual hardware on Venus.

Parkowski blinked and took note of her surroundings. The ACHILLES robot was currently in a deep depression, a long, cracked ridge that traveled east-west along the planet's surface. According to her pre-mission briefing, it was the result of ancient lava flows from the seemingly extinct volcano Sacajawea.

Attached to her ACHILLES unit's waist was a small quadcopter drone. The robot was heavily modified with thermal coverings and redundant electronics for use in the harsh Venusian environment. They were expensive, too - Pham had told her the total cost for the six quadcopters on the ILIAD mission was $100 million - roughly the same price as an F-35A stealth fighter.

She took a deep breath and pulled up the map. Just like in the planning session, the waypoints were clearly marked. Parkowski had to walk the length of the ridge towards the volcano and then climb it - the only difficult part of her mission - and then quickly move to another parallel canyon that would take her closer to the shield volcano's crater so she could release the drone.

After that, Parkowski would turn around and travel back through that canyon until her shift was over and another operator would take over the ACHILLES units' operations.

The engineer began walking at a good pace, the ACHILLES robot mimicking her every move. The ground was slightly inclined, boulders the size of a minifridge littering the path, but Parkowski was able to make good progress as she continued to the next waypoint.

The ridge started to narrow as she progressed onwards. Parkowski began to notice the gigantic shield volcano, named for the famous Native American explorer, off on the horizon. It wasn't a particularly tall volcano, but it was wide, stretching hundreds of miles across at the base.

At one point, the ridge almost turned into a tunnel before opening back up. Parkowski's progress slowed as she had to squeeze the ACHILLES unit between boulders, but sped up as the path widened.

She came to the first waypoint; a blue dot superimposed by the UI on the ridge wall. The top of the ridge was about fifteen feet off of the ground in the direction of the volcano.

The next canyon was only a quarter-mile from the current ridge but the surface between the two was a "hot zone" from a temperature standpoint. It was potentially from the volcano's thermal activity, but more likely from tectonic activity underneath Venus' crust. The ACHILLES robot was rated to operate at high temperatures, but these were at the high end of that range.

The Aering engineers who had done the initial thermal engineering and analysis on the two units had been contacted for this mission. They told Pham and Parkowski that if she spent less than four minutes in that zone, there would be no lasting damage to the heat shielding on the robot. Any more time than that might leave some permanent impact.

Parkowski at first laughed at that requirement. While she wasn't in as good shape as her soccer days, four hundred meters should be a joke. But when she went back and looked at her top speed from the previous mission, she was going to have to push to keep it under four minutes.

First, though, she had to climb. She stood against the wall and found a decent path up, then started free-climbing. Parkowski was no rock climber, but the nimble ACHILLES unit and the low gravity of Venus made it fairly easy to get to the top.

As soon as she made it up, Parkowski started sprinting, or as close to it as she could manage in the VR setup. It was weird running in place, but the display's screen showed her perspective continually moving forward. She wished she had set a timer, but then remembered how distracting the UI was - maybe it was a blessing in disguise.

Per her calculations, Parkowski made the quarter-mile in just over three minutes. "Done," she said over the net, which had been fairly quiet the whole mission. Maybe this time she would be able to finish without any incidents. She dropped down about four feet into the canyon, the ACHILLES leg joints absorbing the impact.

"Good job, Grace," Pham said in response.

Parkowski checked her mission clock. She had four hours from the start to get the drone launched, and she hadn't even used up one of them. Plenty of time.

She started down the canyon. The sides grew taller as she got closer to the volcano and the width narrowed. It reminded her of slot canyons like the one time she went hiking in New Mexico. Thankfully, there were no rocks or boulders like the previous ridge. Rather, the ground was soft and dusty, which the system had enough fidelity to display in great detail around her.

It took an hour, but Parkowski reached the next waypoint, a fork in the canyon where the ancient lava flow had split into two. She had to take the left fork, towards the volcano, which she did.

The incline started to increase as the path widened. It gave her a beautiful view of the ancient volcano; the gigantic shield's size was now apparent and its brown color a sharp contrast to the green-yellow alien sky.

Parkowski was now completely enthralled by the simulation. She and the ACHILLES unit were one and the same, the lag between Venus and Earth was negligible, and the jarring anomalies of the previous mission seemingly a thing of the past. She loved every minute in the VR setup.

She came to an overlook where the canyon's walls towards the volcano were just a few feet high. "Can I launch it here?" Parkowski asked. It wasn't where the mission plan had called for it, but it looked like a good spot.

"Standby," Pham replied, "let me talk to the drone operators."

Parkowski stood still for a few minutes, catching her breath from the long journey. The senior engineer called back after a minute of waiting. "Negative, Grace, they want you to continue and release at the preprogrammed route."

She shrugged. "Sure."

"There's an internal GNC sensor that is already programmed," Pham explained, "and it can't be changed at this point. Just keep going, Grace, you're over halfway done with the mission."

Parkowski put her head down and continued down the path. It was another half-mile or so before the "real" waypoint where she would release the drone. She took her time, walking slowly and carefully, before reaching it after another fifteen minutes of walking.

She took a deep breath. Now, the hard part. Parkowski took the small quadcopter off of her ACHILLES unit's waist and placed it on the ground. It had a small control panel on its top. Parkowski ensured that the communication channel was the same and took a step back, away from the four blades.

"Ready to launch," she said over the voice net.

"Copy," Pham replied. There was a brief pause. "Go ahead and take off when you're ready."

Parkowski pulled up the drone controls from within the UI and coordinated them to her right VR controller. A small picture-in-picture display from the quadcopter's video sensor appeared in the upper left corner of her VR display.

She moved her hand up and the drone's blades began to spin as it started to slowly rise. Parkowski waited until it was ten to twelve feet above the canyon wall before moving her arm forward in the direction of the Sacajawea volcano.

Pham broke in a few minutes later. "Transferring control to the pilot in three, two, one, break," he called out. Parkowski could still see the display, but no longer controlled the drone's movements.

She finally breathed a sigh of relief.

"Ok, great job, you're doing great Grace," Pham said to her. "Now head around and get to the last waypoint."

"Thanks," she said and turned the ACHILLES unit around to go back the way she came.

It was almost over.

But, after only a few minutes of walking down the canyon, Parkowski started to see some graphical artifacts, much like those in her last mission. The terrain went from a high-resolution model to one with lower fidelity, and the boulders and rocks were missing meshes or textures.

The issues from last time had returned.

"Hey boss, seeing some weird stuff," she told Pham. "What's my lag?"

"One minute, forty seconds," the older man replied. "Everything should be nominal."

"It's not," she breathed. There was lag somewhere that drove the graphical anomalies.

Then it happened.

The VR display *flipped* upside-down - paused for half a second - and then tilted another ninety degrees.

Parkowski stopped. What the hell is going on?

The display went out for a brief moment, then popped back with a warped vision of Venus.

At least it was right-side-up this time. It reminded Parkowski of funhouse mirrors - the entire landscape was slanted, turned, and all kinds of topsy-turvy.

She couldn't even think of anything to say over the radio.

The entire environment twisted and turned, making itself large, so large that the ACHILLES robot was just a tiny little pinprick, a speck against the giant Venusian surface.

Then it changed again, this time making the world so small that the robot's legs, torso, and head extended up way above the planet.

Parkowski almost panicked; like she did before, but this time, she remained calm. She wasn't on Venus, she was on Earth at the Aering plan in El Segundo.

She repeated that mantra as she tried to move, to walk forward slightly using her legs, but an error message popped up, covering a large portion of the display. It read ERROR: SPECIAL ACCESS PROGRAM - BRONZE KNOT - SPECIAL ACCESS REQUIRED.

BRONZE KNOT again. But what did the other words mean?

She dismissed it with a flick of her wrist. She tried moving again but the error appeared again. This time it read ERROR: SPECIAL ACCESS PROGRAM - BRONZE KNOT - SPECIAL ACCESS REQUIRED. YOU DO NOT POSSESS TS//SAR-BRK CREDENTIALS.

What was a "SPECIAL ACCESS PROGRAM" and what was it doing on Venus?

The environment then completely disappeared, leaving her with an empty, grayscale room, which was then slowly built up layer-by-layer: skybox, ground textures, meshes for the terrain followed by a fully textured environment, smaller details such as dust and rocks.

The first message appeared again.

It was ancient Greek to Parkowski, a gibberish of words she understood separately, but not in context together. Still, she committed each and every word to memory. She keyed the mic. "Hey, Dr. Pham, I'm getting an error message."

"Standby," he said, a bit of concern in his disembodied voice. "We're getting some error messages too."

"Copy," she replied as the message disappeared. "Standing by."

Parkowski cursed. This was not how today was supposed to go.

She heard a hurried shuffle of feet around her on the raised platform as some of the technicians popped up to help her. "Grace, we're going to disconnect you," Pham said over the radio. "We've lost connection."

Parkowski waited as multiple pairs of hands quickly worked to disconnect her from the wires that hooked her into the Venus VR environment. The error message reappeared briefly before going away for good.

The last thing removed was her headset, but before it was fully off, Parkowski could already feel the tension in the room. At least a dozen people, technicians and engineers alike, scurried about. The large TV screen over the terminals was completely blank.

No one seemed to notice or pay attention to her.

She placed the helmet on the ground and slipped off of the platform, leaving the techs to gather all of the VR setup's components.

Pham was at one of those terminals underneath the TV screen, furiously tapping away at the keyboard.

"How bad is it?" she asked.

The older man shook his head. "Completely lost the signal. Trying to reacquire now, but we're locked out."

He turned his head and looked at her with a forced grin. "Hey, but at least it wasn't your fault this time."

She didn't smile back.

CHAPTER ELEVEN

El Segundo, California

Parkowski packed her bag and headed out. While she had been changing, the techs had reestablished the connection with the ACHILLES units by power-cycling one of the antennas on the relay satellite. But, it wasn't a great link. The signal-to-noise ratio was terrible and they weren't able to fully exercise control of the two robots. But, they were able to get health and safety readings and ensure that both ACHILLES were safe.

Thankfully, the quadcopter had kept its telemetry connection - run through a separate comm pathway than the ACHILLES data - the whole time. The sensor operators reported mission success.

She was scheduled for another upcoming mission. The exact date, time, and details were still up in the air, pending a full recovery of the entire ACHILLES system.

Everything was still a blur. She had done everything right, followed the mission plan to a T, even kept her cool when shit hit the fan, and, most importantly, didn't panic like she had last time. However, she remembered she was just one cog in the machine and a low-level one at that. Parkowski had expected more of a response when she got out of the VR gear, but everyone's attention was focused on getting the integrated enterprise back up and running.

And on deeper examination, who knew if she would even still be on the schedule tomorrow.

#

Parkowski got into her Camry in the parking lot. This was all a lot to process, and she still wasn't sure she fully wanted to.

She started the long drive back to her apartment. As she drove, she thought through the entire bizarre situation. It wasn't going as well as she would have liked.

Parkowski knew that most of the other engineers were angling for the same promotion she was, the same role as Dr. Pham in the NASA-led Io mission that would be launching in the next few years. She hadn't heard about any other anomalies, just hers, so she was seemingly behind the power curve.

If something didn't change soon, she was going to be out of the running. She felt like she was going to have to start asking questions about why it was happening to her.

Parkowski was a naturally curious person. She had driven her parents crazy with questions as a young girl, and had even once taken apart a toy with a screwdriver just to see how it worked. It had been one of many instances that had set her on the path to becoming an engineer.

There was too much going on that she just had to know more about. She didn't work in a classified environment like her boyfriend; there was nothing about the ILIAD mission that should be kept from her. If she wanted her third mission, as well as any future missions beyond that, to go well, she needed to know what was going on with the anomalies.

Parkowski knew from her dad, and her own experience, that unless you had a lot of top cover from your leadership, it wasn't a great idea to blow something up by asking a lot of questions. While some of what she had encountered seemed innocuous, Parkowski had a sneaking suspicion that if she started posing questions to her leadership at Aering, their opinion of her might change, and not necessarily for the better. So, any investigation of hers would have to be under the radar.

But, she could ask her Space Force boyfriend. She had a good idea of what the Space Force did in general, but what DePresti did in particular, she wasn't sure. Maybe he could help her with the weird error and associated message she saw today.

As she drove north, DePresti called. "Hey, want to come hang out tonight? I just got off work."

She laughed. "I was just thinking about you," Parkowski replied. "Yeah, I'm halfway home though. Let me turn around and head back in your direction."

"Come to my place," DePresti offered. "I'll order takeout."

#

An hour later she sat at his kitchen table, eating from a big bowl of Chinese food that DePresti had gotten from a local restaurant. He was still in his uniform, but she had changed into sweatpants and a t-shirt.

"So how did it go today?" DePresti asked, getting up to grab a beer from his fridge.

"Better than last time," she replied. "But not great."

"Any dragons, or even worse, aliens, this time?"

She shook her head. "No, but there was a weird error I got at the end of the mission," Parkowski explained. "They lost the connection to the ACHILLES robots for about ten minutes or so."

"What did it say?" DePresti asked as he took a sip from his bottle.

"Error, special access program, Bronze Knot, special access required," Parkowski repeated from memory.

DePresti spit out his beer.

"It did not," he said, shaking his head in disbelief.

"It did," Parkowski insisted.

"Bullshit," DePresti said, "there's no way."

"Uh, there is a way, because I saw it," she replied. "Just like I saw the dragon."

"I'm more apt to believe you saw a dragon than that error message."

"Why?"

"Grace, do you know what a special access program is?"

She thought for a moment. "No."

He took another sip of his beer and leaned on the kitchen counter. "Let me see if I can explain this without getting myself into trouble."

Parkowski tilted her head slightly. This was getting somewhere.

DePresti took a deep breath. "So, to start, there's three general levels of classification for government secrets. In ascending order of secrecy, they are Unclassified, Secret, and Top Secret." He paused, then continued. "Those are a blanket level of security. Within each of those levels, there are subcompartments that you can only access if you have a need to know *and* have been cleared at that high level.

"For some security levels, in particular Secret, everyone can see what's held at that level, so it's called collateral - a common level. In case information needs to be kept close-hold for whatever reason, it's kept in a special access program, which limits the access."

Parkowski thought for a moment. "So, I have a Secret clearance that I got when I first started at Aering. Everyone did, regardless of what program they worked on. I've never used it though. What does that get me?"

"It gets you access to Secret-level information," he told her. "But nothing more. If you needed information from a special access program - which we call a SAP - you would have to be read into the program specifically."

"Ok, got that part," she said. "So what's the problem? Aering has all kinds of contracts with the military and intelligence agencies in addition to NASA. Maybe Bronze Knot is a part of some other mission?"

DePresti laughed. "Oh, that might be possible, but there's no way that it was in the environment, or even in the same network."

"Why?"

"SAP data needs to be on its own enclosed network," he explained. "There's no way anyone would let it be on an unclassified network. In addition, SAP data needs to be in a SCIF or SAPF."

"What are those?"

"SCIF is Sensitive Compartmented Information Facility, SAPF is Special Access Program Facility, but a lot of SAPFs are called SCIFs," DePresti answered. "Data classified at that level needs to be in a certified facility, it's not stuff you can take home. It's why you'll never see me with anything from work like you have the VR stuff on my gaming PC. Almost everything I do in the office is classified."

She thought for a second. "What does Bronze Knot mean?" Parkowski asked. "It was mentioned in the logs of my first mission, in particular with some of the packets traveling around the same time I saw the 'dragon,' but without any mention of a special access program."

He shook his head. "That's the program name, but it's not one I'm familiar with. And if it's in the logs, then in theory it would be connected to your mission somehow. But, to the best of my knowledge, NASA doesn't have any SAPs. They are a purely civilian agency."

"Any idea as to what the name means?"

"No," DePresti replied.

"There was another error message too," Parkowski continued quickly, reciting from memory. "Error, special access program - Bronze Knot. Special access required. You do not possess TS//SAR-BKT credentials." She spelled out each of the acronyms.

DePresti frowned. "That's worse because you don't have a Top Secret clearance, and that's a huge security violation if you saw anything Top Secret."

"But what did I see that is Top Secret?"

"I have no clue. That's why it's hard to believe what you say you saw," he said carefully.

"I saw what I saw," she replied, a hint of anger in her voice.

"No, I'm not saying you didn't see that," he said quickly, "but there's no way that Top Secret and SAP data was on the VR environment's network. It would be a huge security violation and Aering is smart enough not to do that. There has to be another explanation."

"I saw what I saw," Parkowski said again.

She took a breath and finally took another bite of her food. "Why would someone code an error message to display that?"

"I don't know," he answered. "It doesn't make any sense."

They ate, both of them deep in thought.

"Could there be a data spill?" Parkowski wondered aloud. "Could something from a higher-level network or computer get into the Venus environment?"

"Not likely," DePresti replied. "Most SAP networks are air-gapped - they aren't connected to any other network. And if they are connected, there are multiple security layers, protected by NSA-approved guards. Those prevent Top Secret data tagged as a SAP from going to a lower level - either Secret or Unclassified."

He finished his beer and got up to get another one. "You know, I've never heard of Bronze Knot," DePresti said as he opened the cap, "but there was a program called Onyx Crow that was run during the Cold War."

"A special access program?"

"Yeah."

"What was it about?"

The Space Force captain laughed. "Well, I've never been read into it, but from my understanding, it was a program to let U.S.

Air Force and Navy pilots fly American jets against foreign-built equipment."

Parkowski frowned. "While I get why that would be a special program, that has nothing to do with what I do at Aering or the ILIAD mission."

DePresti took a long sip of his beer and then smiled at her. "I know, the whole thing doesn't make sense. I've never worked with any program with 'Bronze' as part of the codename. But I will say that most of the codenames are randomly generated for security. They usually have nothing to do with the actual program information that they are protecting."

"So, Bronze Knot is meaningless."

"Maybe, maybe not," DePresti said.

"You wouldn't tell me even if you did know," Parkowski said, teasing him.

He laughed, and then his face turned serious. "Grace, even if I did know, I'd at least give you something, anything that would help alleviate your concerns but also keep me out of trouble. But, I do like my clearance."

She didn't say anything. This whole thing ate away at the back of her mind. She had to know why this last mission had gone the way it did, despite her best efforts.

"Have you asked anyone at work about it?" DePresti asked.

"Nope," Parkowski said. "I wanted to avoid that, but I think I have to. I'll do it tomorrow."

"Sounds like a good plan."

"It does. Now, can you get me a beer?"

CHAPTER TWELVE

El Segundo, California

Parkowski cracked open her energy drink and logged into the internal Aering network.

She and DePresti had had a late night.

They had gotten up at six. DePresti looked no worse for the wear, but Parkowski was exhausted. She felt like she hadn't slept at all. Thankfully, it was a slow day, so she could manage.

An energy drink would definitely help.

It took forever to log in to her machine. Parkowski leaned back in her chair and tried to process the last twenty-four hours. In some ways, it was an even more compelling mystery than the dragon appearing in the VR environment.

It was time to get to the bottom of it.

She was sure of what she had seen. The error messages were burned into her memory with indelible ink. Her boyfriend might question her, sure, but just like with the dragon Parkowski knew she wasn't crazy.

Parkowski needed to bring this to someone at Aering, preferably Dr. Pham. But, first, she wanted to do a little research.

Once her computer finally logged her in and she was able to use it, she did just that.

Everything DePresti had told her seemed to be accurate. Special access programs were the crown jewels for the military and intelligence communities, protecting anything from the acquisition of new stealth fighters to special forces operations and even covert associations between government agencies. The requirements for processing SAP data were intense, and definitely not met by the open area that Parkowski worked in.

She then opened the web browser to the internal Aering Space Systems home page. It was a Microsoft SharePoint-based site with collaboration tools for the entire company.

Parkowski was somewhat familiar with the site, but most of her work was done through other tools. Mostly, she used it for stuff like logging her hours worked in the payroll system and doing her required yearly training.

But, today, she was most interested in the site's search feature. By performing one keyword search, Parkowski could crawl through every single web page, document, and archive at the unclassified level for all of Aering's projects going back to the late nineties and, in some cases, even older than that. She had used it in the past to find an obscure Air Force standard for one of her projects and found it to be fairly helpful.

She started with a search for the words Bronze Knot.

The computer took a minute but finally spit out a list of results. There were over two hundred thousand of them.

Parkowski leaned back and took a sip of her energy drink. While she didn't have a whole lot to do today - just go through her emails, write up her after-action report from yesterday, and sit in on a planning meeting for next week - that was a lot of results to go through.

She decided to narrow her search down further. Using a trick she learned from her undergrad program, Parkowski put quotes around the search term, so it was now "Bronze Knot," and hit the enter key.

This time there were no results.

Parkowski blinked and looked again. The web page read "0 results found" in bold letters above an empty list.

That made sense, now that she thought about it. If Bronze Knot was a SAP, likely some kind of military program being built in-house that leaked over to the ILIAD network, it would be blocked from being viewed on the SharePoint site.

She went back to the first search and quickly went through the first page of results. They were all documents using the words "bronze" and "knot" in unrelated contexts - not what she was looking for.

Parkowski wanted to try one more thing before going to Pham.

She used a VPN to log into a NASA network that was located at the Jet Propulsion Laboratory out in Pasadena. Most of the scientists reviewing the data that the ACHILLES robots were collecting were located there, and she had access in case she had to share data with them.

Parkowski tried the same search terms. No dice.

She wanted to have all of her ducks in a row before she talked to her boss. If something was going on and it was somehow related to the ILIAD mission, she needed to have her story straight before she started asking sensitive questions. She pulled up the logging software that she had used earlier in the week to go through her first mission.

Parkowski went to the folder where the logs were kept. It was empty.

She leaned back in her chair and took another sip of her drink. That seemed wrong. Trying again, she refreshed the folder and looked for "hidden" files in it. Still empty.

Parkowski checked the folder size. 0 kilobytes. There was nothing in it.

"What the fuck," Parkowski said to herself. She went up a level to the larger folder containing folders for each of the different missions that had been run. All of them were empty.

The logs were all gone.

She checked her personal folder where the screenshot she had taken with the Bronze Knot reference was kept. Mercifully that was still there.

Parkowski had to make a decision.

She could bring the screenshot to Pham as evidence of the strange SAP's presence on the VR network.

Or, she could keep that piece of information to herself.

In general, Parkowski was a person who trusted authority. She trusted her boss and the management at Aering. They had never deceived her or lied to her. But, the hairs on the back of her neck stood up with this whole Bronze Knot thing.

Regardless of whether something intentionally wrong was going on, Parkowski needed to protect herself.

She emailed the screenshot to her personal email address and deleted it from the local folder.

Then, she stood up to go talk with Pham in his office.

After some brief pleasantries, Parkowski took a step inside of the door and pointed at it. "Can I close it?"

Pham raised an eyebrow. "Sure."

She closed the door and took an offered seat across from the senior engineer.

Parkowski closed her eyes. She didn't know where to start.

"Is something wrong?" Pham asked her.

She tilted her head slightly. "Yes, there is," Parkowski told him. "I was trying to pull up my logs from yesterday's mission, but they weren't in the normal folder."

He didn't say anything, so she continued. "All of the logs were gone. Mine, other people's, everything was erased."

Pham looked confused. "They're there," he said to Parkowski. "I looked last night, and all of the logs were where they were supposed to be."

"Well, they're not now," Parkowski said. "I just peeked to see if I could see them from the end of my mission yesterday and it was all gone."

He put his reading glasses on. "Let me take a look," Pham said, turning to his computer and typing away furiously. A few moments later he turned back to her, seemingly perplexed. "You're right, they're not there."

Parkowski gave a slight smile. "I know."

He leaned back in his chair, deep in thought, and then leaned forward. "A-ha," Pham said, to himself more than to Parkowski. "I remember now. The NASA guy, Dr. Hughes, told me that they took all of the logs to look for an error in the communications system."

"Took them?" Parkowski repeated.

"Yeah, there was some kind of issue with MICS," the Aering Ph.D. told her. "And they wanted to use all of the logs to help troubleshoot it."

"And they deleted our copies?" Parkowski said, a little annoyed.

Pham shrugged. "They're the customer, Grace. They're paying for this whole mission. If they want the logs, they get the logs, and we lose the local copy. It's part of the contract."

That didn't sit well with her. "What if we needed those logs to troubleshoot our system?"

The older man sat quietly for a moment and then answered her question. "I believe they are still in the facility, in the NASA room right down the hall. The entire ILIAD system is currently operational, I even took a spin with an ACHILLES robot early this morning. If we need the logs, we'll go through NASA to get them."

Parkowski crossed her arms. "I don't like it."

"Sorry Grace, but that's just how it is," Pham said. "I wish I had a better answer to give you but I can't. Sometimes the customer, in this case NASA, does things that make absolutely no sense, or in other cases are directly harmful to their own mission. All we can do is point out the flaws in their plan and hope for the best." He took a breath. "I've polled the other operators and no one else has seen a dragon or any other abnormal graphical anomalies. It's only happened to you, unfortunately, but I'm confident that everything has been resolved."

Parkowski nodded. She had one more question for him. "Have you ever heard of the term 'Bronze Knot' in the context of the ILIAD mission?"

Unlike her question about the logs, Parkowski could have sworn she saw a hint of recognition on Dr. Pham's usually inscrutable face when she said the words "Bronze Knot" but it was gone as fast as it had appeared.

He gave her an odd look. "No, I don't think so," he told Parkowski. "Where did you see that?"

She decided to give him part of the truth.

Parkowski felt a little guilty about lying, probably a result of her Catholic upbringing, but some part of her decided that she needed to protect herself. "My last mission, when we lost connection after I released the quadcopter, there was an error message in the VR environment." She didn't tell him about the mention of Bronze Knot in the logs.

"What did it say?"

It was burned into her memory by now. "ERROR: SPECIAL ACCESS PROGRAM - BRONZE KNOT - SPECIAL ACCESS REQUIRED," Parkowski told him, including the punctuation marks.

Pham frowned. "I've worked in that world before, the same one your boyfriend works in, and there's absolutely no link to the ILIAD program. I'm sure of it. I wouldn't have taken this job otherwise. I got very tired of the classified world."

He was lying. Pham wouldn't meet her eyes.

Then, he looked right at her. "Are you sure that's what you saw?"

All of the men in my life are questioning me, Parkowski thought as a hint of a smile came to her face. Everyone thought she was crazy. "Yes." She paused. "And I clearly remember the words "Bronze" and "Knot." They seem so random, so weird and out-of-context, that I committed them to memory."

The older engineer laughed. "Special access program names tend to be like that, but I've never heard of a Bronze Knot." He took a breath. "I've been read into some SAPs in the past and have a pretty good idea of what's going on in the company with regards to our special programs. It sounds like we have another weird error, much like the dragon you saw, probably bringing together some unrelated elements to unfortunately give you some weird visuals in the VR environment. I'll bring it up - quietly - with our developer Panspermia."

"Thank you," Parkowski said. "You've made me feel a little better."

That last part was a lie. If anything, she felt worse.

"No problem," Pham said. "Anything else?"

She shook her head.

"See you at the three o'clock."

CHAPTER THIRTEEN

Marina del Rey, California

The next morning, she went for a quick run to clear her head.

As Parkowski ran through the streets of Marina Del Rey, she started to think of a two-pronged approach to figuring out what Bronze Knot was.

First, she had to use the resources at her disposal.

Her boyfriend, by his own admission, was read into plenty of SAPs for his job at Los Angeles Space Force Base. He had to have access to at least one classified network at his office. It shouldn't be too much effort for him to look around to see if he could find any references to a "Bronze Knot."

Second, she had to up her game at work.

Pham had told her that the logs were moved to the NASA room. Parkowski knew where it was - just down the hall from her boss' office.

Parkowski did not have access to that room. She had been told it was "government-only," meaning for the USSF and NASA factory representatives, but more than once she had seen Rosen or another high-ranking employee enter it.

Parkowski had to get into that room.

But first, she was going to convince her boyfriend to do some snooping for her.

#

DePresti and she had planned months in advance to do some scuba diving, a recently acquired pastime, off of Catalina Island on the Saturday during the long weekend. They had gone through the extensive certification process and done some practice dives in an indoor facility, but this would be their first time with the scuba gear out in the open ocean.

Thankfully, they were going with a group, which was definitely preferable to going alone.

She sprung her request on him while they were sitting in his car as they rode the ferry to Catalina.

"I need to ask a favor from you," she said as they ate In-N-Out burgers in the front seat.

"Sure," DePresti said, his voice muffled as he bit into his hamburger. "What do you need?"

"I need you to go look around at work to try and figure out what Bronze Knot is."

DePresti looked at her, half-chew, in disbelief. "What?"

She took a breath. "I'm not entirely sure how your networks are structured, but is there any way that you can do some kind of SharePoint search or shared folder search in Windows for the term 'Bronze Knot' or any variation of that phrase?"

Her boyfriend pursed his lips. "You just don't do that."

"Why not?"

"Because those networks - of which there are more than one - are continuously logged and monitored," DePresti explained. "Specifically for that reason."

"They don't want you looking around?" Parkowski asked, finishing her burger and starting on her fries and milkshake.

"No," DePresti said. "These systems, they're accredited for a certain security level but sometimes data spills over, usually unintentionally. You're supposed to only use them for official purposes at the security level you are briefed to."

"And you're not briefed to Bronze Knot?"

DePresti laughed. "No, Grace, I'm not. Even if it was an unacknowledged SAP that I'm authorized to lie to Congress and the media about its existence, I'd tell you, just to alleviate whatever concern you have about your mission."

"So what are you briefed to?" Parkowski asked. This was the first time she had ever asked him a sensitive question about his work.

He took a breath. "Don't tell any of this to anyone else."

"I won't."

"I'm briefed to about fifty or sixty SAPs," DePresti explained. "That's in addition to all four 'buckets' of SCI, the big intelligence community quasi-SAP that they put a lot of their information in."

"And you've never heard of Bronze Knot?"

"Nope. Grace, I have just about every space-related SAP there is and I've never heard it mentioned or seen those two words together anywhere."

Parkowski paused. "What if it's not space-related?"

"I think it has to be. Just think about it. If NASA and Aering Space Systems are involved, it has to touch the space environment."

She thought for a moment. "Mike, what exactly do you do?"

He laughed. "Don't worry about it."

The motion of the ferry slowed. They were nearing their destination.

Parkowski tried one last time. "Can you *please* poke around a little, as much as you can without getting in trouble, and see if you can find something about it?"

"It's really eating you up inside, isn't it?"

"It is," Parkowski agreed. "Mike, imagine if you had a really big mission at work, a big event like your launch, and it went sideways for reasons beyond your control. Twice."

"Twice," he echoed.

DePresti paused.

"I'd be pretty pissed," he said, collecting their trash into one bag.

"And everyone tells you everything is fine, but there's one thread that keeps showing up but you can't get any information on it," Parkowski continued.

"I get it, I get it," DePresti said in agreement.

"So can you look for me?"

He nodded. "I'll do some surface-level inquiries, but I can't promise anything. I doubt there's any harm in performing a couple of searches."

"That's all I'm looking for," she said, slightly relieved. "Thank you."

Then, it was time to go scuba diving.

#

The next week started with a quiet Monday.

She tried again to go through the Bronze Knot search results on the Aering internal site when she got a chance but still had no luck. The words were just too common.

Parkowski started to wonder if the lack of results for the two words together was deliberate or unintentional. The SharePoint site's search function seemed pretty intelligent, and considering how many results were there for the two words separately, she thought they would have appeared together, but that was not the case.

She left at three in a funk. Parkowski felt like she wasn't really getting anywhere unraveling this mystery.

DePresti was coming to her place tonight for dinner. He had a meeting at OuterTek in Hawthorne and Marina del Rey was a much shorter drive than Hermosa Beach during rush hour. Plus, her roommate was at her own boyfriend's apartment up by UCLA, so she had the place to herself.

Hopefully, her boyfriend was coming with some good news.

DePresti showed up, late, at six. "Sorry, a meeting ran really late."

"It's ok," she replied. "I got started late, so it's just ready now."

They sat down at the tiny kitchen table to eat the chicken, rice, and mixed vegetables Parkowski had cooked.

"So, how was your day?" she asked DePresti after they got settled.

"Fine, how was yours?"

"Pretty quiet," Parkowski said.

There was a brief, almost awkward pause.

"Did you look into 'Bronze Knot' for me?" Parkowski said quietly.

DePresti gave her an odd look, then smiled. "I did," he said, taking a bite of his chicken. "And before you get your hopes up, I found out very, very, very little, mostly by elimination, but let me walk you through what I did do."

"Ok," Parkowski said. She stood up to get a glass of wine, a little dismayed at DePresti's status report. "Thanks for looking though."

"No problem," her boyfriend said. He leaned back a little in his chair. "First, I took your advice and did some searches on the two main SAP networks we use. I figured a couple of queries wouldn't trip any logging software. There were no results for 'Bronze,' none at all. I checked files, SharePoints, documentation pages, and anywhere where you might see a reference. No joy."

"Got it," Parkowski said. She poured her wine and sat back down.

"Then," DePresti said, "I went to a guy I know, a retired O-4 who is one of the support contractors on base. This dude used to be part of SAPCO, which is the Department of Defense Special Access Program Control Office." He said that last part with a flourish. "He knows *all* of the SAPs, and not just the Air Force and Space Force ones. I pulled him into a conference room and asked him point-blank, that my girlfriend ran into this weird error message at work with a SAP I've never seen before, that she wants to make sure she's not crazy, and that it was a real thing she just accidentally saw."

"And what did he say?" Parkowski asked. This might actually be going somewhere.

"So he said he had never heard of it," her boyfriend replied, "and he told me that was the truth - if it was an unacknowledged or waived SAP he'd tell me if he did since you and I had no idea what it was in reference to; it wouldn't be a security violation."

DePresti took a deep breath. "But, he asked if I had looked around internally at all, and I was honest with him, I had searched on our networks. He did tell me something interesting, if I was looking for a SAP name, or a name that had been or would be protected by a SAP that wasn't on the network, the internal search features wouldn't even perform the search. They would just return a null result as part of the protection features of the system."

Parkowski was about to ask a specific question on the topic of the network but the Space Force captain spoke first. "So, then I went back and did the search again," he said, talking quickly, "and compared it to a different search term. And the system actually searched for the other term - it told me the search took 0.36 seconds - whereas for 'Bronze Knot' it just spit back '0 results' without giving me a search time."

She thought for a moment. "Meaning it's some kind of protected term."

He nodded.

"And that was it?"

"Yeah, that's pretty much all I can do on my end without asking too many questions or getting myself in trouble," DePresti told her. "Sorry."

"No, actually, that was really helpful." She finished off her glass of wine. "I know exactly what I have to do next."

CHAPTER FOURTEEN

El Segundo, California

Parkowski almost skipped into work on Tuesday morning.

She had spent the rest of the night formulating a plan to get a hold of her logs again and see if any other references would help her unravel the Bronze Knot mystery.

The junior engineer knew she had to get into the "NASA room" as Pham had called it, but she didn't have access.

She would have to get in somehow.

Parkowski needed to figure out this mystery. Her promotion - and satisfying her own innate curiosity - depended on it.

That being said, were she to be caught, all bets were off. She'd be lucky to have a job.

After checking her emails, she walked down the hallway towards the room. It had tall ceilings and was well-lit throughout. There were eight offices, four on each side, with the NASA room at the very end of the hallway before it veered off in a 90-degree turn to the left towards a different high bay.

The door itself was not like those of Pham, Rosen, and the other senior engineers' offices. While the other doors were wooden with brass doorknobs, the NASA room's door was metal and painted a matte black. Instead of a doorknob, it had a brushed steel handle with a cipher lock above it. There were five metal buttons with the numbers 1 through 5 next to them in descending order.

Parkowski had never seen a lock like that before, but she assumed that a multi-digit code needed to be inputted for it to open. Whether it was alarmed or not, she had no way of knowing. She knew the risks - there was no valid reason for her to be opening the door and she would at the very minimum get a security violation or write-up. She could be fired in a heartbeat.

However, it was a risk she had to take. Something was wrong here, something that was a risk to the mission, and by association, her livelihood and reputation.

Parkowski had to get to the bottom of it.

Her plan was fairly simple in theory, but complex in execution.

The first part wasn't too bad. Over the last few months, she had seen people go in and out of the locked room. They didn't seem too careful about trying to shield the code as they input it; why would someone want to get into the room who didn't have access? She could easily walk by, strike up a conversation with someone while they typed the code in, and surreptitiously make a mental note of the code.

The next part was a little more complicated. Parkowski was going to have to find a good time to be able to type the code in herself without being noticed, either by another human or by some kind of active or passive security system, do what she had to do inside, and get out cleanly.

She was no spy, no secret agent, and had no clandestine skills. Her one claim to fame was being able to sneak quietly out of her parents' house in suburban Wilmington to go out partying with her friends during high school. But Parkowski was smart, and more importantly, she was observant. Maybe she was overconfident, but she knew she was able to get into the room.

Thankfully, she had no mission to plan for, so she had plenty of free time. No one would notice the nice, young female engineer making the rounds to all her friends and colleagues and being social, and definitely not spending too much time in the senior engineers' hallway.

But, there was more traffic in that hallway than she expected. The special projects division's high bay was the next one over, and for whatever reason, quite a few people were traveling through the

ILIAD mission's high bay to that one. Unfortunately, none of them seemed to be using the NASA room's door.

Parkowski decided to start checking the hallway scientifically, with a pattern. She would get up from her cubicle, speak briefly with Kim or one of her other friends in the cube farm, and then meander over to the hallway and walk towards the NASA room. Just past the door, and the bend in the hallway, was a water fountain. She would walk nonchalantly past the door, take a sip of water, and then walk back as slowly as she could.

She did this every half hour on Wednesday and Thursday. There was a lot of traffic in the hallway, but very little around the NASA door. Rosen slipped in there, twice, as did Pham a few times. She saw a few people associated with the special projects division go in once as a group but didn't catch their exit.

Friday confirmed her suspicions. Dr. Rosen entered the room at noon on the dot. That made three days in a row.

Parkowski surmised that he went in there for some kind of meeting. Why else would he go in at the same time each day?

Making a leap in logic, she assumed that he would be there on Monday. This couldn't be easier. All she had to do was walk up to him as he typed in the code, strike up a conversation, and take note of what he inputted. Then, come back later when no one was around and input the code herself.

#

Parkowski bounded into work on Monday, her plan set and ready to go.

The building was a ghost town - no ILIAD missions were planned. But as she walked in, she saw Dr. Rosen and Dr. Pham up on the raised stage, having an animated conversation with each of them holding a different piece of VR control hardware.

She shrugged and went to a cube to check her emails.

At eleven fifty-five, she got up from her desk and walked out into the hallway. Parkowski got a sip of water from the fountain and turned around to see if Dr. Rosen would go to the NASA door.

He didn't.

She waited a few minutes, but the hallway was empty.

Parkowski was a little surprised - he was off his schedule - but played it off, walking nonchalantly back to her desk.

This was not good.

She was already off of her baseline plan.

Both Pham's and Rosen's office doors were closed. She wondered if something was going on.

She switched cubicles to one where she had a good view of the ILIAD mission area and the entrance to the hallway.

Half an hour later, as she was eating her lunch, she saw Dr. Pham walk quickly through the high bay to the hallway.

On a hunch, Parkowski put down her sandwich and followed him.

Dr. Pham made a beeline for the NASA room's door.

This was her opportunity.

She waited until he was about to input the code before speaking up. "Hey boss, how's everything going today?"

Pham spun around to look at her. "Oh, hi, Grace. It's going well. How is everything with you?"

"It's going great," she replied, leaning against the wall next to the door. "How's your week looking?"

"Not too bad," the Ph.D. said as he hunched over to use the cipher lock. Parkowski peered over. He inputted one, five, three, and two together, then four. "How about you?"

"Staying busy and ready to get back on the sticks," she replied with a smile on her face.

"Ah, yes," Pham said as he opened the handle of the large, heavy door. "Well, I've got a meeting. I'll talk with you later."

"Sure, see you later," Parkowski replied. She walked back to the high bay and her cube as the metal door swung closed with a *clang*.

Parkowski spent the rest of the day checking out where the security cameras in the hallway were. She found four, two near the high bay and two farther down by the NASA door. But, where they pointed and were able to see, she wasn't sure. She thought she might be clear if she stuck to the left side of the hallway and slipped over to the right where the door was at the very end, but she wasn't positive that was the case.

This was her chance, and she didn't want to blow it on a hunch. The cameras seemed to be protecting the classified area beyond the hallway rather than the NASA room, but there was no way to be sure without testing out her theory.

She considered abandoning the whole idea. Parkowski went out to the parking lot to get some fresh air when she saw the security guard sitting at his desk.

Parkowski had another idea.

"Hey, Bert," she said as she walked up to the desk.

The elderly man turned from his paperback to look at her. "Grace!" he said loudly. "Sorry 'bout your Birds. I was rooting for them yesterday."

"I know, I know," Parkowski said as she leaned against the desk. Behind Bert, she could see a number of black-and-white feeds from different security cameras throughout the Aering facility. The monitor changed the cameras every couple of seconds to show different sets of cameras.

"You guys are falling apart, what happened?" the security guard asked as his eyes went back to his book. "I thought they were going to run away with the division."

"Injuries," she replied as she watched the camera feeds out of the corner of her eye. All of the ones for the hallway she was interested in were all on the same screen as the system cycled through. Her brain worked quickly to process them as Bert rambled on about playoff scenarios.

From what she could tell, her initial thought was fairly accurate. She could hug the left wall, and switch to the right side at the very end. If she kept herself in the corner while inputting the code and then slid in with the door as it opened she could avoid the camera positioned diagonally at the end of the hallway staring down towards the special projects bay.

"My Rams have been on a run," Bert finished and took a sip of his Diet Coke can, waiting for Parkowski to continue the conversation.

"Four in a row, right?" Parkowski asked. Her stomach flipped continuously; she was so excited about what was going to come next. She was finally going to get to the bottom of all this.

"Yes ma'am," he replied. "Here's how I see the rest of the year playing out..."

Half an hour later she was back at her desk. The Aering plant was a twenty-four-hour facility, but in practice, everyone was gone by five or six.

Parkowski walked out at five to her car and put her purse under the front seat. She texted DePresti that she was staying late. Then she turned around and went back into the building.

"Forget something?" the evening security guard asked.

She nodded and badged in.

Parkowski then went into the women's bathroom and sat down on a stall. No one else entered.

She waited until six-thirty and left the bathroom.

The high bay was completely empty. It was almost eerie. The lights were on, the computer monitors were glowing, and the only person in the room was a young spacecraft operator, more junior than even Parkowski, tasked with keeping the ACHILLES units alive from a console underneath the giant TV screen.

LAG DELAY

Parkowski paused, wondering if he was a threat to her plan, but he had headphones in and was watching a movie on his computer instead of working.

With a smirk on her face, she slipped past him and into the hallway.

Now the hard part.

She quickly but carefully walked along the office doors on the left side. As she got to the end, she slipped over to the right side and hid herself in the corner between the door's hinges and the wall.

Time to input the code.

One.

Five.

Three and two together.

Four.

She heard a slight click as the lock disengaged.

Parkowski grasped the handle and opened the door.

She slipped inside and closed it behind her.

CHAPTER FIFTEEN

El Segundo, California

Parkowski found herself inside a large, dimly-lit, windowless room. Wide metal desks with cabinets above them lined the outer edge. A large, oval-shaped conference table with expensive chairs occupied the middle. In one corner stood a large server rack, at least a foot taller than her, with lights of every color flashing and blinking.

There was no alarm going off, no flashing red light, no indication that anything was amiss.

If she was going to get fired, it probably wasn't tonight.

She finally exhaled.

Parkowski walked around the edge of the room, looking for any security cameras or other sensors, but found none.

With a shrug, she flipped on the light.

On each of the desks was a pair of computer screens, both of which were attached to a workstation underneath the desk. A few had smaller devices on the desk itself, in between the monitors, which Parkowski figured were KVM switches to use the same set of peripherals for multiple computers.

She bent over and checked one of the computer monitors. It had a yellow sticker on it with the words "TOP SECRET" in a bold font.

Parkowski smiled. This had to be it. Based on her conversations with her boyfriend, this was somewhere where she was *not* supposed to be.

If information on Bronze Knot was in the Aering facility somewhere, it was here.

She moved the mouse to log onto the computer but was met with a login screen.

There was more information here. "TOP SECRET//SCI//NOFORN" read a banner at the top. Parkowski wasn't 100% sure what that meant, but based on DePresti's explanation, it had something to do with the CIA and the intelligence community.

She tried a different computer. This one was different - the banner read "TS//SAP//NF."

A SAP. A special access program. Exactly what the error message had said that Bronze Knot was.

Parkowski *had* to get on this computer. But she didn't have the login. An oversight on her part.

She went to each of the computers in the room. Each had similar stickers on the monitors and either an SCI or SAP banner at the top of the login screen.

The six-foot server rack in the corner also fascinated her. Each of the different computers inside of it had a sticker with a different code on it. Two were SCI and the remaining five had SAP-XXX, with XXX being a set of three letters. Four of them she didn't recognize, but BKT stuck out like a sore thumb.

She thought for a moment. Why was all of this highly classified material inside of the NASA room?

"Because it's not the NASA room, Grace," she said to herself. It was a cover for whatever was really going into the room.

But why was it connected to the ILIAD mission? There was *nothing* classified about her day job - Parkowski was very sure of that. When she had first taken the job, she had asked very specifically if there was any classified work and was told no. Enough of her friends worked on classified projects where they couldn't take any work home, have their phones at work, or even work in a building with windows. All of those things had sounded awful to her.

The words "data spill" loomed large in her head. Somehow, Bronze Knot data had gotten into her VR environment. Maybe the answer as to why that happened - and what Bronze Knot was - lay within this room.

She needed to log onto one of the TS//SAP computers and find out.

Parkowski sat down in one of the chairs around the conference room and thought about how she could gain access.

She knew that a lot of people were lazy with logins, writing them down on Post-it notes and whatnot. But this room had a security posture way above where Parkowski normally worked. Her other option was to go out and come back with some kind of hacking tool - an area where she had little experience but was willing to dive into it head-first to get to the bottom of the mystery.

But who knew if she would get another chance at this. This was a once-in-a-lifetime opportunity to figure out the answer to the mystery that had eluded her for weeks.

Parkowski started going through the room with a fine-toothed comb. Maybe, just maybe, someone left a clue as to how to get onto the SAP system with Bronze Knot information.

After a few minutes, she hit pay dirt in one of the cabinets above the computer monitors.

Someone had committed the cardinal sin of network security.

He or she, whoever it was, had written down their username and password on a small piece of paper that was taped to the inside of the cabinet door.

She had used her hand to feel around in the insides of the cabinet and brushed alongside a scrap of paper. Parkowski carefully removed it from the cabinet door without tearing it and saw that not only had the person carefully written down their SCI username and password, but they had also included the SAP one.

Parkowski went to the first computer she could find with the "TS//SAP" banner on it and used the SAP login information to get on.

It took almost five minutes to get to the desktop, but she was finally in. She opened the file manager and started to look around.

Unfortunately, whoever she was logged in as seemed to have their permissions extremely restricted. When she tried to open up anything on the shared network drive she ran into "permission denied" and "access not granted" error messages.

She tried opening up the browser. Nothing, just another error message. This computer was not connected to the outside internet or any internal network that contained web pages like Aering's SharePoint.

Parkowski sat back, stumped. Maybe this person didn't really use this network at all and just had access as part of something else, hence why they needed to write down their login information. They didn't use it that much, so they needed to keep it somewhere to refer back to when they did access the network.

But why did they have access then in the first place?

There had to be something on this machine that she could get to.

Parkowski tried the network drive again. Still no access.

She tried to get into the computer's own drive - the one physically located inside the computer - but it was locked down as well. But at the top left of the window, she saw the recently accessed folders. Whoever had used this login last, they had left a trail of where they had gone on the SAP-level network.

Finally, a breakthrough.

Parkowski opened up one of the folders named "BKT Logs" and all of the missing files from her previous missions were there, in addition to the ones from the rest of the missions, all the way up until yesterday. Someone had taken them off of the low-side Aering network and moved them to this protected system.

She tried another folder from the recently accessed list. This one was named "SAR-HBX CONOPS and Specifications" and as per the name contained a CONOPS (CONcept of OPerationS) and a series of high-level system specs for a reconnaissance satellite that Aering was offering to build for the government.

Parkowski understood very little of it, this was more up DePresti's alley, but she knew enough to know that it had no connection to the ILIAD mission or Bronze Knot. It was just a different special access program, hence why it was secured on the same network.

The remaining folders that had been accessed were more of the same, some at technical levels well beyond Parkowski's understanding. One was a deep-space sensor, another was a radar warning receiver, and some she couldn't make heads-or-tails of despite her background in engineering and her space experience. They might have made sense to someone more versed in the classified side of the space world, but not to her. None of the others had Bronze Knot data.

She was back to square one.

Parkowski went back to the "BKT Logs" folder and opened a few of the logs. To her surprise, she did learn something new - the fields in the log files for the packets that had been previously blanked out were now filled with numbers or alphanumeric codes. Unfortunately, none of them meant anything to her.

But, she now knew through her conversations with her boyfriend and her own research that the data itself - the ones that had been masked - were considered to be protected under the Bronze Knot program. Why they were protected, and what they were protecting, she still did not know, but part of the SAP was to protect some specific telemetry data between Venus and the ground station on Earth.

But why though? Why would the military care about the ILIAD mission so much that they needed to safeguard some of its data behind the highest level of classification that it could muster?

She opened up each log file. None offered any more information. Parkowski would need a higher-level document, some kind of decoder ring or something, to make heads-and-tails of what she was seeing. Numbers in and of themselves didn't give her any more understanding, they had to be put into context.

On a hunch, she tried to go up a level of the folder directory, to a folder with a vague name.

Access denied.

She tried to go one level up beyond that.

Jackpot.

All of *its* subfolders were locked down, but their names were all readable on the screen.

It was a high-level overview of Bronze Knot. Parkowski quickly scanned the folder names. Some pieces were missing, but Bronze Knot, or at least the piece of it on this network, involved nothing more than protecting certain pieces of data. There was a guard, potentially located in the server rack in this same room, which filtered that data from a classified high side to the low side environment that the ILIAD mission used.

But why? Why would a scientific mission need to protect data, especially at the TS//SAP level? Why were they even connected to a SAP network?

She didn't have the answers. It seemed like every time she figured something out, two new mysteries presented themselves.

There was one file left to open, an .ini file that she had overlooked when she had initially opened the folder.

Parkowski opened it using a text editor. It confirmed some of her earlier suspicions; the box in the server rack was a cross-domain guard that filtered the Bronze Knot data before it hit the ILIAD virtual environment.

She tried to follow the logic in the configuration file but it didn't make any sense. From what she could gather, the data traveled through a path from the ACHILLES robot to the two relay satellites to MICS to the ground station. From there, it *should* go directly to El Segundo - but it didn't. Instead, it went to something called AFAMS-Orlando before coming to the Aering facility.

Orlando. In Florida.

She opened up a few of the log files. Sure enough, there was more evidence there that confirmed that fact.

In fact, the entire ILIAD environment was hosted on a cloud server located in Orlando.

Why Orlando? No one had ever told her that the Venus environment was locally hosted, but no one had indicated that it existed anywhere else, either. That would introduce a small amount of additional lag as packets had to travel via fiber optic lines across the country. That was illogical, no one would ever do that, but here was evidence that it was the case.

There was nothing else here she could do. Parkowski closed out of the folder and logged out of the account. She placed the login information back where she found it and turned off the light.

She then left the way she came, making sure she stayed out of the view of the security cameras.

Parkowski drove back to her apartment with her mind in a swirl. She had completed her "mission" yet had opened up another can of worms; each answer raising another dozen questions.

But she now realized that she was being lied to, by someone, and that was not something she was ok with. The military had to be involved, she was sure of it, as was NASA. But there had to be more to this mission than met the eye.

CHAPTER SIXTEEN

Redondo Beach, California

The rest of the week was quiet.

Parkowski kept framing and reframing the problem in her head but it made no sense. ILIAD was a science mission. They were exploring Venus. There was no connection to the military. None. Zip. Zilch. It was a purely civilian endeavor. The only *slight* connection was the fact that Aering also did military contracts out of the same building where it ran the ILIAD mission.

But then there was Bronze Knot.

It was a special access program, the highest level of classification afforded by the U.S. government. From the research she had done, mostly through Google searches on her phone and her conversations with DePresti, it protected very sensitive technologies, associations, and operations.

And, from what she could gather, Bronze Knot was hiding bits and pieces of packets in the communications pathway between Venus and Earth.

Why was that so important?

She had to find out why. It was the only thing on her mind. The engineer in her needed to know how everything fit together.

"Everything ok, Grace?" DePresti asked as they sat on the couch in his apartment on Saturday afternoon, watching a college football game. They had planned to go hiking, but a rare November rainstorm had ruined their plans.

She nodded slightly. "I'm fine."

"You seem like you've got something on your mind."

Parkowski wanted nothing more than to open up to him, to tell him about the weird "NASA room" with all of the SCI and SAP computers, to tell him her suspicions on what Bronze Knot was, but she wasn't ready to. Not yet at least. "Just some stuff."

"It's not about us, right?" They had fought the night before over what movie to watch, a silly argument that had spiraled out of control.

She laughed. "No, not us, not you, just some stuff at work."

"Got it," her boyfriend replied. "Well, if you want to talk, you know I'm here for you."

He's going to think I'm crazy, fixated on this topic, Parkowski thought.

She did need to talk to someone about it though.

Parkowski considered calling her parents and seeing if her dad had any insight into this, but thought of a better idea.

She would use the screenshot she had saved of the mission log with Bronze Knot, combined with her research, and bring it up with Dr. Pham - who she knew by now had to know more than he was letting on.

All of what she learned in the NASA room was just icing on the cake, an additional confirmation of her suspicions. Parkowski didn't have to bring any of that up. Her own experience inside of the VR environment and the screenshot were enough to hopefully force Pham to spill the beans on what was really going on.

#

Monday was a slow day. A few of the ILIAD team were out of the office and only one mission, an afternoon transit run, was on the schedule. The operational cadence didn't pick back up until the next day.

It was a perfect opportunity to see if she could shake more information out of her supervisor.

Parkowski checked Pham's calendar. He had meetings all morning but was free at eleven.

"Hey, Dr. Pham," she said at five past the hour as she leaned on the doorway into his office, holding a piece of paper with the screenshot printed on it, folded in half. "Can I talk with you for a little bit?"

He looked up at her from his computer. "Yes, Grace, come on in." Pham motioned at the chair across from his desk. "Anytime."

Parkowski closed the door behind her.

He raised an eyebrow but didn't comment.

She sat down in the chair and looked at him.

"Is everything ok, Grace?" Pham asked.

The same question DePresti had asked her over the weekend.

She wanted to just burst with questions, to ask them rapid-fire to Pham and hopefully receive answers back just as quickly, but she held back.

"We need to talk," she said.

The other eyebrow was now raised. "About what?"

Parkowski put the piece of paper with the screenshot in front of him. "This."

Her boss put on a pair of reading glasses and took a look at it. After a quick scan, he looked up at her. "Grace, where did you get this?"

"From the mission logs before they got pulled off of the shared drive," she answered.

Pham shook his head. "You weren't supposed to have seen this."

"What do you mean, 'not supposed to have seen this?'" Parkowski said, a hint of anger in her voice.

Pham looked at the door as if making sure it was closed, and then back at her. "Grace, I..."

"What is Bronze Knot?" she asked her voice up an octave. "You told me you didn't know, but here it is, clear as day, in the ILIAD VR environment."

He sighed. "Ok, you're right. I figured one of you junior engineers would find out sooner or later."

"Find what out?"

"There's a little more going on than we've let on. Nothing that you need to be worried about, though."

That last bit got under her skin.

"But I'm worried," Parkowski said. "Both times I've been on the sticks, things have gone wrong. I want to know why. I don't want it to happen again."

"I know, you're an engineer, you need to know *why*," Pham said, a heavy emphasis on the last word. He leaned back a little in his chair. "Grace, what happened on your missions is easily explained. And it's not related to what you showed me."

A lie.

He had to know more, there was no way he didn't know what Bronze Knot was and how it was connected to her mission.

"Ok, so what happened?"

"The first time the package was incorrectly compiled, hence the dragon showing up. The second time the communications box on the relay satellite around Venus just lagged out. Perfectly normal stuff."

She wasn't convinced. "Ok, so why the secrecy?" She held back on just how much she knew about special access programs.

Pham lied again. "Ok," he said, looking at the door for a second time, "here's the thing. There's rumors of some financial impropriety at Aering making the rounds."

Parkowski hadn't heard that. "Really."

"Yes," the older man said, nodding, "and my understanding is that all of the secrecy is due to the fact that some of the…impropriety was done on the ILIAD mission. With regards to our communications gear built in-house and installed on the robots and relay satellite. And that's all I am comfortable saying at this time."

"So that's why all of the logs were taken away?"

"Yes."

That made even less sense to Parkowski than ILIAD being connected to the military. "And Bronze Knot is then..."

"It's some kind of mechanism for protecting data associated with the ILIAD mission," Pham replied. "I don't know all of the specifics, sorry."

He took a breath. "I know how you feel, Grace, but you need to let this one go."

"Ok," Parkowski said. It was now her time to lie. "Will do."

"I need to keep this," Pham said, showing her the screenshot.

She nodded.

"One more thing," Pham said.

"Yes?"

"We're taking you off the schedule," he said. "At least temporarily. Leadership isn't sure if it's you, or your gear, or just a coincidence, but consider yourself temporarily removed from active duty on the ACHILLES units."

That stung.

Parkowski fought back a tear and nodded.

"It's not personal, Grace," Pham added. "Nothing that's happened has been your fault. We just need to figure out what's going on."

She nodded again.

"Have a great rest of your day," Pham said. "Don't be too hard on yourself. We'll figure it out."

Parkowski finally found her ability to talk.

"See you later, boss," she said in a scratchy voice as she opened the door and left.

Parkowski was furious.

Now, she had to do what she was dreading all weekend - coming clean to her boyfriend about what she had done the previous week.

#

"You did *what*?" DePresti cried out when she finally fessed up that evening at her apartment.

"I got into the locked room using the code," she said quietly.

"Grace, that is a *huge* security violation," the Space Force officer said. He stood up from the table where they were eating pizza. "You weren't cleared for what was in there!"

"So?"

"If they find out they're going to pull your clearance."

"So what?" she said, a little annoyed. This was why she hadn't wanted to have the conversation.

"Grace, in this industry, not being able to hold a security clearance is a death sentence," DePresti explained. "Even if your job, like your current one, doesn't require one, the company you work for wants the flexibility to move you to one that does. If you can't hold a clearance, you're going to have a hard time finding work."

"But I need to know what's going on," Parkowski replied.

"Why? Why do you need to know?"

"Because I've spent the last two years of my life thinking I was doing this one thing, to advance science, to use my engineering skills, to be among the first people to explore Venus," she said angrily. "And now I'm learning that there's some stupid black project, special access program bullshit behind all of this, connected to my ILIAD mission I've busted my ass for. Which makes no sense. And now, you think I'm crazy. That I'm either seeing things that aren't there or am digging too deep into something that I don't need to concern myself with." Parkowski took a deep breath. "And now they've taken me off of the schedule. I'm not crazy, Mike, I know I'm fixated on this, but it's eating me up inside. My promotion, my future at the company, relies on me having successful trips in the VR gear."

He nodded, but let her talk and get it all out.

"We should be having a nice dinner right now but I've been trying to figure out why the military cares so much about my mission to create a special access program for it," she finished.

"Hey, it might not be the military," DePresti said as he took her hand in his. "The intelligence community has them too."

"That's not the *point*!" Parkowski said, with an emphasis on the last word.

"Then what is?"

"That the government is hiding stuff from us, specifically me, that is preventing me from doing my job. And it's impacting my job performance. How would you like it if some black ops bullshit showed up on your performance report?"

DePresti sat back down. "Grace..."

"What?"

"Do you have any idea how many SAPs there are?"

"No."

"I know a guy who's been read into a thousand."

"A thousand?" she said incredulously.

"Yep. And he knew of at least five hundred Navy ones he wasn't read into."

"What does that mean? There's a lot of SAPs?"

"It means that Bronze Knot is just one piece. One amongst many others. It's just a SAP, who cares what it's protecting? You told me over the weekend that no one is saying that what happened during your missions is your fault. Just forget any of this ever happened. If it shows up again, Grace, I promise you, I'll help you figure it out, but right now you need to let it go."

They ate the rest of their meal in silence.

Finally, as they were cleaning up, still not talking to each other, DePresti spoke up. "Grace, you're going to get yourself in trouble."

"I know."

"Just be aware of the consequences," DePresti said, "because I hope it's worth it."

CHAPTER SEVENTEEN

Marina Del Rey, CA

"Shouldn't you be at work?" Parkowski's roommate asked as the Aering engineer sat with her knees to her chest on the couch, watching a trashy reality show, at eight o'clock the next morning.

"Yes, I should be at work," Parkowski said, a little annoyed, "but I'm here. I don't have anything until the afternoon and I worked more than enough billable hours for the pay period last week. I'm fine."

"Ok," her roommate said with a shrug. "Are you hanging out with Mike tonight or do you want me to cook?"

"I'll figure it out myself," Parkowski said. "Don't worry about me."

"See you later."

After her roommate left, she got up and paced the small living room.

Parkowski was scheduled for a Thursday mission with the two ACHILLES robots. She had originally been taken off of the schedule, and replaced with a "training mission" for one of the newer operators. Leadership hadn't wanted to give her another chance. But, the new operator hadn't been available, so Parkowski went back onto the schedule.

She was supposed to spend her week planning for her third time on the sticks, but her motivation just wasn't there. She had debated calling in sick but knew she had to be in the office.

The argument with DePresti last night had left her in an awful mood.

She made herself a cup of coffee and sat back on the couch.

Parkowski had woken up in the middle of the night with a thought. Maybe the reason her boyfriend was so dismissive of her concerns was that there *was* a covert military link to the ILIAD mission. Just before she went to bed, she'd read an article about an upcoming U.S. Space Force launch to cislunar space between Earth and the Moon. The USSF's satellite's orbit was said to be the highest ever achieved, a near rectilinear halo orbit with the Moon as its epicenter.

This spacecraft was supposed to keep tabs on both orbital activity around the Moon as well as the giant volume of space between the Earth and its only natural satellite. Most of the details were classified, but the concept itself got Parkowski thinking.

If the U.S. military was concerned about the Moon and the space around it, why wouldn't they also be concerned about Mars, and by extension Venus? The commercial use of space had exploded over the last decade. There were now two semi-permanent bases on the Moon, one American, one Chinese, and another American one planned for Mars, even though the first astronauts to the red planet had just returned from their long voyage. And where commercial interests went, the military followed, even out into the stars.

The whole Bronze Knot affair seemed illogical unless one went down that rabbit hole.

Maybe DePresti didn't know what exactly was going on, but the U.S. military was a huge organization spread out across the country, with thousands of sub-organizations within it. Maybe someone, somewhere, put some kind of sensors or other military hardware on either the ILIAD landing craft or the relay, as a way to either watch for or defend against Russian or Chinese military activity. The information was held in a SAP, Bronze Knot, at a higher level than what DePresti or even Dr. Pham had access to.

At least that was her going theory.

Parkowski had a sneaking suspicion that one of the two men had some knowledge of what was really going on, just under a different name than Bronze Knot, but she couldn't know for certain.

But what she did know was that there was more information on special programs in the "NASA room" that she had gotten into last week. There had been no indication that anyone had detected her break-in, no negative repercussions at all. Maybe a second time through the TS//SAP workstation would yield her the clues she needed to unlock the secrets of Bronze Knot.

She groaned and got her bag together. Time to go to work.

Parkowski got in at around eleven, but no one seemed to notice her late arrival.

Her first meeting wasn't until one thirty, so she had some time to get settled. Parkowski checked her email and then went out into the hallway to see if there were any changes in the security system from the previous week.

There were none.

No one knew that she had been in and out of the locked room.

She stopped by Dr. Pham's office and had a brief conversation about her upcoming mission. There was no mention of their talk from the previous day.

It was lunchtime. Parkowski grabbed a sandwich and bag of chips at the cafeteria and ate at her cubicle.

She needed to get back into that room. Parkowski had left too early last time without unlocking all of its secrets.

Her plan the last time had been successful. Why change it? She would sneak in after everyone had left, using the same route to get to the room, type in the code, and continue her search for what Bronze Knot really was and why it had manifested itself in both of her missions on Venus.

The afternoon was spent planning for her next time on the sticks.

Parkowski's mission was much simpler than the previous two. She had to get both ACHILLES units to the same point near a larger crater south of the initial landing site. From there, the next operator would take them to an area where a Soviet spacecraft named

Verena 4 in the 1960s had noticed a magnetic field anomaly during its mission.

She had a high-fidelity model of the Venusian surface pulled up on her workstation with a small model of an ACHILLES robot in the center of the screen. She controlled it with the keyboard's arrow keys, much like a video game.

Parkowski had her notebook open as well as the mission planning software as she tried to find the best route for each of the two robots from their starting positions to the final waypoint.

But she was still distracted. Parkowski couldn't remember a time when she was ever as single-minded in her pursuit of knowledge as she was now. She *had* to know what Bronze Knot's association with the ILIAD mission was.

That night, she waited until the Aering facility emptied. Unlike last time, there were a few stragglers, but by eight-thirty, she had the high bay to herself.

Parkowski got up from the cubicle and walked quickly to the hallway door. She peeked out and saw all of the office doors closed and locked.

Game time. She took a breath and slid along the side of the hallway to avoid the cameras and then leaned over to the far right corner.

She remembered the code. Time to get back in.

One.

Five.

Three and two together.

Four.

No click.

She scrunched her nose and rubbed her temples. That was right, she was sure of it, but it didn't work.

Puzzled, Parkowski tried it again.

Still no click.

She heard a rustling in the hallway towards the special projects high bay, a scuffle of a shoe against the floor.

Parkowski panicked.

She threw herself away from the door and started walking back towards the ILIAD area.

"Who's there?" a muffled voice said from beyond the bend in the hallway.

She kept walking into the ILIAD high bay.

"Ms. Parkowski," she heard a voice say from the dark hallway.

She recognized the person now. Dr. Rosen - Dr. Pham's boss.

Parkowski spun on her heel and went back to the entryway.

"Yes?" she said quietly as she poked her head out, her heart beating at a million beats per second.

Rosen stood in front of the door to the "NASA room." He did not look happy. "Ms. Parkowski," he repeated, beckoning her to come closer with his finger. "What are you doing here at this hour?"

"Just finishing up my work," Parkowski said hastily, trying to keep the panic out of her voice, as she walked towards him. "I've got a lot on my plate."

He glared at her.

"Can I leave?" she asked.

"What were you really doing?"

"I was getting a sip of water from the water fountain. I left my bottle at home."

"You weren't, by chance, trying to get into the secure room here?" Rosen pointed at the cipher lock.

Parkowski shook her head. "No."

She was an awful liar. Hopefully, Rosen couldn't pick up on it.

"I heard from the security team that someone without the correct access was trying to get in yesterday," the senior Aering engineer continued. "That wouldn't by any chance happen to be you, would it?"

Parkowski gave him an odd look. "No, that wasn't me," she said, a little surprised. This time she was telling the truth.

Rosen was about to ask her another question when they both heard heavy footsteps coming from the direction of the ILIAD high bay.

She turned around. It was Bert, the old security guard.

Parkowski breathed a sigh of relief. She hadn't liked where the conversation with Rosen had been going.

"Is everything ok here?" he said to the two engineers as he arrived.

Parkowski was about to speak up when Rosen spoke for both of them. "Yes, we were both just leaving," he said as he glared at her.

She nodded. This was probably her signal to get the hell out of Dodge. Parkowski went to her cubicle to get her bag as Rosen stormed out of the high bay towards the facility's exit.

Parkowski turned to go but she found Bert standing in her way. "Grace, what's going on?" he asked, almost innocently.

"I don't know," she lied again. "I was about to leave and went to get a sip of water and ran into Dr. Rosen. He started interrogating me and then you came."

If he detected the lie, he didn't let on.

The older man sighed. "You should go home, bad things happen here at night."

"What do you mean?"

Bert leaned against the side of the cubicles. "Last night, someone with Aering access tried to break into the secure room in the hallway."

"Really?" Parkowski said, intrigued.

The security guard nodded. "Yeah, and that was after they changed the codes and limited the access because last week someone *did* get into it."

"No way," she said breathlessly.

"Yes, but the weirdest thing is, it didn't look like they exfiltrated any data or tampered with anything in the room, they just went in and out."

"Weird," Parkowski echoed.

"Yeah, and the theory is that they tried to break in last night, too," he continued. "But after last week, leadership decided to limit access to only a couple of people, Dr. Rosen included, and to change the code on the lock. I don't think they've told anyone yet though, that room isn't used very much. Hopefully, that deters them."

"Yeah," she said in response. "Hopefully it does."

That was new information, confirming what Rosen had told her. Someone else had tried to get into the room, someone other than her. Parkowski wondered if they were interested in Bronze Knot or in one of the many other programs with data in that room.

"Anyways," Bert went on. The man did like to talk. "I don't know what's going on in there, but I've been here a long time. Almost forty years. If I was able to give you any advice, any advice at all, it'd be to stay away from whatever the hell is going on in that room because I've never seen management here so spun up."

Frustrated, Parkowski went home, this time empty-handed. But now she had even more questions than she had before.

CHAPTER EIGHTEEN

Marina Del Rey, CA

At dinner, Parkowski barely touched the burrito her roommate had picked up for her dinner and went to bed early, around nine o'clock.

It took her over an hour to fall asleep. She tossed and turned, still worrying about her new knowledge that her infiltration of the secure room of Aering had *not* gone unnoticed. She had been as careful as she could, but maybe not careful enough.

Parkowski fell into an uneasy sleep.

A few hours later she woke up.

At first, she wasn't sure why she was awake, but then she heard the steady *buzz* of her phone vibrating.

Someone was calling her.

Parkowski sighed and rolled over to her nightstand and checked the time. 2:04 AM. Who could be calling her in the middle of the night?

She thought about ignoring it, she recognized the Los Angeles area code but not the number itself, but then remembered that the automated Aering remote notification system sometimes used new or unique numbers to reach the company's employees scattered throughout the area.

She hit the green "answer" button on the phone's screen.

"Hello," Parkowski said.

At first, there was no response. Had she messed up whatever the Aering notification system was trying to tell her?

"Hello," she said again.

This time someone spoke up, an unfamiliar, deep, gravelly male voice she had never heard before. "Grace Parkowski," the strange voice said slowly but clearly. "You are endangering national security. Cease your investigation into 'Bronze Knot' before it is too late."

"Wait...what?" Parkowski said, confused, but the call had already ended.

She sat up in bed, bewildered - and terrified.

Ok, Grace, deep breaths, she thought.

How did anyone know about her unofficial investigation of sorts? The only people she had spoken the words "Bronze Knot" to were DePresti and Dr. Pham. The former had admittedly asked around at work but hadn't used her name, the latter she wasn't a hundred percent sure had gone to anyone else. Her roommate had access to her computer and the screenshot on it, but she was significantly less technically adept than Parkowski and likely wasn't snooping around anyway.

The call itself was bizarre.

How could she be "endangering national security" as the caller put it?

ILIAD was a science mission, run through NASA, not some Department of Defense boondoggle like what DePresti worked on. And "cease your investigation before it is too late," was that a threat?

She was a little worried now. Parkowski looked up the non-emergency number for the LAPD and started to dial it, but canceled the call.

Parkowski couldn't sleep the rest of the night. She just lay there, staring at the ceiling or tossing and turning.

At six, she finally got up and out of her bed feeling more tired than when she had gone to sleep. Her roommate snored away in her room next door. Parkowski wanted to do just that; call out of work, tell Dr. Pham she wasn't feeling well, and just stay home all day. But she knew that she couldn't. She had to finish planning her mission and maybe do some more poking around to see if she could tease any more information about Bronze Knot out from the Aering internal network.

#

Parkowski got in at eight, checked in with her boss, and went through her email. She should have finished her mission plan for her mission on Friday morning, less than 24 hours away, but put it off to the afternoon.

After a brief hesitation, Parkowski did some more digging on the SharePoint site. She was particularly interested in anything to do with deep-space sensors or Aering's involvement in any of the cislunar military missions currently on the drawing board.

She surprisingly found quite a bit of both. Aering was working with a smaller business to develop a long-range electro-optical sensor that could detect movement at up to a million kilometers, and all of it seemed to be unclassified. Aering also had recently won a contract to build a small satellite that would be a secondary payload on an upcoming launch to the Earth-Moon L2 Lagrange point. However, all of the details of that mission were classified.

Parkowski had brought her lunch and ate at her cube while organizing all of her computer's files. DePresti had texted her that morning, asking to take her out to dinner that night, but she hadn't responded. She was still kind of upset with him, the two had barely talked since their argument Monday night, and she wasn't sure if she wanted to see him or not. It might just make things worse.

Just as she was finishing her lunch, her cubicle's telephone rang.

She narrowed her eyes at the phone.

It was her normal cube, sure, but they didn't have permanent seating - all of the desks were hot-bunked - and the junior engineers swapped desks fairly often so the phones were usually used for outgoing calls, not incoming ones. Who would be calling her?

Parkowski answered it. "This is Grace."

"Ms. Parkowski, this is James with the security team," she heard in a thick Southern accent - a rarity in SoCal. "There's a visitor here to see you."

"A visitor?" she said. Parkowski wasn't expecting anyone.

"Yes, a visitor," the security guard replied.

"Be right there."

Parkowski hung up the phone and got up from her cube.

She walked towards the Aering building's entrance. Who could be visiting her? Hopefully, it wasn't DePresti coming to try and mend their relationship. She still loved him (that word had been a big step a few months back) and wanted to be with him, but right now she needed a little space. He knew the building, had spent a lot of time there in preparation for the ILIAD launch, but hadn't been there in months. She couldn't think of any other potential suspects.

When she got to the entryway, there was an older man with an elaborate mustache sitting on a couch, reading a magazine. A small briefcase sat next to him. The security guard turned to her. "Ma'am, this man came to see you," he said. "He's got a badge."

"Thanks, I'll go talk with him," Parkowski said. She walked up to the newcomer. "Hey, I'm Grace Parkowski, you came to see me?"

The man looked up from his months-old Sports Illustrated. "Oh, hello," he said in a deep voice, putting the magazine down and standing up. He reached into his pocket and pulled out a small black wallet. Flipping it over, Parkowski saw a picture of the man with some writing next to it - an ID card - and a gold badge. "Special Agent Hollis Everson, AFOSI/PJ," he said, extending a hand. "Pleasure to meet you."

"You as well," she replied, unsettled. Why was a federal agent here? "Sorry, but I don't know what this is about."

"That's ok," Everson said. "I need to talk to you, but somewhere more secure. Can we go get a conference room or something?"

Parkowski nodded, still unsure. She worried about why this man came to pay her a visit. "I guess so, I had a busy afternoon planned but I guess it can wait."

"This shouldn't take too long," the man said.

She got him a visitor's badge and took Everson back through the facility. "I only have a Secret clearance," Parkowski told him as they walked, "and I can only get a conference room cleared to that level."

"That's good enough," the older man replied.

Where she would have gone left to the ILIAD high bay, she took a right and went back to the "classified area" that she did have access to. It was sparsely populated - not much at the Aering plant was done at the Secret level, but they did need an area to process data at that level - so she found a small unoccupied conference room fairly easily.

Once they got in, Everson closed the door. "I'll try and keep my time here short," he said. "But we have a security concern that we need to take care of."

"What is it?" Parkowski asked, her heart racing. Did they know that she had gotten into the secure room out in the senior engineers' hallway?

The older man didn't respond at first, reaching down into his briefcase for something. "Nothing you did," he said gently, noticing her concern as he removed a couple of printouts, "but more what happened to you."

Parkowski was still confused until he flipped over one of the pieces of paper. It was a screenshot of the error message from her second mission in the VR environment. ERROR: SPECIAL ACCESS PROGRAM - BRONZE KNOT - SPECIAL ACCESS REQUIRED - the same words now burned into her memory. "Unfortunately, you saw this when you were doing whatever it is you do virtually on Venus," Everson told her. "And you weren't supposed to see this."

"What exactly is it?" Parkowski asked. "It's been bugging me, I have no idea what it is, but I've seen it twice now in the Venus environment."

"Twice?"

"Well, once in the VR setup, which is what you have here," she explained, "and again when I went through the logs for my first mission."

Everson laughed. "Well, this should cover both times then."

Parkowski tilted her head. "What do you mean?"

He pulled out another piece of paper. "This is a nondisclosure agreement," Everson said, reaching into the briefcase again, "and this is an unauthorized disclosure form."

"What does that even mean?" she asked.

"Let's start with the second one," the AFOSI agent said. "That means you and the government, which in this case means me, agree that you saw something you weren't supposed to."

"What exactly did I see?"

Everson looked at the door and then back at her. "In this case, you saw the name of a special access program," he told her. "In this case, an unacknowledged one where even the name is classified."

"Why?"

He laughed. "I was told a long time ago to not speculate about stuff you don't know or aren't cleared to. I suggest that's what you do here."

"Ok," she said, unconvinced. "What about the other one?"

"This one you need to sign," Everson told her as he pointed at the piece of paper. "It says you won't talk about this program with anyone else unless you want a monetary punishment or imprisonment."

She took a second to let that sink in, then responded. "No."

"No?"

"No, I'm not signing that," Parkowski said, pushing the piece of paper away without reading it. "There's no reason for me to sign it."

She saw it as limiting her options. Parkowski was now more than ever convinced that everything was not on the up-and-up on the ILIAD mission and she felt like she had to protect herself somehow in case it went sideways. Having all of her options open would help her do that.

"Young lady," Everson said, "you are going to sign it if you want to continue working here."

"What are you going to do if I don't?"

"I'll get your clearance pulled faster than you can say A-F-O-S-I," the agent said. "And I'll have you put on an ITAR-restricted list that will prevent you from coming into the building. This is a matter of national security and I'll be damned if I let you threaten that."

But how, Parkowski wondered, how would knowing about a SAP attached to the ILIAD mission impact the country's security?

This guy wasn't going to give her the answer to that, though.

And it was just a piece of paper, right?

"Fine," she said. "Give me a pen."

CHAPTER NINETEEN

El Segundo, CA

"Are you ready, Grace?" Dr. Pham asked.

She nodded. "I guess so."

"Cheer up," the senior engineer smiled weakly. "This time, everything is going to go smoothly!"

If you say so, she thought.

It was Friday, the day of her third mission on Venus.

Parkowski had gotten a good night of sleep and was ready to put the stress of the last few days behind her. It had been a trying week, and she wanted to end it on a good note.

The skies were clear, the communications pathway to and from Venus was working at near-peak efficiency, and there was a crowd in the high bay.

Dr. Rosen, the mission's lead program manager, Anna Khoudry, and a few lower-level Aering executives were present. There were over twenty technicians, double the normal ten, and Parkowski had two backups compared to the normal one.

Her mentor seemed particularly nervous when he had rolled into the office about five minutes after Parkowski's arrival, and his anxiety had increased with every step of the pre-mission walkthrough. Dr. Pham was worried about something specific, but Parkowski hadn't the foggiest idea what it was.

She put her helmet on and waited for one of the technicians to plug it into the VR environment.

Moments later, she returned to the surface of Venus.

Parkowski made some small movements to check the responsiveness of the integrated system and was pleased to see that the ACHILLES unit she was operating, ACHILLES 1, tracked her movement fluidly.

She was pleasantly surprised to see that the graphics settings for the VR environment were turned up to the max, a pleasant side benefit of the clear communications pathway. She could see every nook and cranny on the cracked surface, the detailed starfield overhead, and even the robot's now damaged and dirty exterior. Whatever they were paying the texture artists at Panspermia, it was totally worth it.

The first leg of the trip was short. ACHILLES 1 was only a few kilometers from its final waypoint. Parkowski covered that distance in about twenty minutes without breaking a sweat.

There were some alarms on the UI so she pulled them up. The ACHILLES unit was getting a strange magnetometer reading, which made sense with the context of the mission.

Parkowski had gotten an earful on the relevant science history from Pham and Khoudry before she had suited up. The Russians had never realized the importance of their probe's discovery; the data from *Verana* had been relegated to the dustbins of history with the fall of the Soviet Union before a young researcher had digitized them in the mid-2000s and posted them on an internet repository with little fanfare. A few years later, a CalTech postdoc had discovered the treasure trove of Venusian data and published a prize-winning paper on the planet's magnetic field and its many anomalies. The two Aering senior engineers had compared it to the invention of stealth aircraft, also based on a Soviet researcher's forgotten work, a story that Parkowski had heard too many times from DePresti.

The readings made no sense to her, she was an engineer, not a geologist or planetary scientist. There was a lot of excited chatter on the net from the experts.

Parkowski shrugged - would the ACHILLES unit do the same millions of miles away? So far, everything was going according to plan.

LAG DELAY

She had just switched to the second unit when a new voice broke in on the mission net. "Miss Parkowski, how is everything going?"

It was Dr. Rosen.

"Hey, sir," Parkowski replied. This was odd. "What's up?"

"Oh, nothing," the Aering Ph.D. told her. "I've been reading your after-action reports, Grace, and you have had some interesting experiences in the Venus environment."

She didn't say anything. Where was he going with this?

"Dr. Khoudry and I are here to see if anything...exciting happens on your mission today," Rosen continued.

Were they expecting something, Parkowski wondered? She wasn't sure how to respond.

The senior engineer kept talking. "Great job so far. Keep doing what you're doing."

"Thanks," she replied.

Rosen didn't say anything else.

That whole conversation was weird.

She switched to the second ACHILLES unit, making sure that the sensors on the first one were still active so that the scientists could get all of their readings.

ACHILLES 2 was inside of a network of slot canyons to the far east of its final destination. Parkowski had calculated the distance to be over a dozen kilometers from the current location of ACHILLES 1, but she knew now that number was too low. The canyons were dense, similar to the dry riverbeds of the American west, but they had been created by planetary tectonics rather than running water.

Some of the twisting routes that she had created in her planning software were already not possible. One of the passageways between two canyons that she had hoped to use was blocked with boulders.

Parkowski sighed and pulled up her map within the VR interface. The mapping of this area wasn't as detailed as she would have liked, but it was enough. She manually changed some of the waypoints, adding an extra fifteen minutes to her mission, and started on her route.

While she walked, she called over the net to Pham. "Jake, I've made some slight changes to the mission route. Adding fifteen minutes and four seconds, but still within the time margin."

"Copy, Grace, thank you, let me know if anything else changes," Pham replied.

The path she had chosen was a roundabout one. She went away from the final waypoint before crossing back and taking a parallel, unblocked canyon in the correct direction.

When she was four kilometers away, she started to get an error message. Pulling up the logs, Parkowski saw what the problem was.

One of the robot's leg actuators was malfunctioning. The control system that told the right leg's joints to bend and push forward in a walking motion was throwing up all kinds of error codes, some of which Parkowski had never seen before.

It was the moment when Aering management's decision to use engineers as the ACHILLES unit's operators paid off. Parkowski opened up the code for the leg's control system and scanned it while pulling up a display of the ACHILLES 2's sensor feeds. She called out on the net that she had an issue, but everything was under control.

Comparing a time-series data plot with the expected output from the system's block diagram, she found the culprit. One of the sensors in the robot's leg gave an incorrect output. Parkowski tried to change the gain, but it had no effect. Instead, she told the control system to just ignore the sensor and use the other ones embedded in the leg for feedback.

It worked. She was on her way again, the entire episode having taken just four minutes, which she could easily make up.

As Parkowski came out of the canyon, she increased her speed slightly.

The system didn't handle it well. For the first time in the entire mission, she started to experience some lag.

"What's my total lag?" she asked over the radio.

"One minute, forty seconds," Pham replied. "You should be fine."

"I'm seeing a lot more than that."

"Copy, continue and see if it smooths out."

It did. As she reached the edge of the crater, the sluggishness of the system and the associated graphical bugs disappeared.

Parkowski finished the mission with ten minutes to spare. As the technicians removed her gear, she saw that all of the eyes in the high bay were on her.

She smiled, and as soon as she was able, left the high bay. She checked her phone - DePresti wanted to do dinner.

While she was still annoyed with him, they needed to talk. She texted him back and suggested a Korean BBQ place they both enjoyed. Parkowski then left and went home. Her after-action report could wait until tomorrow.

#

They ate outside on the patio. The conversation started with small talk, both of them being polite, before they got into a more complex discussion about Bronze Knot.

Parkowski was defensive; she hadn't learned anything new about the special access program and its relation to ILIAD, and DePresti couldn't understand why she couldn't just let it go. "Grace, it sounds like you had a good mission today," he told her. "You were able to troubleshoot on the fly and fix a problem all by yourself. Nothing weird happened. No dragons, no aliens, no weird error codes, no strange special programs, nothing. You should be celebrating, not beating yourself up for not figuring out this mystery."

"You just don't understand," she said. "The entire leadership team was there, watching me, waiting to see if I mess up or screw up the whole program. And, yeah, I did fine this time, but who knows what'll happen the next time? I need to know what's going on so I can prepare in case I see anything else strange. I hate not knowing everything going on."

"Maybe you don't need to know everything."

"What do you mean?" she asked, raising her tone slightly.

DePresti paused. "So, when I worked the launch," he said slowly, referring back to the ILIAD mission's successful launch out of Kennedy Space Center. "I was in charge of the seating arrangements for the firing room. I had to make sure that all of the important people, as well as the people actually running the mission, had a seat."

He took a breath. "I thought I had it all figured out until a day before the launch Colonel Hawke told me that two of the seats I had reserved for the Aerospace team had been requisitioned for someone else. I wasn't told who, wasn't told why, just that it happened and we needed to adjust."

"What does this have to do with anything?" Parkowski asked as she crossed her arms. Where was he going with this? Was he going to tell her to stop looking into it? She needed DePresti to be on her side, they needed to be a team, but it felt like he was working against her.

"I'll get there," DePresti said. "So I had to move two members of my team out to a remote site and it wasn't particularly easy to do so, but I made it happen. Day of launch, two nondescript white dudes in suits and sunglasses showed up and watched the launch from those two seats. To this day, I have no idea who they were, but we still managed to pull the mission off.

"Grace, you don't need to know everything. In the aerospace business there's always some kind of weird stuff going on, either because of national security concerns or corporate bullshit," the

Space Force captain explained. "I was able to do my job with the launch despite not knowing why those two seats had to be given up. I think you can do yours without knowing everything about the ILIAD mission."

"So you just want me to drop it," Parkowski said. Her food was getting cold, but she didn't care. "Despite me telling you how concerned I am about all of this, how it's been eating me up for the last month or so, you want me to just let it go."

DePresti sighed. "Grace, you haven't been yourself," he said. Another mistake. "You're always thinking about this and it seems like it's the only thing you want to talk about. Even when we're trying to do something fun, like going scuba diving, you just want to ask me about it. I want to go back to before you had your first mission."

Parkowski teared up. "I can't," she said softly as she pulled out her wallet. This was the last straw. She couldn't take being ignored and blown off anymore, especially by the people closest to her.

DePresti was going to say something but she tearfully held up a hand. "I'm done," she said as she dropped a few bills and wept her way out of the restaurant.

CHAPTER TWENTY

Marina Del Rey, CA

Parkowski was a slug all weekend - ignoring a slew of text messages from DePresti - and then called in sick on Monday.

She wasn't sick. In fact, she felt as healthy as ever. But she just wasn't in the right state of mind to work right now. She was too focused on solving the Bronze Knot puzzle to really do much of anything else.

Thankfully, she didn't have anything to do other than write her after-action report. After her successful mission, she didn't have much to state in it.

Parkowski knew that she had probably overreacted with her boyfriend.

But, she had had enough. Everyone was lying to her, she thought, no one would tell her the truth about what was really going on with the ILIAD mission and Bronze Knot.

She turned on a cooking show at nine and pulled out her personal laptop. Parkowski opened up a spreadsheet and tried to put down all of the different pieces of information that she could remember into the different cells. There was something she was missing, something that could be inferred from the clues she had available.

Parkowski now was more sure than ever that the ILIAD mission, and whatever the Bronze Knot program associated with it was, had much more going on behind the scenes than what was being told to her and the other operators, not to mention the periodic press releases going out from NASA singing the praises of their scientific mission.

There were so many pieces of information that didn't make sense.

For the first mission, there was the "dragon," and then the Bronze Knot-protected packets in the logs associated with the event.

For the second mission, there was the Bronze Knot error message that told her for the first time that there was a special access program involved.

Then there was all of the information that she had learned in the secure "NASA" room. The biggest piece of which was that the VR environment was not hosted on server racks at the Aering facility, but somewhere in Orlando.

Finally, there was all of the stuff DePresti had told her, that there was no SAP data under that program name on any of the networks he had access to, as well as the general education she had received from him on classification and special access programs. She believed him, despite her anger towards him.

Together, they pointed to a military involvement in the ILIAD mission, hidden under the program Bronze Knot, potentially run out of Orlando since the Venus environment was hosted there.

Parkowski remembered that there were some letters before the word "Orlando" in the configuration file she had pulled up on the SAP server - letters she had never looked into further.

She typed "AFAMS" into a search engine. According to the results, AFAMS stood for the Air Force Agency for Modeling and Simulation.

It was located in Orlando - confirming what the configuration file said.

Why was the Air Force involved at all in the ILIAD mission? The only military link was the launch through the Space Force, not the Air Force.

A knock on the door startled her as she absorbed this new piece of information.

Parkowski jumped, knocking her laptop to the floor. She quickly picked it up and checked it for damage - there was none.

She placed it down on the coffee table in the center of her living room and silently crept to the door. Parkowski looked out of the peephole and didn't see anyone.

"Look down," a muffled voice from the other side of the door said.

Parkowski did just that and smiled when she saw the person outside of her apartment.

It was Dr. Pham.

She opened the door. "Hey, boss," the junior Aering engineer said with a slight grin.

He gave a smile back. "Grace, you're not sick, are you?"

"Not physically," Parkowski explained. "But I'm not in the right mental state to go to work today. I hope you understand."

Pham nodded. "I do, I've been there. When Rachel told me that you had called her and told her you weren't coming in I got worried. So I cleared my calendar and drove up."

"You drove up to see me?"

He nodded.

"Why?"

"Because there's definitely something wrong, Grace," the older man said. "A normal person doesn't leave work in a huff after a successful mission."

She didn't say anything.

"Can I come in and we can chat?" Pham asked.

Parkowski nodded and let him into her apartment.

She made herself and Pham cups of coffee and they sat down on the couch and easy chair in the living room to talk.

It was nice to feel like there were people out there who cared about her, despite the funk she was in. DePresti cared too, he had blown up her phone all weekend but she had ignored him. Parkowski wasn't ready to deal with him yet.

She didn't start at the beginning; there were details of her investigation that she wanted to keep secret from her boss. Instead, Parkowski started with the mission yesterday, going more-or-less through the mission in detail. Pham asked a few questions but mostly let her talk.

"Grace, you did a great job on your last mission," the senior Aering engineer said. "What you were able to do with the leg actuator control system, I'm not sure any of our other engineers could have pulled off."

"Thanks," Parkowski said with a slight smile - all she could manage that morning.

"To be honest, you've done a great job overall with all of your missions," he continued. "You've had to deal with the dragon nonsense and multiple communications upsets. Most of the operators haven't dealt with a fraction of that. I have nothing but good things to say, and so does the management team."

"About that," she said, slightly changing the subject. "Dr. Rosen was acting odd yesterday."

"I noticed that," he said in agreement. "But then again, so were you."

Parkowski put her head in her hands. "It's that stupid Bronze Knot crap," she told her boss, finally admitting the source of her issues to him. "And then I got in a fight with Mike last night and I don't know how to fix it and..."

"Grace, this probably isn't what you want to hear," Pham said carefully, "but in this business, there are just things that might not be explained."

"But why?" she asked.

"Because in the space world, so much of what we do, even on the unclassified side, is connected to the classified world," he explained to her. "And that side is a web of lies and deceit and cover stories, and any time you think you have a handle on it, you learn a new piece of information that will throw you for a loop."

He leaned forward. "Did I ever tell you what I did before I worked for Aering?"

"No."

"I worked for the CIA."

"You did?" she asked in disbelief.

Pham nodded. "Not as a secret agent or anything like that. I was an engineer in the directorate of science and technology, working on classified space systems both at the NRO and back at headquarters in Langley. Not what you think of when you think 'CIA,' but it was a great job."

"What got you out here?" Parkowski asked.

"I got tired of the secrecy," Pham said in reply. "Without getting myself in trouble, I can tell you I was working on counterspace systems - different technologies and whatnot that protect American and allied satellites from enemy threats, mostly Russian and Chinese. Most of the intelligence that I had to work from was compartmented, held at the highest levels in the intelligence community and DOD. And to be honest, Grace, it was awful. I had to design and architect solutions without having all of the right assumptions. The only way I knew if I was doing something wrong was if the operators, most of whom were read in, told me I was wrong, or God forbid we got into a war that extended into space and we started losing on-orbit assets."

"That does sound awful," Parkowski agreed. "It's an engineer's worst nightmare, not being able to prove your answer is correct, either analytically or experimentally."

"So I finally got fed up," Pham continued with a nod, "and Gus is originally from the West Coast so I reached out to my contacts out here and got a job lined up. That was over fifteen years ago. And I've never looked back."

He took a deep breath. "Why am I telling you all of this? Because sometimes it's just the way that it is. And it sucks, not knowing everything, but there's nothing you or I can do about that, so why worry?"

She now saw why he was telling her all of this. Maybe he, and by association DePresti, was right. But then again, maybe they were both too far in to be able to see the problem holistically.

He gave her an odd look. "You're not going to stop looking into it, are you?"

Parkowski shook her head.

"Can you at least try to not let it impact the rest of your life then?" Pham asked. "Mike is a good guy and I'm sorry that you feel like he isn't listening to your concerns, but maybe it's not a topic the two of you can discuss. My husband and I have some that are off-limits, maybe this should be one for the two of you."

She shrugged. "I don't know. I feel like he should be helping me figure this out, but he's almost afraid to try."

"There's a line in the black project community, which if I understand correctly he's a part of: don't speculate on what you don't know. He probably doesn't want to get you, or him, in trouble."

Parkowski thought back to the near-miss outside of the secure room. "I guess that makes sense."

"And don't let it impact your work either," Pham continued. "Grace, I can't say it enough, but you're doing great. You're one of our youngest operators but you've done amazing work and are lining yourself up for a promotion."

He cleared his throat. "And, if it becomes necessary for you to be read into any special programs or for you to upgrade your clearance in order to do your job as an ACHILLES operator, I promise I will make it happen. Unfortunately, right now, I can't justify that need-to-know."

She nodded.

Pham sprung up from his chair. "I almost forgot," he said, walking around her apartment, "the other reason I came."

"What is it?"

"Mohammed had to fly home to Michigan today, his dad is in the hospital. He's scheduled to run through a mission tomorrow at ten, the first mission of the day, but he's not going to make it. You're the first alternate and I decided to talk about it with you in person, to make sure you're ready to go."

Parkowski's phone buzzed. It was DePresti again. She turned it face-down on the table.

Maybe the tides had turned. The last mission had gone well and without any anomalies. She might be back on track.

Parkowski turned to Pham. "Yeah, I can do it."

"Great," he said. "Come in early tomorrow, at around seven or seven-thirty, and we can do our planning."

She smiled and walked her boss to the door.

"Thanks for stopping by," Parkowski said.

"No problem, just wanted to make sure you're ok," said Pham.

Parkowski spent the rest of the day watching TV and relaxing on her couch. But that night, she couldn't sleep.

She finally fell asleep at two AM and was still tired when her alarm woke her up at six.

But she didn't have a choice.

Despite everything on her mind, it was time for her to go back to Venus.

CHAPTER TWENTY-ONE

El Segundo, CA

Parkowski drove into work in silence.

There was no one at the security desk, which was odd. She couldn't remember a time when she didn't see anyone manning it.

Parkowski shrugged and badged in. As she walked through the hallways, she saw only a few other Aering employees.

She went straight to the locker room and suited up, then continued to the high bay.

Unlike her previous mission, there was a normal-sized crew in the building, maybe even smaller than normal, but it was still before most of the staff arrived. The most senior person was Dr. Pham; Rosen and Khoudry weren't present.

Pham waved her over to a cubicle and pointed at the screen. "I've got the mission brief pulled up," he told her. "Let's go through it quickly."

After a few charts, Parkowski smiled. It was another fairly easy, more similar to her last one than to the first two. Her job was to use ACHILLES 2 to retrieve the ground-penetrating radar, the same one from her first time in the environment, from its current location. Parkowski would then move it to map a potential cavern system. An operator from a previous mission had stumbled upon it, exciting the geologists.

Once done she would switch to ACHILLES 1 and move that to a waypoint five kilometers away for the next operator to pick it up and continue with the scientific mission.

The two engineers closed the briefing and opened the slow, tedious mission planning software. There were no more changes to be made.

She was in a much better mood today; her eyes were wide and bright and her tone was upbeat. Pham's visit hadn't changed her mind, but it had given her an additional perspective on her situation. She'd have to deal with her DePresti situation at some point, but she used every ounce of her willpower to put that in the back of her head. She had a mission to accomplish.

Parkowski thought about grabbing a bite from the Rayleigh cafeteria but decided against it. Instead, she waited around until about five minutes before the mission started, and then climbed onto the raised platform in the center of the high bay.

A pair of technicians jumped up to plug her in, Pham watching from the floor below. "Good luck, Grace," he said.

"Thanks!" Parkowski replied as she took the VR helmet from the technicians and held it in her hands. Unlike her previous missions, she wasn't sweating from nervousness. This was going to be a breeze. Maybe afterwards, she could collect herself enough to call DePresti and try to smooth everything out in their relationship.

She placed the helmet on her head. The screen was black; Parkowski stared at a field of nothingness, the sensory deprivation overwhelming. "I don't see anything," she said over the radio.

"I know, standby," a female technician said. "We are having an issue with the interface. Give us a minute or two."

"Copy," Parkowski replied.

The screen flickered for a second, momentarily blinding her, then turned off.

She wrinkled her nose in thought. The lag was supposed to be low, as low as her last mission, and there wasn't much traffic planned to be on MICS today. What was going on?

Finally, the surface of Venus appeared on her headset. For a moment, the gray-green clouds and rocks seemed comforting. This was Parkowski's only escape from her mess of a relationship and all-consuming search for the secret behind Bronze Knot. She was starting to feel at home on Earth's smaller cousin.

The display was static; the entire communications pathway hadn't been established. They were on receive-only until the narrowband command path was ready to send commands to the ACHILLES units.

Parkowski was ready, but it seemed like the rest of the operation was not.

She breathed in, then out, then in and out again; performing some mental calculations to keep her mind sharp. She was not particularly good at waiting.

Parkowski tapped her fingers within her glove and waited another five minutes before she said anything. "Hey Dr. Pham, what's going on?" she asked on the net.

There was no response.

Parkowski heard a lot of movement and shuffling of feet outside of her VR setup. She heard muffled voices, but nobody spoke over the voice net.

"What's going on?" she said again.

Without warning she got control of the ACHILLES robot; the sensors on her hands and feet controlling its movement.

She took a step forward and the screen froze. Parkowski saw the error message again: ERROR: SPECIAL ACCESS PROGRAM - BRONZE KNOT - SPECIAL ACCESS REQUIRED.

The error message disappeared, leaving the Venusian surface in front of her. She tried to move again but got the same message: ERROR: SPECIAL ACCESS PROGRAM - BRONZE KNOT - SPECIAL ACCESS REQUIRED.

Bronze Knot was messing with her mission.

Again.

Then the screen shut off. It was pitch black.

She lifted her headset to see what was going on outside of the VR environment in the high bay.

The entire team of technicians and engineers gathered around Dr. Rosen, who had made his way into the high bay. Pham was the only one not in the huddle - he stood off to the side with his arms crossed and his headset off and in his hand.

"Jake, what's going on?" Parkowski asked him quietly.

He looked at her, startled, then crept over to the raised platform. "There's some kind of technical issue," Pham told her in a whisper. "Dr. Rosen is telling everyone that the mission is on hold until it gets resolved."

Parkowski was shocked. "On hold?"

"Yes," Pham confirmed. "It has to do with MICS. Apparently we are getting out-prioritized for a higher priority mission and there's a risk to the ACHILLES units if we operate them knowing that there might be a communications issue." He sounded annoyed.

"Won't they just go into safehold if we lose the connection?" Parkowski asked. In that mode, the ACHILLES units would go into a low-power state until the correct command sequence was given to reactivate.

"Yes, but it takes time to get them back to a normal mode," the older engineer explained to her. "And there's a risk that every time you put them into a protected state, they might not come out of it. Design flaw - blame the team down in Seal Beach who made them.

"Don't get me wrong, I agree one-hundred-percent with my boss with regards to that, there's a serious risk to the robots. I'm more worried about the fact that there's an issue with MICS that I'm not sold on. There's more than enough bandwidth on the relays, there's no way we..."

His voice trailed off as he looked away at the small crowd. Parkowski followed his gaze. Rosen had broken off his discussion and was coming towards them with a pair of technicians. "I'm sorry Ms. Parkowski," Rosen said as the other two men climbed up onto the platform. "But we're going to have to pull you out of the environment."

"What's going on?" she asked, already knowing the answer, as the techs started to unplug her from the system.

"Comm issue," Rosen replied. "We've lost contact with the ACHILLES robots. The mission is on hold until further notice."

"Got it," Parkowski said. The senior engineer's comment left no room for debate.

"I know, it's not ideal," Rosen continued, "but it wasn't my call. NASA leadership at Goddard informed me just minutes before I came in here to tell all of you. They need to take our communications bandwidth," which made Pham's ears perk up, "and aren't sure when we'll get it back."

"Will that be hours, or days, or weeks, or..." Pham asked.

Rosen shook his head. "I have no idea, sorry, Jake. As soon as I hear anything, I'll let you know. I'm just as disappointed as you are."

Parkowski changed and left the facility as soon as she could.

She wanted to investigate further, but the building was packed with people. She would never make it back into the secure room, even if she got the key, and Parkowski had struck out on every attempt at getting anything out of the internal Aering network.

Her curiosity ate at her, and there was no way to satisfy it.

Negative thoughts ate at her mind.

What if they never started the ILIAD program back up again? Her promotion was probably gone, she had somehow screwed everything up so badly that the entire project was at least temporarily shut down.

Would she need to get a new job? Would they move her to another program? Would Dr. Pham still be her boss? The questions got more and more complex as she drove through the midday LA traffic back to her apartment.

The sun was shining and the November rains hadn't started yet. Unfortunately, Parkowski hadn't spent much time outside the last few weeks. She'd have to change that once she got everything sorted out.

She decided to take a shower - she hadn't that morning. While she was shampooing her hair, Parkowski could have sworn that she heard a banging on a wall somewhere in the apartment building, but she ignored it.

When she got out of the shower and started to towel off, Parkowski heard the knocking again. It was on her apartment door.

She groaned and went to check the peephole. It was DePresti, in his Space Force OCPs and carrying a handful of red roses.

Parkowski groaned again. He was the last person she wanted to see right now. She thought she had given him a key to her apartment at one point, her roommate's boyfriend had one too, knowing DePresti he had probably misplaced it.

"Grace, let me in, I know you're in there, I talked with your boss," DePresti said loud enough for her to hear him on the other side of the door. "I called him on the way to Aering and did a U-turn and came here."

She ignored him.

"I want to talk with you about Bronze Knot."

Parkowski unlocked the door and opened it a fraction.

"Grace, goddammit, you were right. I was wrong. Something weird is going on."

She sighed and opened the door all of the way. "Come on in."

CHAPTER TWENTY-TWO

Marina Del Rey, CA

DePresti stepped through the door and took off his hat. "Grace, I have to tell you I'm sorry," he said as he handed her the flowers. "I should have listened to you."

She narrowed her eyes as she took the bouquet.

"Do you know what Bronze Knot is?" Parkowski asked. Maybe she would finally have the answer to her all-consuming question.

DePresti shook his head.

"Then why did you tell me that I was right?"

He sighed. "Grace, go put the bouquet in water and sit down. I want to tell you everything from the beginning."

She went and got a vase, cut off the bottoms of the stems, and put the flowers in, then sat down on the recliner. DePresti went into the kitchen and got one of her roommate's beers and opened it before sitting down on the couch.

"A beer at 11 AM?"

"I need it."

"And in uniform?"

"I really need it."

"Ok, start at the beginning," Parkowski ordered.

He leaned forward. "So, do you remember the big project I'm working on?"

"The classified data link?"

"Yeah."

"Yes, I remember it," Parkowski said, rolling her eyes. "It's the only one you can talk with me about."

DePresti took a sip of his beer. "So, part of that data link is a cross-domain solution, a guard. It prevents data from going from a higher level of security classification to a lower one on the same network."

Parkowski thought for a minute. Those server racks in the secure room...they had guards in them. "Go on, but I don't know where this is going."

"So, for that piece of hardware to operate at the ops site out at Schriever," DePresti continued. "I need an ATO - Authority to Operate. It's a piece of paper saying that I can connect to other networks or data feeds."

He took a breath. "So, yesterday I finally got all of the paperwork done and called over to the AFOSI office at Los Angeles for them to come take a look at it so they could take it to get signed," the Space Force officer continued. "They - the local AFOSI agent - don't sign it, someone at the Pentagon does, but they courier it there for signature. It can't be sent electronically."

Parkowski's mind flashed back to a few days ago. "Was the AFOSI agent an older white guy with a mustache?"

"No, younger dude, Hispanic or Mediterranean," her boyfriend replied, "why?"

She quickly told him about her visit from the AFOSI/PJ agent.

"The two letters after 'AFOSI' tell you what detachment they belong to. That one - PJ - is the same detachment this guy who I saw was from," DePresti said. He took another sip of beer. "That's their special projects division. They handle all of the SAP and SCI data."

He cleared his throat. "Anyways, this dude comes over this morning and is going through my paperwork with me. And I ask him all casually 'Have you ever heard of a program called Bronze Knot?'"

"And then what happened?" Parkowski asked. Her boyfriend's boring work story now had her undivided attention. She was on the edge of her seat.

"His face turned white. Like literally white, Grace, like a light switch. He asked me really nervously where I had heard of it."

"And what did you tell him?"

"My girlfriend saw it as part of an error message at work on the ILIAD program."

"And then what?"

DePresti finished his beer and got up to get another one. "He asked if I was read in, which of course I told him no. I'm telling you, Grace, before you mentioned that program I had never heard of it. I've never seen a program with 'Bronze' in it," he said, sitting back down. "It's not a Space Force program."

She didn't say anything. But, Parkowski's mind was flying at a million miles per hour with possibilities.

"So the guy tells me, and I wrote it down before I left because I wanted to get it right. He says verbatim 'I've been doing this for eight years and Bronze Knot is the scariest shit I've seen.'"

"The scariest shit he's seen?"

"Yup."

"Did you ask what it was?'

"Hell yeah, I asked him what it was," DePresti said with a smile. "I turned into you at that moment, Grace/ I needed to know what's behind the Bronze Knot door." He smiled. "But, the AFOSI agent told me he couldn't. He told me it was a waived SAP - my understanding of that means it doesn't have to be reported formally to Congress - and that I was better off not knowing."

"What the fuck does that mean?"

"I don't know, Grace, I'm sorry," he said. "I pressed him a little more, but I also needed to get this ATO approved so I let him go. He didn't give me anything else, just another warning not to look into it."

Parkowski sat there, processing this new information.

A lot of things were coming together.

"Is that all?" she asked.

DePresti shook his head slowly. "Nope, and I have to apologize again."

"What for?"

"So, before, when you asked me to look around at Space Systems Command for Bronze Knot stuff," DePresti explained. "I did - but only on the SAP-level network I have access to."

"So?"

"So there are other networks," he went on. "The main one being JWICS, which I think stands for Joint Worldwide Intelligence Communications System - don't quote me on that. Anyways, it's the main Top Secret-level network used by the intelligence community."

"Intelligence community?"

"The CIA, NSA, DIA, all of the intelligence agencies, together they make the intelligence community, or IC," DePresti continued. "All of their activities fall under U.S. Code Title 50, the military is under Title 10, which makes a mess sometimes but we deal with it.

"Anyways, I never thought of looking on JWICS. It's not a SAP network, it contains SCI information, which is kind of a SAP, but more importantly, the *entire network* is searchable. If you're looking for information on some random Russian military officer or an obscure telephone technology you just type it in like you search on Google and go."

He finished his second beer and went to get a third. Parkowski thought about saying something, but decided against it. She'd just buy her roommate another six-pack.

"So I searched for Bronze Knot, and as expected found next to nothing," DePresti said as he sat back down. "But I remembered you gave me the trigraph."

"That what?"

"The three letters that represent the SAP in shorthand," the Space Force captain said. "Don't worry too much about it. Your error message said TS//SAR-BKT, the BKT refers to Bronze Knot. They're almost always three letters."

DePresti took another sip of his beer. "So then I searched for the trigraph. And Bronze Knot, or more specifically its trigraph, is an intelligence community program."

Her jaw was on the floor. "No way."

"Yes," her boyfriend said. "I found a document, a memorandum of understanding, between the CIA and USSF, signed way back in 2020, promising to share data on deep space sensor feeds. Much of the document was redacted, even at the Top Secret level, and more information could be found in an appendix classified TS//SAR-BKT."

"But the ILIAD mission is a NASA program, run through Aering as the prime contractor," Parkowski said, almost in disbelief. "Why would the CIA or Space Force data be in the environment?"

"I have no clue," DePresti said. "But I'm not finished. Well, almost finished." He drained his third beer. "There was another hit for BKT - a "BKT Read-In, which was attended by my boss' boss from back when I was working launch, Colonel Hawke."

"A read-in?"

"Yeah, where you are formally briefed into a SAP. This seemed like a fairly large one, they were reading a bunch of people into the program at one time, rather than the one-on-ones that I normally get. From what I could gather from the Outlook meeting invite, it was a pretty big meeting. The CIA and FBI were there, along with the Space Force, Navy, and NASA."

"That's an odd group," Parkowski said. The CIA again. That agency kept on popping up in this whole mess.

"It is," the Space Force captain agreed. "But I couldn't get an agenda or anything. Just some invitees."

"You know," she said quietly. "Dr. Pham was here yesterday, checking in on me."

DePresti smiled. "I thought he might."

"Yeah, and he told me in a lot nicer way than you did to stop looking into Bronze Knot," Parkowski continued. "And told me a really interesting piece of his background."

"And what would that be?" DePresti asked. He put his beer bottle down and looked at the fridge, but decided against it. He seemed to be having a rough day.

"He used to work for the CIA."

"No shit."

"Yup. He was an engineer there before coming out to work for Aering."

"Like at the NRO? That's jointly manned, DOD and CIA."

"Yeah. He said he worked on stuff there, and at the CIA headquarters in Langley. But he got tired of working in a classified environment so he took on an unclassified program out here."

DePresti laughed loudly. "Grace, I was told something once when I got my Top Secret and was read into SCI. No one ever stops working for the CIA."

"What do you mean?"

"Like, have you ever read the Tom Clancy books? Jack Ryan does one little consulting job for the Agency way back in the early part of the timeline, and then keeps getting pulled back in, until he's finally a full-time employee working his way up the ranks."

"No, but that makes sense," Parkowski said. "In a weird way. They want to keep the people who know all of that classified stuff close in a metaphorical way in case they need them again."

DePresti nodded. "Or to make sure they don't spill the beans on what the CIA is actually doing."

He stood up and stretched. "Grace, you need to confront him."

"I already have," Parkowski said, getting a little annoyed again, "and he's told me he doesn't know."

"He knows," DePresti argued. "At least he knows more than he's telling you. Grace, I know what Aering does in El Segundo in the classified realm," he went on. "I know because like I said, I'm read into everything, or at least what I thought was everything. And there's no SAPs being built at your facility."

He paused. "Grace, you were right, I was wrong."

"I forgive you."

And she meant it.

"I thought you would," he said with a smile.

"And I'm sorry too," she said, for all of the overreactions the last few weeks.

He just smiled.

"So what now?"

"Listen, every single thing I've been told tells me to let it go, that it's not worth it," DePresti said. "But, Grace, believe me when I tell you this. I'm read into fucking *everything* that has to deal with space. *Everything*. Because I have to be. Because if I'm not aware of everything going on, I'm making decisions without every piece of information available to me and that could be deadly. I know you joke about my importance at work, but I'm working on the architecture that the country will be fighting space wars with in the future," he continued. "And if I don't know what sensors and weapons we have, I could make the wrong decision.

"And, on top of that, I'm just as curious as you are. I want to know what's going on, especially since it seems like at least some part of it seems to be underhanded."

"Does that mean you're in it with me to get to the bottom of this?"

DePresti nodded.

"What do you think our next move should be?" Parkowski asked, in better spirits than she'd been in days. "I've been doing this by myself for weeks; it'd be nice to have a fresh set of eyes on it."

"Agreed," DePresti said. "Let's lay it all out."

They went back to the very beginning, to Parkowski's first mission in the VR environment, and slowly put the pieces together on a piece of computer paper DePresti took from the apartment's shared printer.

The two engineers ended up with so many notes and pieces of information that they ended up needing three more pieces after a few hours of brainstorming.

"So what do we have?" DePresti said, rubbing his eyes.

"There exists a special access program called Bronze Knot," Parkowski responded as she sat up straight on the couch. "It appears to be controlled by the CIA or the Space Force, but we have no hard evidence that is the case."

"Parts of the network packet on both the narrowband and wideband command pathways are protected by Bronze Knot, but the rest of the telemetry data is unclassified," DePresti added. "The script trigger that made the dragon appear and attack you is likely connected to that data."

"Then, there appears to be some kind of data leak," he said, "or spillage, into the Venus environment that is protected at the same TS//SAP level. That appeared in your second and fourth missions. What caused that, I'm not sure, but likely it's part of the network guard that filters data between the Top Secret enclave and the unclassified ILIAD one."

"That network guard, or whatever it is, is located in the secure room that is protected by the cipher lock in the hallway," she continued. "Along with a whole bunch of other SAP ones and one that is SCI."

"Yet, the environment itself is hosted in an Air Force facility in Orlando," DePresti said. "Despite the fact that there is no indication that it is geographically distant from the Aering facility. In fact, having it that far out..."

"Would introduce unnecessary lag," Parkowski said, finishing his sentence.

She stood up. "So, what do we do now?"

"Two options," DePresti said. "One, we go back to our normal lives and pretend that none of this ever happened."

"And the other?"

He took a breath. "We confront your boss. He has to know what's going on. And we do it together."

She walked over and gave him a hug and brief kiss. "I'm so glad you're on my side now."

"I wouldn't have it any other way."

CHAPTER TWENTY-THREE

Marina Del Rey, CA

After a night of fun and drinking at her apartment, and an early Saturday morning drive down to DePresti's townhouse, they planned their next move.

Parkowski had to confront Dr. Pham - her boss and mentor. There was no other option. He was the key to this whole puzzle. Rosen or Khoudry might know more, but there was no way either of them would be willing to reveal their secrets. With Pham, they had a chance, albeit a slim one.

DePresti helped Parkowski organize her evidence, thoughts, and ideas into a single-page document that detailed everything that she had uncovered. She included all of the information from the secure room as well — things that Pham hadn't known she had learned. It was time to put all of her cards on the table. She printed out a few copies on DePresti's printer, leaving one hidden underneath his desk's keyboard tray for safekeeping. The others she would take to show Pham.

DePresti ran out to get them Starbucks while Parkowski sat and brooded. She was not looking forward to confronting her boss.

But, this meeting was necessary. More than anything else in the world, Parkowski wanted to know the secret behind Bronze Knot.

There was a knock on the door. DePresti was there, holding a pair of iced coffees. He had forgotten the key to his own house. "Thanks," he said as she opened the door and held it wide.

They sat down and nursed their hangovers together with overpriced, oversweetened coffee.

"Have you decided how to approach him? DePresti asked. He was a little jittery, whether from the caffeine or from an overall sense of nervousness, Parkowski couldn't tell. She felt renewed vigor, both from the coffee as well as the recent events that had brought herself and DePresti back together.

"Nope," Parkowski said. "I want to meet him outside of work and show him all I know, and see if I can convince him to let me in on the secret, but I'm not sure how to get there."

"That might be harder than you think, special access program NDAs are pretty ironclad."

"I know, but I think he's starting to get disillusioned with the whole thing," Parkowski argued. "I think he's starting to realize that it has impacted our whole mission. He made some comments when Rosen shut everything down that made me realize that the two of them aren't necessarily on the same page."

"I hope you're right," her boyfriend responded. He paused to finish his coffee. "How about a direct approach?"

"Such as?"

"You have his cell phone number, right?"

"Yeah."

"Text him, give him some information that he doesn't know you have, and ask to meet at a public location."

She got a shiver. "Why a public location?"

"Because, Grace, if we're going to go down this rabbit hole," DePresti said, "we're starting to get into a world that I'm aware of, but barely understand."

"What do you mean?"

"I mean it's dangerous," he replied, "dangerous as shit. You don't fuck around with the CIA or FBI or whoever is behind all of this."

"But it's worth it."

"I agree, but we have to start taking precautions."

"Ok, I text him, give him a new nugget of info, and ask to meet in a public location," Parkowski summarized. "Then what, we go meet him?"

"Yeah, we meet him together," DePresti suggested. "I've ran into him a couple of times, he knows me, and maybe having a military member on your side isn't the worst idea here."

"I just..." Parkowski said, stumbling to find the right words, "I just can't believe that he'd be behind any kind of deception like this. He's such a nice guy, and he's done so much to help me in my career at Aering."

"Grace, I'm sure he's a nice guy," DePresti said. "But he got swept into this, and now is a part of it, whatever it is. And to be honest, I don't even want to speculate on what it could be. He's got to defend himself, and it sounds to me like he's tried to keep you out of trouble as best as he can."

"Yeah, and I just keep putting myself in it more."

She picked up her phone. "Ok, here goes nothing."

Parkowski sent Pham a text message.

"Hey, doc, sorry to bother you on your Saturday. I need to talk with you about Bronze Knot."

To her surprise she got an immediate reply. **"Grace, I thought u said u would drop it."**

With DePresti peering over her shoulder she fired a text message back. **"I know about Orlando."**

It took him a few minutes to respond. **"What do u know about Orlando?"**

"We need to talk, in public," she responded. **"I need to know everything,"** she sent a moment later.

Pham didn't respond.

"You're pushing him kind of hard," DePresti observed, "but that's the only way you're going to get anything out of him."

Parkowski nodded in silent agreement.

She checked the clock on his townhouse wall. It was just after eleven.

"If he responds, where should we choose to meet?" she asked DePresti.

"Shoot, I don't know," the military officer responded. "Maybe a mall parking lot? Or the Home Depot in El Segundo? That's a pretty safe, low-traffic area with a decent security presence. Or maybe the beach, it's similarly populated at this time of year."

Finally her phone buzzed. "**Fine, I can give u some info,**" Pham's response read. She could sense the trepidation through the phone. A message a moment later said "**it's not what u think. I tried to keep u out of it but u asked too many questions. Time to clue u in.**"

"Where and where do you want to meet?" Parkowski asked.

"**One of the piers, either Venice, Redondo, or Manhattan Beach, in an hour and a half**" her boss answered.

"Great," Parkowski responded back.

"I don't want to go to the Redondo Pier, it's too out in the open and we'll be the only ones there. Of the other two, Manhattan Beach is closer," DePresti said quickly.

"**Manhattan Beach**" she shot back in a second message.

"**Are u coming alone?**" Pham replied quickly.

"What do I say?" she asked her boyfriend. "You're coming with me, but I'm not sure if I want him to know that."

"Tell him I'm coming."

"**Mike is coming too, I told him everything. He wants to know too.**"

No response for a bit, then Pham finally got back to her. "**I guess that works. See u and ur boyfriend at 1240 at the Manhattan Beach pier.**"

She put the phone down. "Ok, now what?"

"We need to prepare for the worst," DePresti said. "Grace, I have no idea what the fuck we're getting into."

"What do you mean?"

"I mean, we might not be able to come back here," he said. "We might not be able to talk to our families or go into our jobs or show our faces in public for a while."

He started pacing around his living room. "Grace, what if we've stumbled across something really big? And really bad? Like I'm talking JFK assassination level, or Iran-Contra, or even something as big as a procurement scandal like the tanker leasing crap back in the 90s and 2000s. I don't live in that world, but I have buddies from the Academy who do, and it's scary."

"Ok, so we pack some stuff," Parkowski said. Her boyfriend arrived at the same realization she had experienced weeks ago. This was big.

"I'm probably getting worked up over nothing. More than likely, I think Dr. Pham is going to tell us something mundane, something that's either already on Wikipedia or in a movie somewhere, but that we're spending millions of dollars to protect in a SAP for God-knows-what reason. He'll tell us what we want to hear, we move on with our lives, and both of us have the satisfaction of knowing what is fucking up your missions in the VR environment."

She shrugged. "I hope you're right."

The two engineers spent the next half-hour or so packing up overnight bags; she with clothing that she had left at the townhouse over the last year, and DePresti with what little clothing he had washed, dried, and folded. Parkowski packed a separate bag with water bottles, protein bars, and fruit.

She hoped that all of this was all unnecessary.

And was a little excited that she might finally get to the bottom of all of this.

As he was packing, DePresti dropped something with a *crash* and spilled its contents all over the carpeted floor of his bedroom.

"Is everything ok?" Parkowski asked from the kitchen.

"Honestly, I'm a little nervous," her boyfriend responded. "Don't worry about it. I get worked up when I'm doing this kind of secret squirrel stuff."

She shrugged and continued packing their food bag.

At twelve twenty they were ready to leave. The two engineers carried their bags down the townhouse steps to the parking lot. The sun shone brightly and a slight breeze came in off of the ocean.

"Let's take my car," DePresti suggested.

She opened the Subaru's trunk. "What is all of this?" she asked. She saw what looked like an oxygen tank and associated tubes strewn across the back.

"Forgot to tell you, I bought my own scuba gear last week," DePresti told her. "I want to start doing more once the weather gets nice."

Parkowski shrugged. "Fine by me, but I'm still going to rent mine."

DePresti laughed as he helped her create space in the trunk for their bags. Then they got into the car, the Space Force officer driving.

"Here goes nothing," DePresti said. "To Manhattan Beach."

CHAPTER TWENTY-FOUR

Manhattan Beach, CA

The drive was mercifully short.

However, once they got there, they had an issue. The beach was surprisingly packed with tourists and locals and parking was at a premium. The lots by the beach were completely filled, and street parking was seemingly full as well.

DePresti cruised the side streets, looking for a spot, as he nervously tapped the steering wheel. Parkowski sat next to him quietly as she watched the clock. It was now twelve thirty-five. They were likely going to be late for their meetup.

Finally, they found an unoccupied spot along a residential street. DePresti carefully parallel parked and the two engineers got out.

They started walking in the direction of the beach, the breeze in their faces and the sun beating down overhead. It was warm, in the low seventies, and Parkowski was glad they hadn't overdressed for the southern California weather.

The streets were packed. Parkowski wondered if there was some kind of festival or concert going on, but as they neared the beach she realized it was just a nice Saturday. Families sat enjoying picnic lunches while teenagers played volleyball in the white sand.

In the back of her head, she had a strange sensation, like someone was watching her, but as she scanned the streets everyone minded their own business. It was probably just paranoia, she thought. No one else knew about this meeting other than herself, her boyfriend, and her boss.

She wished she was going to the beach to enjoy it.

But she recalled their meeting with Pham. Today was all business. Time to get to the bottom of whatever was going on.

The pier itself was just as busy as the streets.

Parkowski saw surfers in wetsuits below and anglers with their poles hanging off the side of the structure, trying to catch cod and surfperch.

She and DePresti started looking for Pham. There were plenty of Asian-American men of a similar age walking around, but not the one they were looking for.

Parkowski started to get worried, did they arrive too late, did they miss him, did something happen to her boss? DePresti seemed nervous as well; his eyes darted from side to side as he scanned the crowd.

Finally, they found him at the far end of the pier. Pham sat on a bench down by the Roundhouse Marine Studies Lab & Aquarium at the quay's terminus.

In stark contrast to the rest of the pier's visitors, most of whom were in bathing suits and flip flops, Pham wore a rumpled black suit with dark gray pinstripes that looked like it hadn't seen the inside of a dry cleaner's in years. He looked tired, haggard, like he hadn't slept at all the previous night. The engineer sat on a bench by himself, facing away from the ocean, with his head down and supported by his hands.

"Hey, Dr. Pham," Parkowski said as she and DePresti approached.

He looked up at her and gave her a wan smile. "Grace," he said softly. "Mike," he said to DePresti. "Sit down." Pham slid to the edge of the bench to give them room.

They both did just that, with Parkowski taking a seat next to Pham, as the senior Aering engineer scanned the pier with his tired eyes. He then turned to Parkowski. "Grace, I wish you had just let it go," Pham said to her.

"I know," Parkowski replied. She had prepared for this statement by her boss. "I sometimes wish I had, too."

"And now you brought Mike into this..." he said, his voice trailing off as he stared off in the distance.

Pham was acting strangely, Parkowski thought. He slurred his words slightly and his eyes were glazed over. If she didn't know better, she would have thought he was drunk, but Parkowski knew that he wasn't a drinker.

"Anyways," Pham said, "Grace, you were right."

"Right about what?" she asked.

"About everything."

"What do you mean?" DePresti asked, speaking up for the first time.

Pham ignored him. "I went to the facility today, I was going to try and troubleshoot the MICS issue we saw yesterday," he said in almost a monotone. "I couldn't sleep. I was worried about the mission."

He took a pause. "The high bay was completely closed, Grace. My badge wouldn't get me in. I went to talk to the security desk and was told that men in suits with government badges came in the middle of the night and closed the entire ILIAD mission room up. I couldn't even get to my office."

"Did they say what agency they were from?" DePresti asked.

Pham answered this one. "No, but I have my suspicions."

He was still being vague. Parkowski needed to move the conversation along. "Dr. Pham, Jake," she said, feeling the folded printout in her pocket that she had prepared to give him. "Can you tell me about Bronze Knot?"

"No, I'm not allowed to, but I need to," Pham replied. "Like I said in my text back to you, it's not what you think it is. Bronze Knot is just a cover story for..."

His voice trailed off as he turned his head slightly towards the east.

"Dr. Pham?" Parkowski asked.

Pham didn't respond. He just stared out ahead towards the entrance to the pier.

Parkowski followed his eyes. She didn't see anything at first. Everything appeared to be normal; Pham was just nodding off.

Then she saw them.

There were four, walking slowly side-by-side and almost in lockstep as they came from the shops near the pier's entrance towards where Parkowski, Pham, and DePresti sat on the bench.

She initially thought all were males, but as they got a step closer, she realized that one of the four was a woman.

They were easy to pick out. Like Pham, they were severely overdressed for a casual spot such as Manhattan Beach. They all wore trench coats, two in tan and two in a dark gray, with wraparound sunglasses on their heads obscuring their features.

DePresti saw them too. Parkowski noticed his leg started twitching.

Just like when the dragon appeared in the Venus environment, Parkowski froze. She knew she needed to do something, to run, her lizard brain screamed for her to get away.

But she just sat there, rooted to the spot.

Pham just stared.

The four were about a quarter of a mile away from the two Aering engineers and the Space Force captain when they stopped. The one in the middle-left position raised his arm as they stood in the midst of the tourists, fishermen, and sightseers.

All of the trenchcoat-wearing individuals reached into their coats and pulled out matching metallic objects.

Parkowski couldn't believe what she was seeing.

Firearms.

They were short-barreled and had long, banana-shaped clips jutting out from the lower part of their receiver.

The four individuals fired indiscriminately into the crowd as Parkowski stood up and watched in horror.

An angler went down, his chest a puff of red as the strange assailants' submachine guns tore into him. A teenager tried to run past the four but a quick burst took him to the pier's wooden floor, motionless, dead. A woman screamed and put her hands up but was cut down. The shooters were firing seemingly at random at their victims, causing panic as well as death.

It was a massacre.

And it happened in the blink of an eye.

The junior Aering engineer started to react.

DePresti leaped to his feet, staring at the four shooters with his hand over his eyes, shielding them from the sun. "What the fuck..." he said under his breath.

"We need to go," Parkowski yelled.

He nodded. "Hey, doc, time to go," he said to Pham.

Pham didn't respond. He was frozen to the spot, watching in disbelief as the four shooters cut down the crowd as they slowly marched forward.

Then Parkowski made a horrifying conclusion.

The four shooters weren't firing indiscriminately.

They were coming straight for them.

All four of them had their eyes trained on Parkowski, DePresti, and Pham. They were only a hundred meters away now, leaving a trail of bloody bodies in their wake as they cut down the people on the pier one by one.

"Jake, we *have* to go," she said loudly.

"They're here for me," the older man finally said. "We need to get out of here."

He stood up and staggered a step backward, then forwards to the pier's edge.

One of the shooters looked right at Pham.

He raised his submachine gun and fired a short burst.

Pham's body jerked as if he had been shocked by an electrical current. He fell to his knees.

"No!" Parkowski yelled.

Another one of the shooters, the woman, fired a burst from her own weapon. Two of the men paused to reload.

Pham fell face-first onto the wooden pier. Blood seeped from his body and stained the deck red.

The shooters had momentarily paused their killing spree.

At least forty bodies littered the ground behind them. People ran off the beach towards the safety of the buildings, screaming, as they finally realized what was happening above them.

The other two reloaded and they fell back into a lockstep.

Parkowski and DePresti slowly backed up towards the aquarium at the pier's end as the four shooters stepped towards them.

Parkowski knew what she had to do.

She made a break for the edge. DePresti followed her a split second later.

The four shooters opened fire but it was too late.

They were already in mid-air.

CHAPTER TWENTY-FIVE

Manhattan Beach, CA

Parkowski hit the water hard feet-first.

She heard the submachine guns' rounds cut through the air around her, but, mercifully, none struck her body. The killers weren't as good at hitting a moving target as they were at gunning down innocent people on the pier.

Parkowski sank to the bottom. It was about seven to eight feet deep. As she opened her eyes, she saw a school of fish pass by in front of her through the murky water.

Dazed, Parkowski floated back up to the surface, but was snapped out of it by DePresti appearing out of nowhere.

He grabbed her arm and shoved her to the bottom.

Parkowski gave him an angry look- they needed to go up for air - but realized what was going on when she looked up and saw the streaks of the bullets, fired from the four shooters still up on the pier.

The saltwater slowed the projectiles. They fell harmlessly around DePresti and Parkowski and sank to the sand below.

She was shocked at how many bullets had been fired at them. There seemed to be hundreds, all around them.

DePresti took the lead again and started pulling her south, away from the pier.

Parkowski grabbed his hand, their brief scuba diving experience coming in handy now. She squeezed it, then pointed at her neck and chest with the other one.

DePresti nodded and pulled her slightly towards the shore, near where the large waves were breaking.

He pointed at the cresting wave above them, let go of her hand, and pushed off towards the surface. DePresti thrust his head out of the water for a second, getting a breath of fresh air, and then dove back down towards the bottom.

LAG DELAY

A hail of bullets followed him. The shooters on the pier had seen him.

Parkowski, almost out of breath now, waited a second, then two, and did the same.

She aimed for a spot far away from where DePresti had taken a breath. Parkowski closed her eyes and pushed the lower half of her face out of the cold Pacific, exhaled, then inhaled, and threw her body back towards the shallow ocean floor, opening her eyes back up on the way.

They didn't fire at her, or if they did she didn't notice, but she didn't take any chances as she pushed her body flat against the sand next to her boyfriend.

DePresti grabbed her hand again and she gave it a squeeze.

He pointed in the direction away from the pier, south, and let go of her hand as he kicked off in that direction. Parkowski waited a second then followed him.

Her boyfriend went up for air after an excruciating thirty seconds then dove back down. Parkowski did the same.

This time she looked around quickly. They were a decent distance away from the pier now; far enough that she couldn't make out if the shooters were still there or not in her brief inspection.

She played it safe, diving back down to the bottom after filling her lungs with air.

DePresti wasn't so cautious. He was about halfway between the surface and the sea floor, swimming quickly.

It was probably safe by now - she didn't see any bullets enter the water. Parkowski swam up to join him.

They swam underwater for at least ten to fifteen minutes, coming up carefully for air then diving back down, as they hugged the Pacific coast going south towards Hermosa Beach.

Then, they swam back up to the surface, Parkowski first, and swam another five or six minutes in the same direction.

DePresti overtook her, and started turning in towards a surprisingly empty beach for one o'clock on a Saturday. She estimated that they were half a mile from the pier, near the Manhattan/Hermosa dividing line. It must be safe.

The authorities must have cleared the beaches after they became aware of the massacre happening just up the road. The only people Parkowski saw on the beach were the lifeguards, and instead of looking out towards the ocean for a swimmer in distress or the occasional shark, they were looking at the far-off Manhattan Beach pier.

DePresti swam easily through the waves and surf towards the beach with Parkowski closely following him. She knew he had grown up going to the beach, his parents had a beach house in Ocean City, New Jersey and he was an excellent scuba diver, but she hadn't realized just how powerful of a swimmer he was.

Unfortunately, Parkowski wasn't quite as strong of a swimmer as her boyfriend. She got caught in a rip current that took her back out to sea. She may not have been as powerful as DePresti, but she was just as intelligent. Parkowski let the current take her in the wrong direction while swimming south, perpendicular to the beach. DePresti had made it ashore and was watching her. Finally, she got free, and with a few overhand strokes made it to shore.

"What happened?" her boyfriend asked. He was soaked, his shorts dripping onto the sand and his wet t-shirt clinging to his thin frame. "I thought you were right behind me."

"Rip current," Parkowski replied. "You either swam through it or just missed it."

"Must have been the adrenaline," he responded. "Grace, what happened back there...?"

"I almost don't want to talk about it," she said. "Dr. Pham...he was my boss, but he also was my friend."

DePresti was about to say something but she interrupted him loudly. "And then they tried to kill us!"

He put his finger to his lips. "Shh!" he said in a loud whisper. "Yes, they did, and we need to get off the beach and somewhere safe."

"But where is safe?" Parkowski demanded. "They almost just murdered us in broad daylight."

DePresti didn't answer, he didn't have a good answer. Instead, he turned and started walking nonchalantly up the beach towards the houses of Hermosa Beach.

Parkowski followed him closely. She couldn't be completely calm - she had just been shot at - but she tried to give off an air of coolness as she walked in her soaked gym shorts and t-shirt away from the Pacific.

The beach was eerily quiet.

They watched as an ambulance, speeding with its lights and siren on, drove parallel to the road north to Manhattan Beach.

"That was bad," Parkowski said.

"Yeah, really bad, and I don't even know how we got out of that one alive," her boyfriend responded. "Those people were professionals, Grace, professional killers. They just gunned people down without thinking about it, men, women, children, it didn't matter. Dr. Pham was the target, and everyone else was just collateral damage."

"You think so?" she asked.

He nodded. "That's why they killed everyone else. To hide who the real targets were."

"You read too many books," Parkowski said as they walked off of the beach onto the sidewalk. This was like something out of an action novel. But, deep down, she knew her boyfriend was right. Someone wanted them dead - but why?

Parkowski knew it had to be related to Bronze Knot. Pham was going to tell her something, something important, but it was so important that he was killed for his secret before he was able to reveal it.

However, even if he hadn't agreed to meet them, she had a suspicion that she and DePresti would have been targeted for elimination regardless. Whoever had killed Dr. Pham would have killed them too, eventually. The secret was too great to let anyone in on.

But what was that secret? Parkowski had no idea.

Pham said something about a "cover story." What was that? Something to worry about later.

Neither of them were wearing shoes, their flip-flops lost in the vast ocean to the west. The pavement was warm but not hot under her toes as they crossed The Strand and started the half-mile walk back to their car.

As they strode along the sidewalk, Parkowski checked her pockets. Her phone was there, likely dead from extended water exposure, as was the document she had created for Dr. Pham and her wallet.

DePresti didn't speak. He was a man on a mission, trying to get them back to his car. She watched as he pulled out his car keys and wallet - but surprisingly no phone - out from his shorts' pockets and checked them before putting them back in.

"You didn't bring your phone?" she asked.

"Nope," DePresti replied. "Old habit from work. I can't bring my phone into the office with me, so I leave it in my car."

It was half a mile back to his Subaru, and her feet hurt like hell by the end of it. Parkowski breathed a sigh of relief as DePresti unlocked the car and got in. He took his phone, an older Samsung model, and opened up the back to get to the battery.

"What are you doing?" she asked him.

"Taking the battery out so we can't be tracked," he responded. "Grace, I hate to break it to you, but we're now on the run."

CHAPTER TWENTY-SIX

Manhattan Beach, CA

Parkowski twiddled her thumbs while DePresti fumbled to get the battery out of his phone.

Finally, he gave up.

DePresti chucked the cell phone out of the car's window into a bush outside the house they were parked in front of.

"What was that for?" she asked.

"Whoever attacked us on the pier, they can track us through our phones," he explained. "I've seen it in movies."

"In movies," she repeated, incredulous at the suggestion.

"And I know that anything transmitting via an antenna can be triangulated," DePresti said. "So I want to be better safe than sorry." He looked at her. "Grace, this is serious business now."

"No shit," she responded. "We almost just died."

He didn't have a response.

"And Dr. Pham..."

His silence continued.

"What now?" Parkowski asked.

"We need to get out of here," her boyfriend answered. "And we can't go back to my house or your apartment. We don't know if we were the intended targets or not."

"Ok, so we go to the police?"

"We can't go to the police," DePresti argued. "We have no idea who those four people were on the pier. They could be from our government, a foreign government, an NGO, or a corporation coming from God-knows-where. For all we know, they could be in cahoots with the local cops."

They sat in the car quietly.

"Can we go to one of our friends' houses?" Parkowski asked.

DePresti considered it. "That's not the worst idea. Reggie lives at the far side of Manhattan Beach up by El Segundo off of Rosecrans. He's working from home today. Let's pay him a visit."

He started to back out of the parking spot and froze. "Cop car," DePresti said quietly.

Parkowski saw it in her side's rear-view mirror. The black-and-white SUV was coming towards the Subaru slowly, its lights on, but no siren blaring.

She sat as still as she could manage with her heart beating a thousand times per minute. Had they been caught? Why else would a police car be here, blocks away from a recent massacre? They had to be coming for them.

There was nothing they could do. Parkowski and DePresti sat motionless as the police SUV approached.

But it didn't stop. Instead, the car with the flashing lights slowly passed their parked Subaru and continued down the residential street.

DePresti let out a short laugh.

"What's so funny about that?" Parkowski demanded.

"I forget just how big the government is sometimes," her boyfriend explained. "If the shooters on the pier were in cahoots with the government somehow, it'd take a dozen people to get through all of the layers needed to get down to the local cops. And that takes time, which means we have a chance to get out of this."

"And if they're not part of the government?" Parkowski asked. "I have a hard time believing that the U.S. government would indiscriminately murder people in broad daylight."

"We'll come to that if we have to," her boyfriend said. "Right now, let's just get out of here."

He deftly pulled out of the parking spot and started driving north toward his friend's apartment.

They stuck to the residential streets rather than the main thoroughfares of Ardmore Avenue and CR-1. The drive was silent; DePresti focused on driving while Parkowski kept an eye out for anything out of the ordinary.

She had a sick feeling in her stomach. Whatever had happened back there was her fault. If she hadn't been so invested in figuring out what Bronze Knot was, her boss and all of those innocent people at the pier would still be alive.

"If I remember correctly, his apartment complex is off of this street," DePresti said as he made a left onto a two-lane street.

She saw a black, late-model Chevy SUV with dark tinted windows parked alongside the street in front of a house in the opposite direction that she and DePresti were traveling. Parkowski couldn't put a finger on why she felt a sense of danger, but the car had its lights on and engine running; seemingly just sitting and waiting for someone.

"Mike, don't pull in," she told her boyfriend.

"What?" DePresti asked. They were almost at the turn-in for the apartment complex, the only one on the street.

"Keep driving," she repeated, "Something's wrong."

"Ok." He increased his speed slightly and drove past the apartment's entrance.

She turned around in her seat. The SUV had pulled out of its spot towards them.

"We're being followed," she told DePresti.

"Fuck," he said, rolling through the stop sign at the end of the street and making a right to go towards CR-1. "That's not good."

"We should have switched cars," Parkowski said, realizing their error. "Or stolen one."

DePresti didn't respond.

"What do we do now?"

"We lose them."

He got onto CR-1 going north, the famed Pacific Coast Highway, which had lighter traffic than expected at this time of day.

Parkowski turned around and looked again. The black SUV was still there, two or three cars behind them, and if her eyes weren't deceiving her, there was another SUV, the same make, model, and color, coming up from the south.

"I think we've got another tail," Parkowski said to DePresti.

"Fuck," he said again. "Just keeps getting better and better."

"Can you lose them?"

"I think so," he replied. "But, if we do, where do we go? Is there anywhere we can go? Or are we just going to be on the run until we get caught or forgotten about?"

"Can we go back east?" Parkowski wondered aloud. "That's where both of our families are; they can help hide us somewhere until this all dies down." If it dies down, she thought but didn't say.

"Maybe?" DePresti said. "I think long-term that's a good strategy. But man, there's a lot of stuff I think we'll have to do first."

"Like what?"

"Like, Grace, I'm in the military, and they're going to expect me to show up to work tomorrow," DePresti said. "Otherwise, I'm AWOL. I'm going to have to figure out a plan to explain why I won't be there."

"Oh."

"And they'll expect you at work at Aering, too," DePresti continued as he made a left onto Rosecrans, now heading west towards the Pacific. "We'll have to figure out that one too."

The two SUVs still followed them. "Both of them turned with us," Parkowski said.

He nodded. The huge Chevron refinery was on their right as they drove down the avenue. Traffic was starting to pick up as they got closer to Los Angeles International Airport. "Keep track of them."

"What are you trying to do?" Parkowski asked.

"I'm trying to get to the airport and lose them in the mess there," her boyfriend responded. "And if that doesn't work, get on the freeways and try to get rid of our tails there."

Parkowski almost asked him why he was going away from the airport - CR-1 going north would have taken them right to the airport terminals - but realized why when DePresti made a right going north on Vista del Mar. The road here was almost completely empty, giving them a lot more room to maneuver, while CR-1 became bumper-to-bumper as it neared LAX.

Unfortunately, that also gave the pursuing vehicles more room too.

"They're gaining on us," Parkowski said, a hint of panic in her voice.

DePresti didn't respond, rather, he gunned his Subaru's engine and barely made it through a yellow light.

The two SUVs kept coming.

They managed to get through another yellow light just twenty yards ahead. The chase had moved to the city El Segundo as they traveled north. DePresti made a right at Imperial Highway, just south of the Blue Butterfly Preserve, and headed east towards the airport.

Parkowski watched as both of the SUVs made the same turn and continued their pursuit.

After driving down that road for a few minutes, there was trouble - a huge accident and police response just before the left turn to go under the runways at LAX going north. The road was blocked.

"Well, shit," the Space Force captain said. "There goes that plan."

"What do we do now?"

"Did you ever meet Andrew Chang?"

Parkowski thought for a moment. "No, but the name is familiar." She knew that DePresti had mentioned it at some point, but couldn't remember in relation to what.

"I used to work with him at Space Systems Command," DePresti said as they stopped at a red light. The SUVs were a dozen cars behind them, stuck in the snarl of traffic as well. "We were in the same units twice, in both launch and space superiority. Chang got out of the military and bought a spread out in the Barstow area where he works remotely for some LA-based defense contractor. I've never been there, but I've talked to him a few times since he moved. I think that might be a good place to hide out."

"But, if I remember the conversation correctly," Parkowski argued, "he's kind of crazy, right?"

"Yes, but right now that's what we need," DePresti replied.

She flipped around to check the SUVs, then back to the front. "What do you mean?"

"He's paranoid about being tracked online and in person, both about the federal government as well as large corporations," the military officer explained as he drove. "I think he's completely off of the power grid, and any kind of internet connection that he has is likely untraceable. Chang probably has a lot of supplies and other things that might be of help to us as well."

Parkowski nodded - she didn't have any good arguments. Or a better plan, for that manner.

They were almost at the I-105 onramp, just before the Aering Space Systems facility where this had all begun. She checked back again. Somehow, the two SUVs had covered the ground between them much quicker than she had anticipated.

"Shit, they're here," Parkowski said.

"What?"

"They're almost on top of us," she said as they stopped at a red light just before the onramp.

She turned around and saw one of the SUVs, the closer one, draw its window down. A submachine gun, the same one used by the shooters on the pier, appeared. Any doubt she had that the two groups were related - or even one and the same - evaporated.

This weapon had something else on it though, a long, cylindrical attachment on its barrel. A silencer.

"Get down!" she yelled and pulled her head down towards her chest.

"What?" DePresti said.

The submachine gun fired.

With a muffled *pop-pop-pop* a hail of bullets struck the Subaru, shattering glass and thudding into the back seats.

Neither DePresti nor Parkowski were hit.

The light was still red.

"Fuck this," DePresti said. He slammed on the accelerator and the car shot forward, narrowly missing a minivan traveling north on California Street towards the airport.

This was it. They were going to die.

Despite her terror, Parkowski looked back. The two SUVs were running the red light as well.

But then they got a stroke of luck.

A large truck, not quite a tractor-trailer, but still huge, barreled down the road towards the intersection.

It tried to stop but the huge vehicle, probably laden with cargo bound for the airport, slammed into the lead SUV - the same one that had shot at them moments before. It struck the Chevy just behind the passenger's side rear door, tipping it up on its side as it slid across the pavement with a sickening metal screech. Parkowski heard the sound clearly from their vehicle a hundred feet away.

The second SUV tried to stop but it collided with the truck too. Its front crumpled and the car came to a halt.

"Looks like we lost them," Parkowski said.

"For now," DePresti added as he sped up to get on the freeway. "Grace, go back and see how much damage there is."

She unbuckled and climbed to the back seat. At least ten bullets had struck the car, most of which went through the window, through the car's interior, and through the floor. Parkowski looked out the window - all of the tires looked ok - and then through the tiny holes in the car's floor. It didn't look like any of the lines had been hit.

"I think we're good," she said as she slid back into her seat. "They didn't hit anything vital."

"I guess we won that one," DePresti said as he changed lanes. "So, are you good with my plan?"

Parkowski nodded.

"On we go to Barstow."

CHAPTER TWENTY-SEVEN

Los Angeles, CA

They continued east on the 105 in relative silence.

Parkowski tried again to digest everything that had happened.

They had been shot at, not once, but twice. Dr. Pham had been murdered - in cold blood - just feet from where she had stood. They were now on the run, a decision she initially questioned, but after the short chase and gunfire, wholeheartedly supported.

She tried to talk to DePresti, the silence killing her slowly, but he seemingly wanted to focus on the road. Parkowski didn't blame him one bit, though it would have been nice to have someone to talk to.

The traffic started to pick up as they hit the beginning of the evening rush hour.

She also kept an eye out for any other cars trailing them, but didn't see any.

The Aering engineer was able to start a conversation with DePresti once they got off the 105 and onto I-605 going northeast around the city of Los Angeles proper.

"What's a cover story?" she asked DePresti.

"It's basically a lie," he answered. "A sanctioned lie, covering up some information or technology with a sanitized version. They're very common in the IC and the classified military world."

It seemed like he wanted to say more, but he didn't. Parkowski decided to move the conversation along. "Dr. Pham said that Bronze Knot was a cover story."

"I heard that too," DePresti said, "and I was kind of confused by that."

"What confused you?"

"Because a special access program usually has a cover story to protect it from people who aren't read in," the Space Force captain told his girlfriend. "Dr. Pham said that Bronze Knot *was* the cover story. That's odd, and not a mistake that someone who used to work for the CIA would make."

"So was it a mistake?"

DePresti shrugged. "Maybe? Maybe not? I don't know, Grace, I really don't. I just want to get to Barstow."

"Do you know how to get there?" she asked.

"To Barstow? Yes. To Chang's house? No," DePresti answered. "I know he's north of the city, up in the hills somewhere. I figured we'd stop at a gas station in that area and ask if they knew a crazy Asian guy living off the grid."

Parkowski chuckled. "I guess that's a better plan than nothing."

"Well, it's the one we have right now."

They continued northeast, the traffic getting heavier and heavier, eventually switching over and traveling due east on Interstate 210. Parkowski kept looking for a new tail, but it never came.

The Subaru passed through the eastern part of Los Angeles County before crossing over into San Bernardino County.

As they traveled away from the ocean, the terrain outside transitioned from green to brown. The wooded Angeles National Forest out their driver's side windows gave way to the shrub and brush of Mt. Baldy and Timber Mountain.

Parkowski had never made it this far northeast of the South Bay area; she had driven in from the East Coast through Orange County. While it was still a pretty area, she would have preferred some more foliage.

At least her clothes were drying in the dry air.

As they passed north of Ontario, she started to doze off.

"Hey, Grace, are you still checking behind us?" her boyfriend said, jerking her awake?

"Wha..." she asked, sitting up in her seat and rubbing her eyes. "What's going on?"

"I think they found us again."

"What?" she said as she turned around.

This time, she saw it easily. Three black SUVs, driving side-by-side in formation, coming down the 210 towards them about a kilometer in the distance. There were maybe three or four cars between the Subaru and the oncoming pursuers, but that was it in the way of cover.

"I see three of them," Parkowski said.

"Fuck," DePresti said. His voice was shaky. "Three?"

"Yup."

They traveled at over seventy miles per hour now, well above the speed limit, but the SUVs were rapidly gaining on them. The road in front started to clear up as they reached roughly the halfway point between Los Angeles and the city of San Bernardino.

"Same assholes as before," Parkowski added. "Black Chevys."

DePresti floored the accelerator. His car in theory, was faster than their pursuers, but who knew what modifications they might have made to their SUVs to improve them. "Christ, they're pulling out all of the stops." He swerved around a late-model minivan, and had more or less an open road in front of him.

The three SUVs were now right behind them. Parkowski braced herself, expecting them to try to fire on them again, but oddly no submachine guns appeared from the heavily tinted windows.

Instead, they had broken their formation and were trying to surround the Subaru.

Maybe their tactics had changed. Instead of trying to eliminate her and DePresti, perhaps they were now trying to capture them by boxing them in.

DePresti drove erratically, trying to shake them, but the pursuing cars closed on his vehicle. "Grace, we've got to do something," he said, swerving to the right around one of the few remaining cars on the freeway. "Traffic is going to start picking up once we hit San

Bernardino, and they're going to be able to trap us once we slow down. I don't know how much longer I can keep this up."

She nodded. "What do we have in the car?"

"Our bags, my bike helmet, my scuba gear," DePresti said. "Not much. I just cleaned it out."

"I'll go check back there." She unbuckled and climbed into the Forester's back seat, almost flying out the shattered window as DePresti swerved to the left into the freeway's shoulder. Parkowski was shocked that there weren't any California Highway Patrol cars or even local cops on the road, but maybe that was by design. Whoever were in these SUVs had seemingly unlimited resources.

There wasn't much available in the trunk to her. Everything DePresti had said was there, plus an emergency kit and some trash. But nothing jumped out as a possible course of action.

An idea came to her.

"Mike, how do you feel about your scuba tank?" she yelled to the front.

"If you need to use it, use it," he yelled back.

Parkowski threw everything from the trunk into the rear seat except for the tank, then climbed into the trunk herself. "Unlock the car," she yelled.

A moment later she heard the *click* as DePresti did as she requested.

She grabbed on to the back of the seat with one hand and used the other to open the Subaru's rear door.

The wind from the outside blew in her face as she was now exposed to the elements. It was a dry, warm air, and if they weren't in a life-or-death situation, it would have felt good on her face.

Parkowski saw the three pursuing cars now, weaving in and out of traffic as they tried to get in a position where they could box DePresti's car in and force them to stop. Their windows were all tinted, she couldn't see any of the occupants, but mercifully there weren't any submachine guns pointed at her. She waited until one of the cars, the middle one, was diagonally to her left and flung the scuba tank out of the Subaru.

The former high school athlete timed her throw perfectly. It impacted the SUV's driver's side windshield and went cleanly into the vehicle.

Unlike in the movies, the tank didn't explode. Instead, she could see the cracks in the windows of the SUV as the high pressure tank bounced around; the vessel had been breached somewhere along its exterior.

The black SUV careened off the road.

Both of its twins were slow to respond. The car to Parkowski's left was able to accelerate and avoid the impacted Chevy, but the one to her right was not. Its front bumper slammed into the rear of the SUV that Parkowski had hit.

The SUV that had originally been counterattacked went airborne, flipping over back-to-front before skidding and sliding towards the median, upside-down. The second SUV went slightly off-axis, the right side tipping up and the entire car putting all of its weight on the left two tires, before coming back down. It, too, turned sideways from the collision and slammed into the railing on the other side of the freeway.

That, Parkowski briefly thought, was like the movies.

She closed the trunk and quickly climbed over the back seat.

"I got two of them," she told DePresti with a smile.

"Great, but that means there's one still left," he said. Their victory was apparently short-lived. He was pushing the Subaru as fast as it could go, but the SUV was gaining on them.

They were going well over a hundred miles per hour and she wasn't wearing a seatbelt.

She was terrified.

Her fears were realized when the Subaru received a sudden jolt. Parkowski fell forward into the driver's seat. She felt a slight pain in her neck but was otherwise unhurt.

"What the fuck was that?" she asked.

"Our friends in the last Suburban rammed us," DePresti said. "Do you have any more tricks back there?"

"Do you have any more scuba tanks?"

"Fair point."

She went over the rest of the scuba gear, but there wasn't anything heavy enough to throw.

The only thing left was the emergency kit. Parkowski quickly went through it and smiled. "Mike, have you ever opened this kit up?"

"No, I just bought it and threw it in there, why?"

"You have road flares."

He started to say something in response when they heard the now-familiar sound of gunfire. Parkowski dove to the floor as another round of bullets slammed into the Subaru.

"They're firing again!" she yelled.

"I'm painfully aware of that," DePresti responded. He drove the car to the far right lane and up onto the shoulder.

Parkowski poked her head up. The SUV followed them, cutting across all four lanes of traffic.

The rear driver's side window was completely shattered now, the interior littered with shards of glass. Parkowski was aware of a few cuts on her legs but none of them seemed to hurt or be bleeding particularly badly. The adrenaline rush made up for all of that.

The SUV was almost alongside them now, ready for another deadly volley.

Parkowski quickly read over the instructions for the road flares. They were similar to lighting a match; brush the removed cap against the tip to start it. There were all kinds of warning labels about not doing it inside your vehicle, but she ignored them. Desperate times called for desperate measures.

She lit a flare and peeked out the window. The SUV was only a car's length away from them, both of its rear windows open. She could see darkly dressed occupants inside of it, two of them with submachine guns - the same type that was used at the pier and near LAX - at the ready.

Parkowski aimed and threw the lit flare.

She missed.

"Fuck," she thought, and lit another. Parkowski took aim again and launched it towards the SUV.

This time the other vehicle's driver swerved to avoid it. They were getting smarter.

Both of the shooters aimed their submachine guns at the Subaru and fired as Parkowski dove back down.

This time, they hit her square in the upper arm just below the left shoulder.

Parkowski groaned as she hit the glass-covered floor. It felt like Mike Tyson had just hit her with a punch. "I'm hit, I'm hit."

"Oh shit," DePresti said, more than a hint of panic in his voice. "Where?"

"My shoulder," she yelled, daring to take a look. There was a lot less blood than she expected, but it was there, seeping out of a dime-sized hole. Parkowski felt around her back and found a slightly smaller one. Blood slowly seeped out of both wounds. "I think it went through."

"Jesus," DePresti said. "Press something up to it...I think. There's a first aid kit back there if you can reach it. Let me try something, if this keeps up, we're going to both die here." He paused. "Hold on!"

Parkowski held onto the back of his seat with her bad arm - which hurt like hell - while holding her other hand to the exit wound. She looked out the window again.

The SUV had fallen back but was coming around for another pass.

DePresti turned the wheel hard to the right, then turned left into the other vehicle. Their opponents hadn't anticipated an offensive move.

He caught the SUV accelerating. The taller automobile angled up slightly on its left wheels as DePresti pushed the accelerator all of the way down. The SUV then tipped over, its wheel spinning in the air as the car skidded across the freeway.

DePresti deftly turned left and continued east.

"How are you doing back there?" he asked Parkowski.

"I'm bleeding, but it's not that bad," she responded, a lot braver than she felt inside. "I think it went all of the way through, and didn't hit any bones or anything."

"Do we need to stop? Go to a hospital or anything?"

She shook her head. "No, keep going. I don't see any more of them."

Parkowski poked her head around. The highway was somehow almost empty.

DePresti took a deep breath. "I guess they're gone."

CHAPTER TWENTY-EIGHT

San Bernardino, CA

Parkowski climbed back into the passenger's seat, her arms and legs a terrifying sight from the broken glass.

Her real concern was her shoulder.

She used some gauze from the kit and painfully put it on both wounds. Then, she grabbed a windbreaker from DePresti's backseat and managed to tie it around her armpit. The blood from the entry wound had seemed to stop somewhat, but the exit wound still bled slightly.

There was a roll of paper towels under the seat, which she grabbed and started to clean up the superficial cuts on her arms and legs.

The pain had started to set in though, a deep ache in her shoulder that she felt every time she moved. Parkowski would have done anything for a painkiller, but DePresti didn't seem to have any in the first aid kit.

DePresti kept his eyes glued to the road as he took the ramp for I-15N towards Barstow. Parkowski checked the mirrors for a reappearance of the small army of SUVs that had terrorized them since they had left El Segundo. They chillingly had seen no police cars.

He turned the radio on. After a few minutes, he found a local news station. "A brazen mass shooting at the Manhattan Beach pier today left fourteen dead and another twenty wounded," the male announcer said.

"Holy shit, fourteen people, just to get Dr. Pham?" Parkowski said. And us, she didn't add.

"Shh," DePresti said.

"Believing it to be a terrorist act, authorities are on a multi-county manhunt for members of an Islamic militant group that they believe to be behind the heinous act," a female newscaster said. "They are searching Los Angeles, Orange, and San Bernardino counties and we will let you know more when it comes in."

"None of the shooters at the pier looked the least bit Middle Eastern," DePresti said quietly as they switched to a weather update. "Not that they couldn't be Islamic converts, or from the Balkans."

"I concur," Parkowski agreed. "There was no mass shooting."

"No, I agree," DePresti said. "They were gunning right for us and your poor boss."

"Oh, Dr. Pham," Parkowski said, putting her head in her hands. She felt like a horrible person. "Why did I have to push the issue?"

"We didn't know," DePresti said. "We had no idea that it was going to trigger that kind of response."

"I know we didn't, but should we have?" she asked, not expecting an answer. DePresti didn't have one.

They drove in silence for a bit. The news station had no more information than it had already offered, so DePresti turned it off.

The freeway passed through the mountains now, the terrain becoming drier and drier as they drove into Southern California's interior. The dry air whipped in through their shattered windshield, but after a while Parkowski got used to it.

Her shoulder throbbed. "How much longer?"

"Just under an hour," DePresti answered. "Are you going to be ok?"

"I think so." She checked the exit wound. The bleeding had started to stop, but she had begun to feel a little light-headed.

"Drink some water," DePresti suggested. "Once we get to Chang's place, we'll get you checked out."

She was exhausted, in pain, and not much seemed to be going right. Parkowski took a sip from a bottle and curled up on the seat.

The sun was starting to sink below the horizon. Parkowski kept an eye out for any more SUVs, but she had a sneaking suspicion that there weren't going to be any more. Their opponent - whoever they were - made their move, and had failed. They would likely try again soon, but it would take time to gather those resources.

The desert north of San Bernardino was brown, dry, and to an East Coaster like Parkowski, ugly. It all looked the same as it scrolled past the window.

Parkowski wanted to talk through everything with her boyfriend, to try and process together what they had been through, to make sense of it with all of the other pieces of information. But she was too tired, too weak, and just plain exhausted. That discussion could come later.

Eventually, they reached the outskirts of Barstow.

DePresti drove to a well-lit gas station and backed the car into a parking spot.

"Stay here," he told Parkowski. "I'm going to go get a map and some stuff."

She nodded.

A few minutes later he returned, holding a large map book under one arm and a paper bag in the other. "We need to keep moving," DePresti said, "but here's some medical stuff. I can do it, or you can while I drive."

Parkowski groaned. "I'll do it. Let's get moving."

"Hold on, not so fast. I want to use this map first," he said. "I have a general idea of where I'm going, but I want to double check."

She laughed. "Just imagine, in the age of cell phones, virtual reality, and space travel, someone using a map."

"I'm glad I learned how to read one at the Academy," DePresti said as he spread out a local map of the Barstow area. "I thought it was stupid at the time, but it's coming in handy now."

DePresti pointed at a road on the north side of the city. "He told me his address a while ago, it's off Antelope Road here. I remembered the road, but not the house number. But, look how long Antelope is."

It starts in Barstow proper, goes all of the way northwest to the town of Randsburg, and his complex could be anywhere off of there."

"Complex?"

"Trust me, it's a complex."

"Sure."

"Anyways, it looks like a gas station here," he went on, ignoring her jab. "I'm going to stop here and ask if they know Andrew Chang. He's a hard guy to miss."

"Sounds like a plan," Parkowski said, digging into the other bag. There were painkillers, more gauze, and a wrap that had been missing from the kit, in addition to a pair of sodas and some snacks. "Thanks, Mike."

"Don't mention it," he added as he pulled out of the parking spot, map in hand. "Thank me when we finally get there."

They slowly drove out of the gas station and back onto the main roads. The autumn sun had completely set and the evening was in full swing. They were far enough from the Los Angeles metro area that light pollution was less of an issue. She couldn't remember the last time she had seen a sky as full of stars as they danced against the pitch-black sky.

Parkowski cursed again at the arrhythmia that had prevented her from ever becoming an astronaut. Maybe, someday, she would get a chance to go up there.

As they left the city of Barstow, the houses became less and less frequent until there were almost none along the road. DePresti continued onto the Barstow-Bakersfield Highway and then made a right onto Antelope Road. The two began their journey through the desert towards what they hoped was Chang's residence.

Parkowski popped a few of the ibuprofen and tried to wrap her shoulder with the gauze. She thought about taking off her top but decided to bandage over the t-shirt. "Sorry about your windbreaker," she said to DePresti, who didn't respond as Parkowski tossed the bloody jacket into the backseat.

After a few failed attempts, she managed to do it. A little blood seeped out, but it'd have to do until they arrived. Then, she used the wrap to hold the gauze in place. It hurt like hell and made her shoulder hard to use, but it worked.

"You didn't get anything to clean it, did you?" she asked. DePresti shook his head to confirm her suspicion. That'd be something they'd have to do eventually.

The road wasn't well marked, and the various driveways and unmarked paths were hard to see. They were no longer in a major metropolitan city or even in a suburb. There were no streetlights to guide them, no road signs. It was truly the middle of nowhere.

Parkowski thought that they had gone too far and was about to tell DePresti to turn around and go back to Barstow. But, she finally saw the neon light of an old Sinclair sign that had to be almost a century old off in the distance.

"That's the gas station," she said.

"I know." DePresti smiled. "I can read a map, dear."

As they got closer she noticed that the gas station was completely empty of cars, save for an old Camaro parked in the back. DePresti pulled right up to the station and got out of the car with his map. "Be right back," he said.

Parkowski waited for an eternity.

She drank one of the water bottles in the back and nibbled on an energy bar. Her boyfriend was taking forever.

Another five minutes passed. She thought about getting out of the shot-up Subaru and going in, but thought better of it. If DePresti was in any kind of trouble there in the gas station, she wouldn't be much help in her current state. Better to just wait.

Finally the Space Force officer left the tiny, ancient building with his map and a huge smile on his face. "Sorry, Grace, the guy in there was a talker," he said. She smelled a hint of whiskey in his breath. "Gave me a shot and talked my ear off."

"Are you ok to drive?"

He nodded. "I just had one. I'm fine. And I know exactly where to go. Three miles back, make a right, go down about half a mile. He knows Andrew pretty well."

Parkowski tried to shrug but wasn't able to with her wrapped shoulder. "Works for me."

DePresti followed the directions, turning off of Antelope Drive onto an unmarked dirt road. "This must be his driveway. Just a little more and we're there."

Up ahead, Parkowski could barely see a small, one-story house with a carport next to it. None of its lights were on. It was as if no one was home. "That's his house," she said as she pointed at it. "Go there."

He nodded and pulled up behind a large, dark-colored Ford pickup truck with a raised suspension, then stopped the car. "Ok, I'll get out and walk around."

"I don't think you will," a low, deep voice said from just outside the Subaru.

Parkowski whipped her head around - a painful gesture - to see the barrel of an ugly, pump-action shotgun pointed through the broken driver's side window right at her and DePresti.

"You have thirty seconds to tell me why I shouldn't blow both of your faces off."

CHAPTER TWENTY-NINE

Barstow, CA

DePresti spoke first. "Andrew, it's me, Mike, from work," he said slowly. "We've known each other for four years."

"Mike who? I worked with a lot of Mikes."

"Mike DePresti, from Space Systems Command," the Space Force captain added.

"Philly?" Chang asked as he stepped closer to the car.

"Yeah, it's me," DePresti said. Must be a nickname from work, Parkowski thought. "The other person is my girlfriend, Grace. You've never met her."

The shotgun barrel didn't move. Chang said nothing.

"We need help," Parkowski said, trying to break the awkward, dangerous silence.

"How the fuck did you find me here?"

"You told me you bought a place off of Antelope Road. I found a gas station on Antelope Road and asked if anyone matching your description has moved to the area in the last year and the guy working the counter pointed me in your direction. Russell says hi, by the way."

"He's an idiot. Should have kept his big mouth shut."

"Andrew, my girlfriend has a bullet hole in her shoulder. We need to come in and take a look at it."

"And you had to drive all of the way from the South Bay to do that?"

"We didn't have much of a choice," Parkowski said, getting a little annoyed despite having a weapon pointed at her. "Mike and I have been on the run all day from a group of people who seem to want us dead. We've been on the go, nonstop, since noon. Please, just let us come inside."

"Ok," Chang said. The gun lowered for a second, then went back up. "So you led them here?"

"No, we lost them somewhere back around San Bernardino," DePresti said.

The shotgun finally went down and stayed there, pointed at the dusty desert soil. "Philly, you shouldn't have come here."

"We didn't have any other options."

The other man sighed. "Ok, come on in. Grace, is it? Let me take a look at your shoulder."

Parkowski opened the car door and took a few uneasy steps, the first she had taken since they had gotten into the Subaru on the Manhattan Beach residential streets. It was only a few hours ago, but felt like an entire other lifetime.

DePresti rushed over to help her, as did Chang. "Easy, easy now," her boyfriend said. "Let's get you inside."

The two men carefully helped her inside the small house. It only had a few rooms, and was dimly lit, so Parkowski couldn't see much.

They took her to a tiny eat-in kitchen with some cheap-looking furniture. There, she got her first look at Chang. He was short, maybe an inch shorter than her, and his left arm had a full sleeve tattoo. Chang's black hair had started to recede. However, his most striking feature was his jaw. He had a serious look practically embedded onto his countenance, his chin jutting out at all times. She almost shuddered thinking about how easily he had pointed a weapon at them just a few moments ago.

"What were they shooting at you?" he asked her quietly as he took a look at Parkowski's shoulder.

DePresti answered for her. "MP-5s, and on three separate occasions. Thankfully they were only accurate the last time. She says she took a clean through-and-through, but I haven't been able to confirm."

"And you were able to evade them?"

"My Grand Theft Auto skills were finally put to good use."

Chang slowly removed the bandage. "Ma'am, you are one lucky lady," he said. "This is as neat of a hole as I've ever seen." He took a look at the back. "Mike, we won't even need to cauterize it. We'll just clean it, wrap it, and it should heal itself."

DePresti tried to say something, but Chang spoke over him. "Let's do it now, and then I'll get you guys to a bed to rest. I can stand watch overnight and we can talk in the morning."

Parkowski started to feel weak. She nodded in DePresti's direction.

She wasn't sure if he saw her, but he agreed. "Sounds like a plan. Thanks for taking us in."

Chang laughed, the first sign that he had a sense of humor. "I just want to hear the story, man. Two normies like you, one of you with bullet wounds, it has to be one hell of a trip."

He went into the small kitchen and got out a bottle of antiseptic from one of the upper cabinets, then returned to Parkowski. "Sorry, but this is going to sting," he said.

Parkowski nodded again. "Just do it," she said weakly.

Chang handed it to DePresti, who poured a little on Parkowski's bullet wound.

It hurt like hell. It hurt even more than when she had been shot. Parkowski screamed.

DePresti grabbed her hand and handed the bottle to Chang. "It's ok, it's ok," he said as the other man put the bottle down and quickly put a new strip of gauze over her shoulder.

She barely remembered the next few minutes.

The two men wrapped some kind of bandage over the gauze and then DePresti half-carried, half-dragged her to a small bedroom located near the house's main door. He put her into a queen-sized bed and pulled up the covers.

Parkowski passed out moments later.

She woke up at the crack of dawn to the sound of a rooster crowing.

The Aering engineer sat up in the bed's stiff sheets.

Her shoulder still hurt but it was more of a dull, throbbing pain rather than the acute hurt she felt yesterday.

Using her good arm, Parkowski got herself out of bed and started looking for her boyfriend or Chang.

The house looked even smaller in the daylight than it had the night before. There were only four rooms: the eat-in kitchen, a sitting room, and two bedrooms, plus a full bathroom, with the bare minimum of furniture in each of them. There were no decorations on the walls, no signs that any particular person lived there. It almost seemed unoccupied.

An old-school analog clock over the back door told her it was six o'clock. She was starving. Parkowski hadn't eaten a meal since lunch yesterday.

She opened up the ancient refrigerator and was shocked to find it empty. Thankfully, her bag from yesterday was right by the front door. Parkowski gulped down a granola bar and ate an apple.

Parkowski stepped outside into the dry wind of the Mojave. Unlike the previous day, it was not hot - she estimated it to be in the high forties. She shivered as she walked out onto Chang's "complex."

A German Shepherd, dirty from the dust and sand but obviously well-fed and friendly, bounded over to her and rolled over for pets.

She sighed and bent down to scratch the dog's belly with her good arm. Where were they?

The area around the house seemed deserted.

The house itself was at the top of a small, gently sloped hill. The roof was falling apart, the siding was starting to come off, and it looked like it had been transported from the early part of the previous century. It didn't seem to fit.

There was a structure a hundred feet from the house, which by closer inspection she found to be a chicken coop, a satellite dish up on a ridge pointed due south, and a small well that didn't look functional. Chang also had an old, dilapidated barn that looked empty.

She found two other vehicles on the property other than DePresti's Subaru and the giant pickup truck, a rusted Chevrolet Silverado that looked older than her but still seemed functional and a Buick from the sixties or seventies that was most definitely not. A mangy-looking cat jumped out of the latter vehicle as she inspected it.

What was this place?

DePresti had told her that Chang was a former Space Force officer, obviously an educated man, who had left the military for a high-paying consulting job as a contractor for the federal government.

Why would he live here, in the middle of nowhere, in such a dilapidated environment? How did he work? There was no computer in the house. Parkowski doubted he had a wired internet connection, and there was no way he had cell phone service out here. Chang would have to use the satellite dish for his connection, but the infrastructure required, the computer, router, networking equipment, all seemed to be absent.

She went back to the Subaru and marveled at the amount of damage done to DePresti's formerly pristine vehicle. There were dozens of small bullet holes alongside the driver's side of the vehicle. One had even gone through DePresti's driver's side window and gone into the dashboard. Parkowski dug around until she found one of her own sweatshirts jammed under one of the seats. It had a little glass on it, but that was easily brushed off.

There was still no sign of either DePresti or Chang. Puzzled, she walked back inside the house.

Parkowski sat down at the kitchen table with a warm water bottle and energy bar from the Subaru and popped some ibuprofen. She was confused. Why would they just leave her here? They couldn't have gone far; all of the vehicles were still at the house.

She wondered if they were playing a cruel trick on her, but quickly pushed that thought out of her head. DePresti was too nice of a guy to do something like that, especially with her being injured, and Chang seemed too serious.

Then she heard voices.

Two of them, male, both spoke loudly but very muffled. And if she wasn't going crazy, they were coming from underneath her.

Parkowski got up and carefully lowered herself to the floor with her uninjured arm.

It was DePresti and Chang. Those fuckers.

She got herself up and started looking for an entrance to the basement, but couldn't find one. The doors in the house either led to rooms or closets. There didn't seem to be a basement at all.

Parkowski stood in the kitchen, annoyed. The voices started getting louder.

Finally, the edge of an ugly red area rug started lifting, seemingly by itself, off of the floor.

Her jaw dropped to the ground.

Below it was a concrete structure. It continued rising until one edge was almost at the ceiling. Inside was a set of stairs. An entrance to the basement.

Moments later, DePresti and Chang appeared at the top, talking quickly about something Space Force-related that Parkowski didn't understand.

She stood and tapped her foot.

DePresti saw her first. "Oh, Grace, you're awake."

She lost it. "Woke up? I got out of bed and no one was there. We're in the middle of the freaking desert and you left me here in a bed and didn't tell me where you or your friend went."

Chang grinned.

DePresti was apologetic. "Sorry, Grace, I should have probably told you where we went. But, trust me, when you see what I've just seen, it's worth it."

"Seen what?"

Chang smiled even bigger. "Alright, Grace. Follow me. I'm about to show you why I decided to live out here, in one of the most desolate spots in the country." With that, he turned around and went back down the stairs."

DePresti extended an arm. "After you, dear."

Parkowski groaned and followed Chang down into the basement.

CHAPTER THIRTY

Barstow, CA

"I thought there weren't many basements in California," Parkowski said as she carefully went down the concrete stairs into Chang's lower level. "Because of all of the earthquakes."

"Ma'am, you are correct," the former Space Force officer said. "However, that assumes that you are in a basement."

"Huh?" Parkowski said.

At the bottom of the stairs there was a long hallway, much longer than the length of the house. Metal doors on either side lined the passageway.

Parkowski turned to DePresti. "Is he crazy?" she asked.

Her boyfriend laughed. "Just eccentric."

"How did you afford a supervillain lair?" she asked Chang.

"Oh, eight? No, ten years ago, I made some good investments," he replied. "Did a little cryptocurrency trading."

"How much did you make?"

"I ended up with over three and a half million dollars."

"Million?"

"Million."

"And what did you do with that?"

"I doubled it again."

"Holy shit," Parkowski said.

"Yup. But before then, when I was sitting with a cool two million in the bank, I started the process of designing my dream home, which you are in right now, while contracting out the start of the construction work that would prepare the ground for all of the structures," Chang continued. "I considered a few different areas, but my family is all from the SoCal area, so I settled on Barstow. I can show up at family functions while still living by myself without anyone bothering me."

Parkowski laughed. "I think there's an Everybody Loves Raymond episode about that."

"There is, and believe me, it went into consideration when I chose my location."

"So how did you do it?"

"I built this level, and then paid a ridiculous amount of money to cover it with sand and dirt. Then, I toured a couple of older, failing California rural communities and found the house that you slept in. Then, I paid an exorbitant amount of money to have it relocated on top of it. Finally, I had to connect the underground portion to the house above and put on the finishing touches."

Chang started walking to the end of the hallway. DePresti turned and whispered to Parkowski, "Enjoy the show, I just got the tour too."

She snorted and followed the short man to the end of the hall.

He opened the first door. She recognized the smell almost instantly. "Here is my grow room."

The room was full of marijuana plants, arranged in rows with a sophisticated irrigation system suspended from the ceiling.

"And your smoke room?"

The man shrugged. "That too."

He closed the door and led Parkowski and DePresti to the next room.

"Here is my hydroponics suite."

The room was the same as the marijuana room, except with vegetable plants suspended in water substituted for the narcotic plant.

Chang closed that door, then switched to the other side of the hallway.

The next door hid a large studio apartment, at least five or six hundred square feet, with a television, king-sized bed, eat-in kitchen, and small bathroom. "Here's where I sleep."

Parkowski laughed. "Was Mike there with you last night?"

Chang laughed back at her. "No, he was next door."

He showed her the guest room, or at least one of them. "Here's where Mike spent the night."

She gave her boyfriend a punch on the shoulder with her good arm. "And I had to sleep upstairs in the cold."

DePresti got defensive. "You were so weak, so tired, we wanted to get you in a bed," he said. "The one upstairs was the closest one. And you were out as soon as we got you under the covers."

Parkowski laughed. "Fair enough."

Chang hurried them down the hallway. "This is my work area," he said, showing DePresti and Parkowski a good-sized room, twice as large as his living space, with strange blue-and-green lighting. It had both a computer console with an oversized seat and six monitors spread out in front of it as well as a virtual-reality area with tape on the ground off to the side. "I spend a lot of my time here."

"I can tell," DePresti said.

The next door held a server room which reminded Parkowski of the secure "NASA room" she had broken into. The basement also contained a storage room, full of emergency rations, "in case shit really hits the fan," as Chang said, an armory, another guest room, and strangely enough, a wine cellar, in addition to a couple of storage areas.

It seemed like Chang spent most of his time underground.

"This is it," he said, showing her the final storage room. It looked like he bought a lot of things in bulk from Costco and Sam's Club. "This is what a cool two million will buy you in the California desert."

She laughed. "So, are you completely off the grid?"

Chang laughed. "As much as I can be."

He took a breath and then explained. "I have solar panels, but I'm unfortunately tied into the grid there. Even in the desert, I just don't get enough for everything I do.

"For internet, I have two sources: OuterTek's StarServe service, and a Brazilian GEO communication satellite that I've been able to hack, their security is atrocious. I use the StarServe IP address for my day-to-day job, looking for vulnerabilities in Rayleigh ground station software and reporting back to my government point-of-contact what I find. For more...esoteric activities, I use the satellite dish and go through my Brazilian 'ISP'."

Parkowski shook her head. "This is crazy."

"No, it's not," Chang argued. "The government is watching everything and everyone at all times. The only way to be truly free, to be independent of the feds, is to live like this, away from the connected world."

She didn't respond to his comment.

"How is your arm feeling?" DePresti asked.

"A little better," she replied. "I think we should probably change the bandage though."

"Agreed," Chang broke in. "I think all of the medical supplies are upstairs. Let's go check on your wound and then we can talk down here in my office."

They did just that. Parkowski had another white-hot burst of pain shoot through her shoulder when it was exposed to the air and another, even more painful jolt when DePresti cleaned it out with the antiseptic. They wrapped it up again and Chang gave her a choice of pills. "One is ibuprofen, the other is oxycontin," he told her. "Take your pick."

She chose the ibuprofen pill and swallowed it.

Chang shrugged. "You sure you don't want the good stuff?"

"Nope."

"Fine," he said, leading DePresti and Parkowski back to the hidden concrete entryway to his basement. "Let's go back down."

He led them, snacks and water in hand, into the dimly-lit office space, turned the LED lights on, and then excused himself to get a couple of extra chairs.

Parkowski turned to her boyfriend. "Your friend is nuts, you know that, right?"

"I know he's nuts, and I think he knows it too," DePresti replied. "But he's our best chance at making it out of the situation we are in alive."

She sighed.

Chang came back with a pair of folding chairs which he set up in the virtual reality area. He then sat down behind his computer console and broke out a vape pen. "You guys don't mind, right?" he asked.

DePresti and Parkowski both shook their heads.

He inhaled and then put his feet up on his desk. "Ok, so since you've experienced my warm hospitality, and since it seems like you haven't been followed." He turned briefly to his computer and pulled up a GUI with a map, then sent it away. "And we haven't had any unwelcome visitors," he continued. "The least the two of you can do is fill me in on how you went from your boring, lame, safe lives in El Segundo to being shot at and your car trashed and ending up out here with a burnout like me."

Parkowski and DePresti looked at each other.

"Where to even begin?" the Space Force captain asked.

Parkowski smiled. "I'll start at the very beginning."

She started with an outline of the ILIAD mission, including her selection to be an operator, and how she met DePresti during a Ground Operations Working Group (GOWG). "I actually got frustrated with him," Parkowski said with a smile. "He wasn't letting any of the Aering engineers go into the OuterTek hangar at LC-39a after encapsulation. I had a side conversation with him after one of the GOWG sessions and that led to getting dinner together to continue it, and we're still together a year and a half later."

Chang laughed. "How come I never met any cute girls while I was on active duty? I feel like I worked with nothing but old white and Asian dudes the whole time."

"I'm just lucky, I guess," DePresti said with a chuckle.

He spoke now, telling Chang about the launch.

"Was there anything odd about the processing campaign or launch sequence?" the former Space Force officer asked.

"Nope," DePresti said. "Some minor anomalies and whatnot during the launch but they all quickly resolved and adjudicated. We hit the insertion accuracy within three-sigma and everything was nominal on the coast to Venus."

"And when did you stop working the program?"

"After the launch service contract closed out," DePresti answered. "As soon as we paid out the last progress payment I PCA'ed across the street."

"And then you took over once they reached Venus," Chang said as he turned to Parkowski.

She took a sip from her water bottle. "Not exactly. When the ILIAD probe reached Venus' orbit I was still in training. There was a separate team, I believe the same team who built the spacecraft, but not the robotic probes, who did the separation of the relay satellite from the rest of the probe and then landed it on Venus. I stayed out of that as much as I could."

Parkowski took a breath. "Then, once they landed, the senior engineers like," she paused, "Dr. Pham," she paused again. Just saying his name made her feel awful, a sick feeling at the bottom of her stomach. "They did all of the initialization and checkout stuff for the two robots and ground support gear while we finished our training. Then, once the ACHILLES units were calibrated and ready to go, we - the junior engineers - started operating them."

Chang nodded.

She then went into a rapid-fire summary of the last two months, starting with her first mission in the virtual reality environment and encountering the simulated dragon. Parkowski then told Chang about all of the references to Bronze Knot showing up in the logs and inside of the environment itself. The man nodded, this was a familiar topic to him.

"And this is where I started bringing Mike in," she told Chang. "I asked him to start looking around on base for any references to Bronze Knot."

"Were there any?" he asked DePresti.

"Nope," the Space Force captain said. "At least, not right away."

She told Chang about the secure room down the hall from the high bay and her late-night break-in. Parkowski kept going, telling the rest of her story until she asked Dr. Pham just yesterday to meet up with her and DePresti and finally fess up about his involvement in Bronze Knot.

Chang put a hand up. "I'm going to go grab a beer," he told the other two. "Do either of you want anything?"

"No," DePresti and Parkowski both said.

He came back a moment later with a can of PBR. "Ok, keep going."

"Do you want me to take this part?" DePresti asked her.

She nodded.

DePresti told Chang about the pier, their escape, and then the two surprisingly brief car chases, one through El Segundo and the other through the outskirts of San Bernardino.

"Holy shit," Chang said once DePresti had finished. "And then you came here?"

"Yes," Parkowski said. "And we're not sure what to do next."

Chang sat up in his chair and took a sip of the beer. "Are you looking for advice then?"

Parkowski and DePresti both nodded affirmatively.

"Ok, so here's what I think is going on, and what we should do next."

CHAPTER THIRTY-ONE

Barstow, CA

Chang took another sip of beer.

"So, you two probably know this already, but you've stumbled onto something big. And bad."

"No shit," Parkowski said.

Chang nodded. "It has to be something like a faked Apollo mission, or the CIA killing JFK, or anything along those lines. The levels of security, the quick response to Grace's incursion into the secure room, we're dealing with either a high-functioning government agency or its private equivalent."

"What do you mean, high-functioning government agency?" Parkowski asked.

The short man laughed and pounded the rest of his beer. "Most of the government is beyond fucked-up. The majority of the federal government is a jobs program, first and foremost. Every single member agency of the intelligence community is absolute trash. However, there are smaller, less well-known government entities out there that do this kind of thing."

"What kind of thing?"

Chang laughed. "A lot of different things, actually, but what it really comes down to is secret keeping."

He threw his empty beer can away. "Information is power. It's always been the case, from the ancient Egyptian priests being able to predict the flooding of the Nile to the high-tech information warfare that took place during Operation Desert Storm. What did the U.S.-led coalition forces take out first? The tanks, planes, and guns? No, they went after Saddam's C2 structure, removing the Iraqi military's ability to receive reports from the field and give orders to their forces."

"What does that have to do with the U.S. government?" Parkowski asked.

"The U.S. government hoards information. Always has, always will, it's their best chance at staying a step ahead of everyone else, foreign and domestic. They hide that information in classification schemes, HIPAA laws, the Privacy Act, and more or less give themselves a monopoly on controlling that data." Chang paused to take a breath and then resumed his monologue. "But, what happens when someone not in the government gets a hold of a valuable piece of information? Something so important that would put the ability of the U.S. federal government to either rule its own citizens or present our image as the 'city on the hill,' the 'world policeman,' to the rest of the world in jeopardy."

"They have a problem," Parkowski answered quietly.

"Bingo," the former military officer said. "They have to get information supremacy back. That piece of data cannot be released free into the wild. It's why the intelligence community went so hard after Assange and Snowden."

"So who does it then?"

Chang laughed. "To be honest, I don't know for sure. But I know that organizations dedicated to removal - of both people, objects, and information - exist."

"How can something like that stay secret?" Parkowski asked. "That seems insane. Rogue U.S. hit squads going after private citizens sounds like something out of a dystopian novel."

"Let's go through your example that you and your boyfriend are living in right now," Chang said. "Yesterday, when you texted Dr. Pham and asked him for a meeting, that crossed a red line. Either you, he, or the two of you were under heavy surveillance because, shoot, I don't know, the Bronze Knot information would put a U.S. agent in China at risk or something. Make up your own story, the why isn't important, just the how." He cleared his throat. "So, when he agreed to the meeting, that triggered a response. Somewhere in some classified document there exists a flowchart that probably says something like 'if Bronze Knot information is to be exposed to non-BKT individuals do X, Y, and Z,' which in your case is to terminate both the potential leaker as well as the person being leaked to."

Parkowski's mouth hung open. "You're just making this up."

Chang opened his mouth to speak but DePresti responded for him. "No, he's not. I've heard of things too. Just rumors, sure, but I never believed them. Now, I think that some of them might be right."

"You're both crazy," Parkowski said. "The government just doesn't do that. It has to be someone else. The Russians or Chinese or some kind of mega-corporation, sure. But not the United States government."

They both shook their heads. "It happens, Grace," DePresti argued.

"Fine, whatever," she said. Parkowski still wasn't convinced.

Chang snickered. "That's some of the least crazy shit I've heard. Some guy who used to work NRO launches out of the Cape told me that some of the Apollo unmanned missions were cover for the Illuminati launching people in cryosleep to the far reaches of the solar system."

She shot him a look.

DePresti laughed.

"It's almost irrelevant who killed Pham and chased you here," Chang said, trying to change the subject. "Hell, it's almost irrelevant what's behind the Bronze Knot curtain."

Parkowski stared at him.

"What's really important is how to fight back," the short man finished.

"Oh, enlighten me, please," DePresti said. "I want to know how to fight back against an assassination squad."

Parkowski laughed, but deep down she agreed with her boyfriend.

Chang snorted. "Come on, you're an Academy puke, you had to have read the Art of War, right?"

"Read it, and believe it, or not I enjoyed it," DePresti responded. "Military strategic studies was one of the few classes I enjoyed outside of my engineering ones."

"I've read it too," Parkowski chimed in. "My dad recommended it to me when I started dealing with some Aering internal politics. I found it to be extremely helpful."

"Well, I'm going to butcher this quote, sorry Sun Tzu," Chang said, "but it goes something like the ultimate art of war is to subdue a superior enemy without fighting."

DePresti and Parkowski were confused.

"How can we beat an enemy, especially one with superior forces, intelligence, and experience?" Parkowski asked.

"Ok," Chang said, turning his chair around and sitting in it backwards facing them. "Let's go through a thought exercise. What do our opponents - whoever they might be - fear the most?"

"I think that's fairly obvious," Parkowski said quickly, looking over at DePresti who nodded. "They want to protect Bronze Knot at all costs."

"Precisely," Chang said. He turned to DePresti. "Are there more like her out there?"

DePresti ignored him. "So, they want to keep Bronze Knot and whatever is behind it a secret," he said. "I get that part. But how does that help us?"

"It's simple in concept, but the execution is going to be much more difficult," Chang said. "The two of you, with help from me now that you've dragged me into this, need to figure out what Bronze Knot is."

DePresti laughed. "Oh sure, we couldn't figure it out once Grace had physical access to the ILIAD networks and I was able to get on base to get into all of the SAP stuff, what makes you think we can do it now, on the run, with limited resources?"

"Well, before, you didn't have me," Chang said. "And Mike, you know me well enough by now, if there's something out there I can get my hands on it. I wouldn't say you have limited resources...just different."

"So what do we do, just hang out here and try to put our brains together to solve the mystery?" Parkowski asked.

"Maybe some of that," Chang said, "but we're going to have to move too. You can't be a fixed target."

"Are you sure that you want in?" DePresti asked him. "I mean, we kind of forced ourselves on you here. If you want us to leave, we can. Grace's shoulder isn't going to kill her."

"No, I'm in," Chang said firmly.

"So what is our next step?" Parkowski asked, hopeful that they might be finally taking the initiative from their mysterious enemies.

Chang held up a finger and then stepped out into the hallway. "Be right back," he said.

Moments later he reappeared, dragging a large whiteboard on wheels behind him. "We need to get all of our data points, all of our pieces of the puzzle, down on this. I'm an engineer like the two of you, even though I went to the far superior MIT rather than your respective trade schools, and if there's anything we like to do, it's write stuff down on chalkboards and whiteboards."

"Oh, man, I always wanted one," DePresti said as he stood up. "I think I need to get one now if this ever all blows over."

"*When* it all blows over," Chang corrected.

He went into his jeans pocket, fished out a dry-erase marker, and handed it to Parkowski. "Draw a line in the middle," he told her, "then on the right side I want the architecture for the entire ILIAD mission."

"The whole thing?" she asked as she got out of her chair.

Chang nodded. "The whole thing."

Pointing at the left side of the whiteboard, he said, "And here we'll put down all of the Bronze Knot data points that don't go on there."

Parkowski shrugged. "This sounds as good as any place to start."

It ended up taking them all morning. The ibuprofen had worn off so Parkowski popped some more.

The whiteboard was full.

The right side of the board had a diagram of how data flowed between the ACHILLES robots, the ILIAD relay satellite, the L2 relay, and MICS, down to White Sands to the environment hosted in Orlando and back to the mission control center in Aering's facility in El Segundo. The narrowband command path and wideband return path were both noted with arrows indicating direction.

The left side was a jumble of random notes and scribbles.

It was lunchtime. They ate quickly and went back down into Chang's office space.

Now, it was time to see if there were any weak points in the Bronze Knot chain.

CHAPTER THIRTY-TWO

Barstow, CA

An hour later, Parkowski stared at the whiteboard.

"Either they're all weak spots, or none of them are," she said. "I don't know how we can get back into Aering, Orlando's on the other side of the country, and I can't see us getting access to White Sands. All of them are bad options for our next step."

She needed another ibuprofen. Not just for her shoulder anymore. All of this made her head hurt.

DePresti held up a finger. "Can I add something to the diagram?" he asked.

"Go for it," Chang said. He had gotten another vape pen and was going to town. His eyes were red, and Parkowski figured he was pretty baked at this point.

The Space Force captain got up and grabbed a red marker. "We're missing part of the architecture," he said, "or at least how I've been taught to understand the architecture of an integrated system."

He drew a Shrike Heavy rocket on the side of the diagram where all of the Earth-based segments were located.

"The launch segment should be represented too," DePresti said. "It's not a part of the current architecture, sure, but it's necessary for the rest of the mission to happen."

Parkowski slowly got up.

"I'm going to get some more painkillers," she told the two men, "but first I want to add something too."

She drew a large oval on the diagram, then connected it to the hosted VR environment in Orlando and the Aering facility.

Inside of the oval she wrote "Panspermia Game Studios."

"They're the ones who created the whole environment," Parkowski told Chang and DePresti. "And they still have links to Aering. They're in LA County, even, located in Pasadena by JPL."

"How do you know that?" Chang asked. "The second part."

"Because when I was figuring out the dragon bullshit, Pham had a reachback to one of their developers," Parkowski explained. "Whoever he talked to confirmed that the dragon was accidentally compiled into the ILIAD environment and appeared by accident. Panspermia is likely still supporting the mission."

"If there even still is a mission," DePresti said. "I thought Rosen shut everything down."

"He did," Parkowski admitted. "But that doesn't change anything for us. If we want to have the power to get them to stop them from trying to kill us, we have to figure out what Bronze Knot is protecting." She took a short breath. "Come on, you guys are both acquisitions people. The contract with the prime isn't going to magically end just because an Aering senior engineer says it does. It will probably run through the end of the ILIAD mission in six months, plus probably another six months after that. They might not be as invested if we're not currently running missions in the environment, but they should still have some people supporting it."

He nodded. "Ok, makes sense."

Chang stood up. "So, which segment do we target first?" he asked.

DePresti pointed at the rocket he had recently drawn. "I vote OuterTek. I know them intimately, I spent years working in their facility, and I think we can get some information out of them that we won't out of any of the other players. The launch team has to know everything about the payload - RF frequencies that it's sensitive to, shock environments, software interfaces, et cetera. OuterTek maintains all of that information in huge databases that anyone with access to their internal networks can get into."

"And you can get into those networks?" Parkowski asked.

"Yes, but I think I can only do that from on-site," he answered. "My VPN access is no longer valid, but I've heard that they keep user accounts around for far longer than they have to."

"Not the worst idea in the world," Chang said, "but I've got a different solution."

He put his vape pen down and got up, then pointed to the NASA ground station at White Sands that handled the MICS terminal. "I've worked with NASA before and they are a bunch of idiots. All of them. Diversity and legacy hires with no idea how to do 'space' in the twenty-first century. Their security is probably atrocious."

"What are we going to learn there that we haven't already?" Parkowski argued. "I've seen the MICS logs."

"But I haven't," Chang said, "and I'd love to take a look at them."

"As would I," DePresti added.

Parkowski shook her head. "I think the first place to look is here," she said as she pointed at her own freshly-drawn oval. "Panspermia makes video games, they're not a defense contractor or government agency. They don't even have the word 'security' in their vocabulary."

"That...that actually makes a lot of sense," Chang said. "Nintendo got hacked just last year and the source code for a whole bunch of Pokémon games got released out into the wild. They apparently had a repository which was using an old version of version-control software that had an exploit already out and floating around. The software's developer had patched it, Nintendo just hadn't bothered to install the fix because they don't care about security. And that's *Nintendo*. I can't imagine Panspermia is much better."

"There's a history of video game companies being hacked," DePresti continued. "Valve, Microsoft, Sony, EA, Capcom, they've all been hacked in the last twenty years or so. I think the number of creative types there fosters a collaborative environment, which is good for development, but not much so for security."

"Sounds like a weak spot," Chang said.

Parkowski frowned. "But, do we need to go in person?"

DePresti tilted his head towards her. "What do you mean?"

"I think White Sands is out, at least for now," the Aering engineer replied. "That's a multi-day trip, and the other two locations are just a few hours away. But, you said we need to go in person to OuterTek. We don't to access Panspermia."

Chang smiled and rocked back and forth slowly. "I like how you think."

She turned to her boyfriend. "Can you get me into the OuterTek plant, or do I need to wait in the car?"

DePresti thought for a moment. "Shoot, I'm not sure if I can get you in," he said slowly. "Aering is part of the American Rocket Alliance, OuterTek's main competitor for government launch contracts, and I doubt they're just going to let you in. However, their Wi-Fi is notoriously open. I bet if you have a laptop in the parking lot you could get access. I'll write down the passwords and one of them should work."

Parkowski shrugged, a painful gesture with her injured shoulder. "Works for me."

"Great," Chang said as he clasped his hands together. "It's about four o'clock now, it'll take me the better part of today and tomorrow to get everything together. How about we spend tomorrow planning and making sure that we have everything ready, and then you two drive into Hawthorne bright and early?"

#

DePresti and Parkowski ate a quick dinner of Chang's leftovers, which were surprisingly good, while he made some phone calls. Chang came back while they were finishing up and doing the dishes in the dilapidated house's kitchen.

"So, good news first," he said while getting a frozen dinner out of the refrigerator. "I've got a guy who will come and fix up your car. He'll do all of the work here, no questions asked, as long as he's paid in cash."

"How much does he want?" DePresti asked.

"Thousand bucks for labor, plus parts," Chang replied. "I'll cover you until you can pay me back."

"Thanks," DePresti said with a smile.

"But that's going to take a while," Chang said. "Which is the bad news."

"How long?" Parkowski asked.

"Three to four weeks. Mostly for him to get all of the parts together."

"Damn," Parkowski said. "So if the Subaru is out of commission, how do we get back to the city?"

"I've got two trucks, you guys can take the Chevy," Chang responded. "It's older, and has a lot of miles on it, but works great."

"What about making sure no one comes looking for us?" Parkowski asked. "I've got a week of work before the plant shuts down for the holidays. Plus, if my parents don't hear from me in the next few days they're going to start to worry."

"I'll get a VOIP line set up via my Brazilian pirate satellite," he said. "You can make all of your calls through that. It's completely untraceable unless someone wants to pay a visit to a Sao Paulo ISP."

"Got it."

They changed Parkowski's bandage again, this time a little less painfully, and went to bed.

Parkowski slept well next to DePresti in the guest room downstairs.

The next morning she called in to work. "Rachel, I don't think I can come in today," she said when she finally got a hold of her friend.

"I heard about Dr. Pham and I just can't do it. I've been a wreck since I heard the news."

And then some, she thought.

"It's ok, I'm one of the only people here," Kim responded. "Dr. Rosen told those of us who came in about it. There's tape and plastic over everything, Grace, it's almost like they're going to shut us down for good."

"Did he say anything about that?" Parkowski asked.

"No, other than he said that the ACHILLES units were safe and he wasn't sure when we'd be on the sticks again."

"Copy. I don't know when I'm going to be coming back in, probably not before the Christmas shutdown."

"Got it. I'll let the leadership team here know. Is everything ok?"

"As good as it can be."

She then called her mother and told her she wouldn't be home for Thanksgiving. Her mom was surprised, and a little disappointed.

DePresti did the same with his commander and his parents.

They were now free of any commitments.

#

The next morning, they slept in, and then had a quiet brunch.

At noon, Chang brought them the Chevy's keys and a small bag, which had the flash drive and a pair of burner phones that he had been saving, as well as a pair of laptop bags and DePresti's map that he had bought at the gas station. "Keep them off the internet if you can," he explained. "They've never been connected to anything. The OuterTek network is fine, but don't do Starbucks or anything like that. They'll need to be wiped if they're connected to any public nets."

"Got it, thanks," Parkowski said.

He handed her a large, old-looking cell phone as well. "This is a satellite phone. Please try to use it as little as possible, I have to pay an arm and a leg every time a call is made."

"Got that too."

Chang nodded and went back inside the house.

Parkowski smiled and handed the keys to DePresti. "You drive."

CHAPTER THIRTY-THREE

Hawthorne, CA

The drive from Barstow back into the city was uneventful.

They didn't speak much. DePresti focused on the drive while she kept her head on a swivel. She was high alert for a tailing vehicle.

The two of them grabbed fast food for lunch and drove back through Los Angeles County towards El Segundo.

The OuterTek plant was just a few exits east on the 105 freeway from the area around the airport that contained both Los Angeles Space Force Base as well as the Aering plant.

Parkowski had never been to the huge, sprawling facility, but could easily tell where it was from the interstate. A giant, two-hundred-foot-plus rocket, looking more like a smokestack than a launch vehicle, loomed over the complex from its stand just outside the main building. It was the first Shrike 9 that OuterTek had launched and recovered on an autonomous barge off the coast of Florida. Rather than reuse it like they did their other rockets, their founder and CEO, an eccentric South African-born billionaire, had put it on display.

She couldn't figure out why it looked more like a smokestack than a rocket, but then it dawned on her - there was nothing on top! No capsule, no fairing, not even a nosecone. Nevertheless, it was an impressive feat of engineering. It had taken NASA and the might of the U.S. government years and billions of dollars to design, test, fly, land, and reuse the Space Shuttle orbiter; OuterTek had managed to do it in a fraction of the time and with a significantly smaller budget.

DePresti pulled off of the freeway onto Crenshaw Avenue, and Parkowski finally saw just how big the OuterTek facility was. On the left side of the road was a giant, ten-story parking garage, on the right side was the main OuterTek building, a former Southron Aerospace building that had been built and expanded until it was the size of a city block.

Sprawling out from the main building were a number of smaller ones, with tiny roads and paths between them. She knew from DePresti's description that those were mostly test facilities for things that couldn't be done in the main, office-like building, but others were office buildings that OuterTek had absorbed as it went from a startup to a ten thousand employee corporation.

There was no guard at the entrance to the parking garage. DePresti turned into it and started looking for a spot.

To both of their surprise, there were none to be found. The entire garage was full.

The reason for the filled garage was found on the ground floor of the concrete structure as they came back down a spiraled loop from the top floor. Over half of the lowest level was roped off as construction machines and workers scurried around.

"What's going on?" Parkowski asked, not expecting an answer.

DePresti smirked.

"One of OuterTek's sister companies, The Looping Company - originally part of OuterTek - does what they call 'hyperloops,'" he explained. "They're trying to build high-speed mass transit underneath urban areas. Think a Japanese bullet train but on a frictionless air bearing instead of on tracks. They're in theory building one starting here all of the way north to San Francisco, but to be honest, I think it's a boondoggle. They started back when I was at the Academy but haven't made much progress. Every once in a while The Looping Company puts out a press release on some new technology, or promise to link LA with Las Vegas or Denver, but to the best of my knowledge, no one has ever ridden on it."

Parkowski laughed too. "So what have they done?" she asked as he checked through the garage for a spot again. Every single one looked full.

"They did a small-scale prototype almost ten years ago," DePresti said, "that supposedly worked well. I think it went just over a kilometer. But nothing's happened since then." He sighed. "I don't think there are any spots."

"So what do we do?" Parkowski asked.

"Let me try something."

He drove out of the parking garage and stopped at the intersection between it and the main OuterTek building. "Get your Aering badge out," he told Parkowski.

"What?"

"Just do it."

Parkowski rolled her eyes and gave him the badge as DePresti drove across the street. Almost instantly a security guard on a golf cart drove up to their truck. "Excuse me, I need to see your identification," the nondescript white man in his forties asked.

DePresti handed over his OuterTek badge and Parkowski's Aering ID. "Here you go," he said.

The guard scrutinized them intensely.

"Does she have a green badge?" he asked the Space Force officer.

"No, I'll have to get her a red badge at the front desk. They know she's coming," DePresti lied.

The guard nodded and handed the ID cards back.

He pulled the golf cart aside so DePresti could drive through to the small parking lot in front of the main building.

DePresti looked for a visitor's parking spot but those, too, were all full.

"Well, hot damn," he said softly. "What do we do now?"

"Can you pull into one of the other spots, the ones with numbers on them?" Parkowski suggested.

"No, those are reserved for OuterTek big-wigs or VIPs coming to visit," he replied. "We can't park there." He looked at the clock.

"Actually, I take that back. It's almost three. They should be pretty much done for the day. I think we should be safe."

"You think?"

"It's better than going back to Barstow empty-handed," he argued.

"Fine," Parkowski said, pointing to a "4" on it. "Park there."

"Aye, aye," DePresti said sarcastically as he pulled in. He stopped the vehicle and took out a pen and notepad from his bag.

"What are you doing?" she asked.

"I'm writing down all of the different wireless passwords we used while I was spending time at OuterTek," DePresti explained as he jotted down a dozen phrases. "They cycled through about ten or twelve while I was working that program. Hopefully one of them will still work and you can get into their network. Make sure you pick the guest one - it'll get you access to all of the stuff you're looking for. And here," he continued as he wrote a few more lines below it, "is my username and password. They still work as of last week."

"And if none of this works?"

"Then hopefully I find something while I'm inside," he said as he opened the door to the truck. "If I'm not back by six, just take it and drive back to Andrew's. I can find my own way out of the city."

"Good luck," Parkowski said as she reached around with her good arm for her bag. She gave him a brief kiss.

DePresti stepped back as he attached his green OuterTek badge to his shirt. "Good luck to you as well."

Parkowski sighed as he walked off. She hated the feeling of losing control of the situation, but her boyfriend was right. She could do more good outside in the parking lot than inside of the massive complex.

Maybe the answer could be found inside the OuterTek networks. Thankfully, Chang had told her that it was ok to connect to them.

"We'll just have to put the laptops in the do-not-use category afterward," he had joked. "They'll be tainted."

She pulled out the year-old HP model from the bag. Time to get to work.

Parkowski booted it up and started looking for a wireless network to get on.

There were five to choose from. But, she remembered DePresti had said she wanted the "guest" one. She chose the one with "guest" in the name and was asked for a password.

Parkowski looked at the list that DePresti had given her and tried the first one, "The Red Planet," an obvious reference to Mars - the colonization of which was an obsession of OuterTek's founder.

It didn't work.

She sighed again and tried the second one, "Highway to Mars."

Same with the third one, "Fourth Rock from the Sun," and every other one on the list.

None of them worked.

I should have known as much, she thought, reaching into the bag for an energy bar and water. Remembering what video game was coming out next? That was something her boyfriend would have burned into his memory. Her birthday? Sure. But recollecting a Wi-Fi password he had used months ago was too much to ask.

Parkowski selected a different wireless network and went through the list of passwords again. And, again, none of them granted her access.

She tried the other three networks with the same result.

The Aering engineer rolled her eyes. What a waste of time, she thought. Hopefully, Mike would be more successful inside.

Parkowski ate her energy bar and a bag of grapes while she watched the company's employees file out of the building in groups of twos and threes before walking to their vehicles in the parking garage across the street. She tried all of the passwords on the "guest" network for a second time, but still, none of them worked.

Something nagged at her, though. A voice in the back of her head was telling her that she hadn't exhausted all of her options. But she had, hadn't she? She had been through every single permutation of passwords with networks. And none of them had worked.

She got the notepad back out and looked through them. DePresti's handwriting was strangely clear and easy to read - he might be the only engineer on the planet with good penmanship. Parkowski went down the list and checked for any typos or misread words, but there were none. None of them worked.

"Fuck," Parkowski said to herself, slamming the keyboard with her fist in frustration. She didn't like to feel helpless, but here she was, stuck in an old Chevy truck in the OuterTek parking lot.

Parkowski went through the list again. She had the feeling that something was wrong with the passwords - that DePresti hadn't remembered them correctly - but nothing jumped out at her as being incorrect.

She went line-by-line, word-by-word. Same thing. All twelve phrases were logical passwords for a space- and Mars-obsessed company to use.

Parkowski slammed the laptop closed. Nothing was going right.

Suddenly, she had a revelation, based on an experience that Parkowski had had her first week in Los Angeles.

Parkowski had been talking with Rachel Kim and another female Aering engineer over lunch in the Rayleigh cafeteria about her commute into work from her apartment in Marina del Rey down to the Aering plant south of LAX. She had described her route to the point where she got onto I-405 South, "the highway," as she had called it.

Kim and the other woman had quickly corrected her.

"Freeway," Kim had said. "In California, they are all 'freeways.'"

"What do you mean?" Parkowski had asked. "A highway is a highway."

"Unless it's in California, where it's called a freeway," the other engineer - whose name Parkowski couldn't remember - had said.

DePresti, like Parkowski, was from the East Coast and called an interstate a "highway."

OuterTek was located in Hawthorne, California. Where an interstate was called a *freeway*.

She grabbed the notepad and looked at the list. Where had she seen "highway?"

The second entry was "Highway to Mars."

Parkowski grabbed the pen and scribbled out "Highway." In its place, she wrote "Freeway."

She opened the laptop back up and selected the guest network.

"Freeway....to...Mars," Parkowski said to herself as she inputted it on the HP's keyboard.

It took a few minutes, but finally, at last she was connected to the wireless network.

"Yes!" she said as she pumped her fist into the air. Parkowski was in.

She opened up a browser window.

Bang!

There was a loud knock on the Silverado's door.

CHAPTER THIRTY-FOUR

Hawthorne, CA

Parkowski jumped. The laptop went a few inches into the air and then back down into her lap.

She put the laptop on the driver's seat and looked to see if DePresti was back from his site visit to the facility.

It wasn't him.

Instead, a harried-looking young Asian woman stood there, her arms crossed and an unhappy expression on her face.

Parkowski's heart raced with panic. Had the real reason for her boyfriend's visit to the OuterTek facility been discovered? She carefully rolled down the passenger's side window. "Can I help you?"

"I need you to move," the woman said, annoyed. "The lead singer of the band Muse is coming to visit our founder, and this is the spot that I told his driver to park in."

Parkowski blinked. "What?"

"You need to move your truck," the woman said. "Now."

The Aering engineer didn't want to cause any trouble. The last thing that she needed was for the other woman to call security.

"Fine, no problem," Parkowski said as she painfully switched seats over to the driver's side, her shoulder burning every step of the way. "Can I park in a visitor's spot?"

"Sure, whatever." The woman flipped her hair. "Just don't be here."

Parkowski nodded and turned the ignition. She had never driven a pickup truck before and now, with her bad shoulder, wasn't a good time to learn. But it wasn't as different from driving her little Camry as she had thought. She managed to back up out of the "4" spot, drive fifty feet closer to the small parking lot's entrance, and park in one of the now-empty visitor spots.

Satisfied, the woman turned on her heel and went back inside.

Parkowski exhaled. That could have been a lot worse.

She grabbed her laptop and got back onto the OuterTek guest network after having momentarily lost connection. Parkowski opened up the web browser first. She was greeted with the OuterTek internal splash screen - the browser was smart enough to take her automatically there.

There was a username and password location on the top right of the screen. She inputted DePresti's login information and was taken to a second screen showing his personalized homepage. Almost everything there had to do with the Shrike Heavy launch that took the ILIAD probe to Venus. It had been the twenty-first flight of the launch vehicle, so much of the data was abbreviated SH-21. The numbering and naming conventions took some getting used to, but Parkowski adapted quickly.

OuterTek used two main systems to track their software and hardware designs and data and to manage their agile approach to launch vehicle and satellite design.

The first was called Mosu, short for *Mosura*, the Japanese name for Mothra from the *Godzilla* movies. All of their engineering work was done in that tool via issue tracking and workflows.

The second was Sangam, a documentation tool from the developers of Mosu named after the Sanskrit word for a river confluence. All of the notes and evidence for engineering decisions were kept there. It was somewhat more locked down than Mosu, but DePresti's account still had limited access to it. It also had an integrated calendar that linked to the Microsoft Office suite and direct hooks into the Mosu database.

Thankfully, there was a wealth of data available to her. As a part of their government contracts, OuterTek had to provide almost all of their data to their customers. Then, the Space Force performed a pedigree review of that data and looked for errors or gaps that could impede mission success.

Parkowski of course knew none of this until she met and started dating DePresti, and now she knew more than she ever wanted to know. She never thought she would use any of it until now.

The first thing that she looked for was any obvious links to the program Bronze Knot or its trigraph BKT.

She searched for "Bronze Knot" and "BKT" in the search bar, looking for any indication that OuterTek was involved with that special access program. And, she did find one, but just one - a BKT Read-In on an executive-level calendar. More interestingly enough, that call-in had people from the CIA on the invite - their email addresses linked back to the agency's website.

The CIA again.

OuterTek was most definitely involved.

But why, she wondered, why would the launch company have to be read into a special access program protecting something about the ILIAD mission? They were just the ride to orbit, NASA took over once the probe separated from the second stage.

It probably had to do with the launch processing. Whatever was so special about the ILIAD probe or the ACHILLES robots that had to be protected at the highest levels, it was probably obvious to the OuterTek technicians and engineers installing the payload on the top of the payload attach fitting and then integrating the entire stack onto the rocket's second stage. Those people - and their management over them - would have to be read in so they could protect that secret.

That was a good place to start - the second stage and the PAF (payload attach fitting). Those parts would have the most contact with the ILIAD payload and the most likely location to contain a link to Bronze Knot.

Parkowski dug into the engineering database in Mosu.

The second stage and PAF were both common between the Shrike Heavy and the Shrike 9 single-core rocket. They had been flying with small modifications for hundreds of flights over the last fifteen to twenty years. There were gigabytes and gigabytes of data for those two assembly-level parts of the launch vehicle.

She filtered out everything except the SH-21 data. Everything looked nominal.

The post-launch data analysis looked great. The second stage had nailed the orbit insertion for the transplanetary path that would take the ILIAD probe to Venus. The three first stages had all been recovered. Everything looked as good as it could get, at least to Parkowski's level of understanding.

Prior to launch, OuterTek had delivered data packages on every part on the bill of materials (BOM) for the launch vehicle for review by Space Systems Command and the federally-funded Aerospace Corporation. The packages were standard, sterile, like they had put the information together and submitted them dozens of times before - which they had. This was normal.

Parkowski got out another water and took a sip. There was something here, there had to be; some clue as to what Bronze Knot was.

Or, maybe that was just wishful thinking on her part.

She went to the BOM itself inside of Sangam. It was the list of parts on the rocket itself, complete with part numbers and descriptions. It was DePresti's most-accessed file according to the OuterTek interface. Parkowski checked it carefully, nothing was out of the ordinary.

Just for fun, she compared it to the pre-launch acceptance test packages that OuterTek had given to the government for review. All of the part numbers matched and lined up, nothing was out of the ordinary.

On a hunch, she checked the post-flight reports.

Most of the reports for each of the second stage's main components were extremely detailed, down to the part number and qualification history. Some of the part numbers were different from what was in DePresti's BOM.

In fact, roughly a third of the pieces on the second stage and PAF - but not any of the three first-stage cores - were different from what was supposed to be on the launch vehicle.

And, they were big parts too: the fuel tank, the nozzle, all of the avionics parts. All of the smaller parts were correct, but the large ones were all different.

What did that mean?

OuterTek was notorious for replacing parts, even on the launch pad, and not informing their customer or even their upper management. DePresti had complained about it during the entire launch campaign. Was this just another case of that?

Parkowski was no launch expert. She would have to ask her boyfriend.

She switched to the Mosu tool and started poking around for those part numbers. Maybe she could find a work order or a ticket that explained why those parts had been replaced with different ones, or where the parts that were supposed to have been on the rocket had gone.

Her first few attempts got her nowhere. The system wasn't smart enough to filter out just those parts. The search feature was much less helpful than she had anticipated.

Gritting her teeth, she tried a different tactic - search by date. She checked the computer's calendar and found all of the work order tickets that had been created or closed out during the SH-21 launch campaign.

There were thousands and thousands. Too many to go through one by one.

She focused on those closest to the launch date. If OuterTek made a parts switch, it would have to be near the end, when the government oversight was the most overtaxed and exhausted from the long launch campaign. Likely, it would have been backdated and documented after the fact, so that no one from the government would catch it.

There were a number of tickets, numbered sequentially, with a "BK" header on them, from three days before launch.

BK.

Bronze Knot.

She had found the jackpot.

Parkowski dug in.

It appeared to her that several parts on the second stage were changed - all due to BK requirements. Bronze Knot requirements, but without the trigraph that would catch someone's suspicion.

The notes were straightforward, basic one-for-one swaps of small parts, not the large ones that were incorrect in the BOM. The instructions in the tickets told the next person on the workflow to update it in their internal part tracking system that fed the BOM.

The parts were small, sensors and thermistors and wiring harnesses and whatnot. But, all of them had tickets at the top stating that they were "BK," which to Parkowski had to mean Bronze Knot.

She was finding more questions than answers. The only thing she knew for sure was that OuterTek was definitely involved in Bronze Knot.

Maybe there was an updated BOM with all of the changes made? Or they had changed everything and just included some of the part swaps in Mosu.

Parkowski went back to the post-flight data. Sure enough, there was a BOM provided, but it had been updated with the changes made in the Mosu tickets. It still didn't match the pre-flight one though - the part numbers that she found in the post-flight reports were there in the post-flight BOM.

How could a rocket's parts change from processing to the post-flight data review?

She shook her head. None of it made sense.

Parkowski checked the clock - it was 4:30 PM - and went back to the post-flight reports. Maybe she could find something she had missed.

And, in a "propulsion performance" folder, she found it.

CHAPTER THIRTY-FIVE

Hawthorne, CA

Parkowski was curious how the rocket had actually done performance-wise on its mission. She had seen the executive-level summaries, how they had "nailed the bullseye" and whatnot, but as an engineer she wanted to see the raw data and analyses that had led everyone to conclude that the mission was a success. There were processed data in the post-flight report, but this was the raw, unfiltered data that had been used to produce the summaries

There was only one engine on the second stage, as opposed to nine on each first-stage booster, so there was significantly less data for it. But, in the folder with all of the engine data and analysis, there were two copies of everything. One set had raw data, spreadsheets, and charts had "DELIVERY" in all-caps before the real filename.

The other set did not.

Curious, she pulled up a chart deck with both the DELIVERY tag and the one without and compared the two.

The one that said DELIVERY was exactly like she had expected. The second stage had separated from the first and immediately did its first burn, getting on its transfer orbit for the Hohmann maneuver that would end with it on its interplanetary orbit to Venus. Then, once it reached the second planet, the second stage would burn again to reach an orbit around Venus before separating the payload and putting itself in a disposal orbit that would decay until it burned up in a few years in Venus' hellish atmosphere.

That one made sense.

What didn't make any sense was the other chart package.

It showed a completely different burn sequence, with much longer coasts and a longer mission duration than Parkowski remembered from when she followed the launch closely.

The data was there, in separate files, backing up that burn sequence as well.

Parkowski, once again, was no expert, but it looked like the second stage got to the same location from a distance-traveled perspective. But the number of burns, as well as their durations, were very different from those labeled DELIVERY.

She wasn't dumb.

OuterTek had delivered one set of data files and the associated chart packages to the Space Force.

And, in their internal records, kept another set for their own use. But why?

Parkowski had two possible answers.

One, OuterTek had taken a different route to the final destination for their second stage. Maybe they didn't get enough performance out of their first stage cores and had to use a different burn sequence to get the ILIAD probe to the right place by the correct date. She knew that there was a strict time requirement in the contract with penalties in place if they didn't make it. NASA - and Aering - needed as much time as possible with a short communications pathway with Venus for the VR controls of the ACHILLES units to work properly. It would be hard to hide that from the Space Force and NASA, but it was still possible.

The other option was something that had been sitting in the back of Parkowski's head. She hadn't found anything in her investigations at Aering and OuterTek to rule it out and she had found evidence to confirm it.

Her current running theory was that there was an extra payload added to the mission at the last minute. Something needed for the Space Force or the intelligence community or some other secret group within the government. A weapon, a sensor, whatever it was, it didn't matter to her, just that something was there.

That payload was put on right before the launch. All of the development of it, its concealment of it on the ILIAD mission, and all of the things that happened post-launch were hidden under the special access program Bronze Knot.

It was dropped off at some point along the path to Venus. Where it was placed, Parkowski wasn't sure, but once again, the actual location wasn't important, just that it was dropped off somewhere along the hyperbolic orbit to its final destination.

If her suspicions were correct, the payload even used the same communications pathway that the ACHILLES robots did back to the White Sands ground station; its narrowband and wideband packets intermixed with those of the mobile explorers that she had controlled from the Aering facility.

All of this secrecy, all of the subterfuge, all of the violence on the pier and the car chase through southern California, it all was to protect this payload if her theory was correct. Dr. Pham was killed to keep it a secret.

Whatever it was, it was worth killing for.

Parkowski took a deep breath. What the hell was it? She looked for some more information in the data delivery folders but couldn't find any.

Parkowski closed out of Mosu and Sangam. Then, she went to a different folder, the one containing all of the day-of-launch data and information, as well as all of the media content.

OuterTek launches were an event. Their webcasts were top-notch, with production values rivaling that of a cable news show. All of their launches, either out at the Cape or on the West Coast a few hours north of Parkowski at Vandenberg Space Force Base, were well attended. Each launch was captured on video on the live webcasts starting about half an hour before T-0 and ending when the satellite was either in the correct transfer orbit or its final orbit.

Parkowski had a suspicion that some more evidence supporting her theory could be found in this area. She wanted to see if there were any slips in the webcast as to the trajectory - she knew for a fact that the version she had seen contained the public, nominal one rather than the secret one that the launch company hadn't given to the government. OuterTek's security, as she had found, was surprisingly lax, and she assumed that the creative types that made up the company's public affairs and media types would be no different.

She was right.

Everything was accessible from the SH-21 media folder. Videos of the launch pad, webcast graphics, scripts, it was all there for her to poke through. Parkowski looked up to see if DePresti was coming back but there was still no sign of him.

The videos on the webcast were all exactly what she had expected. But, once again, Parkowski had a feeling that there was something here, a clue she just wasn't seeing yet. OuterTek was slick, but they weren't that slick. The "BK" notes in the Mosu tool were a huge security violation, but the launch service provider just didn't seem to care. If they were careless in their engineering documentation, she knew that their media people had to be even more so.

She started opening up the video files' properties, looking for some kind of connection to Bronze Knot or the parts switch, but again there were none.

Maybe the public relations people were smarter than she thought.

Parkowski switched to a view with an expanded list of properties and something jumped out at her.

Almost all of the video files were created on the same date: June 26, the same date as the launch.

But a small subset of them had *earlier* dates than that. They ranged from November of the previous year to the March before the ILIAD launch date.

She wrinkled her nose. That didn't make any sense.

Parkowski opened one of them up. It was an internal view of the second stage's fuel tank. The supercooled RP-1 glowed blue as it rippled inside of the large volume.

The video was hours long, with a T-count displayed on the bottom, overlaid over the footage from the camera located inside of the tank near the flow valve. Not much happened until the stage separation occurred. Then, Parkowski could see the fuel slowly flow out of the tank until the first burn was over. Small globules of RP-1 then floated around as the second stage coasted, waiting for the next burn of the engine.

In theory, this video should have taken place the same day in June as the launch. Instead, it showed a March date on the timestamp at the bottom right - the same one that was in the "last modified" field in the properties page in the directory.

Parkowski went back and checked the launch schedule. The date matched an OuterTek launch of a Kuwaiti communication satellite. The video was included in the webcast itself as the presenters switched between feeds inside and outside of the fairing with those from the fuel and LOx tanks.

Why would a video from another launch be included with those from the SH-21 webcast?

There were other videos that she flipped through. One was that of the payload stack, consisting of the two ACHILLES robots and their associated gear on top of the lander and the relay satellite, sitting on top of the PAF. Parkowski watched as they separated over a stormy, orange Venus as the lander sped towards the surface while the relay satellite drifted off into its synchronous orbit.

She checked the date. May 31.

That made no sense. It had taken the ILIAD probe months to get to Venus, but this video was from *before the mission even launched.*

There had to be some kind of mistake.

Parkowski changed tactics again and started flipping through the launch notes from the OuterTek mission manager.

Again, at first glance, nothing was out of the ordinary.

The OuterTek team had worked closely with the government and Aering on the launch campaign. Each day, at the end of the workday, they had an end-of-day meeting between the three parties to provide status and make sure that they were all on the same page. Her boyfriend's name appeared often as the GMIM, working between the Aering team both at the Cape and back in El Segundo and OuterTek.

She went through them temporally, working from the oldest to the newest.

Oddly, as they got closer to launch, the notes became less complex and informative, which was counterintuitive to Parkowski. She would have thought they would have had more issues, not fewer.

Then, she discovered another folder.

There had been an "executive level" meeting after the end-of-day status, one that DePresti hadn't been invited to. There were only a few participants, and the military members were higher ranking than him.

Those notes were sparse and full of acronyms that Parkowski wasn't familiar with. But in a document dated one day before the launch date, there was one that she had seen before.

BK.

Bronze Knot.

The meeting with that reference had notes that stated: "BK MAIN SERVER NODE MOVED TO NASA HANGAR AZ ON CAPE CANAVERAL SPACE FORCE STATION.

CONNECTION TO ORLANDO HAS BEEN ESTABLISHED."

The next day said. "ALL BK DATA CONSOLIDATED AT MAIN NODE."

That was a lot to unpack.

There was a main server node for the Bronze Knot program. It was likely built into the ILIAD communications pathway, if Parkowski's theory was correct, with all of the data for the ACHILLES robots flowing through it while the Bronze Knot data was either stripped out or filtered out for use by that compartmented program.

And it was located in a NASA hangar named Hangar AZ.

Parkowski knew that there were several hangars there at the main part of the sprawling facility, built for various missions over the years. She didn't know which one was AZ, but she had a general idea of where it was located.

Finally, it had a connection to "Orlando," which to Parkowski meant AFAMS, where the ILIAD environment was located.

A lot of pieces started to connect, but they needed to travel cross-country to Florida to solve the mystery.

She looked up at the clock. Five. One hour until DePresti had told her to leave if he wasn't back yet.

But there he was, walking out of the main OuterTek facility with a dejected look on his face.

"I hope you found something," he said as he got into the passenger's seat. "I completely struck out in there. They denied everything and didn't give me any information that I didn't already have."

"Well, I found some pretty interesting stuff," she said. "Let me tell you about them on the drive."

CHAPTER THIRTY-SIX

Hawthorne, CA

DePresti told his story first as Parkowski drove one-handed through the heavy rush hour traffic back towards their current home in Barstow.

"I got nowhere," he said, always coming back to that phrase. He was frustrated.

"What exactly happened?" Parkowski asked.

He told her what had gone on inside the plant.

DePresti had first tried to pump an old worker and fellow Academy grad, retired Colonel Harris Stein, for some information, but had failed. The man had stonewalled his every attempt for information, laughing at his suggestion that something classified was tied to the ILIAD mission.

He paused. Parkowski used the moment to take in their surroundings. They were on the 605 now going north. Traffic had been picking up slowly since they left and now was choking the roads.

Her boyfriend hadn't been paying much attention, so she took stock of the cars around them. None of them were suspicious. There was an old, maroon Dodge van a few cars back that seemed out of place but Parkowski ignored it for now.

Parkowski started to worry a little but kept quiet. It was only one vehicle, not a swarm of them. The level of danger was currently low.

DePresti continued. He had then sought out the Space Force uniformed plant representative, a fellow captain who was assigned to the Defense Contract Management Agency (DCMA), and asked if he could get into the OuterTek SCIF. To his surprise, the female DCMA officer agreed. She led DePresti into a SCIF, and there they had a brief discussion lasting about fifteen minutes. The plant rep had to go to a meeting so she had left DePresti by himself in the small, windowless room.

He had then tried what Parkowski had been able to do in the secure room at Aering. DePresti had successfully logged onto the internal classified network and poked around on their shared drive.

There, he had thought he had hit the jackpot. He had found a list of all of the different SAPs that OuterTek had people read into. Unfortunately, Bronze Knot was not one of them.

The female captain had then returned. Luckily for DePresti, she had inputted the door code incorrectly multiple times before typing it in correctly, giving him time to hide his activities.

Dejected, he had left the facility and walked out to Chang's Silverado empty-handed.

Parkowski didn't want to break him, but she knew that she had gotten a lot more out of the trip to OuterTek than he had.

She started with the battle to get onto the OuterTek network. DePresti almost slapped himself. "Sorry!" he said to her as they got back on the 105 going east. "I keep calling them highways."

"It's what they are," Parkowski said in agreement. "But it took a while to figure it out. I knew that one of them was wrong, but I had to work through them one by one."

She checked their surroundings again. The minivan was gone. Maybe she was just getting paranoid.

Parkowski then described how she had gotten into the Mosu and Sangam tools and how she had found the part differences between the launch vehicle that OuterTek had launched the ILIAD probe on and the one that the Space Force and Aerospace had done their pedigree review on.

DePresti didn't seem that surprised. "The only thing about it that sticks out is the number of parts, and the centralization of their locations," he told his girlfriend. "OuterTek pulls this shit all of the time with almost every single customer."

"The part swap?"

"Yeah, and normally someone in the LC-39a or SLC-40 hangars will catch them in the act, forcing a quick pedigree review of the new part," DePresti explained. "Sometimes it's to test out a new part or box, other times they realize they made a mistake somewhere and just don't want to own up to it. OuterTek would like us to be like their commercial contracts, where there's almost no mission assurance, but the Space Force and the NRO are never going to agree to it. Our payloads are too expensive and too critical to our national defense." He cleared his throat. "On the other hand, OuterTek has a vested interest in launching successfully, so really it's just a game."

"Got it," Parkowski said. She then explained the difference between the "DELIVERY" post-flight reports and the one without that modification.

This time, DePresti was stunned and a little stumped. "That makes no sense," he told her, "absolutely none at all."

"It's what I saw," she argued. "I pulled some of those files to the laptop, you can take a look in Barstow."

He scratched his head in thought. "I remember looking at the final burn and trajectory files, and there was nothing out of the ordinary."

She then told him about the trajectory change.

The Space Force captain sat up quickly. "There's no way," he said, "no fucking way."

"Why?"

"Because we used Space Force terrestrial and space-based tracking assets to track the ILIAD probe as it left Earth's gravitational well and went to Venus," DePresti said. "I remember because I had to beg, borrow, and steal resources to make it happen. They gave us all of their raw, metric data and none of it was anomalous. The second stage took *exactly* the trajectory we thought it would."

Unless they were in on it too, thought Parkowski, but she left that unsaid. She wanted to share her last piece of information before she told her boyfriend her theory.

She finished with her discovery of the "executive" post-day meeting and its associated notes, and the physical location of the Bronze Knot data node at Cape Canaveral.

To her surprise, DePresti knew about the higher-level summit.

"Col Hawke always went and then back-briefed us afterward," he told her. "They weren't hiding anything, or at least I didn't think they were."

"Well, they talked about Bronze Knot, or at least its data center location," Parkowski continued.

DePresti nodded, seemingly unsurprised by that revelation. "Do you think it's still there?"

"Yes," she confirmed. "And I think we need to go there."

She then told DePresti her theory as to the additional payload added to the SH-21 mission.

He didn't confirm or deny it.

"That's the most likely thing I've heard all day," her boyfriend told her. "OuterTek has been changing parts on rockets for ten years. Adding an additional satellite to the PAF - especially one blessed by the Space Force - wouldn't hurt my brain one bit." DePresti paused, then continued. "I was with the rocket the whole time. I was away from it maybe once, and my boss was there when it happened. It's unlikely, but possible. We just need to figure out exactly what it is."

"And then we do what?"

DePresti thought for half a minute.

"Then, if Andrew's theory is correct, we will hold all of the cards," he told her. "The government agency or private corporation that has been after us since Sunday will have to deal."

"And then hopefully this will all be over," Parkowski said, "and we can go back to our normal lives."

She got a series of nods from a tired-looking DePresti in response.

They were just outside Barstow now, near the turn to the road that would take them to Chang's compound. Parkowski noticed a couple of black Suburbans parked on the side of the road near a power line, but they looked deserted.

They looked like the same ones that had chased them just a few days ago.

She took a quick breath. "Do you see those?"

"Yes," DePresti confirmed.

"Should we keep going?"

"Yes," he repeated himself. "It's probably a coincidence. Chang would have called us via sat-phone if he had been in trouble."

Parkowski nodded and kept driving.

The sun was almost down now at the end of the short autumn day. She had to squint in what remained of its light to see the narrow, windy road out of Barstow.

When they got to Chang's house, his lifted truck was there in the carport.

Everything appeared to be normal.

She took a deep breath of relief and pulled up behind it.

CHAPTER THIRTY-SEVEN

Barstow, CA

Parkowski turned the truck off and carefully got out, grabbing her bags as she went. DePresti did the same on the other side.

He stopped and held up a hand as they walked towards the small house's front door. "Do you hear anything?"

She frowned. "No, why?"

"Exactly. It's too quiet."

The complex was almost entirely pitch-black now, save for the house's porch light.

The Aering engineer squinted and scanned her surroundings. Chang's place looked deserted, the animals she had seen the last few days were either asleep or hiding.

The homestead itself was surrounded on three sides by short, rounded hills that branched off of a larger formation that ran west-to-east outside of the city. Chang's land was nestled snugly between them.

The hills were topped by scraggly brush, a common theme in the Mojave. Parkowski could barely make out the outline of a few bushes and tumbleweeds in the dim light.

She walked to the door with DePresti in tow and tried the doorknob. Finding it unlocked, she turned and pushed it open, her boyfriend following closely behind her.

It didn't seem like anyone was home.

Parkowski felt a strange sensation on the back of her neck. The house was deadly silent. Chang was nowhere to be found.

She wrinkled her nose. There was an odd smell to the house that hadn't been there earlier, something pungent that was very different from the weed-and-air-freshener odor that normally permeated it.

DePresti didn't seem to notice it. He stepped forward and methodically searched each room for any sign of Chang.

"He's not here," she said as she crossed her arms and remained in the entryway. "If he was here, he'd come out to see us."

"Maybe he's downstairs," he suggested.

Parkowski wasn't so sure but really wasn't looking forward to the alternative. And she wasn't so sure that those black SUVs parked along the road were here for something else entirely.

DePresti knelt next to the hidden entryway to the space below, then removed the rug. The concealed metal door was locked. "How do you open the stupid thing again," he said to himself.

She didn't answer him. Instead, after finding the hidden switch disguised as a GFCI reset button, she pressed it.

"You haven't been paying attention, have you?" Parkowski said as the two of them heard the floor panel unlock.

"Apparently not."

They descended into the dark basement. Parkowski fumbled for a light switch and eventually found one. Flipping it on, she saw the long hallway that Chang had carefully planned his entire complex around.

There was still no sign of the former Space Force officer. All of the doors were closed and there were no sounds that would indicate that Chang was behind any of them. The smell of marijuana was strong, stronger than normal, but there was a hint of the odor in the upstairs as well.

"Shit," she said softly to herself. Parkowski had hoped that their friend was just hanging out in the hidden main level of the structure; high, drunk, or some combination of the two, and just had ignored their return.

They went room by room, looking for any sign of Chang, but there weren't any to be found. His room was in its normal untidy state with clothing askew on the floor and the bathroom looking like it hadn't been cleaned in months, if ever. The office looked like he had gotten up in the middle of something and just left. His main computer was still logged in, displaying a web browser with a dozen tabs open, the lights were all on, and a half-finished beer was next to the keyboard. A black handgun was on top of one of the other desks, safety off. Parkowski didn't check to see if it was loaded or not.

"I don't like this," Parkowski said quietly.

"Me either," her boyfriend agreed. "Let's keep checking. Maybe he fell asleep somewhere weird."

The other rooms were just as deserted as the last.

"I don't get it," Parkowski said to herself.

"Why would he leave without telling us? He had to have a pretty damn good reason," DePresti offered.

"Maybe he got robbed."

DePresti laughed. "He would have put a full magazine into them," he told her. "Did you see the pistol in his office?"

"I did."

"That's his favorite, a Glock 17. He always has one on him regardless if it's legal to carry or not. Andrew used to be on the Air Force competitive shooting team. He's really, really, good. If someone came here to rob his place, he would have mag-dumped and then hid the body. I didn't see any sign of a gunfight or any struggle, did you?"

"No," Parkowski admitted. "I get it. So what do we do now? Call him again"

"Let's go back up and look around again," DePresti suggested. "Maybe we missed something."

They went back up the stairs to the main level.

Parkowski made her own search now of the upper level while DePresti grabbed a soda out of the refrigerator.

In the bedroom she had spent her first night in, right under a slightly opened window, she found a cylinder roughly the size of a tall can of beer.

She didn't pick it up, instead squatting down to get a better look. Parkowski couldn't make out the color in the dim light. It had a small black protrusion at its top and a small silver handle along its side.

"Mike," Parkowski called out. "Come here and take a look at this."

DePresti entered the room a few seconds later. "What's up?"

"Do you know what this is?"

He squinted, then stepped back in shock. "Grace, get out of here!"

Her lizard brain, fight-or-flight reflex kicked in. Parkowski stood up and sped out of the room, followed by DePresti a moment later.

Nothing happened.

They stood, panting, for a minute in silence.

She yawned and turned to her boyfriend. "Care to explain why the fuck we just ran out of that room?"

DePresti frowned. "Grace, that's a grenade. It's going to explode."

"It doesn't look like a grenade."

He sighed. "It's a smoke grenade."

"Oh."

"And," he said, peering back into the bedroom, "it looks like it already went off."

"Why would there be a smoke grenade in Chang's house?"

"I'm not sure," DePresti said as he scratched his head, then yawned. "It's cold to the touch, so it's been here for a while."

"Is it his? Do you think he dropped it or it went off by accident?"

"I said, I don't know," he repeated.

Parkowski was tired - suddenly really, really tired. It had been a long day and her shoulder hurt. "I think I'm going to lie...down..." she said as she leaned on the bed.

Her boyfriend's eyes, which had also been closing in a fit of drowsiness, went wide again. "Fuck," DePresti said as he slowly stepped towards the still-open window. He tried to push the grenade - if that's what it was - out of it but failed.

She shook her head to wake herself out of the stupor she was mysteriously in and watched as he expelled the object out into the cold desert night.

"What the hell..." Parkowski said, her voice trailing off.

DePresti frowned. "I think that had some kind of incapacitating agent in it, not smoke for concealment."

"What?"

He tilted his head, then cracked his neck, trying to get out of whatever fugue he was in.

"It's a common trope in movies," DePresti began, "some kind of gas that can incapacitate people in seconds to minutes without killing them. In reality, that's supposed to be impossible - it can't work that quickly. But there are rumors that the intelligence community developed something that was fast-acting enough for a snatch-and-grab operation."

"And they used this grenade to put it into the house?"

He nodded. "Precisely."

"But why would they want to grab Chang?" Parkowski asked, keeping the "they" vague, and almost not wanting to know the answer.

DePresti shrugged. "Honestly, there's a ton of things, and not just related to what we're working on," he said carefully. "As you've probably figured out, he does some shady stuff here. I know for a fact that he buys drugs and weapons through less-than-legal methods, and he's also got some enemies within the government for his work in the Space Force. And on top of that, he's been looking into Bronze Knot stuff from here. And who, I have no idea either. It could be the same people who have been tracking us or it could be the FBI or someone else entirely."

Parkowski sighed. "Sorry, I know I've been asking you a lot of questions knowing that you don't have the answers."

DePresti smiled weakly. "It's ok. I'm worried now; it's becoming pretty obvious that he didn't go out for a walk."

"Same," she agreed. But Parkowski didn't like where this was going. She was tired, even without whatever lingering effect was still in the house from the grenade.

"I'm going to go grab a soda too," she told her boyfriend.

"Grab me another one too," DePresti asked.

Parkowski went into the small kitchen and took two Diet Cokes out of the refrigerator.

She snuck a peek out of the window over the sink.

The sun had completely set, but the full, bright moon was up over the desert. The rays from the sun bouncing off of the moon bathed the area in a silvery, almost ethereal glow.

As she opened her can of soda, Parkowski took in the hills surrounding Chang's complex again, just like she had before they had reentered the house. It was fascinating how well it fit into the natural surroundings.

The hairs on the back of her neck all stood up at once.

Some part of Parkowski's brain alerted her to danger.

But what was it?

The engineer listened for movement, some kind of danger outside of the ranch house.

It was eerily silent. The only sound was a slight breeze outside the open window in the bedroom down the hall.

She peered up at the ridgeline off in the distance. It was littered with brush and tumbleweeds.

Then, one of them moved.

That was normal, she thought. Tumbleweeds blew in the wind.

Then, as she watched in horror, a tumbleweed stood up.

Illuminated by the moonlight, Parkowski saw the figure of a person against the slightly lighter night sky behind them.

And they were carrying a weapon.

"Fuck."

CHAPTER THIRTY-EIGHT

Barstow, CA

"Mike!" Parkowski yelled as she ran from the kitchen into the hallway, spilling her Diet Coke onto the cheap laminate floor, "Mike, they're here!"

"What?" DePresti yelled from the living room.

"There's people outside. Up on the ridge."

"Shit," he said as he ran towards her.

"What do we do now?"

"Fuck, I don't know," DePresti replied quickly.

"How much time do you think we have?"

"Maybe ten minutes before they'll be at our front door."

This was not good. Parkowski thought for a moment. "Doesn't he have an entire arsenal downstairs?"

If whoever took Chang was going to storm the house again, they needed to be prepared.

He nodded. "He does. Let's go."

They hurried down the stairs. Parkowski opened the handle on the large metal door and swung it open. The room beyond was small, maybe twice as large as the bathroom back in Parkowski's apartment.

But it had exactly what DePresti and Parkowski needed. Weapons were everywhere.

It was a gun-lover's paradise.

Most surprising to Parkowski was how clean and organized Chang's arsenal was. Despite his careful planning of his complex, he was a slovenly man. However, he kept the most important things to him - his guns and his computer setup - meticulously clean.

DePresti swooped like a bird from weapon to weapon.

"Who are they?" Parkowski asked.

He didn't answer. Instead, he grabbed a long black rifle off of the rack on the wall and tossed it to Parkowski. "Here, catch."

She grabbed it by its three-point strap.

"What is this?" Parkowski asked.

He laughed. "To be honest, I don't know what it is exactly," he told her, "but it's some kind of AR-15."

Parkowski looked at it in shock. She had held a weapon once in her entire life, on a skeet-shooting trip in high school. Now, the rifle was going to be crucial to her survival.

She checked the rifle. The weapon was seemingly unloaded - there was no magazine inserted into it - but she still treated it like it had a round chambered, pointing it at the ground and away from her.

DePresti grabbed a rifle off of the wall that looked like a twin to Parkowski's and set it down. Then, he took a second rifle, a longer bolt-action one with a large optic on its top, and set it down next to the first one.

"That should do," he said to himself.

"Great, we have weapons now," Parkowski said. "What about some ammunition for them?"

DePresti frowned. "You haven't seen any yet?"

"Just a couple of boxes of...nine millimeter, plus a few loose rounds," she responded.

"Fuck."

"Yup."

"Any magazines?"

"No, none of those either."

"Huh," DePresti said, confused. "There's no way that Chang doesn't have a whole bunch of loaded mags ready in case of trouble."

"Well, if they're here, I don't see them," Parkowski said, a little frustrated. "Where could they be?"

Her boyfriend knelt beside her and they quickly went cabinet by cabinet. No magazines of any kind, rifle or pistol, could be found. "Fuck," DePresti said quietly.

They were running out of time.

"I'm going to go check his room," he said as he got up. "I'll be back in a sec."

Parkowski kept looking. Something was weird about the cabinets, she thought.

She took a step back to look at them.

They were metal, with wooden tops; probably a custom design. There had to be something in there.

Parkowski picked one of the cabinets at random and took a good glance at it. There were two rectangular drawers, a smaller one at the top, and a larger one at the bottom roughly twice the size of the top.

The top contained tools; screwdrivers, wrenches, the normal things that one would find in a workshop.

The bottom had a collection of spare stocks for AR-15 style rifles.

Parkowski closed both drawers and stared at the bottom one. It was wrong, but she couldn't figure out why.

Then it clicked.

The interior of the drawer was half the size of the exterior.

Parkowski opened it back up and felt around for a way to open up the apparently false bottom.

At the back, she found a pair of plastic tabs that had previously gone unnoticed. She pressed them together and heard a click. Parkowski used the tabs to lift the false bottom out of the drawer and peered into the cavity below.

Inside were a horde of neatly stacked AR-15 magazines.

She grinned for the first time since they had arrived back at the complex.

"Mike," she called, "I found them."

He came back into the room with a pair of civilian-grade night vision goggles (NVGs). "Found what?"

Two minutes later, they had a duffel bag full of magazines for their AR-15s, DePresti's bolt-action long rifle, and a pair of Beretta pistols that they had selected from the cabinets.

"Are you sure this is all necessary?" she asked her boyfriend. "Maybe they'll get bored and leave. I bet they didn't even see us."

DePresti snorted. "There's no way they missed us showing up in Andrew's truck," he told her. "No, they're going to try and grab us too."

He didn't elaborate, but he didn't have to.

After watching her mentor be gunned down on the Manhattan Beach pier just a few days ago, Parkowski knew what would happen if they were caught.

DePresti quickly showed her how to use the rifle. He cleared the chamber - it was empty - and then helped her insert a magazine and pull the charging handle back to load the first round. She put the stock on her good shoulder and aimed it at the ground, making sure the safety was on.

He then put one of the NVGs on her head. "They're already configured," DePresti told her. "Just pull them down when we get upstairs."

Her heart beat a little faster. She might not be overthinking it after all.

He slung the bolt-action rifle on his back and picked up his own assault rifle. "Ready?" DePresti asked as he grabbed the duffel bag.

"Ready," Parkowski responded. But she wasn't - how could she be? She was no soldier, no warrior. But her life was at stake. And she only saw one way out of this.

"Ok, here goes nothing," her boyfriend said with an obviously false sense of bravado.

Parkowski followed him out of the armory and up the stairs.

Right before they reached the top, DePresti stopped and turned to her. "Take these, I almost forgot," he said as he handed her something small. It was a pair of earplugs.

"You're going to want them," he promised.

Parkowski shrugged and put them into her pocket.

They had only been in the basement for eight minutes. The main level was just as dark and quiet as it had been before they had armed themselves.

She slipped to the kitchen and looked out the window at the ridge beyond as her boyfriend checked the front of the house.

The moon was a little higher in the sky, but the rest of the desert landscape, or what she could make out in the limited light, looked the same.

Parkowski peered at the ridgeline. The same bushes were there, or at least she thought they were. She heard a loud cracking sound - almost like someone snapping a large branch in two - coming from the ridgeline and then echoed off of the hills below.

The window spider-webbed.

And a large-caliber bullet slammed into the wall behind her.

CHAPTER THIRTY-NINE

Barstow, CA

Parkowski dove towards the cheap tile floor.

She cursed as her rifle slammed into the ground first, followed by her hands and knees. A searing pain shot through her injured shoulder as time slowed down, much like it had on the highway. Parkowski rolled towards the refrigerator as she heard another *crack* of a supersonic bullet.

The glass broke again, this time in a different place, shattering it and littering the kitchen with fragments.

DePresti sprinted into the kitchen and knelt in front of the dishwasher to the left of the sink.

He pointed at his ears.

She gave him a blank look.

DePresti shrugged, pulled his NVGs down, from the top of his head to his face, and readied his assault rifle. He carefully and deliberately swept the muzzle up to the window.

He then aimed and fired three times.

Boom, boom, boom.

The report reverberated through the small kitchen.

Parkowski's ears burned. The noise hadn't shattered her eardrums, but they hurt like hell. She dug the earplugs out of her pocket and jammed them into her ears.

DePresti ducked, then popped back up and fired another couple of rounds.

This time, it was more of a dull roar, but still loud even with the protection.

She crawled on her hands and knees, rifle dangling precariously under her, to her boyfriend.

He didn't speak but breathed heavily. She saw his chest heave up and down in the dim moonlight.

Parkowski tilted her head slightly, as if to ask a question, but didn't say anything either. She probably could yell and get through to him, but she didn't want to make any noise that would give away their position.

DePresti pantomimed his most recent action - firing into the ridge - and then pointed at Parkowski and finally at the entryway.

She understood. Her boyfriend wanted her to cover the front of the house.

Parkowski painfully crawled out of the kitchen into the entryway.

There were three rooms located on that side of the house: one of the two smaller bedrooms, the master bedroom at the far end of the house, and the living room at the other end.

Parkowski chose the living room.

It had a large window overlooking the carport and sweeping driveway, the one direction not protected by the hills and ridges. There was less moonlight on this side of the house, and Parkowski could barely make out the road.

In a brief moment of calmness in between those of pure terror, she noticed that between the house and the road were a number of boulders and mounds, some natural, others created by the dirt removed when Chang had dug out his underground lair. She figured that if their unseen assailants were coming towards them, they would use those for cover.

Parkowski got up, ran towards the window, and slid down to the left side.

A pair of bullets streaked into the house from the window, leaving dime-sized holes. They both impacted the old couch on the far side of the room.

She quickly put her NVGs on. They made the world a fuzzy green; giving her the perception that everything she saw had a slight glow around it. Then, she peeked out of the window.

Behind one of the boulders, over a football field away, she saw a hint of movement.

Parkowski used her thumb to move the rifle's safety to the "single" position.

Placing its butt against her good shoulder, she leaned out to the window and put her eye against the rifle's optic.

Whatever had been there was gone.

Parkowski was about to pull back when she saw a dark figure lean out of the boulder's right side.

She moved the rifle so that the crosshair was right over it and fired.

Big mistake.

The Aering engineer had forgotten that the glass was mostly still there.

It shattered, blowing shards everywhere, including one back into the rifle's scope.

The spent piece of brass bounced on the worn hardwood floor.

"Shit," she said. Parkowski leaned back to check her rifle's optic as a hail of bullets slammed into the house.

Thankfully, the walls were thick enough to stop any from penetrating through them.

The rest shredded Chang's couch.

Her scope was fine. A piece of glass had gotten into it, but she deftly removed it and threw it on the floor.

Parkowski leaned back and fired, almost blindly, into the night.

One, two, three, four trigger pulls.

One, two, three, four rounds went out towards the boulder.

The first was fairly accurate.

The next three went wild, all high.

Parkowski leaned back as the assailants - there had to be more than one - returned fire.

Even with her earplugs in, she could hear the supersonic bullets slam into the house.

Only a few pieces of glass remained in the corners, the rest of the window completely obliterated. The rest had been shot out by her opponents.

She was no firearm expert, but the people outside - whoever they were - seemed to be firing different weapons than the submachine guns in the frantic chase from Los Angeles to Barstow. From their description, Chang had told her that their weapon of choice was a Heckler and Koch MP-5 submachine gun, firing a 9 mm round that matched her shoulder wound, with a distinct chatter. The rounds being fired at her now were larger, with a louder report, probably from a rifle not unlike her own.

Did that mean that they were with a different organization?

Or did it mean that they were experts, who had selected a different weapon with increased range?

Parkowski did some mental math. There were thirty rounds in the magazine to start, and she had expended five. That left twenty-five before she had to reload.

But she realized she had been trying to do too much. Parkowski had neglected to grab an extra magazine from the duffel bag.

She took a deep breath and poked her head around the edge of the window, just enough to see the expanse between the road and the house.

This time, she didn't see anything.

As she pulled her head back, another hail of bullets slammed into the house, most just above where her crouched body was.

They had night vision - or even worse, thermal - goggles too.

"Fuck," Parkowski said.

Another coordinated volley came in from the boulders.

She wasn't sure what their endgame was. They hadn't made any attempt to communicate, to ask for their surrender. They had just started shooting when she appeared in the window with her rifle.

Parkowski became hyper-aware of a different sound, a lower, harsher crack close to her position.

Her boyfriend had switched weapons.

She leaned out and fired another pair of bullets in the vague direction of her assailants, then leaned back to safety.

Just what were they trying to do?

Her heart beat faster than it ever had before. One wrong move, one miscalculation, and she would die under a hail of bullets fired by people much more skilled than her.

Parkowski wished more than anything she could talk with her boyfriend. DePresti was an acquisition officer, an engineer - the farthest thing from a combat expert - but his time in the military had rubbed off on him. Whatever basic combat training he had experienced was definitely paying off. He seemed cool, collected, and ready to defend the house. But, they hadn't figured out any method to communicate once the bullets started flying.

They hadn't had time.

There was a strange lull, a pause in the response by their enemy.

She wasn't sure why.

Parkowski poked her head out, kept it there.

No response.

She leaned back. "Mike!" she screamed, barely able to hear the sound of her own voice through her earplugs.

A moment later he appeared next to her.

DePresti's face was bloody, but he looked coherent and his hazel eyes were locked in.

"What happened?" Parkowski asked as she carefully took a fingernail-sized shard of glass out of his cheek.

"Window exploded into me," DePresti said loudly. "I'm fine, it missed my eyes."

"What are they doing?" she questioned.

The Space Force captain shrugged. "I honestly have no idea. If I were them, I'd coordinate my assault so that one group can advance while the other pins us down, then repeat the process. I don't know what their end game is."

"Me either," Parkowski said. "Do they want to capture us, or do they want us dead?"

DePresti shrugged. He handed her a pair of magazines. "Use these wisely."

Parkowski smiled and accepted them.

Her boyfriend smiled back, his teeth glistening in the dim light, and went back to the kitchen.

She poked her head out again and this time she was met with a new round of bullets. There were fewer, but they came from a different direction, near where the hills that surrounded the complex started their rise. They were also now visible to her; white lines tracing across the black sky.

The bastards had repositioned.

Parkowski swore to herself and carefully crawled underneath the window to a new position in the corner. If they were to move slightly more up the rise, they could reach her through the window on the next wall.

Something big - probably a large caliber bullet - hit the back of the house.

"They moved!" DePresti yelled, barely audible.

"I know!" Parkowski screamed back.

Her repositioning saved her. Another bullet hit the spot she had been crouched in a moment ago.

"Fuck fuck fuck," she said to herself.

There was a silver lining, though. Her assailants were now using tracer rounds. She knew exactly where they were.

Parkowski switched her rifle to her bad shoulder - the adrenaline pumping through her dulled the pain - and leaned out in the opposite direction she had previously.

She fired a dozen rounds.

The AR-15 jammed.

"Shit." She opened the bolt and tried to get the stuck casing out of it.

A new noise - a dull thud - came from just inside the window.

Parkowski looked up in horror to see a cylindrical grenade, the same as the one that had been used to incapacitate Chang, lying on the floor.

Even in the fog of the NVGs, she could make out a small stream of smoke escaping from it.

CHAPTER FORTY

Barstow, CA

Parkowski threw her rifle onto the ground and dove to the grenade. A familiar pain spread from her shoulder to her back as she crashed down next to it. She groaned as the rest of her body followed onto the wooden floor.

Grabbing the grenade with her good hand, she rolled slightly. It was hot, not hot enough to burn her hand, but definitely increasing in temperature. Like she had thrown the scuba tank out of DePresti's Subaru, she aimed an arc out of the house's window and threw the grenade out of it.

Parkowski felt slightly sleepy, just like she had earlier in the bedroom, but that quickly passed.

It was another incapacitating grenade. That answered her earlier question to DePresti. They were trying to capture them like they had Chang.

The problem was that they hadn't gotten the drop on them like they had their friend.

"Mike!" she screamed as she crawled on her hands and knees back to her still-jammed rifle. "Mike!"

"What?"

"They're trying to grab us too!"

"What?"

A torrent of bullets, tightly grouped, slammed into the window on the side of the house, littering her new cover spot with fresh glass shards.

"A grenade, like the other one we found," she finally got out.

"Did you give it back to them?"

Parkowski didn't respond at first. She almost had the stuck brass out of the ejection port. "Yes!" she yelled as the enemy outside began a new tactic. They fired a shot every few seconds, coordinated between at least two or three shooters. She wouldn't be able to poke her head out to fire like she had been doing.

The Aering engineer finally worked the stuck shell out of her rifle.

She took a breath and removed the spent magazine, then inserted one that DePresti had given her.

Did they get close enough to throw the grenade? Or was it propelled from some kind of grenade launcher?

"Mike!" she yelled again.

"What?"

"Cover me."

Parkowski heard rustling from the other side of the wall that the living room shared with the kitchen.

DePresti had repositioned.

She heard the long bolt rifle boom, again, and again, and again, in a rhythmic beat.

"I hit one! I hit one!" DePresti screamed in celebration.

"What?"

"I hit one on the arm," he said, soft enough that Parkowski could barely hear him.

"Good job," she said, not loud enough for him to hear, as she pulled the charging handle back to chamber a round.

The coordinated fire had stopped.

Parkowski poked her head out of the newly shattered window.

They were close now, maybe a hundred feet away. She could make out three, no, four different shooters; likely a separate team than the one on the ridge.

She had a fleeting thought. This was supposed to be a highly trained team, government or otherwise, coming to extract her and DePresti and take them wherever the hell they had taken Chang. But, their tactics were weak and easily countered by the inexperienced pair in Chang's house. Granted, they had a proverbial arsenal available to them and had a strategic advantage in position, but they had already held out for a ten-minute firefight.

That shouldn't be possible.

Parkowski shouldered her rifle again and fired a pair of rounds at the indistinct figures at the nearby boulders.

She was met by a return of coordinated fire.

They were using different weapons now, and if her dulled hearing could be believed, they were the MP-5 submachine guns that the men and women in the SUVs on the way out to Barstow, as well as the ones on the pier, had used.

Parkowski snuck a peek out and confirmed visually through the hazy green light of her NVGs. She saw a man with an MP-5 with a long, distinct banana-shaped clip run from one boulder to a small rise on the hill surrounding the complex just twenty yards from the house.

Well, that confirmed it. All three groups were related, if not the same. But, who were they?

She fired again, and again, and again.

Her shoulder burned with a white-hot pain, as intense as anything she had ever felt.

This time there was no response. Were they trying for another grenade attack? No, Parkowski thought quickly, they wouldn't.

The windows of the house had all been shot out, at least on two sides.

The incapacitating gas would just leak out and leave DePresti and Parkowski slightly woozy at the worst.

She understood why DePresti had described it as he had, as an urban legend rather than something used on a day-to-day basis. It was hard to get enough of the knockout agent together in a large volume to cause that kind of impact on a person's nervous system.

But, what did that mean?

Then it dawned on her. That's why they were moving in. They were going to try to pin them down and then sneak into the house and grab them while they were otherwise occupied.

Shit.

Parkowski fired twice, then got back down on her hands and knees and crawled back under the window towards the entryway and the front door, holding her one extra magazine in her hand.

She made it to the other side, and then pulled her right earplug out.

There was a rustling noise outside.

Parkowski put the barrel of the rifle out of the window and blind-fired in the direction of the sound and then pulled it quickly back.

No bullets came back in response.

She was about to call out to DePresti when the door slammed back into her.

Her night vision goggles slipped off of the top of her head.

Parkowski dropped her rifle and staggered back.

A dark figure rushed through the entryway and crashed into her.

They tumbled together towards the cheap, old wooden floor.

Parkowski struggled against the invader, who was definitely more skilled in hand-to-hand combat than she was.

She - Parkowski instantly realized she was a woman - expertly grabbed Parkowski's good arm and twisted it to the side.

It hurt like hell.

Parkowski had no advantage, no strategic edge, and no training.

The only thing she had was her rage and will to survive.

She fought like a tiger, rolling with the assailant's twist and surprising the woman into letting go of her grip slightly.

Parkowski went on the offensive.

She brought her left arm - her bad one - back and hit the woman square in the face

It was an error. Parkowski's arm was too weak, too damaged by the bullet passing through it just a few days ago. She gave the woman a weak blow, hitting her just below her eye.

Her opponent grabbed her arm and twisted this one now, putting her whole weight into it as she rolled away towards the living room.

Parkowski cried out in pain.

The other woman started to pull her left arm to Parkowski's back.

She was going to try to handcuff or otherwise disable her arms.

What could she do?

The assault rifle was four feet away, just out of reach. But, her right hand could feel the dropped extra magazine. It was plastic, but it was better than nothing.

Parkowski wriggled her right arm free and slammed the magazine into the woman's head, right on her ear.

She felt the grip slack off again.

Parkowski hit her again, then rolled away towards the interior of the house.

DePresti was still firing. It hurt her ears, but that was a good sign. He hadn't been captured yet.

The woman sprang to her feet.

Parkowski did the same.

They squared off, the other individual in some kind of martial arts stance, Parkowski in what she thought a boxer looked like.

The woman started circling to her left, barely visible in the scarce moonlight.

Parkowski matched her step for step.

Her opponent tensed for a strike.

Then, through her unplugged ear, Parkowski heard a strange high-pitched whistle.

The other woman heard it too.

She looked right at Parkowski, although the Aering engineer couldn't make out her features in the darkness, and then dove through the broken window to the cold desert outside.

Parkowski stood there in shock.

Then she remembered she was in the middle of a running gun battle.

DePresti had gone back to the assault rifle, its thunderous report echoing throughout the old house.

She grabbed her rifle and plastered her body against the wall, then used her foot to move her NVGs close enough for her to pick up and put back on.

Parkowski peered outside of the front window.

There was movement, but it was further back to where she had first shot at the oncoming enemies.

She fired a couple of shots and paused, waiting for a violent response.

None came.

Parkowski peeked out again, this time catching the indistinct form of a person against a large boulder just at the start of the hill.

She raised the scope to her eye, aimed the crosshair at the figure, and fired.

Parkowski never expected it to hit. It did.

She had aimed at the person's body but caught them in their left leg.

The enemy figure fell to the ground. Another figure, smaller, perhaps the woman she had fought, appeared over them.

Parkowski fired one, two, three, four, five times.

All of them went wild.

The second shooter pulled the one Parkowski had shot behind the boulder.

She ducked back, then fired again until the magazine ran out.

No shots came from the distance.

A few seconds later, Parkowski heard DePresti's rifle go silent. She put her own down and carefully crept to the kitchen. Her boyfriend was surrounded by a horde of spent brass, glistening in the moonlight from the shattered window.

DePresti looked exhausted. He grabbed his night-vision goggles and put them on the counter.

"Are they gone?" Parkowski asked.

He nodded. "For now."

CHAPTER FORTY-ONE

Barstow, CA

Amazingly, the firefight had only lasted an hour. But it had been an exhausting sixty minutes.

As soon as they confirmed that the mysterious enemy team of gunmen had gone, Parkowski relaxed slightly. The adrenaline had worn off. Parkowski's injured arm hurt like hell. It had felt better over the course of the day, but firing the rifle and getting into hand-to-hand combat had aggravated it.

She dug around in Chang's bathroom downstairs and found some prescription painkillers. Parkowski had to be careful - there were a lot of drugs in the cabinet, including some hallucinogens - but the oxycontin was clearly labeled. She popped a pair and knocked them down with a sip of water.

DePresti stayed up top, alternating between checking out the front of the house and the rear, but it appeared their opponents had departed the area.

They slept in shifts.

Parkowski took the first one, sleeping in the bed she had slept in that first night, while DePresti kept watch.

He woke her up at midnight. "I hate disturbing your sleep, but I'm about to pass out on the job."

"It's ok," she responded as she slid out of the covers and off the bed. "Go get some rest."

"Thanks," he said as he got in.

Parkowski grabbed his AR-15 and went to the kitchen. She got out a Diet Coke - one of the last ones - and opened it. The caffeine helped. Ten minutes later she felt fine.

Both sets of night vision goggles had run out of batteries. They could go look for more in the basement, but the threat seemed to have passed.

The moon was fully overhead now. Her eyes adjusted quickly. The desert night was devoid of movement.

She sighed and sat down in a chair. The painkillers made her slightly loopy. Hopefully, there wouldn't be another attack.

After a few minutes of sitting, Parkowski stood back up and walked to the front of the house. She now noticed that all of the windows were shattered, not just the two she had been standing near when they were shot out. Brass from her rifle littered the ground.

Interestingly, there were no footprints from her opponent in the brief hand-to-hand skirmish.

Parkowski carefully walked through the living room, taking in the scenery outside. It was still.

Deathly still.

She spent the next hour or so switching back and forth between the rear of the house and the front, looking for any signs of movement on the ridge or on the flat plain between the road and the house.

There were none.

Parkowski woke DePresti up at 3. "Ding, dong, your turn," she told her boyfriend.

He groaned. "I was sleeping so well too."

She handed him the rifle, climbed back into bed, and quickly fell back asleep.

Parkowski dreamed; the contents of which she forgot moments after she woke up. But what was important was a sensation of warmth, of heat, on the side of her face.

She blinked her eyes open.

The sun was coming up over the hills, warming her face and spreading its rays through the broken window.

Parkowski rolled out of bed.

She was sore, stiff, and exhausted.

DePresti was in the kitchen, drinking the very last Diet Coke.

"Mornin'," he said in an exaggerated accent as the Aering engineer slowly made her way in.

"Anything exciting happen?" she asked as she took a seat.

He shook his head. "No, I would have woken you up if it had."

"What do we do next?"

DePresti had seemingly thought this through. "Let's go check outside. See if they left anything behind."

They quickly ate what little food was left in Chang's upper kitchen and went down to the lower level. Parkowski grabbed an Israeli-made Uzi, while DePresti grabbed a couple more magazines for his AR-15. The two of them then headed back up the stairs and out the front door into the cold desert morning. She wished she had brought a jacket.

Parkowski and DePresti walked out towards the road in the direction of the boulders that her opponents in the gun battle had taken cover behind.

She had an odd thought. How could they have been shot at for over thirty minutes, with their opponents expending hundreds if not thousands of rounds, and neither she nor DePresti were hit once?

She knew that they were trying to capture them, not kill them, but the odds of neither of them getting hit had to be astronomically low.

Even more shocking was the complete lack of brass around the boulders.

"There's no way," Parkowski told her boyfriend. "I watched them fire at me from this spot," she continued, pointing at the rear of a large, distinct rock.

DePresti frowned. "I don't see anything, outside of a few hits that must have been from your weapon, here," he said as he pointed at a few small holes in the rock.

"Yes, I know," Parkowski said. "But they were firing at me from here."

"They must have policed their brass," he said, crossing his arms.

"But how? They weren't picking it up in the middle of a firefight."

"Maybe they came back at night and swept it all up into bags," DePresti suggested.

She was about to protest but he raised a hand. "Listen, I'm just spitballing here," he said, "but it looks like they wanted to remove any trace that they were here."

A few yards away they found a blood stain on the dusty desert floor.

"I hit one of them," Parkowski told her boyfriend. "It must have been here."

The whole previous night was a blur.

There was a short trail to the next rock, then it stopped. She knew what had happened here.

"They bandaged whoever I shot, then got them out of the combat zone," Parkowski said.

DePresti gave a slight nod.

They looked for something, anything that they could use to identify their attackers, but there was nothing. After reaching the road, the two headed back to the house.

There was no food in the upper portion's refrigerator, so they raided Chang's studio apartment for some ramen and beef jerky for lunch. It wasn't enough, but it had to do.

"What do we do now?" Parkowski asked.

"I guess we can go check the spot on the ridge where they were firing at the house from," DePresti suggested, "but I think we both know what we will find."

"Nothing."

"Precisely. These people are professionals, Grace, they're not going to leave a trace."

"So what do we do now?" she repeated.

Her boyfriend had no answer.

They weren't in a good position.

Chang had taken them in, sheltered them when they had nowhere else to go, and helped guide their investigation into the Bronze Knot mystery. And now he was gone, taken by the mysterious adversary that had dogged them since the Manhattan Beach pier.

They were rudderless.

She recalled the other two suggested investigative branches: the NASA complex at White Sands and Panspermia Game Studios, the developers of the virtual environment. But, Parkowski quickly ruled both of them out.

White Sands was just a ground station, a pass-through for the data coming from Venus through MICS to Earth. She had already seen the logs, seen the Bronze Knot references. It was unlikely that they would find anything new if they were to travel in person to the NASA site.

Panspermia was the same. Parkowski already had all of their data, including the entire virtual environment, in her cloud storage drive. The environment took in inputs from external sources and displayed them in virtual reality. It was totally dependent on those inputs, which is what Bronze Knot seemed to be protecting. Unless Parkowski could pin down exactly who coded and documented the interface to the Bronze Knot data, a trip there would be for naught.

All of their leads in Los Angeles had been played out or were otherwise unavailable to them.

That left one place to go.

"We need to go out to the Cape," Parkowski told DePresti.

He snorted. "That's a long trip."

"It is," she agreed, "but it's the only way out of this."

"How so?"

"We need to stick to the plan," Parkowski explained. "Get as much information on Bronze Knot as we can, threaten to go public with it, trade the information with these people to get them off our backs. I think the only chance we have to get that information and figure out what's behind Bronze Knot is to go east. To Hangar AZ."

"To where it all started," DePresti said with a smile.

"Yes."

He thought for a moment. "It's not the worst idea," the Space Force captain said. "I was the government manager for the launch, sure, but there's plenty of spooky stuff that happens at the Cape that I wasn't aware of. There could have been some kind of addition, some kind of dual-use technology that would be protected by a SAP that was done either above or below my level. And that Hangar AZ reference that you found, that could be the place where we break the whole thing open."

"So what are we waiting for?"

"Nothing. Let's go east."

CHAPTER FORTY-TWO

Cocoa Beach, FL

They made it to Florida in one piece, driving Chang's old Chevy truck cross-country without stopping, and checked into a small, locally-owned motel in the beach town of Cocoa Beach.

With no alarm, Parkowski slept until eleven. She sat up in the small twin bed in the old-fashioned motel room with a start. DePresti still snored away on the other bed. The sun shone through the two windows at the front of the room.

Parkowski wondered why she had slept for so long, but then remembered that in the last three days, she and her boyfriend had driven almost twenty-five hundred miles. It was mentally and physically exhausting. Plus, the three-hour difference in time zones probably played a big role too.

She let DePresti sleep and ran out to a donut shop and got a box of donuts and a pair of coffees. It was warm in Florida, but not overwhelmingly so. She understood why people wanted to spend winters here.

By the time she got back, DePresti was awake. They quickly ate and then set up all of their equipment and paperwork in order to plan their next move.

DePresti had a pretty good plan, Parkowski thought. They would go on base with all of their gear in the truck. From there, they would find a secluded spot on the base and wait. Security was mostly concerned with keeping people without access to the Cape off of it, not preventing the movement of accessed people once they got on. They could literally just sit in the truck, or even better, in the back with the windows blocked, and wait for the day shift to leave the facility. Then, they could find Hangar AZ, break in, and finally solve the Bronze Knot mystery.

She breathed a sigh of relief. It was almost all over.

They showered and DePresti shaved. After packing everything they'd need, including the two pistols Chang had given them, Parkowski and DePresti grabbed lunch at a Wawa and headed back up Florida A1A towards the Space Force Station.

Parkowski ate on the way while DePresti drove. It was relatively peaceful, the early rush to the beaches was over, and just a few tourists were walking back to their rental houses and hotels. It was warm, roughly the same temperature she had experienced in LA, and the smell of the Atlantic was again refreshing to her senses.

They got off of A1A towards the cruise ships. One of the two that Parkowski had seen the night before was gone, the other still in port but in the process of loading up with passengers. She smiled at the juxtaposition of family-friendly cruise ships with the military launch facility just up the road.

After going through some rumble strips, they got to the gate. DePresti put out his hand and Parkowski gave him his CAC as well as her Aering badge. At least a dozen cars were coming out of the facility while theirs was the only one entering. DePresti pulled up to the leftmost guard shack and handed the gate guard, an Air Force airman first class, the two ID cards.

The other man promptly saluted and went into the small shack with the IDs.

"What's going on?" Parkowski asked as soon as the A1C was out of earshot. "Is that normal?"

DePresti shook his head. "No, they normally just give it a cursory scan and hand it back to you. Something's up."

The security forces E-3 came back to the Chevy truck. "I'm sorry, sir, but y'all ain't on the list."

"What list?" DePresti asked.

"The list of people supporting the NROL-204 launch," the other man said.

DePresti's mouth fell open in shock - there was something they had missed despite all of their planning - but Parkowski was quick on her feet. "That's why we're here," she told the gate guard. "We just got into town. We might not be on the list yet."

"Sorry," the E-3 said with a shrug. "If you're not on the list, you can't get in. This is a highly classified launch, and security is a lot tighter than normal."

"How long is it going to be like this?" DePresti asked.

"Until they launch the thing," the enlisted man said. "And that's not for another week or two."

"Oh, ok, thanks," DePresti said, realizing that they were defeated. "I'll call our boss and get it all sorted out."

"Works for me, sir," the E-3 said. "Good luck! If you could turn around up here," he continued as he pointed at a turnaround fifty feet in front of them, "and head back towards the cruise ships that'd be great. Hopefully, it all gets worked out."

The Space Force captain nodded. "Thanks, sorry about that," he said to the guard as he pulled forward and turned around, heading back the way they had come in.

They just missed hitting a giant turtle that was crossing the road. DePresti swerved to avoid it and the reptile continued its path to the other side. Parkowski made a note of the turtle's size - it was massive.

As soon as they were off of the base DePresti hit his hand on the dashboard next to the steering wheel. "Goddammit!" he yelled.

"What?" Parkowski asked.

"I should have checked the launch manifest," her boyfriend said. "Fuck. I had no idea that there was a processing campaign going on right now. It's all on the internet, too, but neither of us thought to look."

"Why is security so tight?" Parkowski asked, a little annoyed. "I don't remember it being like that for your launch or you would have said something."

"It wasn't," he said. "Shit, it's not even like this for any other NRO launch, you just can't get near their processing facilities while they're preparing their spacecraft. You can still get through the gate."

He got back on A1A and started back to the hotel.

"Is this launch different from any other NRO launches?" Parkowski asked.

DePresti thought for a minute. "It might be. I don't work the IC stuff much, I'm read in, but all of my stuff is Space Force. I have a few guesses as to what it could be, but none of it will mean anything to you."

He sighed. "And it's probably not related to Bronze Knot or the ILIAD mission either."

They drove in silence until they got to the motel.

It was well into the afternoon now, the clock showing five minutes past two, and the rest of the day was pretty much shot.

Parkowski was devastated. How did they not think to check if they could get into the Cape with their badges? They assumed too much. It put a lot of self-doubt into her mind. What if they got to Hangar AZ and couldn't get in? What if the Bronze Knot information had been moved to another location? She was very worried that this would be yet another boondoggle.

DePresti started going through his documentation from his GMIM job, looking for a loophole or flaw in the security processes that would allow them access to the facility and let them onto the Cape proper.

Parkowski spread out a map of the area onto the motel room's table and took a look at the facility. It was huge. After taking a look at the scale, Parkowski was shocked at how large both the Space Force base to the south and the NASA complex to the north were. It would have been nice to have been able to visit in person to give her preconceived notions a basis in reality, but that unfortunately wasn't currently possible.

From her initial inspection, there appeared to be extremely few points of entry to either of the sections of the Cape.

She would have thought the NASA, civilian side would be easier to gain access to, but it looked like it was just as buttoned-up as the DOD section of the launch complex to the south. There were less than half a dozen gates, and DePresti told her that between them were ten to fifteen-foot chain-link fences, most of which were electrified. Security cameras were on posts behind the fence at fifty-meter increments. There were likely other, unseen, sensors as well, but neither Parkowski nor DePresti had any insight into them.

Unless they could talk themselves through one of the gates, the facility seemed almost impenetrable.

She sighed and got out some snacks that they had brought from Barstow. DePresti was deep in thought, focused on something on his laptop, so she left him alone.

Instead, she went back to the map.

Parkowski started at the top of the Cape, at Kennedy Space Center on Merritt Island, and worked her way counterclockwise along the edge of the controlled area. There was nothing. No way in.

Her finger reached the southeast corner of Cape Canaveral, on the other side of the port past the docks and cruise ships, and stopped.

"There's nothing," she said to herself.

"I know," DePresti said, agreeing with her. "It's one of the most secure areas in the country. The launch complexes are worth trillions of dollars in materials, and even more than that in their intrinsic value. They, and the ones out on the west coast at Vandenberg, are our only access to space and can't be easily replaced or rebuilt."

Parkowski took a deep breath. "Are you getting anywhere?"

"Nope."

She took another look, tracing her finger around the map again, and just getting more frustrated.

"Can you try calling someone and get at least your name on the list?" the Aering engineer suggested.

"I think that's a bad idea," DePresti replied. "We're trying to keep as low of a profile as possible, and a guy not currently working launch or with the NRO would raise a lot of eyebrows."

She didn't respond.

There was something she was missing. This couldn't end here. They had come too far, worked too hard, to just give up. Parkowski traced around the map again and stopped.

She had something.

"What about coming in from the water?" she wondered aloud.

DePresti gave her an odd look. "Explain," he said.

"How much of the security presence is looking outwards towards the ocean?" Parkowski asked.

He thought for a moment. "Most of it is focused at the gates, or on keeping unwanted intruders from sneaking on base through a hole in the fence or something like that," the Space Force captain answered. "There's some small government-owned motor boats that travel up and down the coast, but they are most active during launches making sure that the exclusion area is clear. I think there might be some beach patrols too, but they're limited in scope too."

"Any kind of passive sensors?" Parkowski asked.

He shrugged. "I don't know of any, but that doesn't mean that they aren't there."

A plan began to formulate in her mind. "What if we rented a small boat and some dive gear and at night anchored a few hundred yards off the coast," Parkowski suggested, "and traveled that distance with scuba gear underwater? Once we get there, we hide our gear and book it to Hangar AZ and get inside."

DePresti smiled. "That's not the worst idea you've had."

She smiled back. "Better than any you've come up with."

CHAPTER FORTY-THREE

Cocoa Beach, FL

DePresti found a nautical map of the Cape Canaveral region in their hotel room.

Parkowski put it down over the topographical map she had been studying and the two engineers began to closely examine the shallow waters off of the coast of the launch complexes.

Her boyfriend traced a path from the interior part of the port - where most of the boat rental places were located - along the Atlantic up Landing Zones 1 & 2 where OuterTek landed their first stage boosters, just two miles east of the main gaggle of buildings that contained their final destination of Hangar AZ.

She shook her head. "No, no, we can't go right there," Parkowski argued. "That's too suspicious. We need to go out to sea and then hook back towards the Cape."

"Fine," DePresti agreed, "we go out here," he said, pointing at a spot a little over two and a half miles off of the coast, "outside the security zone, set anchor, and then come back to LZ-1."

"Why do we need to land there?" Parkowski asked.

He laughed. "It's two miles from the hangars," DePresti told her, "and that's the closest point along the Atlantic side. We're going to swim two-plus miles and then walk another two-plus to our destination. I'd like to keep it as short of a trip as possible."

"Gotcha," she replied.

Parkowski checked the clock. It was four-thirty, almost time for dinner. She needed some sense of normalcy before they embarked on their mission.

"Want to go grab something to eat?" she asked her boyfriend.

The Space Force officer nodded. "Yes, but let's go get some gear first."

The pair got back out on A1A and found a dive shop. Inside, they used some of the cash Chang had given them to rent tanks, masks, buoyancy compensators, flippers, and respirators, as well as to buy a pair of wetsuits. The water around Cape Canaveral and Cocoa Beach was warm, staying in the low seventies even in the winter, but if they were going to have to swim miles to and from the boat, especially at night, having the neoprene shorty suits would be beneficial. DePresti also picked up a dive knife, a waterproof satchel, and an underwater flashlight.

After paying for all of that in cash, they drove farther up A1A to the seafood restaurants located just before Port Canaveral.

The wait was too long at the first one they tried, but the second one had none. They ate outdoors along the dock. The weather was perfect, absolutely perfect, thought Parkowski, and there weren't any bugs or seagulls to ruin the setting.

She ordered a crabcake sandwich while her boyfriend got blackened, freshly caught tuna.

They ate mostly in silence, Parkowski's mind elsewhere, as the second of the two cruise ships departed the port for the open waters of the Atlantic.

"Are you sure you want to do this?" DePresti asked, seemingly out of nowhere.

Parkowski nodded. "I need to figure this out, Mike. I need to know what Bronze Knot is. Even if it's something mundane." She paused. "It's bigger than the both of us now."

"I know how you feel," he said in agreement. "I've felt the same way ever since we had to jump off of the pier. Not only is that the only way for us to get out of this mess, deep down I need to know why the government and a bunch of defense contractors seemingly need to kill people in order to protect a secret."

After dinner, they headed back and went to bed early. Tomorrow was going to be a big day.

Unlike the previous day, they both woke up early at nine.

There was a rare morning rain shower, large raindrops beating against the motel room's window as the two engineers packed their gear and got their scuba equipment ready. Their two handguns and one of their laptops went into the waterproof satchel along with some food and maps.

Parkowski only had half a dozen dives under her belt, and only one in the open ocean, but she felt ready for tonight. It wasn't like she had much of a choice. They were either going to uncover the secret behind Bronze Knot or slink back to Los Angeles with their tails figuratively between their legs, hopeful that the people who had killed Pham and all of those innocent people on the pier had forgotten about them.

After a quick lunch, they put on bathing suits underneath their street clothes and headed to the boat rental shop they had selected the night before.

The elderly man in the Navy hat running it was kind and understanding. No, they didn't need to use a card, cash was fine as long as they paid a $500 security deposit, taking most of DePresti's remaining reserves. Yes, he would show them how to use the boat (Parkowski and DePresti had both piloted small craft before, but it had been many years since the last time they had done it), yes, they could keep the small fifteen-foot Boston Whaler overnight, just make sure it was returned by the morning.

The whole process was a lot easier than Parkowski had thought it would be.

DePresti practiced driving it up and down the beach, before the sandbar, while Parkowski went to the local Wawa and picked up sandwiches and snacks for dinner.

To kill time, they took the boat down to Melbourne Beach, just a few miles down the coast from Cocoa Beach, and back.

Parkowski would have enjoyed it a lot more if her mind wasn't stuck on the mission.

DePresti let her drive a little, but for the most part, he stuck to the wheel. The beaches, while not packed, had plenty of people on them and the waters had more traffic than they had expected.

At five, they headed out for the open ocean through a gap in the sandbar clearly marked by buoys. Storm clouds lurked far out to the west, but they weren't supposed to hit the area until closer to midnight. The sea was calm, almost too calm, Parkowski thought.

They anchored and ate a quick dinner. DePresti and Parkowski did a once-over on their gear and equipment before slipping their clothes off and their wetsuits on. Their clothing went into the waterproof satchel.

The next step was to put the scuba gear on. After their tanks, respirators, buoyancy compensators, and masks were put on, they checked each other to make sure they had done it correctly.

Parkowski nervously kept checking the water around them for a patrol craft from the Space Force Station or Kennedy to pass by, or maybe their mysterious pursuers, but there were no other ships or boats present. The beach two miles in front of them was deserted as well. All of the precautions they were taking, coming in underwater so as to not be seen from land, didn't even seem necessary, but she knew deep down that they were. Nothing was ever as easy as it seemed.

When they were ready, they flipped off of the boat backward into the calm Atlantic, DePresti carrying their gear in his bag.

The water was murkier than she had expected. Visibility was low, maybe seven or eight feet, but it was enough. She stayed about two or three feet under the surface and started swimming.

They were in about forty or fifty feet of water according to the NOAA chart they had looked at yesterday. Parkowski had a fleeting thought - what if there were sharks? She shook it off and continued towards the coast of Cape Canaveral.

As the sun set, the visibility underwater worsened. Parkowski just kept going and going. There wasn't much of a current, and the calm seas made it easy. DePresti swam just a few feet in front of her. He surfaced every couple of minutes to make sure the heading on his compass was still accurate.

Nevertheless, two miles was a long way to swim. After about twenty minutes she started to feel fatigued, but Parkowski pushed herself to keep going.

At the halfway point, DePresti stopped. He was tired too. They took a five-minute break and then continued their path towards the beach.

When they finally reached it, Parkowski was exhausted, but she knew she still had a long way to go. They quickly took off their flippers and ran across the beach to the safety of the grass and shrubs beyond.

The two quickly stripped off their gear and placed it in a pile at the edge of the sand in a tangle of brushes and tall grass. DePresti made a small rock cairn to indicate that this was where they had put it, but it wouldn't mean anything to anyone who didn't look too closely.

They then put their street clothes back on, including their sneakers. Parkowski got out the map and figured out where they were. They were in between the defunct LC-12, an old Atlas pad, and LC-36, owned by a private space company and currently under construction. The spot they had landed was just short of DePresti's target of Landing Zones 1 & 2, but it wasn't that far off.

Somehow, they hadn't been spotted.

Parkowski and DePresti had just broken into one of the most secure military facilities in the country. It wasn't quite Area 51, but it wasn't that far off, either.

She shook her head in amazement. Parkowski had expected security to be a lot tighter, especially with the NRO launch currently processing. But, it worked out in their favor.

Parkowski tingled with excitement. She had never been this close to solving the Bronze Knot mystery. Hopefully, they would be able to get to Hangar AZ without the Air Force security forces catching them.

They wolfed down energy bars and set off for the main section of the Cape.

DePresti and Parkowski kept off of the main roads as much as they could. A couple of times they saw a vehicle, but on both occasions they were far enough from the main road to not be spotted. It was a weak, waxing moon and there weren't many artificial lights on the Space Force Station. Someone would basically have to be on top of them to detect their presence.

There were some bugs, but surprisingly little wildlife to be seen as they passed through the green, preserved areas between the roadways.

Parkowski was exhausted. The only thing that kept her going was the promise of solutions to all of her unanswered questions.

After what felt like forever, they started to see lights off in the distance.

"Is that where we're going?" she quietly asked DePresti.

He nodded. "That's the main complex," he answered in a hushed whisper, "and somewhere in there is Hangar AZ."

CHAPTER FORTY-FOUR

Cape Canaveral Space Force Station, FL

They continued towards the main part of the base.

It seemed so easy. They were finally going to get to the bottom of the mystery.

Parkowski and DePresti passed through a mess of structures. There were large, multi-story buildings comparable to Aering's high bay, shorter, lower hangars that looked like they had been built back in the Apollo days, and more modern three or four-story office buildings.

"I had no idea this was all here," Parkowski said to DePresti.

He smiled. "I didn't either, not until I started spending a lot of time out here. It takes a great deal of work that goes on behind the scenes to make the rockets go up and the pretty webcasts happen," DePresti told her in a low voice. "And the footprint here is only going to get bigger as more and more launches take place."

It was almost like a town now, with stoplights and crosswalks; well-lit with streetlights suspended over the roads. The parking lots were mostly empty; the majority of the people working on the Cape had left for the day, but there were still a few cars parked. Operations at the launch complexes were twenty-four/seven.

Hangar AZ was located at the far end of the complex from where Parkowski and DePresti had entered it, built along the Banana River that flowed between Merritt Island and the Cape. The two-story building with a semicircular roof reminiscent of an overgrown Quonset hut was sandwiched in between Hangar AE, a NASA facility, and Hangar AO, a former Space Shuttle auxiliary building that was leased by OuterTek. If there was a naming scheme, Parkowski couldn't figure it out.

They crossed Phillips Parkway, the main north-south thoroughfare on the Space Force Station, and passed by the small AAFES shoppette before they reached Hangar Road. There, DePresti and Parkowski had to wait for a small convoy of work trucks to pass by going south towards the main gate before they could continue through the parking lots and towards Hangar AZ.

Unlike the two facilities on either side of it, the hangar looked deserted. No lights were on at the entryway, or inside that they could see through the dirty glass door. The badge reader appeared to be nonfunctional. Not that they had any badges that would work on it. Paint peeled from the sides of the buildings, and unlike the hangars on either side, no cars were parked in its small parking lot.

Parkowski and DePresti crept around the facility, probing for a way in.

They found a pair of doors on either side, all of which were locked, and a large vault-style door reminiscent of the one that Parkowski had gotten through weeks ago at Aering with a similar cipher lock above the handle.

That one was locked too.

"Shit," Parkowski said, "what now?"

"We keep looking," her boyfriend responded. "There's got to be a way in."

They walked around a second time. Parkowski focused on the roof and upper level, maybe she could find a way in there but was unsuccessful.

DePresti found a manhole that was unlocked on the far corner of the building, on a small concrete slab that seemed to have been placed just for that purpose. "Want to try this?"

"Sure," Parkowski responded.

He opened it and climbed down the ladder. His girlfriend followed him, closing the cover as she cleared the opening.

At the bottom, they found themselves in a concrete tunnel with a stagnant inch of water on its floor. Dying light bulbs were strung along the top every fifteen feet or so. It had a musty smell of stale water. Apparently these passageways were rarely used.

It appeared to travel forever in both directions.

"How do we get up into the hangar?" DePresti asked.

Parkowski tried to re-orient her internal compass. "I think we go that way," she said, pointing toward what she thought was Hangar AZ.

They walked for a minute before coming to a dead end.

"I don't think that's the right way," Parkowski said, "sorry."

DePresti grunted and started the other way. She followed close behind.

They came to a fork and took the left path, which should have taken them in the direction of their desired destination, but that was a dead end as well.

"Do you want to give up and go back up to the surface?" DePresti asked.

She shook her head. "No, let's try the other way, and if that doesn't work we'll go back up."

They took the other way at the fork. It took them on a winding path with another fork that they took the left hand at. Thankfully, it led them back in the direction of Hangar AZ.

At its terminus, instead of a dead end, there was another ladder. At its top was a gunmetal gray door with the letters "AZ" on it in faded red paint.

"Ladies first," DePresti said with a grin.

Parkowski carefully climbed the ladder and opened the unlocked door. Beyond it, the room was pitch black.

She stepped forward so DePresti had space to get in, and started fumbling around for a light switch. She stopped when she realized how futile it was.

A few moments later she heard her boyfriend, huffing and puffing, pass through the door. "Shit, it's dark," DePresti said.

"Shh," she warned as her eyes continued to adjust to the absolute lack of light.

Eventually, Parkowski felt comfortable enough to start feeling around again. She walked forward slowly and after a couple of steps came to what felt like a wall or a door.

She ran her hand along the wall at roughly the height of where she thought a light switch would be. Parkowski found a corner and continued her search.

She found a lone switch, then flipped it up, and immediately shielded her eyes.

She and DePresti were in a small utility room lit by a pair of naked light bulbs. There was an additional, decrepit wooden door on the far wall. She walked to it, DePresti closely behind her, opened it, and stepped through.

Parkowski was in a Spartan, featureless hallway with doors on either side. The only light was from the room behind her.

DePresti got his flashlight out of his satchel and shone it down the hallway. It made a right turn at the end. The other end of the hallway made a left.

It was a fairly standard design for government buildings. The majority of the offices were spread in a loop around the exterior of the structure. On the inside were either more offices, likely for lower-ranking individuals or support contractors, or just as likely, the building's SCIF or secure area.

That was where they wanted to go.

They walked softly around the hallway, looking for a way in.

LAG DELAY

There was only one door into Hangar AZ's interior. It was like the one at the rear exterior of the building and the one in the secure room at Aering El Segundo, a large, metal bank vault-style door with a cipher lock.

DePresti and Parkowski paused in front of it.

"Any idea what the code is?" the Space Force captain asked her.

"I only know one code," Parkowski said, "and they changed it after I got in the first time at Aering. But it worked that one time."

"Well, what are you waiting for?" DePresti asked. "Go ahead and try it."

The code was burned into her memory.

One.

Five.

Three and two together.

Four.

Parkowski heard the satisfying *click*.

"No fucking way," DePresti breathed.

She grabbed the handle and turned the door inwards. "Yes fucking way," Parkowski said with a big, dumb grin on her face.

That room was dark too.

DePresti shone his flashlight around to reveal a room that was nearly a carbon copy of the secure room in El Segundo.

Parkowski saw a lot of differences, but the overall theme was the same. Server racks in the back, workstations around the edge of the room, a large conference table in the middle, and a projection screen at the front.

"Are all classified rooms like this?" she asked her boyfriend.

He shrugged. "No, but I've seen plenty that look like this one," DePresti replied as he walked back to the server rack. He opened it and scanned the rack up and down. "There are stickers on the different server blades here for a whole range of SAPs, a bunch of which are old and the programs have been closed. There's one I don't recognize..." his voice trailed off, "and there's one that says BKT."

Bronze Knot.

Parkowski grabbed the laptop they had brought out of the waterproof satchel and walked it over to DePresti.

He fiddled around in the back and came out with a network cable.

"Plug it in," he said.

She did and booted the laptop up.

The computer that Chang had given them connected to the network for the special access program that they had worked for so long to get access to.

She quickly learned that all that the server in the room was doing was taking data from the NASA MICS network and passing it along to the ILIAD virtual environment hosted at the Air Force facility in Orlando. The data was the sensor feed from the ILIAD mission on Venus, with the same BKT identifiers that she had seen while she was troubleshooting the dragon from her first mission.

It was a huge disappointment.

Parkowski checked and double-checked. There were no huge file directories, no security classification guides, and no documents that would help shed a light on the mystery.

It was yet another dead end.

She groaned and looked up at the ceiling.

"Let me try," DePresti said.

Parkowski gave him the laptop. "Because you're so much smarter than me?"

"No," he said, "I just want to get another set of eyes on it."

He too came up empty.

"I don't get it," he told Parkowski a few minutes later. "Why would a special access program, one that is even worth killing over, just be a bunch of fields in telemetry packets coming from a NASA science mission?"

"I don't know," she said, reaching out for the laptop. "Let me look again."

This time, she dove into the packets that she had looked at on her Aering workstation so long ago.

She pulled up five, ten, twenty-five, fifty different telemetry logs.

The BKT data was there, but here, on the high side, was clearly identified.

Interestingly enough, every five packets, there was something injected into it from a specific IP address into one of the sensor values.

"Mike, write this down," she told DePresti. "One-seven-two, dot, one-six-eight, dot, one hundred, dot, fifty-five."

"Ok," DePresti said, fumbling in his bag until he got out a pen and a small notepad he had gotten from the motel. "Got it. What about it?"

"Is there any way of telling where this IP address is located?" Parkowski asked. "I remember seeing a list of IP addresses in one of the packets from your launch."

"Hold on," he said. He took the laptop and pulled up a document consisting of one large table.

"The IP addresses on the Cape are configured by building," DePresti explained, "and the first two numbers indicate what building the workstation or server is. What were the first two values?"

"172 and 168."

"172 and 168," DePresti repeated as he scanned the table. "That is in...Huh, that's weird."

"What's weird?"

"That's for building A99," he said, surprised, "but that doesn't follow any of the building numbering schemes I've seen for Cape

Canaveral or Kennedy Space Center. They're either hangar-something or have a three-digit number."

"Huh," Parkowski said, confused now. "So we go there?"

"We're going there," he confirmed.

"I don't think the two of you are going anywhere," a third, gravelly voice said, causing Parkowski and DePresti to both jump in shock.

She turned to see Special Agent Hollis Everson, the AFOSI/PJ agent who had visited her at Aering, and two other men, one on either side of him.

In his hand, pointed directly at her forehead, was the largest handgun she had ever seen.

CHAPTER FORTY-FIVE

Cape Canaveral Space Force Station, FL

Parkowski opened her mouth to say something, but nothing came out.

The new arrival grinned beneath his mustache. "Cat got your tongue?"

"Who are you?" DePresti asked him, stepping slightly towards Parkowski.

Everson laughed. "The young lady here knows me as Special Agent Hollis Everson," he said with gusto, "but I flew on a commercial flight out here as James Baker. I've also spent time as Dmitri Gustavovich, Mohammed El-Farsi, Petr Cenek, and any number of other names. You can guess which one, if any, is real."

DePresti didn't respond.

"Go ahead and sit down," Everson said as he waved his oversized pistol at DePresti and Parkowski. "We're going to have a quick chat."

Parkowski, still in shock, did as she was asked to, taking a seat at the conference table. DePresti did the same.

Everson sat down, pistol still aimed at Parkowski, as the two other men stood on either side of the door.

She couldn't believe that they had let their guard down. They had gotten too cocky.

"So, you want to know what Bronze Knot is," Everson said softly, gun still aimed at her forehead. He laughed. "You know what, I'll tell you."

"You will?" Parkowski asked.

"Sure. It's quite simple, really. Bronze Knot is a special access program that protects the linkage between the ILIAD mission and an unnamed organization." He seemed like he was about to say more, but then he stopped himself. "And, that's really all it is," he added after a few seconds of silence. "There's much more information, of course, but that's all protected in another special program. I'm actually surprised that neither of you was able to figure that part out."

"Who do you work for?" DePresti asked, a slight hint of defiance in his voice. He wasn't as scared as Parkowski, or at least was trying better to hide it.

Everson snorted and then smirked at the Space Force captain. "That's what you want to know? Not, how did we track you here, why haven't we killed you already like poor Dr. Pham, why are we so interested in your little investigation?"

Neither DePresti nor Parkowski responded.

The man holding the gun didn't seem to care.

"Bronze Knot protects one of our most closely guarded secrets," he began, "and when our man in the Aering facility told us that you were starting to look into it we weren't initially concerned. No offense, kid," he said to Parkowski, "but you're not the type that I'd have expected to blow this whole thing open."

She frowned but didn't respond to the slight.

"But, when you got access to the SAP room at the Aering plant," Everson said, "it got serious."

"Why are you telling us this?" Parkowski asked.

Everson ignored her. Even if he had given her an answer, she wasn't sure she would have liked his answer.

"I had to send a team out to Los Angeles," the older man said. "And we started tracking you, your boyfriend," he nodded in DePresti's direction, "and everyone else involved with ILIAD. We had to prevent a spill, a leak. We had to make sure that the only people that knew what was going on in the SAP were the carefully vetted people who had been read in."

"To include Dr. Pham?" she asked.

"Yes," Everson said, "who wasn't our most willing participant, but he was read into the high side." He went on. "Then, we tried to make you stop. A phone call directly to you, having your management tell you to stop, even a visit from yours truly," Everson said. "But, Ms. Parkowski, you are quite determined to get to the bottom of this."

He took a breath. "Then, you went to Dr. Pham. You forced the issue. We were similarly forced to take drastic measures, ones that I did not want to have to do, but that were necessary. Our leadership believed that based on the information we had at our disposal, Dr. Pham was going to reveal the crown jewels of the operation, the big secret that everyone wants to know."

"And what would that be?" Parkowski asked, a little annoyed.

Everson ignored her again. He wasn't going to tell them anything that Parkowski and DePresti didn't already know.

"I had to make the call to one of the other organizations that exists within our larger one," he continued. This was almost like a carefully prepared monologue to himself, like DePresti and Parkowski weren't sitting there in front of him. "They eliminated the threat - Dr. Pham - and attempted to eliminate the two of you as well. However, you escaped the initial attack and somehow eluded our pursuit. We lost your position at San Bernardino. From there, you could have doubled back to Los Angeles, gone to Barstow or Las Vegas, or cut south to Riverside and Orange County.

"We started to search for you but our leadership pulled us back. They had another idea. The two of you, particularly you, Ms. Parkowski, got frighteningly close to unraveling what my organization has spent years planning. If you could do it, given your relative lack of experience, other people could do it, too."

Parkowski's mouth fell open again, this time in horror. She knew what he was going to say next.

"We went from elimination mode to reconnaissance mode," Everson explained. "We didn't initially know where your base of operations was located, but we knew it was in the Barstow area. It was easy enough to keep tracking teams in the city and trail you on your excursion in and out of Los Angeles as well as your road trip across the country until we lost you in Texas, but we knew your final destination. We even had a fun time staging a shootout at Chang's house - neither of you was really in any danger. Your friend is fine, by the way, just in federal custody until we can take care of this issue. We had to keep you moving along in your investigation.

"We briefly lost contact with you today, and to be honest I'm not entirely sure how exactly you got on base, but we had sensors placed at all of the relevant BKT buildings for the launch campaign that we reactivated yesterday. We were already on base, working on another project, when we realized that someone had gotten into our hangar. And imagine my shock when I found you here. Now, we can close all of the doors that you opened and lock and bar them so that no one else can learn what you did."

It was her worst fear, something that she had suppressed for days. It had been far too easy for them. They had been allowed to get as far as they did because Everson and whoever he worked for wanted to make sure that no one would ever travel down the path they had taken again.

DePresti gave a short, nervous laugh. "You're part of some spooky, unnamed intelligence agency," the Space Force captain said. "I've heard of organizations like yours. You get funded off the books through the CIA or DIA or whatever agency they funnel the money through, but your name and purpose remain hidden. The IC is full of people like you. You're totally unaccountable to Congress and to the taxpayer."

Everson laughed back at him. "What makes you think we're part of the intelligence community, or really, part of the government at all?" he said, refuting DePresti's central argument.

"The American intelligence community is a mockery of the word intelligence," he continued, pointing a finger at DePresti with his free hand, "if they told me the sun was going to come up tomorrow, I would have to go out in the morning to verify it. We work in the shadows, in the cracks, to advance our interests forward."

"And what would those be?" DePresti asked. Parkowski was still in shock. She had led herself to believe that they had outsmarted and outmaneuvered their pursuers; instead, they had just let them see how far they could get so they knew which holes to patch.

Everson didn't answer her boyfriend's question. Instead, he just sat there, handgun pointed at Parkowski.

She finally worked up the courage to talk. "I know why you told us all of that," Parkowski told Everson, "you're not going to let us out of here alive."

Everson smiled. "You've got a smart one here, Captain DePresti. I'm afraid Ms. Parkowski is correct. I'm going full, open, and honest here because you are never going to be able to tell anyone what you've learned."

Her heart sank. That confirmed her worst fears.

"And, the best part," Everson continued, "is that you're going to go to your graves never knowing the full story behind Bronze Knot."

He leaned back. "I could tell you the truth, or, hell, I could make up a good story about aliens or dragons or whatever I wanted to," the man said in his deep voice, "but to be honest, the two of you have pissed me off so much over the last few weeks that I'm not going to give you that satisfaction.

"Instead, you're going to answer a few questions for me."

Everson transitioned to interrogating DePresti and Parkowski. He wanted to know just how much they had been able to figure out.

They refused to give him what he wanted.

Parkowski was surprisingly aware of her own mortality. She had come to grips that she was likely going to be killed within the next hour or so. Everson seemed like a hard, mean man, and the other two men who had come in with him even more so. They looked like former special forces types with scraggly beards and wraparound sunglasses and intimidated her without saying a word.

Any one of those three would kill her without blinking.

These could be her last few minutes alive. Regardless, she didn't give the mysterious operative what he wanted.

But, if Everson had grown annoyed at her and DePresti, he didn't show it.

"Very well," he said after getting nowhere with his lines of questioning. "We're going to take the two of you for a drive. We can't splatter your brains all over government property."

He waved the handgun at Parkowski as he stood up from his chair. "Get up, both of you."

They did as he asked.

One of the two silent men opened the door to the secure room while the other one walked out into the dark hallway beyond.

Everson motioned with the weapon and Parkowski and DePresti followed him out into the interior of Hangar AZ.

They continued down the dimly lit hall until they came to the entrance of the building.

The fake AFOSI/PJ agent pulled a card out of his pocket and scanned it on a reader, unlocking the glass door. Then the five of them walked out into the parking lot.

It was pitch-black. All of the lights that had been on just an hour ago had been turned off, save for a few on the far side of the gaggle of buildings. Everson snapped his fingers and, seemingly out of nowhere, an older paneled work van with government plates turned on and headed towards them at the front of Hangar AZ. Parkowski couldn't see inside the front as it came in their direction; the window was heavily tinted but it was too dark to see anyway.

It pulled up and the two men who had accompanied Everson opened the rear door.

"Get in," the older man said.

Parkowski and DePresti didn't have a choice. They followed Everson's command and got into the back of the van.

All three of their captors got in after them.

The van then sped off into the dark Florida night.

CHAPTER FORTY-SIX

Cape Canaveral Space Force Station, FL

They sat in the back as whoever was driving the van took them on a journey around the sprawling facility.

Parkowski sat on one side of the van's interior, DePresti on the other. One of Everson's goons held a pistol - a much smaller one than the lead agent was armed with - against her forehead, while the other did the same to her boyfriend.

Everson sat at the far end of the van from the door, his handgun next to him. He sat quietly, his eyes never leaving the two young engineers.

They hadn't bound or gagged either of them.

They didn't have to. Parkowski and DePresti were both terrified.

Parkowski's eyes darted from side to side like a caged animal, looking for a way to escape. Her arms and legs were tense, and she wanted nothing more than to leap free from her captors. She would have if not for the cold steel of the pistol pressed against her temple.

DePresti was almost in shock. He was a military man, sure, but his desk-bound Space Force career hadn't prepared him for this moment. The officer probably hadn't been in a physical confrontation since his unarmed combat training at the Air Force Academy. He had initially shown quite a bit of resistance to Everson, but that had trailed off as the realization that these could be his final moments had kicked in. He held his head against his knees and rocked quickly back and forth.

She wasn't sure how they were going to do it, though. Were they going to murder them here, at the Cape, executing them on a grassy bank in the middle of the night and feeding their bodies to the alligators or sharks? Or would they take them out into the water and throw them overboard with weights attached to their legs? Parkowski's imagination ran wild.

LAG DELAY

The van turned around, making a full one-hundred-eighty-degree turn before going back in the direction they had come from.

Parkowski made up her mind.

She was going to get free, escape, go to the authorities or the media or whoever would listen to her story of a rogue intelligence apparatus of the United States killing her mentor and trying to kill her and her boyfriend. There was a lot that they could cover up, but they wouldn't try and hide that. That, or she would die trying.

However, she needed to get a hold of DePresti.

Her boyfriend wasn't paying any attention to her or their captors. He sat, seemingly hoping that the entire problem would vanish.

But, how could she get his attention when she had a gun pressed up against her head?

She thought and thought.

There was no way that she was going to go down like this.

The van hit a pothole, slightly skewing their arrangement in the back. No one wore seatbelts.

Parkowski's eyes darted over to the van's rear door. There was a small window at the top - a detail she had initially missed - and a latch that when swung downwards, would open the door outwards.

Her captors had failed to lock it.

They hit another pothole, jostling them again. But, she had come up with an idea.

The next time the van jolted, she nudged DePresti's foot slightly with hers.

His eyes met hers. "What?" he quickly mouthed.

Parkowski's eyes darted to the door latch, then back to DePresti. She blinked twice, slowly, deliberately.

It took a moment for him to process. When he did, his eyes widened.

Another pothole. Another jostling of the passengers in the back. The Space Force really needed to maintain their roads better.

The next time they hit one she would strike.

Parkowski coiled her right arm, the one closest to the man with the gun to her head, like a snake ready to pounce.

She was ready.

It felt like the moment to strike would never come.

The road underneath the panel van became smoother. They must be on a different section of the base, she thought. There were no more potholes.

Parkowski felt the pressure of the cold weapon against her head lessen just a fraction. Her captor was getting sloppy.

If she was going to make a move to free herself and DePresti, it needed to be soon. She locked eyes with her boyfriend again, then nodded just a fraction. DePresti responded with the same gesture.

If not a pothole, another disruption to the rear of the van would have to do.

Just a few moments later, the van's driver provided the opportunity.

They took a left turn just a little too quickly, throwing the occupants of the back of the van around haphazardly.

Parkowski's watcher took the pistol off of her head for just a second to right himself.

She took a deep breath and allowed for everything around her to slow down slightly.

Her captor was in the process of placing his pistol back against her head when Parkowski grabbed her right fist with her left hand, and, using the force of both of her arms, slammed her elbow into the ribs of the man next to her.

She got lucky. He wasn't wearing a bulletproof vest or any armor. Her elbow went right into his solar plexus, pushing it upwards and knocking the wind out of him. He doubled over in pain.

DePresti made a similar move to his captor's face and neck. Less than half a second after Parkowski struck her opponent, her boyfriend jammed his fist into his captor's throat. Instead of pulling it back for another strike, he kept pushing after the initial impact, sending the man off of the seat and to the front of the van, towards Everson.

Parkowski was already moving towards the door. She grabbed the handle and swung it down. The door opened up and swung outwards with her hanging onto it.

Looking back she saw Everson grabbing for his pistol but the heavy handgun was hard to manage. Neither of his goons would be of much use - the one she had hit clutched his side while the other held both hands to his neck from DePresti's brutal strike.

The van was traveling about thirty miles per hour along a two-lane road. It wasn't pitch black anymore; there was quite a bit of light coming from a huge launch complex to the right side of the road.

Parkowski squinted as she swung outwards to see if she could make out where they were. The launch pad was well-lit, dozens of floodlights illuminating a single-core white rocket with black scorch marks on it, topped by a long, extended fairing. Next to the rocket was a large gantry with a crew arm extended at the top towards the rocket. At the top of the gantry was a single white lighting rod. Just to its right was a giant water tower with the OuterTek logo on it.

Her mind whirred as she rotated with the van's door. She knew where she was. That was LC-39a, the same launch pad that had launched the ILIAD mission. It was the only pad with that configuration - they had finally come full circle. They had crossed over onto the NASA side of the cape and were now on Kennedy Space Center.

The moment the door was fully extended, Parkowski let go of the handle. She fell hard onto the pavement below, thankfully landing on her good shoulder rather than her injured one. It still hurt like a bitch, though. She rolled towards the grass on the side of the road.

DePresti had leaped out of the van as well and landed hard but upright on his two feet. He took a couple of quick steps in the direction of Parkowski and then broke into a full-blown sprint away from their captors.

Parkowski got to her feet as she heard a shot fired, the bullet hitting the asphalt about two feet to her right as she headed away from the road.

She stumbled and almost fell. DePresti grabbed her arm and got her back to her feet.

Parkowski didn't hear the van's engine anymore. They must have stopped and gotten out to pursue them. A bullet whizzed over their heads as they scrambled away, trying to put as much distance as possible between them and their pursuers.

DePresti and Parkowski headed for a grove of mangrove trees along a small decline that she couldn't see past in the darkness.

He grabbed her hand as they reached the trees and led her through the maze of trunks and branches until suddenly they fell into the water beyond the trees.

The water wasn't particularly cold, but it still shocked her system.

She could smell a hint of salt right before they hit the water, but it wasn't the same as when they had traveled underwater, not the same as the ocean. Parkowski wasn't a hundred percent sure of the geography, but she guessed they were in a brackish estuary or river that ran parallel to the coast to their east.

The water was slightly murky. As she sank, Parkowski opened her eyes to look around.

To her shock, there was a giant, twelve-foot alligator on the riverbed not a dozen feet from her.

Parkowski opened her mouth to scream but remembered she was underwater, expelling precious air as a bubble rose to the surface. She closed it quickly.

There wasn't just one alligator, either. She counted at least four of the massive beasts - three on the bottom and a slightly smaller one floating on the surface, nostrils poking out of the water.

This was it, she thought. She was going to die here. Either she was going to be eaten by alligators, or their pursuers were going to execute them on the side of the road.

Parkowski did everything in her power to not panic.

Her boyfriend was next to her, floating near the bottom of the six-foot depth of water. Surprisingly, he didn't seem to panic. She looked at him and, incredibly, he smiled.

Then, he gave a thumbs-up.

It was time to panic. Something was wrong - DePresti was either hallucinating or just completely losing it.

He slowly but deliberately went up for air, then went back down, taking care not to make any sudden movements. Parkowski did the same, filling her tired lungs while making as little of a sound as possible.

When she submerged again, the Aering engineer saw DePresti carefully swim along the side of the bank, to the south, away from their pursuers.

What the hell was he doing? He was going to get them all killed.

A fish - she couldn't tell what kind - swam in front of her.

It was huge and thankfully not a threat. If it was, she'd have been in some trouble.

Another one, this one even bigger than the first, swam right by her legs. Parkowski guessed they had to be some kind of grouper, and had to weigh at least twice what she did. There was no way that they were naturally here, this close to the shore, in a mostly saline environment.

How did such a fish come to exist in a small, remote area?

Then, it clicked.

Parkowski smiled when she realized the answer, then followed her boyfriend deeper into the estuary.

It might just get them out of this one.

CHAPTER FORTY-SEVEN

Kennedy Space Center, FL

Parkowski knew why the fish were so big. And why the giant alligators were so docile and uninterested in her. It was the same reason the turtle they had seen while turning around at the gate seemed so big.

They were in a protected area, one of the few spaces in Florida that was completely closed to hunters and fishermen. The Cape and Kennedy were government facilities, closed off to the general public.

The alligators, groupers, and other creatures had no natural predators. They were at the top of their respective food chains.

No humans were there to hurt or kill them.

The alligators didn't attack Parkowski or DePresti because they didn't have to. They were well-fed on whatever lived in this brackish river, and unless threatened would remain in their relaxed state.

DePresti had to have known that, hence why he didn't panic or freak out when he saw them. It just took her a little longer to come to the same realization.

They swam slowly, almost bumping into a juvenile alligator. Seemingly, they weren't spotted.

Her boyfriend rose to the surface and stayed there, his nose, eyes, and ears above the water. Parkowski did the same. She scanned the area to see if she could see their pursuers or any other threats.

In the faint light from the far-off launch complex, she could barely make out the three figures along the edge of the water. But they were there, just half a football field away, one of whom was swinging around a flashlight.

They were armed.

And they were loud.

"Shit, my ribs hurt like hell," one of the men - the one she had hit - said loudly. Parkowski heard the words clearly as they traveled well through the crisp late autumn air. He was the one with the flashlight. "Where did they go?"

"I don't know," the other bearded man said. He spat, his saliva striking the water with a hiss. "Fuck, man, I can't believe they got away."

Parkowski and DePresti remained perfectly still. She didn't dare breathe. One false move could give away their position to the killers on the bank.

"They got away because you got cocky," Everson said, his gravelly voice carrying across the water as the man with the light shone it in a random, haphazard pattern. If he hoped to get lucky and find them that way, it probably wasn't going to work. "Why didn't you tie them up?"

"Because you didn't tell us to, boss," one of the men said. He kicked a rock into the water.

Parkowski saw a movement in the water, a slight ripple that she was just barely able to make out in the dim light.

"Fuck this," the man said. He raised his weapon - an MP-5, the same submachine gun used by the shooters at the Manhattan Beach pier, and fired a short, jerky burst into the water.

The other goon did the same, running through his whole magazine. The water rippled with waves from the bullets.

"What the fuck?" Everson said.

The first man who had fired shrugged. "Just want to kill them and get this over with."

"You aren't going to hit shit," his boss replied.

Parkowski felt movement in the water. Their captors had poked the proverbial bear. Something bad was about to happen.

"Stop, I hear something," Everson said carefully.

"I do too," one of the other men said, "fuck, is it them?"

The two in the water remained still, breathing slowly.

A creature, either a bat or an owl, flew overhead.

Something brushed against Parkowski. Despite her fear, she ignored it. She wasn't the threat. The people on the bank were. Her heart pulsed as she waited for the next shoe to drop.

"It's a gator!" one of the men yelled and opened up with his pistol in the direction of the river, using the flashlight to guide his fire. The attacking reptile - the juvenile they had seen - came on fast, much faster than Parkowski had expected.

The other man and Everson opened fire as well, Everson's pistol giving an unearthly *boom* that shattered the silence of the historic launch area.

The three of them fired until there were no more bullets in their magazines. Parkowski couldn't see the alligator, but there was no way it could have survived that. It was probably ripped to shreds.

"Got the fucker," one of the operator types that had guarded Parkowski in the van said. He turned the flashlight off.

There was a new disturbance in the water, more of a wave than a ripple.

Their captors had disturbed the larger alligators' sleep.

Parkowski watched in part horror, part satisfaction as the giant alligators that she had seen resting peacefully on the bottom rose to the water's surface and started swimming slowly but deliberately toward the three men.

They initially didn't notice. "We smoked him," one of the goons said, more quiet than his boastful brags before, as he knelt beside the dead animal. The other goon and Everson reloaded their weapons. "That's what lead will do to you."

The larger alligators had reached the bank and were almost on the shore.

Parkowski squinted, but could barely make out what was happening.

The lead gigantic reptile struck first. It grabbed the kneeling man by his arm and started dragging him down the bank into the dark water.

"Fuck!" Everson yelled. He aimed carefully and fired off a shot with his giant handgun while retreating.

The third man took off and ran back towards the van.

Everson took a few steps back and squeezed off another shot. The loud, large-caliber pistol hit something solid.

It looked to Parkowski like he had hit the lead alligator that had grabbed his subordinate. The alligator dropped the man, either from fear or from pain.

The other alligators kept coming towards them.

Everson pulled the fallen man, who screamed inhumanly, away from oncoming reptiles, firing a pair of shots.

"Fuck, let the gators have them," the third man yelled as he ran away. "I'm getting out of here."

Parkowski didn't hear a response from Everson.

She and her boyfriend waited until they heard the van turn on and speed off towards the north side of Kennedy Space Center.

"Fuck," Parkowski said softly.

DePresti didn't respond. He grabbed her hand and led her toward the far side of the bank. He helped her up and out of the water.

Parkowski shivered. It was cold and her wet, dirty clothes didn't help. "Did you know what was going to happen?" she asked her boyfriend.

He nodded.

"The NASA and Space Force guys are always talking about how big the wildlife is here," DePresti said softly. "And also how docile the animals generally are."

The Space Force captain paused, recollecting something.

"There's a story from about five or ten years back about a Taiwanese guy who was visiting for a launch almost losing an arm," he continued. "He was trying to take a selfie with a fourteen-foot 'gator and got a bite taken out of his arm. It was told to me as a true story, but I used to think it was an urban legend.

"When I was out here for my launch last year, a bunch of drunk lieutenants from some unit on the Space Force station went and did the same thing - and they got some amazing pictures. The alligator didn't care at all that they were maybe two or three feet from them taking pictures. They got in trouble for messing with the wildlife, but no one got hurt."

"So as long as we don't bother them, we're ok," Parkowski said.

"Yup. They may be big - the area we were just in is called the 'fishbowl' because of the giant fish that live there - but they want nothing to do with us."

She sighed, "What do we do now?"

DePresti didn't have a response for her. "We failed," he told her. "We never figured out what Bronze Knot was."

"At least they think we're dead," Parkowski said quietly.

He laughed. "That's true. It'll be a big surprise for whoever is monitoring you at work when you show back up at Aering in a week or so."

"You don't think they'll go after us again?"

"I'm not sure, but I don't think they will," he said. "We have nothing on them. Just bits and pieces. And, most importantly, they know what we know now - and it's nothing, or next to nothing. We don't have the big secret, whatever the fuck it is. We can't prove anything, and I think we're no longer a threat. They saw how far we could get, and then when we couldn't pierce the Bronze Knot veil, we were no longer useful. With no evidence, no one is going to believe us."

Parkowski's eyes began to well up with tears.

There was something out there, a giant secret that a shadowy government agency was willing to kill over. So many people had already been impacted by it. But, thankfully, despite not coming away with a better understanding of what was behind the Bronze Knot curtain, Parkowski was happy that at the moment it looked like they were going to make it out of here alive.

She still wanted to know what it was. But, she wasn't convinced about her boyfriend's last statement. "They tried to kill us before. Hell, they were going to kill us just a few minutes ago," Parkowski said as she wiped the tears away.

"I know, but they had us dead to rights," her boyfriend retorted. "As long as we can get back to civilization, I think we're safe. They aren't going to try and kill us and shine more light on them when they know we know nothing."

It made sense to her now.

"Do we have to walk all of the way back to our scuba gear?" Parkowski asked.

DePresti thought for a moment, then shook his head. "No, I know where they keep a bunch of GOVs," he said, referring to government-owned vehicles. "There's a small cluster of buildings maybe a mile south of here on this side of the estuary. I know for a fact that they never lock them because I used them repeatedly during my launch campaign."

"So, we just drive back to where we left our gear, and then swim to our boat?" Parkowski asked. "We can't just drive off base and get our boat another way?"

"No, they're checking the exits, I saw it when we were at the gate," he answered. "And, remember though, we have to swim back on the top of the water. Our air tanks are empty. That should be easier than coming in. Plus, I want to return all of our stuff - abandoning both the boat and scuba gear would draw a lot of unwanted attention."

She sighed. "To the GOVs."

CHAPTER FORTY-EIGHT

Kennedy Space Center, FL

In the blackness of the humid Florida night, Parkowski and DePresti walked south along the side of the river.

Any joy that she had felt in escaping the harrowing situation had evaporated.

She couldn't shake the sinking feeling in her stomach. Parkowski knew that she would never understand why things had gone so wrong in the ILIAD environment, why Dr. Pham was murdered along with all of those innocent people at the pier, why Chang was kidnapped, and what the Bronze Knot program was protecting.

Her arms and legs ached. The constant activity, since they leaped backward off the boat, had depleted her stamina. She hoped that her boyfriend was right and they could get access to a vehicle at the cluster of buildings that they headed towards.

Parkowski wasn't sure she could swim to the anchored boat, let alone walk miles and miles to get their gear.

After a few minutes of walking, her eyes adjusted to the almost pitch-black environment. If she squinted just right, Parkowski could make out the outlines of a half-dozen buildings in front of them; their square, artificial shapes a sharp contrast to the trees and water behind them.

It only took them about twenty minutes of walking. Normally, that would be nothing for Parkowski, but she was exhausted. She stopped to catch her breath as her boyfriend kept walking.

There were about ten vehicles in a small parking lot with one entrance leading out to a rough, two-lane road headed south along the riverbank. Around the parking lot were five buildings - she had miscounted - two large, four-story tall high bays and two smaller, one-story buildings alongside one that didn't look like much more than a garage. Strewn around the area were cinder blocks, pallets, and other construction-type garbage.

"What is this place?" she asked.

"It's an old SMC processing area," he answered. "It was used for processing of the old DSP - Defense Support Program - missile-warning satellites. But, when they went to SBIRS fifteen years ago, this whole area was abandoned. Or, at least that's what they told me when we came to get the GOVs here to ferry around VIPs. That's all this area is now, a parking lot," he finished with a laugh.

"Why did they abandon it?" Parkowski asked.

He shrugged. "Those birds are processed at Astrotech down the road," DePresti explained. "I think the facilities here are so specialized that it'd cost too much to refurbish them for another purpose or to support another mission, so they just left them in place."

Even in the dark, Parkowski could tell that the buildings had seen better days. Part of the roof of one of the smaller office buildings was falling off, probably damaged from a hurricane, and she spotted a hole in the garage. Regardless, the vehicles, mostly small SUVs or large sedans with a pair of pickup trucks rounding out the group, were all less than a few years old.

She stood and tried to relax while DePresti started trying to open up the cars and get the keys, which he told her were always kept in the glove compartment.

He wasn't having much luck.

"Fuck," DePresti said after his third failure. "I was here less than a year ago, and all of these were unlocked. It was an open secret on base; you need a GOV, you take the right just before the NASA Parkway and take that road all of the way up until you come here."

"I wonder if some policy changed," Parkowski said, finding a seat on a concrete block and sitting down. "Or if someone got in trouble."

DePresti didn't respond. Instead, he kept trying to open car doors. Eventually, he ran out of options.

"Well, shit," he said. "There goes that plan."

"Maybe they moved the keys inside one of these buildings?" Parkowski suggested.

He looked like he was going to angrily reject her idea, but then nodded. "Go look, I'll keep trying."

Parkowski swung herself off of the concrete block and walked over to the garage-like building.

The door was locked, but Parkowski was able to see through a small window next to it. In the darkness, she could see the building was just one room and it was completely empty. There was some serious water damage on the floor.

No keys in there.

The next closest building was one of the high bays.

Parkowski pushed her tired legs forward to the tall building.

There must have been a cloud over the moon, obscuring some of its reflected light, because as the Aering engineer walked towards the structure it was bathed in light.

She felt a pang of sadness as she saw an American flag painted on its side near the top, half of the stripes faded away and the rest hanging on by a thread. It didn't seem like anyone had been in the high bay in years.

Her eyes skipped to some writing above the American flag. "SPACE AND MISSILES SYSTEM CENTER PROCESSING FACILITY A98."

Parkowski's heart skipped a beat.

A98.

The same numbering scheme they had seen on the packets in the secure room in Hangar AZ. In fact, just one number off from the building they were looking for.

This story wasn't over yet.

"Mike," Parkowski said.

"What?" DePresti yelled while he tried to yank a sedan door open.

"I think you need to take a look at this."

He grunted and stepped away from the GOV. "What do I need to look at?"

Parkowski wished she had a light as she pointed a finger at the top of the building. "What do you see?"

"I see that it's a processing facility run by SMC."

She wanted to slap him. "Keep reading."

"...A98. What's so important about that?"

Parkowski did slap him. "Idiot!" she said loudly. "Don't you remember your network decoder ring from back in Hangar AZ?"

"Yeah."

"The Bronze Knot data was coming from A99. Maybe it's one of the other buildings here."

"Shit, I forgot," DePresti said, scratching his head. "Are the other buildings numbered?"

Parkowski did a quick check of the garage. B16. "Yeah, and in the same scheme."

DePresti walked off to check the office buildings while Parkowski strode over to the other high bay, located at the other side of the parking lot from A98.

The building was in even worse shape than the others. The paint was falling off in chunks from the humid Florida air, and the front door looked like it was barely hanging on, although Parkowski saw a second, more secure door past it.

It didn't have an American flag, but it did have a military logo with writing at the bottom. Parkowski squinted to read it. "SPACE & MISSILES SYSTEMS CENTER."

"That's the old SMC logo before it became Space Systems Command," DePresti said, walking next to her and putting an arm over her shoulders. "But that changed over about five-ish years ago. I guess no one has gotten around to updating it."

"Mike, I don't think anyone has been in these buildings in *fifteen* years," she responded. "Look how beat up it is."

"That's what a dozen tropical storms and hurricanes a year will do," the Space Force captain said. "I don't see a building number, do you?"

Parkowski shook her head and stepped closer, almost to the front of the building. Her boyfriend followed her.

On the caved-in metal door she saw in faded letters "A99."

"This is it," she said, breathing heavily with excitement. "A99."

DePresti looked confused. "There's no way," he said. "There were active packets coming from a machine into Hangar AZ. This building is abandoned. I don't even know if it has power."

"So either your 'decoder ring' for the IP addresses was wrong..." Parkowski's voice trailed off.

"Or there's something going on inside," DePresti finished. He took another step forward. "Wait a sec."

He cupped his hand to his ear. "Do you hear that?"

"Hear what?" Parkowski asked, crossing her arms in front of her.

"There's a humming sound," DePresti said, pointing to the side of the building. "I'm going to go check it out."

With a sliver of hope, Parkowski followed him.

About five feet from the dilapidated side of the building was a green electrical box. DePresti walked up to it. "Do you hear it now?"

She did. It was a low-frequency hum and had to be coming from the box. "I do."

"That's active," her boyfriend said. "That building has power."

Parkowski was skeptical but held her tongue.

"Let's see if we can find a way in. Maybe they're using a small part of it for something and decided to stash all of the keys to the GOVs there as a security measure."

She shrugged. "Sure."

Parkowski followed DePresti around the building, looking for an easy way in.

On the far side of the electrical box, facing a small stand of large oak trees, was a metal door. It looked newer than the doors on the front and had no peeling paint.

It also had a massive padlock that prevented them from getting into the building.

Her heart sank while DePresti snorted a laugh.

"What's so funny?" she asked.

"If they're using a low-tech lock, we can get in," her boyfriend responded. "A padlock like that can be broken. Come on, let's go get one of those cinder blocks from the parking lot and see if we can't break it."

A minute later DePresti slammed the cinder block onto the padlock.

"Oof," he said, dropping the block with a slam. "That's harder than it looks."

"Can I try?" Parkowski asked.

He nodded and stepped back. "Be my guest."

Parkowski picked it up. It had to be at least thirty or forty pounds.

She raised it to shoulder height and paused. Then, the Aering engineer let the force of gravity do the work, unlike her boyfriend, who had tried to brute-force it and smashed the cinder block into the top of the padlock.

It fell to the ground with a metallic clang.

"Work harder, not smarter," she said quietly to herself as her boyfriend clapped his hand on her shoulder in celebration.

"Shall we?" DePresti asked.

She nodded.

He swung the door open and stepped inside.

They stood in another dimly lit hallway, similar to that in Hangar AZ. Only a single naked bulb at the top provided any light.

DePresti was right. The building *did* have power. And at the end of the hallway was another metal door.

They walked to it together. "I'll let you have the honors," DePresti said.

Parkowski grabbed the handle and opened the door.

After her eyes adjusted to the bright light of the cavernous room beyond she stopped in a state of shock.

She didn't believe what she was seeing.

CHAPTER FORTY-NINE

Building A99, Cape Canaveral Space Force Station, FL

Beyond the door was a massive high bay, easily twice both the height and size of the former satellite processing facility that the ILIAD mission had used at the Aering plant in El Segundo. It was just as clean and well-kept - someone had spent a great deal of time, money, and effort renovating the place.

There were no windows. It looked to Parkowski like a former clean room that had been converted for another purpose. The walls were beige and the floor was a shiny white tile that reflected the incandescent lights suspended on beams just below the ceiling, creating a glare that blinded Parkowski and DePresti.

On the far side of the room was what looked like a payload stack ready to be put on the second stage of a rocket. Parkowski couldn't make out what it was with all of the glare. Next to it were two halves of a rocket fairing.

The stacked payload was connected with wires, both to large outlets in the high bay's walls and to a mess of electronics on white folding tables, which was connected to a rack of servers against the wall that ran almost the length of it. Rounding out the room were eight small cubicles in two rows at the end of the server farm.

"What the..." Parkowski said. She was at a loss for words.

All of this looked new, or at least built in the last few years. The floor gleamed like it had barely been walked on. It was all such a sharp contrast to the outside of the building, which made it appear to be falling apart. Inside, it was as clean and well-kept as any modern aerospace facility.

After adjusting their eyes from the darkness outside to the overbearing light inside, Parkowski and DePresti walked across the high bay to the payload stack. It looked very familiar, but she couldn't put a finger on where she had seen it before.

On the top of the ten-meter stack was a large, two-meter-wide jumble of metal and composites. She wasn't sure what it was. In the middle was a large ring with different antennas and sensors sticking out of it. At the bottom was a wide, short metal cone that was painted black.

Parkowski stood about ten feet from it, studying it further, while DePresti walked up to it.

He stood there, mouth open, speechless.

"There's no way..." he said, his voice trailing off, "there's no fucking way."

"What's 'no fucking way'?" Parkowski asked.

"I never thought I'd see it again."

"See what?"

DePresti pointed at the stacked payload. "That's the ILIAD stack. The lander is on the top there," he said, "with the two ACHILLES units and all of the associated ground gear. In the middle is the relay satellite, built on an ESPA ring, and at the bottom is the payload attach fitting that goes on the top of the second stage."

Parkowski was confused. "So, they built a second one and stored it here?"

He shook his head vigorously. "No, no, no, there's no way they could, or even would," the Space Force captain said. "They spent four or five billion dollars on the entire stack. There's no reason to build a second one." DePresti paused for dramatic effect.

"They never launched it."

Everything clicked into place for Parkowski. She knew what Bronze Knot was protecting. "Holy fucking shit."

It all made sense. The robots had never left Earth's surface.

They had never gone to Venus. They had been here the whole time.

Parkowski was willing to bet that the server racks next to the payload stack were some kind of virtual environment - another level into the simulation.

The ACHILLES units were programmed to operate in that virtual world, not on the solar system's second planet.

The operators at the El Segundo facility were plugged into it like they had thought, but all of the sensor feeds coming into it were spoofed.

Aering's decision to have a video game developer and not a simulation design firm create and maintain the Venus environment made so much more sense. The operators weren't piloting a high-tech robot. They had been in a simulation - playing a game.

She sank her knees down to the cold tile floor. It was too much to take in at once.

DePresti stepped even closer to the stack. "Those bastards."

"What do you mean?" his girlfriend asked.

He turned to her. "I spent years of my life working on a lie." DePresti shook his head. "Those fuckers did a full second stage swap, to include the payload, and I had no idea. I don't even know how they could. Something of that magnitude would be impossible without a bunch of other people finding out."

Parkowski nodded in agreement. "It'd take an army to make it happen."

DePresti snapped his fingers. "Wait a sec," he said, "when we were about to transport the encapsulated fairing from Astrotech to the launch site, the day before the launch, I was absolutely exhausted. I had been watching OuterTek perform processing operations and closeouts for almost twenty-four hours straight. Col Hawke told me to go back to the hotel and get some sleep before the launch, and that he would monitor the transportation activities. That's when they did it. They traded out the ILIAD probe for the other second stage, which had to have been prepared in advance, and put it on the flatbed to come over to LC-39a."

He breathed slowly. "Goddammn it, how could no one have noticed?"

"No one said anything?" Parkowski asked.

"Nope. And that's what is so confusing. We had cameras inside of the fairing the whole time, not to mention string after string of sensors all over the second stage. If something was wrong, or the payload was different, we would have known immediately."

Cameras. Videos. Something clicked in Parkowski's brain.

She stood back up. "They - OuterTek - tricked you with the videos," she explained. "When I was in their system, I found all of these videos of the launch for the webcast, but the dates were all wrong. The files had all been created before the launch date."

"I remember you saying that," DePresti said, eliciting a smile from Parkowski, "but I didn't appreciate it at the time." He paused. "And, during the launch, when they went to jettison the fairing, the video remained the same - fairing still attached to the second stage - before they cut the feed. I bet someone fucked up and went to the live sensor feed before they went to the canned video."

Parkowski had nothing to say. She just nodded. It all made too much sense.

"And after the launch, they just pretended everything was fine," DePresti continued. "And gave NASA and Aering fake data until the probe 'arrived' on Venus."

"I have a theory," Parkowski said, "the servers here are creating a virtual Venus in terms of sensor inputs that are fed into the Panspermia environment that the Aering operators control the ACHILLES units in. It closes the feedback loop and makes you, the operator, feel like you're really controlling the virtual robot when really you're just talking to a virtual state machine here. Even the lag is fake."

"That makes too much sense," her boyfriend responded, "and is probably the cause of all of the anomalies that you saw while you were in the VR gear."

"That's what Bronze Knot is protecting," she said in agreement. "The fact that the virtual environment isn't calling Venus at all - it's calling this building, A99, out here. We just didn't see it because we didn't have the full network architecture. They didn't need to protect the details, or the 'big secret' if you will, *because they didn't have to*. All they needed to do was to conceal the fact that the data from Venus wasn't being pulled from MICS through White Sands. We had the answer all along but just weren't able to put it into the right context."

DePresti put a hand up against the PAF and sighed. "All of this, and for what?"

She didn't have an answer for him. But, all of the things that she had found over the last few weeks, large and small, now fit in place.

There was no real-time interface between the Panspermia environment and the feed coming in from MICS because it wasn't needed - all of the packets coming in were artificial. Since whoever had integrated all of this had control of both sides of the interface, there was no need for data conditioning.

There was lag - artificial lag - that was needed in order for the Panspermia environment to react as it had been programmed in. It was expecting a ninety to one-hundred-twenty-second delay, and if it didn't receive that, the virtual environment software wouldn't work as planned. When it had gotten smaller than that in some of her missions, the errors had started, leading to the cryptic messages exposing the Bronze Knot name.

The changes in part number for the second stage of the Shrike Heavy were real and poorly documented by OuterTek. Given their history of last-minute configuration changes, a few swapped part numbers wouldn't be totally out of the ordinary.

It was a lot to take in.

Her entire job for the last year had been a lie.

She joined him next to the OuterTek PAF with the ILIAD probe on top of it.

"If this is here," DePresti mused as he ran his hand along one of the thick wires that connected the ILIAD probe to the wall and gave it power. "Then what went up on the Shrike Heavy?"

Parkowski had no idea.

Her mind flashed with a million possibilities, each more implausible than the next, but none of them made any sense.

"I don't know," she said.

"I don't either," DePresti said in response. He laughed. "I'm not sure it matters now, does it?"

"Nope." It was another mystery, sure, but Parkowski felt a great deal of satisfaction in solving the one that had bugged her for months. "At least we know what Bronze Knot is."

They followed the cables to the scattering of electronic gear on the folding tables. DePresti and Parkowski both instantly knew what it was. "That's a flat-sat," she said, pointing at the contraption, referring to a set of satellite parts, mostly avionics, arranged on the ground for rapid testing of software upgrades. "But for what satellite?"

DePresti bent over it, studying the components. He turned to her. "It's a MICS simulator and a very high-fidelity one at that. Those are all space-rated parts or models of space-rated parts. I bet you're looking at close to a million dollars of hardware there."

Parkowski blinked. "Why would you spend that much on a simulator?"

He laughed. "Grace, the payload stack there cost over a billion dollars. A million dollars is a drop in a bucket to these people."

It took a bit for that to sink in.

"Why would someone pay over a billion dollars to build a science probe that never launches?" she asked rhetorically.

"To be honest with you, I have no idea," her boyfriend responded. "I bet this launch was going in the direction of whatever they switched it with and they just swapped the payloads. I wonder if they're going to declare a mission failure, claim they lost contact with the ACHILLES units, and then cannibalize it for parts. Or, they could pull another swap and roll out this payload stack for another, real launch since they have the infrastructure in place."

Another piece clicked. The OuterTek post-launch report, with all of the weird burns.

She recounted it again to DePresti.

"But why would they need to make so many different burns?" he asked her. "Did they provide a trajectory map?"

"No, just the performance data," she answered.

"That's weird," he said. "They always provide some kind of trajectory depiction, usually with the accuracy data. But, in this case, I get why they didn't."

Parkowski's mind still raced. But, she had a warm feeling come up through her that made her surprisingly happy despite the predicament that she and DePresti were still in.

She had solved the Bronze Knot mystery.

CHAPTER FIFTY

Building A99, Cape Canaveral Space Force Station, FL

Parkowski and DePresti still needed to escape the secure facility and make it back to civilization.

They spent a few more minutes observing the ILIAD payload stack and MICS simulator as well as the server racks. Parkowski hoped for some more SAP stickers; some new trigraphs for her to further her investigation, but there were none - just BKT.

Then, they moved to the small cubicle farm. It almost looked out of place to Parkowski but she remembered that she, too, worked in a cube farm located inside of a satellite processing high bay - an odd symmetry to the whole affair.

Each of the cubicles had a workstation with a pair of monitors and a thin client, meaning that the desktop environment was physically located elsewhere, probably in the server rack. Parkowski tried to log in, but they were locked down tight. To get in, she would need a username, a password, and a code from a two-factor authentication keyfob. Even if she had been successful at getting login information like she had at Aering and OuterTek, she didn't have the two-factor keyfob.

In the drawers, though, they hit the jackpot.

DePresti held up a handful of car keys. "I think these are what we were looking for," he told Parkowski. "Which one do you want?"

She laughed. "Just pick one. It doesn't really matter."

He grabbed one and threw the rest back into the cubicle's desk drawer.

Parkowski looked for something to record what they had just learned.

The Aering engineer knew what they had seen here, no one would believe them. The ILIAD launch and mission were national news. Fox News and CNN had both carried the launch live, and it had warranted a front-page New York Times article the morning after. NASA released regular updates on the scientific value of the mission, both to keep the public informed as well as to push for funding of future missions to other planets.

Unless they had hard evidence that the ILIAD mission was sitting in an obscure hangar on Cape Canaveral; that the data that NASA was presenting to the public was fraudulent, they would be dismissed as cranks or conspiracy theorists.

She, too, got lucky.

In one of the bottom drawers, she found a trio of smartphone boxes, each with an older smartphone inside next to a charger.

Now, it was Parkowski's turn to laugh. "Why would they leave these here?" she asked DePresti with a smile on her face.

He took a look at them and snorted. "These were the ones we issued the NASA and Aering ground crews when they were here for the launch campaign," DePresti told her. "A lot of them had service providers that didn't have great coverage here. It was easier to just buy them phones and let them use them for the launch campaign. Afterwards, we gave them back to the Cape Canaveral support team, and I didn't know what became of them. Turns out they ended up here with a bunch of other junk."

That's what was in the rest of the drawers - junk from the Shrike Heavy launch. Launch notebooks, remove-before-flight tags, tools and hardware, press pamphlets and scripts, it was all there. This was where the local Space Force team, who must have been in on the Bronze Knot deception, stored everything after the rocket went up.

Thankfully for Parkowski and DePresti, that included the GOV keys and the smartphones.

Parkowski took one of the phones out of its box and plugged it in. She got lucky again. Not only did the phone boot up on its first try, there was no passcode. And, to top it off, the phone had service, getting three bars from a nearby cell tower.

She waited for the phone to get about a quarter-charged and then removed it from the charging cable.

Parkowski then went to the area of the high bay that the payload and flatsat were in. She took dozens of pictures, showing the payload stack from every possible angle, as well as the flatsat and server racks

The Aering engineer then recorded a short video explaining the situation and why it was important, especially to her.

Afterward, she looked at her image on the phone's screen and frowned. Parkowski looked like hell. Granted, she had been through the most grueling, both mentally and physically, stretch of her life in the last six hours or so. But the payoff had been worth it.

She uploaded the video and images to three different cloud locations and then shut off the phone.

"I wish we still had that waterproof pack," Parkowski said to her boyfriend.

He shrugged. "Beggars can't be choosers."

They then left the building.

The moon shone directly overhead and the sky was clear. Despite the lack of light, Parkowski's eyes adjusted easily to the conditions.

DePresti clicked the key's "lock" button until they found the car he had chosen, a late-model Hyundai sedan.

Parkowski got in the passenger's seat. Her legs felt like jelly. She was not ready for a long swim, but she didn't have much of a choice.

There were no other cars on the Cape roads. Parkowski wasn't sure if that was by design - was someone letting them escape - or just because it was the middle of the night. The sedan's clock read twelve forty-five. When this was over, she needed a full day's worth of sleep. It would probably be weeks before she recovered from all of this.

DePresti drove carefully on the side streets to the main north-south thoroughfares. They were less lit, but in theory, had fewer cars on them. They didn't see a single one.

They came to the eastern edge of the installation. DePresti pulled over to the side of the road and got out, followed shortly after by Parkowski.

Their gear was there and didn't look like it had been touched. They helped each other get their scuba equipment on, then walked carefully to the edge of the water. It was low tide now, the small waves slowly lapping up against the shore. Parkowski waded out slowly in her flippers behind her boyfriend before diving into the three-foot water.

Thankfully they had brought snorkels in addition to their now-empty tanks. Parkowski swam slowly on the surface, her flippers helping slightly but also making her tired leg muscles burn.

DePresti didn't seem as affected though, and if he was, he didn't show it. He just kept swimming at a steady pace.

At the halfway point, they paused. Parkowski wasn't sure she was going to make it. She gulped for air and her muscles felt like jelly. But the speedboat, their end goal, was in sight. It slowly rocked back and forth with the ocean less than a mile away.

"Are you ok?" her boyfriend asked.

Parkowski nodded. "I think so."

"Let me know if you can't make it," he said. He was panting too. "I can go to the boat myself and swing back to pick you up."

"No, I can make it," she said defiantly. Parkowski wasn't going to give up now when the end of the physical ordeal was so close.

Parkowski dug deep within her and pushed off swimming again. She swam in a breaststroke, save for a few pathetic attempts at an overhead freestyle stroke, and her arms were just as exhausted as her legs now.

The boat got closer and closer. Her body wouldn't give up now.

Finally, she reached it. DePresti helped her get on deck and they removed each other's equipment. Their clothes were soaked - they had worn them under their wetsuits - and dried slowly in the damp Florida air.

Parkowski lay down on the speedboat's stern as DePresti pulled up and stowed the anchor.

Then, they headed back to the rental shop where they had gotten the boat from.

She finally caught her breath about two-thirds of the way there. "How can you even stand?" she asked her boyfriend.

DePresti chuckled. "If the military has taught me anything, it's to stand for long periods of time," he said in response. "We used to have noon meal formations at the Academy that lasted for hours. I'm just as tired as you are, just as exhausted, but I have more experience with it."

And what an experience it had been.

If someone had told her a few months ago that she would be fleeing a secure government facility after uncovering a secret worth killing for, Parkowski would have laughed in their face. Now, she had just escaped Cape Canaveral, with evidence that would prove to the world that the ILIAD mission was a sham, a lie.

There was time for that later. Now, they needed to get back to the safety of shore and get back to Chang's resource-rich compound in California. From there they would plan their next move.

As expected, there was no one at the dock when DePresti pulled the rented speedboat in. He tied it up with a few knots and helped Parkowski get out and onto the wooden structure.

She took a few unsteady steps before getting comfortable.

DePresti gave her a look but she waved him off. She was fine.

He shrugged and dropped the keys into a drop box, then took the Chevy's keys out of his pocket. How he had kept that through everything they had been through Parkowski would never know, but he had them.

They got into the truck and drove back up A1A to their motel.

Parkowski and DePresti walked into their room and changed into dry clothes, then collapsed onto their respective beds.

The two of them slept until one PM the next day.

Parkowski woke up with her muscles more sore than they had ever been in her life. It was like she had played an entire season's worth of soccer games in a twenty-four hour period.

She groaned and willed herself out of bed.

After popping a few painkillers and eating some snacks, Parkowski felt a little better.

DePresti snored away in a deep sleep. If history was any indication he wouldn't be up for a few hours.

Parkowski grabbed a water bottle and some more snacks and turned on the TV, keeping the volume low so her boyfriend could sleep.

She tried a few different channels before settling on a cable news channel.

None of the news was good - South Africa was on its way to a civil war, an earthquake had struck Chile, and America's internal politics were just as messed up as they always were. Parkowski watched for a few minutes and was about to turn it off when one of the stories crossing the news ticker at the bottom of the screen caught her eye.

NASA MISSION FAILS, LOST CONTACT WITH INTERPLANETARY PROBE.

She snorted and put the remote down.

A few minutes later, after a commercial break, the cable news network had the story.

NASA had held a press conference that morning while they slept, announcing that they had lost contact with the ILIAD mission on Venus. Both of the ACHILLES units were not responding to commands sent from the ground. The prime contractor, Aering, and

NASA were jointly troubleshooting the issue but had no expected response.

Parkowski threw the remote at her boyfriend. "Hey, asshole, time to wake up," she said over his protest. "There's something good on TV."

"What," he groaned.

The TV feed cut to a young, attractive black woman standing in front of the Aering facility on Imperial Highway - the same one that Parkowski had worked at for the last few years.

The Aering engineer held her water bottle in one hand and pointed with the other. "Hey, I know that place."

DePresti laughed. "So do I. And we know her, too. It's my buddy Reggie's girlfriend."

Parkowski recognized her as well.

They had just had dinner with her and Thibeaux a few weeks ago.

She gave a fairly standard piece on the story, highlighting that the ACHILLES robots had been controlled at this Aering facility in El Segundo, and giving no new information, before handing it back to the main anchor at the cable news network's flagship location.

"That's interesting," DePresti said as the channel went to another commercial break, "but I think we kind of expected that to happen."

"I know."

"Well, I think we need to hit the road."

"You don't need to tell me twice," Parkowski said with a grin. "Let's pack up."

CHAPTER FIFTY-ONE

Cocoa Beach, FL

After a quick dinner at the Preacher Bar in the city of Cape Canaveral, they left at eight on their way back to California.

The two took a different route back, taking I-95 north to I-10 and taking that route all the way west to Los Angeles. From there, they took the same route they had taken weeks before up to Barstow.

Parkowski looked but didn't see any cars following them.

It was night when they pulled up into the carport at Chang's homestead. She felt surprisingly rejuvenated despite the long journey.

They had cut an entire day off of their return trip by driving through the first night. One of them drove while the other one slept. They had then slept in a Walmart parking lot in Tucson during the second night and continued their journey the next day. Unfortunately, they got stuck in Los Angeles traffic and didn't make up to Barstow until just after seven.

Chang's dog came out to greet them, but there was no sign of the homeowner himself. DePresti's Subaru was there, looking as good as new. Chang must have had someone come out to fix the bullet holes. The house itself was repaired as well - it didn't look like it had been through a gunfight just a few days ago.

They walked carefully into it. The lights were off. Parkowski switched them on. From all appearances, the house was deserted. "What now?" she asked DePresti.

"I don't know," he answered. There was a brief, uncomfortable pause.

"Should we go check the basement?"

He nodded.

They were just about to reveal the hidden staircase when they heard another vehicle pull up outside.

Parkowski froze.

A moment later, she heard Chang's familiar boisterous voice outside of the front door, accompanied by two other people, one male, one female, which she didn't recognize.

Then the door opened. Parkowski tensed - she didn't know what to expect.

"Hey," Chang said as he walked in looking no worse for the wear, followed by a man and woman, both in military fatigues.

Parkowski breathed a sigh of relief. If he was walking in that nonchalantly, they were in no danger.

One of them - the woman - Parkowski had seen before. It was DePresti's commanding officer, Lt Col Michelle Thorne.

The man, she knew only by reputation. He was Col Hawke, DePresti's former commander when he worked in the launch unit.

The three stood in front of Parkowski and DePresti.

She stood breathless, not knowing what to expect.

"Well, I guess you're wondering what's going on," Chang said.

Parkowski remained silent. DePresti nodded.

"When the two of you went back into the city, I had a SWAT team come and pay me a visit," Chang said. "Something to do with FCC violations. I was held in a cell in downtown LA for forty-eight hours and then released with a warning."

"Was it the same people who attacked us at your house?" Parkowski asked in a softer-than-normal tone.

Hawke shook his head. "From my understanding, no," the Space Force colonel said. He pointed at Chang's restored living room. "Come, let's sit down and chat."

The two senior Space Force officers then gave their side of the story to Chang, DePresti, and Parkowski.

Hawke had been fully read into Bronze Knot since before the launch. Thorne had been read in more recently when Pham had been killed.

Other than Hawke admitting that he knew about the payload swap, they didn't have much more to add in the way of new information. They just confirmed what Parkowski already knew. Some third-party had a payload that they wanted launched on top of the Shrike Heavy, and they moved the NASA payload off of the mission to put it there.

"So who is behind all of it?" she asked. "And why?"

The two FGOs looked at each other and then back at her. "To be honest, I'm not sure," Thorne - the less talkative of the two - said.

"There were some weird groups at the launch from the State Department," Hawke added. "And that's just the government side. Who knows if there was a private company or companies involved."

There was an uncomfortable pause.

DePresti asked the question that was on her mind. "So what happens now, sir?"

Hawke gave a small smile. "If the three of you can keep your mouths shut, I think you're in the clear."

Parkowski didn't believe that. "I've almost been killed half a dozen times over the course of the last few weeks," she told Hawke. "And I'm just supposed to drop it and move on, without looking over my shoulder?"

He nodded. "I can't tell you exactly who told me, but I can stake my professional reputation on that. The powers that be - the ones behind Bronze Knot - recovered your recordings from the cloud and the phone they were taken on and have already cleansed the facility at Aering. The only loose ends are the three of you, and the Department of Defense was able to convince them that having you alive, rather than dead or imprisoned, is in the country's best interests. So, stop looking into it, don't tell anyone, and yes, Grace, you can stop looking over your shoulder."

"So we'll never figure out what was really launched?" DePresti asked.

"Mike, I don't know myself. I don't think any of us ever will." Hawke responded.

Parkowski didn't ask any further questions.

#

Six months - and one proposal - later, in late May, they found themselves again at Rock 'n Brews in El Segundo. This time, it was for DePresti's going away. He had been picked up for a special assignment at the National Reconnaissance Office in Chantilly, Virginia, and was leaving the next week to report. Parkowski would be joining him there too, having taken an internal transfer that would take her to Aering's R&D division located near Dulles International Airport.

It was a perfectly clear night as DePresti and Parkowski left the restaurant, loaded down with going-away presents and plaques, and walked to her Camry. Despite the light pollution from the city, they could see plenty of stars.

Parkowski put down the large plaque she was carrying and looked up.

"What's up?" her fiancé asked, stopping as well.

"Just wondering, whatever went up there on the ILIAD launch, it's still up there, right?" the Aering engineer said as she gazed up at the heavens.

"Probably," DePresti responded.

Parkowski laughed. It was probably a dumb question. "I wonder where it went."

EPILOGUE

Vicinity of Jupiter, Sol System

The second stage of the Shrike Heavy rocket launched from LC-39a the previous June, traveled towards its final destination.

It had been a cold, lonely journey for the RP-1/LOx powered upper stage. After launching into what had been the ILIAD mission's initial transfer orbit, it had done a low-energy Hohmann maneuver once it was out of range of any Earth-based sensors that would detect the change in trajectory.

The intermediate target was Jupiter.

The second stage, with its mysterious payload that had been attached at the last minute, would use a fraction of its remaining fuel to slingshot itself around Jupiter and use the planet's mass to propel itself forward; transferring all of the orbit's potential energy to kinetic energy.

Its flight computer monitored the sensors, computing the optimal solution in both the planet-based as well as the sun-based reference frames. Most of the trajectory had been computed on the ground, long before the system had launched. Still, this burn to put them on a path for the gravity assist had so many different complex parameters that it was best done closer to its destination.

Thankfully, the stage was roughly where it needed to be. The flight computer sent a couple of commands to the thrusters and aligned the stage to be on the right path.

The rocket's upper stage was soon grabbed by Jupiter's gravity well.

The massive planet dwarfed the Shrike Heavy upper stage. But, the math worked out in the smaller body's favor. The stage swung out of orbit with a much higher velocity than it had come in with, conserving its precious fuel for later.

It then headed out on a trajectory that would take it out of the solar system into the great void beyond.

Also by Ryan M. Patrick

Grace Parkowski Thrillers
Lag Delay

Standalone
Low Frequency
The Martian Incident

Watch for more at www.ryanmpatrickauthor.com.

About the Author

I am a USAF and USSF veteran currently working as an aerospace engineer, writing in what little spare time that I have. My books are my creative outlet from a math & science-heavy, technically-demanding job. I primarily write in the science fiction and technothriller genres but I may branch out to others in the future.

While I'm originally from the Philadelphia area, I currently live in Northern Virginia with my wife, four daughters, and dog.

Read more at www.ryanmpatrickauthor.com.

Milton Keynes UK
Ingram Content Group UK Ltd.
UKHW030848111124
451035UK00001B/235